POWERLESS
A Superhero Novel

Tony Cooper

Third Edition

Cover by Harry Corr
harrycorr.co.uk

***

Also in this series:
KILLING GODS

ACKNOWLEDGMENTS

Thanks to my wife Lyn for her support and understanding while I make this slight change from my previous career path

Thanks to my mum for always encouraging me to be creative from an early age

Thanks to Sharron for showing me how bad a writer I am through her fantastic editing work

Thanks to you for buying this third edition of POWERLESS

PROLOGUE
PRESENT DAY

"…and when I look back I realise the team broke up because we experienced a shared nightmare. We did the most horrible, unimaginable things and we all knew what we had done. We couldn't bear to look at each other. When we did, we saw our own terrors reflected back in our eyes. None of us could judge each other, none of us could help each other.

Since then we have all scattered to the winds and tried in our own ways to either regain what we lost or to hide from our own dark thoughts. Have we succeeded? Are we happy? Are we fulfilled? I say no. We are lost, stuck in the past forever. The truth is he won. He beat us all. And nearly twenty years on we are still paying for what he did.

And are we still the heroes of 'The Pulse'? Will you still idolize us after reading my words? Can you forgive us by remembering only the good things we did: the people we saved, the city we saved? Or are our heroic deeds forever tainted by my admissions?

Would it help at all if I admit that I am going to die? Right now? In fact… I think he's in the kitchen. He just bumped into a chair, trying not to make a noise in the dark.

Don't even contemplate thinking of me as some kind of martyr though. I am as weak and as powerless as we all were. I only hope that what I have written here will somehow end the torment, free us of our demons at last, even if it is the death of me.

He's in the hall. Even through the medication I can hear his mind screaming my name.

Ah well.

The end."

***

The bars of orange street lighting slicing through the half-closed blinds shrink and split as a large figure silently settles between them and Vincent. As the silhouette stands there, breathing loudly, he pops another sleeping pill and washes it down with half a glass of whisky.

"Not… trying to kill myself you know", he says aloud, "doesn't affect me like everyone else, it just helps block out the voices."

He studies the broken light refracting in the glass.

"Not that there are many voices out here anyway. Apart from yours, bellowing in my head." He carefully places the glass on a worn green coaster on the table next to his chair.

There is silence.

"It's finished you know. And I'm not telling you where it is."

There is more silence.

"Surprised? Thought I'd be cowering by now? Thought I'd still be the weak-willed, whimpering Vincent you could intimidate by just being there?"

The figure seems to shift slightly.

"Well sod you. I've had a long time to think about everything that happened. I knew this was coming. Someday. And I'm not cowering, not for you."

The silhouette grows larger. The bands of light behind it are almost completely obscured. Vincent's breathing quickens and his neck starts to pulsate. His hands bounce up and down involuntarily on the armrests.

"I love this chair...", he says rather too loudly, "had it since I left the unit and got this place. Just seems to get more comfortable by the... aww, no." The air starts to smell of heat, as it shifts and begins to glow. "That's it eh? Not even a word for old Vincent? Nothing?" Then the glow. Then the heat. All the beams of window light are blocked out now. Vincent is panting. He starts beating his fists on the chair.

"It's all in there you bastard! All of it! Everything you want to hide, and you're never going to find it. Martin will make sure of that. Martin will make sure you never even touch it! It's gonna get out there, on the bookshelves, on the internet, wherever, and you're gonna learn you can't hide from yourself!"

He smells his hair singeing as his eyes dry up.

"You fucker..."

The blue pulse rips him open from neck to pelvis, spreading darkening organs and an arm flying outward like grotesque, unfurling wings. His head, loose, drops over the back of the chair and hangs there. A small black patch of material falls from the rear of the chair, grey curls of smoke rising from the hole it reveals.

The figure steps back and beams of light cut their way across the remains. A carcass. Hollowed out and empty. No more voices for Vincent.

The intruder begins searching.

CHAPTER 1
THURSDAY 13TH SEPTEMBER 2012

The first bird calls of the day filter through the ventilation system. The pale blue-grey light of an overcast dawn lazily floats through the vaulted glass ceiling and drapes itself over the shop frontages that stare emptily out onto the wide, dim interior. The glass and chrome fountain sculpture is dry and sleeping. A McDonald's milkshake cup pokes from the mouth of a dozing swing-bin, having been gently gummed all night. The tick-tick of an unseen security system, echoes across the cool ceramic tiles. A muted primary colour window display, "20% off".

He stands in the centre of a giant blue and gold floor mosaic of an old sailing ship, directly underneath the highest point of the roof, eyes closed, breathing slowly and deliberately, arms down straight by his sides. He is listening. He breathes so slowly that the folds in his pale blue shirt barely change shape, only the sewn-on shield symbol on his left breast rising and falling betrays the fact he is alive. Fingers outstretched he feels the air slipping between them thickly, like a soft current underwater. Every sense is heightened. The silence is at once imposing, pressing in on his skin, forcing him onto the floor and yet at the same time lifting him up, pulling him outside his body. Through his boots he feels every crevice, every crack and texture of every tiny tile under his feet. Through his eyelids he sees the leaves stuck to the top of the glass roof, the seagulls patrolling the ledges, the city beyond.

He likes it like this. Silent seats. No voices. Just listening to the world. Listening to the buzzing.

***

There was a faint yet persistent buzzing, like an alarm clock being forcefully smothered by a pillow. He felt himself slip across the rooftops, accelerating, before slamming back into his body. He exhaled a huge breath from his barrel chest. It was already time.

Despite carefully and slowly opening his eyes, the sudden rush of visual information stunned him momentarily. Abstract shapes and colours violently forced themselves into his consciousness and hurriedly coalesced into recognisable structures. As his pupils adjusted, the reverie faded and he was now firmly in a reality that was less than before. With his senses swamped he could no longer hear the buzzing, but he knew it was still there. He cracked his fat knuckles, rolled his heavy shoulders back, briefly checked he remembered how motor control to his legs worked and turned round.

The security office was two floors up in the management section of the New Merlin shopping centre. It occupied an innocuously small room in the "gallery" area, a line of offices with one-way windows that overlooked the main lower aisle and first floor mezzanine. One wall had a long, shallow desk, above it the ubiquitous mosaic of flat screen monitors showing a persistent, uncomfortably bleached version of the key thoroughfares and entrances. The opposite wall had another desk and a filing cabinet forced up against it. There was very little space between them and the chairs for each desk jostled for dominance in the middle of the room. This second desk was covered in papers, folders and sticky notes – some deliberately placed, some having peeled off a large whiteboard above it covered in marker pen grids entitled,"Shifts", "A.A.Strong delivery timetable" and "Emergency contacts (management)". The third wall, just inside the door on the right, had two tall dark blue lockers leaning against it.

As he came into the room, the buzzing started again. A large black intercom phone at the far end of the security camera desk blinked a frustrated orange light at him. Fighting with the chairs for supremacy he held the speak button.

"Hello, can I help you?"

"Martin you dick, Mary's freezing her tits off out here!"

"Can I confirm your security ID please?"

11

"Your mother's so fat the Japanese want to harpoon her for science!"

"Be right down."

He wiggled the mouse and the solo screen hurried into life. With a few clicks, the staff door alarm was disabled and he headed back down.

People. Damn. People. Shit. Damn. People. Martin braced himself with several quick breaths in and out, rolling his shoulders. People. He could do it. He knew these ones. They were OK. He had been working here for the past five years now, always night shift. He liked the solitude. He needed it. It was the handovers he hated the most. Not the people themselves but forcing himself to speak, forcing himself to engage with their chatter and humour after a night lost in himself. Not that his colleagues weren't interesting or funny, just that he would prefer to engage with them on his terms. Which were pretty much "not at all". Actually these ones were OK. He liked them.

Turned out that most other security guards tended to be individuals that preferred their own company, so they all gave each other the requisite amount of personal space, just the right amount of conversation, just the right level of black humour.

He was good now, the breathing exercises had helped.

When he got to the side door Barney was peering through the glass, forehead pressed against it, hands either side of his head like a cheeky boy staring at a lavish Christmas shop window display. Behind him stood three women talking to each other. All of them had visible breath. Barney shook his head as Martin unlocked the door with a fist-sized bundle of keys.

"Fucking slacker." He pushed his way in, slipping off his woollen hat, his bald head beaming red. The sudden presence of people around Martin was jarring. His head started to swim. He tried to remember that this wasn't his space, it was work, that this was OK. His head cleared but he had a crushing urge to force himself into the grooves of the wall and hide there.

"Morning Barney, how's you? Morning ladies."

Mary, Emma and a new oriental girl whose name he couldn't remember slipped in past him through the narrow corridor as he held the door for them.

"Ooh, cold enough to freeze your bits it is!" said Mary. "And it's only bloody September."

"It's *tits* love!" called Barney from round the corner.

Mary made an "oh isn't he awful" face and took the set of cleaners' keys Martin had brought down with him. As he closed the door the breeze blew a fire safety leaflet from a cork pin board down the corridor. The oriental girl picked it up and handed it to him.

"Good night?" she asked with a slow drawl.

"Quiet... thanks," he smiled back, and pinned the leaflet back. Their chatter and bodies and smell and mannerisms were intruding into his calm space now. He liked them as colleagues but he didn't want to have to think about their thoughts, he just wanted his own.

"Hope you've got the fucking kettle on you twat!" bellowed Barney.

***

With everyone settled into their tasks and the security shift handed over uneventfully, Martin grabbed his jacket and backpack from the locker and made his way through the random etch-a-sketch corridors below the gallery. Four more cleaners had arrived and one of the admin staff on an early shift. His space was now full of chatter, clattering keyboards and dragging buckets. He couldn't wait to escape.

He walked faster and faster, the passageways seeming to narrow around him so much he felt he needed to turn sideways so as to not scrape the walls. Finally, the exit. He swiped his card on a small silver box. It happily beeped green and he pulled the heavy door open and relaxed as he felt the cool swish of air around his face.

Making sure he heard the magnetic lock click shut behind him, he adjusted the strap of his backpack and took a few clear breaths. Across from him, he spotted the lights in a small French styled café flickering to life. Looking down the main aisle, several other stores were waking up, one metal shutter complaining about being forced open. A loud radio station starting up in the girls' clothes store next to him made him jump.

"Jesus!", he said to himself, and for a moment tried unsuccessfully to recognise the electronic music thumping through the floor.

He zipped himself up to the neck and went across to the café. He was their first customer of the day whenever he was on night shift. The owner, a small fussy man with dark curly hair, gave him a free cup to check whether the machine was heating up properly. Most of the time it had. When it hadn't he got a free biscotti.

***

He found himself smiling as he left the centre, coffee in one hand, crunching on a biscotti. Emma locked the doors behind him, gave him a little wave and went back to shining the glass.

He took a deep breath of the crisp air and immediately felt lighter, his chest relaxing, the tremor in his hands fading. He was no longer locked in a box with people. He only had to survive the supermarket, which was thankfully quiet at this time of the day, and then he would soon be safely home again. His own space.

The early morning sky was puffy and overcast like a giant grey duvet smothering the world. The familiar sleepy shrugs of people were wandering to work, the odd car crawling round the deserted roads. He liked this time of day. He liked knowing that so few people saw the world like this through his eyes. He crossed the plaza in front of the centre, a group of dozy pigeons half-heartedly getting out of the way.

As he debated in his head whether to go home through Element Park or to go out the back entrance of Tesco instead, there was a sudden commotion in the distance. Screeching tyres. A hard rev of engines. He immediately became nervous, a tingle of uncertainty zipping down his arms. He stepped back from the zebra crossing he was near as an unmarked police car with a small lopsided and painfully flashing blue light on its roof whizzed past. Following it intently was the Team Element City One van. Electric red with blacked out windows and emblazoned with their logo, website address and a small line of plain white text reassuringly stating: "Working with the authorities for a power-safe city!"

Martin had to wait until they had both disappeared into the far distance before he could exhale. After a few seconds he could feel his hands again and shook his arms out, spurting coffee from the small mouth hole in the lid over his sleeve.

As he wiped his arm dry with a small tissue from his pocket he couldn't help but think about the van. He could imagine the team in the back, prepping for whatever they had been called to do, most likely a drugs bust at this time of the morning.

Their hearts would be pounding but they would busy themselves checking equipment, going over the intel. They would be practicing their powers, like athletes stretching and warming up their muscles before an event. They would be confirming the plan and what their roles were to be: scout, entry, offensive, crowd control, etc. They would be nervous, yet calm and professional, keeping an eye on everyone else, supporting each other, because they knew that a single mistake by one person could endanger them all. And the team sticks together, always.

CHAPTER 2
FRIDAY 16TH APRIL 1993

"Can't this fucking tin can go any faster?"

The van glances off a kerb, almost sending Maria flying into the computer desk.

"Better my dear?" comes the reply from the front.

She mutters curses under her breath as she unsteadily reclaims her seat and finally decides to fasten herself in. She doesn't look at anyone else.

A tight corner makes me slide forward in my seat, the harness digging into my pecs so hard I can almost feel it. I settle back, rubbing my chest, and look around to distract myself from the stunt driving.

Despite The Pulse team van actually being a large converted security truck, the four of us in the back are strapped into slim racing-car style seats packed into the smallest space possible, two either side of the rear doors. I have to sit like a child trying to hide in plain sight: thighs pressed tightly together, shoulders rolled forwards and squeezed in, hands in my lap holding my mask, all to give Inna next to me enough room to sit normally. Not that I think anyone would ever complain, but I don't want to be "that guy" taking up somebody's space on the armrest with my bulk.

Apart from the four of us, the rest of the space is taken up with computers, miscellaneous rescue equipment, gadgets and bits of hardware I've never managed to identify, all either strapped to the walls, fixed to shelves or jostling around in storage containers. Spare costume pieces hang on two poles separating us from the driver's cab, their thin plastic covers creating static as they crinkle against each other. Underneath them are a rack of boots and shelves holding several sets of night vision goggles, gloves and face masks.

Screws and fixings complain loudly as the truck bounces over speed humps, while upturned rainbows of wiring and a collapsible plastic nozzle swing from the ceiling. Irregular black shadows cut through the blue gloom from the monitors, the only light in the rear.

A stack of white medical stretchers rasp against each other next to Maria's ear, making her pale face tighten more and more with each jerk of the van. She is staring at the computer screen diagonally opposite her with a look of grim attention, as her long black bob swings side to side. In fact, as The Black Witch her costume is entirely black: dress, shoes, choker and jewellery. In the near darkness of the van she looks like a white mask and a set of four mannequin limbs dangling off the wall.

I try to catch her eye but her gaze doesn't alter. She is always so serious while on a mission, so utterly focused it's like she's switched personality with a Marine.

Mitchell sits next to her, a figure not much bigger than Maria. A skinny lad of nineteen, dressed in a loose fitting custom made dark blue top and trousers, a silver electric bolt symbol affixed prominently on his chest. We're still ten minutes away from the scene but he already has his helmet on, painted blue like his top, with his goggles flipped down. Looks like he's sweating. Kid still has a lot to learn about the practicalities of going on missions. To be fair he only joined us a few months ago and still needs to learn these things for himself.

He sits as far away from any electrical equipment as possible, his electric charge ability making him a liability around sensitive equipment. He's already fried seven Mega Drives and two microwaves since he started. His seat in the van is a specially earthed one, just in case. As always he seems anxious to be somewhere else, repeatedly whipping his head round to crane out the rear door window and absent-mindedly shooting sparks between the fingers of opposite hands like a ghostly cat's cradle.

Next to me, outline etched in the blue monitor glow, sits Inna, hands up at her shoulders holding the harness straps like a parachutist about to leap to her doom. She is expressionless. She blinks infrequently and, when she does, slowly. Our stoic Ukrainian blonde goddess. She's the only one in the team other than Jack who can get away with wearing skintight spandex. The figure-tightening white and gold leotard costume with matching knee-high boots doesn't leave much to the imagination. Naturally this has made her a paparazzi magnet, which she seems typically impassive about.

I did briefly try a spandex version of my costume, but Maria said that seeing me move in it was like watching two pit bulls wrestling in a sleeping bag. Not an image the team wanted to plant in the public mind. After that it was back to the comfy cotton two-piece and waistband. Tan and dark brown. Not the nicest of colours, but the cheapest when it came to making my own when I was solo. I had hoped for a redesign after joining the team, something flashier, but instead I got a better quality version of the same thing. Something about keeping my Hero identity consistent. Still wish it wasn't brown.

Something squeaks incessantly near the front of the van. If it's bugging *me* I know Maria will be ready to murder someone by the time we get there.

"You OK?" I say to Inna.

Don't know why I said that. Desperate to listen to anything but this van shaking itself to pieces I guess.

Not sure she can even hear me, but after a short pause she slowly turns her head.

"Yes."

Even that single word is smothered in a thick accent. She turns back and adjusts her hands on the straps.

"Good. No, that's good." I nod slowly.

Maria is staring at me. I try to shrug, but the seat and straps constrict me and I end up hunching forwards like I'm gently retching. She blinks and looks at the screens again. Suddenly she and Mitchell slide forward, straining into their straps. Maria gasps out loud and Mitchell lets loose a small burst that briefly lights up the rear doors.

"Fucking hell!" screams Maria when she gets her lungs back.

A beeping from the computer suddenly makes her alert. She pops her straps and leaps over to the empty chair in front of the screens. Her black dress expands in the air and suddenly lights up, black sequins scattering bright monitor-blue sparks of light around the cabin, black silk seams and edgings curling like eels in the gloom. She firmly plants herself in the seat and secures herself in.

"OK, we've finally got a link to the drone we sent off before we left."

She hammers at the keyboard and goes to grab the mouse, only to find it's hung itself over the edge of the desk by its own cord. She snatches it up and slams it on the desk.

Inna has bent her head forward for a look, so I have to strain the straps and tilt my head to get a look at the furthest of the three screen setup, angled more or less towards me.

A fuzzy black moving picture appears. Streaks of light pass from one corner to another. White, orange, red, white. Strange patterns, rectangles, a Tetris nightmare. Maria is cursing about the zoom function not working when she hits the right command and within seconds the night-time cityscape comes into view.

The drone is hovering over the Mellfields area of the city, just south of the river, before the main centre. High-rise flats pass beneath it, then shops, rows of older houses, car lights cutting between them at right-angles. South Bridge is lit up yellow and looks like a cardboard cutout pasted over the inky river beneath it. Then blackness, as all it shows is water.

"Oh for fuck's sake." Maria is glued to the screens. "We need a faster drone. We'll be there before that fucking thing arrives."

"Only on account of my astounding driving!" calls Charles.

We're all staring at the screens. Still black.

This is the worst bit. When you're about to find out what you're up against and, in this hanging moment it could be literally anything. You're going to have to assess the situation and work out a plan in a matter of seconds, and you're going to be there in minutes. I can hear Mitchell mouthing, "Come on, come on…"

Still black. Only the occasional white snaking ripple of water breaks the darkness. Then, all at once a river boat burns next to its moorings. Fletcher Drive is covered in debris but no movement. A road joining it is also empty and they form an orange vein cutting between the black meat of the city. Then the drone breaks over the main square and Inna gasps. Police cars are scattered, some overturned and burning. Officers on foot, officers on horses, all seemingly in disarray, run suddenly in a group. Riot police with shields hold a line while a barrage of people slam into them, the line collapses, trampled on. Then the swarm of people, just as quickly and just as bizarrely, retreat like a wave being sucked back out to sea. Maria has to zoom the camera out even further.

"Oh fuck."

Chaos. Swarms of people run in groups, break apart, reform like split mercury. One blob splits off to slam into a bus stop. Glass smashes, people tumble and become trapped and squashed under it as the weight of bodies uproots it from the pavement. Then the group urgently changes direction as a canister of tear gas lands next to it. It moves right over it and moments later the canister arcs back towards a huddle of officers hiding behind a police van on its side. Other groups slam their bodies into shop frontages and giant windows collapse into waterfalls of glass. An explosion. The petrol tank of a car has ruptured. People are thrown back, some on fire. They all pick themselves up and start running again. The burning ones push to the front and leap on a car trying to three-point turn its way out of trouble. They smash in the windscreen and pile onto the driver. Two passengers jump out but are forced back in by the throng. The inside of the car is alight.

As the drone reaches its pre-programmed destination and starts circling around the square I can see more people moving down side streets. Some are being chased, some run to join the crowd.

"What the hell is going on? Those people are on fire you know? It's like they don't care!" Mitchell's face is pale behind his goggles.

Maria studies the scene intently.

"This is definitely a psychic phenomenon. Vincent? What are you getting now?"

"A headache," comes another voice from the front. "I've never felt anything like this before. It's a force of will covering the centre of the city like an iron blanket. Incredible."

"Is this The Controller?"

"If it is he... aah... he's more powerful than any of us reckoned him to be. I'm seeing those same pictures you are. There must be hundreds of people in his thrall, with more joining all the time. I'm trying to keep us all psychically shielded but there is so much background noise from this it's... a struggle."

"You have to keep us safe Vincent, otherwise we're all completely fucked."

"Don't worry...", a whimper, "I know all too well..."

"You'll do fine by us buddy, don't worry." I call. He doesn't reply. I know he's trying to concentrate.

Without warning the radio bursts into noisy clicks and crackles making me wince.

"Pulse to team, rendezvous at the corner of Passmore Road and Element Park. The police have set up an Emergency Incident Area there. I have new information, we need to update our plan. Over."

Maria immediately hits the reply button. "OK, en route. Five minutes. Over."

"Element Park it is!"

Charles brakes hard and filters down a side street. He flicks a switch and the siren drowns out all other noise. It's a relief in one sense. We hurtle between parked cars, only inches either side. The movement of the van is more erratic now and I can hear Charles muttering under his breath.

"Getting busy up ahead. I think we're going to have to go the wrong way across Heroes Bridge."

"Right... what?" says Maria.

Too late. I hear car horns as we cut between traffic islands into oncoming traffic, then we're onto the bridge. Looking out the back I see the tail end of a large queue on the northbound side

"Are you fucking insane?"

"I'm perfectly sane my dear, less vehicles this side, although they *are* travelling a mite faster..."

We suddenly swerve across lanes and in front of cars braking in our wake.

"Shiiit, this is like some action movie yeah? The good guys racing to the scene you know?"

"Hah! That's the spirit my lad!"

"Except they usually get there alive don't they?"

"And this isn't a fucking action movie!"

"Well I can turn back and wait politely in the queue until the riot is finished sometime early tomorrow morning, but I thought it expeditious in...". We swerve, a car horn changes tone as it goes past us "...the circumstances."

Maria mutters curses louder. She knows she can't argue the point and stares at the screen instead, blinking out her frustration.

The wires of the bridge whizz past, orange streaks against a velvet purple sky. Sliding pairs of red lights bend around us. I'm steadily hypnotised by them as the wailing siren fades from my consciousness.

Abruptly, the bright orange glow of the bridge falls away from us as we hit land again. Out the back windows I see pedestrians scatter in all directions as we jump a crossroads. Some are running full pelt on their own, some in pairs or small groups holding on to one another. An old man clutches his head, blood on his face. A crying boy stumbles around confused.

"Ah, shit man, this is well fucked up," says Mitchell, face screwed up with worry.

He's bricking it. The last thing we want is him electrocuting civilians in a panic. Need to keep the kid grounded. Routine. These missions are all about routine.

"Don't worry Mitchell", I tell him, "we'll meet with Jack, find out from the police what the situation is, where we're needed and what we need to do. Trust me, when we have a plan the fear will go. It's just that first leap into the unknown that gets your guts twisting about."

Mitchell looks at me, forces a smile and creates a tiny ball of electricity between his hands.

"Don't worry about me man, I'm well ready you know?"

Even with the jostling of the vehicle I can tell he's shaking. I smile back.

"I know. You'll be fine."

We take a few corners sharply, slowing down more and more as the streets become busier with people coming in the opposite direction.

"Almost there!" shouts Charles from up front as he turns another bend. "Ah, bugger."

The van comes to a halt.

CHAPTER 3
THURSDAY 13TH SEPTEMBER 2012

Martin walked through the door and stopped until it clicked shut behind him with a satisfying double thunk of the lock. He stepped back and pressed the crown of his head against the door behind him. He breathed in, held it, waited until he could no longer hear the echo of the lock in the corridor outside then breathed out slowly. Immediately relief flooded up through the centre of his chest, choked him at his neck then spread out across his scalp. He stood there, leaning back on the door, the sharp edge of horizontal mid rail digging into his skull. He rocked his head side to side. There was the sickly rasp of muscle being ground between bone and wood. Martin felt nothing, but he needed to hear the noise.

The supermarket hadn't been any busier than usual, but only three of the self-service checkouts were working. He had to queue between two chattering schoolgirls and a young bloke buying a box of doughnuts and several bags of cookies and biscuits, who was standing just a bit too close behind him. The girls discussed boys with high intensity and little shame. Their conversation somehow wound its way from a friend's break-up, to a new Hero music group, to how boring seventies Hero history was, to whether they would get friction burns from having sex with Zip Taylor, all within a minute. The unstable verbal whirlwind almost sent Martin running. He had visions of him running terrified past security, his shopping flying out of his hands, scattering and sliding across the floor around him, before throwing himself out of the sliding doors, chest first onto the pavement and rolling into the gutter, clutching at himself like a terrified child.

He had to mentally shut them out in the end, pretending their words were noises, not to be interpreted as having meaning. When that was done he could more easily ignore the noise itself, push it into the background and focus on something else.

This was a trick that Vincent had taught him once. Of course his friend had to do it constantly, did it automatically, but it was a useful technique for non-psychics too. The problem was that with the girls shut out, he was now hyper-aware of the proximity of the man the other side of him. Every tiny move the man made felt like that of a lover in bed, hugging him from behind. Every sound he made felt like it came from inside his own head. The man cleared his throat, Martin clutched his. Now he felt squashed, threatened. He slid slowly forward until he was equidistant between the two forces either side. This gave some relief, although the queue didn't move for a while after.

The keys went on the key hook by the mirror with their usual tinkle and tock as they hit the wall. He placed the Tesco carrier bag on the floor next to the wooden shoe store, took off his jacket and hung it up opposite. He flicked the light switch. There was the familiar faint crackle of electricity inside the wall and the soft yellow light near the top of his head lit the narrow hallway. A strip of slate blue carpet led the eye to a hazy rectangle of sunlight from the living room.

He picked up the shopping bag, took it into the kitchen and dropped it on the counter by the sink. From it he produced a microwaveable beef cannelloni meal for one, a pack of eight suspiciously small pro-biotic yoghurts, a two litre carton of milk, (he could never finish a four litre one before it started to ripen), a pack of sliced chorizo for his midnight sandwiches, a box of limescale prevention tablets for the washing machine and an energy saving light bulb, (the one in the spare room stopped working just the other day).

The kitchen was small and narrow with two walls taken up by pale wood units and the sink at the far end. A folded down plastic topped table and one chair were pushed flush against the other. The food went in the tall silver fridge-freezer, out of which he grabbed a can of Czech beer. The limescale tablets went under the sink next to the bleach and cooking foil. Picking up the beer and bulb he went into the bedroom. He stood on the small chair that he had left under the light fitting, opened the packet and slotted the bulb in place. He was startled when the bulb lit up straight away. He must have left the switch on. Never mind, he was glad it was working again at least. He glanced around the room. Plain bed linen, a small chest of drawers in the corner, tiny table next to the bed and a small plain mirror on the wall. Neat and tidy. Looked good.

Turning the light off before it had time to whiten he went into the bathroom. The pull cord clink-clunked and the harsh strip light seared his eyes. "There must be an energy saving bulb that can go in that fitting...", he mused to himself. He washed his hands and face. As he dragged his hands down from his forehead to his chin he stared at himself in the cabinet mirror. He mentally filled in the patches of male pattern baldness stretching back from his temples, dipping his head slightly to check he still didn't have a bald spot. His hair was short, dark and cropped close to his head. Number two all over. No style at all really. It kept things simple and had made visits to the barbers nice and quick, until they started to talk and pry too much so that he had to buy a hair clipper from Argos and do his own.

He poked at the bags under his eyes. They looked puffier today, emphasising the crease underneath them. Turning slightly sideways, he traced the outline of his nose, over the bump down to his top lip. His square jaw at the bottom of his square head led straight down to his neck. Turning portrait view again he grimaced, revealing his coffee stained teeth. One day he was going to treat himself and get those whitened. Tipping his head up this time, he felt under his chin with a fingertip for the line of beard hair bristle that he could somehow never manage to shave to the skin. He looked like a boxer who had never been in a fight, as Charles used to say to him. Utterly unexceptional.

"A face like any other.", he reassured himself and went into the living room, turning the light off behind him.

The living room was a simple affair. A solid red leather three seater sofa sat facing the windows, with a rectangular dark walnut coffee table in front of it. The table was covered in free newspapers, junk mail and chocolate wrappers. Opposite sat his old "fat" TV on a glass stand. He wasn't bothered about replacing it with a flat screen one until it broke, and it had done him well for almost ten years now. A small bookcase with drawers filled up another wall space. He only had three books on it. Two of them were gifts, one from his mother many years ago and the other from Charles, a free copy of his autobiography that he found sitting on his welcome mat one morning. The third was a non-fiction book he had bought for one pound fifty in a charity shop. He occasionally read parts about the old fifties and sixties Heroes and their battles with the Communists to avoid nuclear war. Another shelf had an old Polaroid picture in a frame, fuzzy and with colours a bit too intense. A picture of his mum and dad, him as a two year old in her arms and his older brother, about four, standing between his parents looking inexplicably grumpy.

He sat down heavily on the sofa. It gave its familiar sigh then gently eased down to its normal sitting height.

One heavy swallow from the can of beer and a deep sigh of his own and his upper eyelids were tapping their lower cousins. He shook his head to stay awake. He didn't want to fall asleep on the sofa like yesterday morning, only to wake up when the postman delivered pizza menus. He didn't want to fall asleep on the sofa like every morning. Well, there was something to be said about routine, he thought to himself. Good old sofa.

He patted the dark red leather seat next to him. He sometimes imagined that there would be someone else sitting there. A woman. Sometimes she would be blonde, sometimes dark. But she would be wearing a Hero costume. Old fashioned, with a V-neck, not one of the modern S&M styled ones. And they would talk. They would talk about how different things were back then. She would talk about her life in the 1960's and 70's and they would compare it with his exploits in the 90's. They would both laugh at the similarities and the strange differences. Then they would talk about today, and how there was no character to anything any more. Everything was distant and so precise, the human element stripped out so methodically, as if it had always been some inconvenience. Heroes were now "assets" with strict rules of engagement drawn up by the UN and individual governments. How could they inspire people any more? How could they give people any sense of hope that the ills of the world could be sorted? They couldn't. That was the point. They had been neutered by governments terrified of losing their relevance.

Nothing was the same. Nothing was going to bring back the old days.

Then there would be silence between them for a short while before she leant over and kissed him on the cheek. He would wake up when the postman delivered pizza menus.

He turned on the TV to stave off the inevitable slumber for a moment longer. On the breakfast news there was already a report about Team Element City One successfully aiding the local police in a large drugs bust. Nine arrests on the scene, over a hundred kilos of heroin, over thirty thousand in cash, several weapons including a handgun, a handful of marijuana plants and a variety of drugs paraphernalia. Team boss Reverb stood proudly next to the detective in charge, who made certain to say that the police had been gathering intel and planning the operation for seven months, before thanking the team for providing, "essential support in apprehending the criminals".

Reverb himself was given a brief moment to speak, in which he reiterated the hard work of the police, and said the whole team was proud to be working closely with the local law enforcement officers. He thanked the team's sponsors for their continued support.

Martin wasn't sure how much was genuine or how much was heavy sarcasm. Reverb certainly wasn't giving anything away with his body language. Very controlled. Fixed grin, hands behind his back, looking straight at the detective as he returned to the microphones, quietly nodding at the right moments, being visible yet remaining respectfully distant. The cameraman also seemed to forget he was there and zoomed back in on the detective, leaving the Hero off screen.

Reverb reminded Martin very much of Jack. In fact, Team Element City One was pretty much the modern day equivalent of his old team.

In many ways they had been ahead of their time. Jack would personally organise sponsorship and licensing deals. All communications to the public or press went through him. Eventually they hired a PR company to manage their image. They became the template for dozens more teams, at least until the Innate Power Registration Bill passed, when it all disappeared in a day.

Before then, Heroes still had free reign as long as they didn't involve the general public in their affairs. Every week there was some villainous escapade to be dealt with. Bank robberies, an attack on the police, some new Hero gone wild, a powered gang trying to assert their dominance over a part of town. Things were fluid. New Heroes appeared, joined teams, fell out with teams, swapped allegiances, disappeared under mysterious circumstances and were either found floating in the river, spread over several square miles of city, or slipped back into anonymity. It was an exciting time. People needed them, the police more or less tolerated them, the government accepted the necessity of having them around. But now...

Martin chuckled to himself. He slapped the side of his head to stop himself going through all that crap again. He had to remind himself that was eighteen years ago. Those schoolgirls in the queue weren't even born when the team split up. That made them ancient history. A Wikipedia entry ripe to be copy pasted into an essay. Nothing more. In any case, he would be able to unload his mind this Sunday when he went to visit Vincent.

Apart from the old psychic, he spoke to no-one else from The Pulse any more. He and Vincent were close friends when they were in the team and now each was the only person the other could bear to be with for any length of time. The only company they both needed.

He knew Maria sometimes came to visit, and he made sure he would never be there at the same time. He couldn't face that. Funnily enough, he and Vincent always started by saying that they wouldn't talk about the old days, and they always ended up talking about the old days. Still, it was a change of scenery. Someone for Vincent to talk to apart from the community support workers who visited him fortnightly. It was a chance to get safely drunk on whisky before grabbing the last bus home. Something to look forward to, other than sitting on the sofa with cheap beer, half listening to the TV.

What was it now? Business news. Shares in Pullman Enterprises have gone up after they announced they would be completing their government contract early and under budget. Well at least Jack was still doing well for himself.

The beer was finished. He didn't remember drinking it all.

He shifted on the sofa, the cool patches where he hadn't been felt nice.

His eyes felt heavy again. They were harder to fight to stay open this time.

Sports news. Fallout from the Paris 2012 Olympics where one of the Azerbaijani athletes had been identified as having innate powers and disqualified from a running event. She was in tears being interviewed, saying she didn't know, and still had no idea what her alleged power was and whether it would have given her any advantage. Stern faced officials saying it must be a level playing field for all, questioned once again the need for a Superlympics, standard reply that individual national laws and cultural attitudes on the use of powers make this an impossibility.

Martin huffed and remembered when Heroes were looked up to as examples of how good and decent humanity could be. Even those without powers aspired to be as honourable and brave as them. Nowadays you were tested at birth, controlled if need be and made to hide your powers, like it was something to be ashamed of. Living your life never knowing your full potential. What a waste.

He thought about his days in The Pulse and all the good things they did.

And then he woke up when the postman delivered pizza menus.

"Ah bugger."

CHAPTER 4
FRIDAY 16TH APRIL 1993

"Ah bugger."

"What is it?"

Maria presses the quick release button on her seat harness and runs to the front of the van. She grabs the handle on one of the side door and pulls. It folds out and up into three sections that overlap each other and tucks itself into a recess in the roof.

I look past her, through the doorway. The road ahead is lined with small boutique shops and stretches for about two hundred metres up to the corner of Element Park. Normally it's busy with cars filtering off the main central roads and those heading towards the city centre car parks. Now it's filled with a stream of people stumbling away from the chaos. Some are spattered with blood, others sobbing and looking lost, most seem dazed.

Just ahead of them a bus has collided with two cars while trying to escape. One car was on its side. Behind the bus the full length of the road is jammed with abandoned vehicles. A couple of cars are on fire. A paramedic is in the road with a young woman who has been hit.

I twist my head and look out the rear. The people flow past us. Somebody leans on the van, sweating and gasping for breath. A group of youths with metal poles and a cricket bat are heading in the opposite direction.

"Maria, your turn at the wheel! Martin, Inna, with me."

"We should try a different route..."

"Trust me my dear they will all be the same. This may not be the easiest path but it is the shortest."

Charles jumps out of the driver's seat. I hit my release button and the straps whip away round my sides. I can move my shoulders again. Relief! I hear Inna freeing herself as I pull my mask over my head and fit it under my chin. It's time to do this.

I push down the handle and the heavy door nearest to me opens with a slight squeal. I jump out onto the road with Inna right behind me. She is quickly away round the side of the van as I look back in to Mitchell.

"Keep cool, we'll be there soon."

He just nods. Looks like he's going to be sick.

I close the door and follow after Inna.

The first thing I notice is the noise. The inside of the van is well soundproofed and we couldn't hear anything going on outside. Out here it's as if hundreds of people are reading off the same script of screams, cries and roars but have started from different places, their voices overlapping each other chaotically. The effect is of an eerie demonic chant that laps slowly around the buildings, tickling my skin as it brushes past me. Even Inna looks around anxiously. I've never felt so claustrophobic.

"Guys! Front!"

We move round the side of the van, trying not to bump into people. A man runs up to Inna.

"Sunlight! My parents! I lost them somewhere back there." He urgently and repeatedly points up the road. "I couldn't find them, the Police said I had to move back, but I can't leave them..."

She takes him by both shoulders and looks at him intently.

"Do not worry, we are on our way."

He visibly relaxes with relief as tears stream down his face. He mouths "Thank you" as we join Charles at the front.

The tallest of the team, Charles's physique is trim, but he doesn't look skinny. His dark red curly hair is clipped at the sides and he has a slightly paler, well trimmed goatee today. His facial adornment varies constantly from full beard to clean shaven and all styles in between. His garish red, orange and white spandex top reflect the glare of the street lights, his dark red trousers and boots complete the costume. His costumes are the most expensive of the whole team. They are all specially made from the very latest heat and fireproof materials and are hand tested to destruction by him, to make sure he isn't going to set himself alight mid-mission. He changes the design every few months and argues that the cost is offset by the increased merchandise revenue, urging the rest of us to consider doing the same. His "summer" top comes halfway down his biceps, showing off his tanned, freckled arms, thin curls of hairs glowing bright yellow in the van headlights behind him. His chin is lifted and he is carefully surveying the road ahead as we line up next to him.

"Remember people, Hero names only from now on. Under the circumstances I doubt anyone would notice, but always better to err on the side of caution."

The oncoming flow of people starts to part further up in front of the van as if expecting us to move forward. I guess we must project some invisible barrier of confidence as we stand here. The, "wall of purpose", as Jack puts it. It's all about poise, how you speak, and looking like you have purpose. As a wail of screams rustles through the trees I flick away the instinctive urge to run. I think I'm going to need to practice that a bit more.

I look into the cab behind us. Maria is busy adjusting her costume and fighting with the seat position levers, while Vincent sits awkwardly to one side, elbow resting on one knee, cradling his head in his hand. He looks in pain.

I always felt his costume was the strangest choice but now, and I hate myself for thinking such a pointless thought while he's obviously in distress, he looks like a sad boy at a fancy dress party.

I know they were going for a mystical look, his Hero name being The Seeker, but I do wonder which native American communities we are offending with the faux tribal patterned top and mask. Not to mention the cheap looking white cape with oversized eyelets and gold rope tying it at the front.

He shifts as if a bad dream is rousing him from sleep and opens his eyes a crack to look out of the window. He seems to be looking past everything, until his eyes flick down to mine.

I give him a smile and a thumbs up. He nods and closes his eyes again.

I turn back and see Charles has stepped in front of us.

"OK chaps, here's the plan..."

***

It takes us nearly ten minutes to reach the corner. I push or roll cars to the side of the road to make room. Inna disintegrates others with her light beam, making sure, as Charles is swift to remind her, that there is no-one inside. Meanwhile Charles sucks the flames out of the burning cars and, with his calm authoritative voice, manages to get the panicked citizens to stay mostly on the pavements. Maria follows slowly and closely behind us in the van.

Eventually we make it to the top of the road by Element Park. A small group of police cars and ambulances have made an impromptu checkpoint on the small plaza in front of the park's iron gates. They form a haphazard line across the road leading towards the pedestrianised centre, their light bars causing the buildings and trees to flash blue and white. Beyond them the silhouettes of ragged, inconsistent lines of police in riot gear form a jagged wall of black. Beyond them the night is purple and orange and angry.

Dozens of police, medics and fire crews form small, intense groups as a multitude of insistent voices shout orders and alerts at officers and into radios, piercingly loud messages being relayed back to them. Some run back and forth, to and from the front line, through the gaps between the vehicles. An officer, face covered in blood, sits on the back step of an ambulance as a paramedic looks at his head wound. Another police van arrives on the scene through the route we just cleared. Armed officers jump out from the back and head straight towards the large group in the middle of the plaza, gathered round an unmarked car. In the middle of this group stands Jack. Pulse.

While we took the long route he flew ahead under his own power to assess the situation. In his silver and blue one-piece costume he is stillness and calm personified, as if the world has been sped up around him. He has one earpiece of a small set of headphones pressed close to his head as a small grey haired policeman talks urgently at him, gesticulating wildly. As our van creeps round the corner, Jack waves us over.

Mitchell hops out the back and Maria tries to park somewhere out of the way. The young lad runs over to me, completely ignoring Vincent who almost drops out of the passenger seat onto the tarmac and slowly and unsteadily follows us, holding one side of his head.

"Seriously, we should get a fucking jet. One of those ones that can go, you know, vertically and shit? Save us getting caught in traffic all the fucking time."

He is crackling with anxiety. Can't blame him. Ten minutes of listening to that hideous wailing noise while we picked our way into a war zone and I'm anxious too. Got to keep him calm though. I know how to steel myself, but he hasn't learnt that yet.

"Well you never know Buzz, if we save the city tonight we might be able to buy one."

"Oh that would be so fucking cool you know? My brother is in the RAF you know?" I know. "He could be our pilot! He'd fucking love it you know?"

Vincent arrives and stands swaying behind the rest of us as we face Jack and the officer, who he introduces as Chief Inspector Pace. We have of course assisted the police before, but this is the first time they have asked us for help. Pace starts off by explaining clearly this very fact, making very sure we know we're here by police request and as a last resort. He warily eyes all of us as he speaks, frown lines hardening across his forehead. Jack reassures him that we are here to help with crowd control as they need it, and to track down the psychic who is causing this.

"Don't forget these are civilians caught up in this, they're not villains for you to beat up yes?" says Pace.

He's worried. Not just from the unfolding situation, but also that his desperate decision to officially involve us isn't going to horribly backfire on him. Maria, who has appeared from nowhere, manages to reassure him and the whole group, subtly using her mood altering abilities to calm them and increase their trust in us. Just enough so they are not aware it's being done.

Finally certain, CI Pace explains the situation in detail. Just over an hour ago two officers attempted to move on a homeless man from a bus shelter and were attacked by him. After a vicious struggle, they finally got him on the ground. When they attempted to cuff and arrest him the other people queuing at the stop suddenly attacked them too. The small group stood at the stop screaming as the officers retreated and called for backup. After two more police cars arrived, things escalated. The group started doing a bizarre swarming movement. They attacked anyone who came close then rushed into a small supermarket before crashing back out through the windows with everyone who had been shopping in there. A major incident was announced and the whole force was mobilised for riot duty. Since then the crowd had become increasingly violent and unpredictable and the initial defensive police lines had to be repeatedly moved back. For the last fifteen minutes however, the crowd had been contained and, while it had threatened to break through the police lines, it hadn't made any committed attempt.

While containment is top priority, there are still officers and unaffected civilians inside the cordon who need to be brought to safety. Pace succinctly sums up the evening's events as, "hell on earth", stretches one hand across his forehead and tightly squeezes his temples before pointing at a fold-out map of the city centre spread across the car bonnet.

He shows us where he needs backup for his men, mainly in the narrower and darker side streets, locations where he knows officers are trapped and danger areas where the crowd has been most active.

Jack turns to us and gives us our orders. He grabs Mitchell and flies off to try to reach the stranded officers. I'm to escort Maria to a vantage point where she can try to calm the crowd mentally, while the others are to take Vincent and track down the psychic.

Pace picks up his radio and lets everyone know to let us through their lines in both directions if they see us.

We regroup beside our van.

"OK", says Maria, "best vantage point for the main square is the Merlin Centre. If the two of us can get to the roof I should be able to see the whole pedestrianised area and down most of the side streets too."

"You think you can affect that many people at once? While they're under psychic control?"

"It's… something I have to try." She almost shrugs.

"In any case, my fellow Heroes," said Charles, "you are but one part of the plan. We need a vantage point of our own too. One where our resident psychic detector here can pinpoint his location."

Vincent is leaning against the van. He looks shaky.

"Too… busy down here to focus."

"Exactly! Sunlight and my good self will find you somewhere nice and quiet to do your best work." He slaps down on Vincent's shoulder and his knees nearly buckle. "Well, seems as if we're walking

45

today chaps. Once more unto the breach and all that."

The three of them head towards the park gates and disappear into darkness.

Maria and I look towards the police line. It suddenly splits open before being quickly reinforced by officers at the back charging forward. The crowd howls its disapproval like a wolf chorus.

"Hmm. Don't fancy that much. How about we take a quieter route? If the police don't mind us doing a spot of breaking and entering that is." I slap my fist into my palm.

Maria twists one side of her mouth into a smile and holds out her hand towards the buildings along the road we just cleared.

"You lead the way."

I nod, "Let's do this", and we walk towards the chaos.

CHAPTER 5
THURSDAY 13TH SEPTEMBER 2012

"Our policy on personal mail clearly states that we do not allow any. No letters, let alone packages or parcels. It really is very clear on this."

Martin was standing in the corridor outside the gallery security office where Simon had been waiting to catch him with a large brown envelope. The guy was a good fifteen years Martin's junior and about a quarter of his weight. Even the smallest uniform size hung off him, making him look like a sad schoolboy on the first day of term. He had a topping of light brown hair above his long gaunt face and strangely pale blue eyes that faded into his corneas, leaving a small black dot of a pupil that would never lose contact with yours. This disturbed Martin greatly and he avoided the young man whenever he could.

Not that he had any problems with him personally. He was very a diligent assistant office manager who gave everyone equally good praise or criticism, whatever their job title or status. This of course meant most people hated him passionately.

Martin suspected he had been bullied as a child, like he had. It was strange how you could tell. He felt a slight kinship in that regard, an unspoken connection. But whereas Martin's escape from that mental prison had been to reach out and help others, Simon's was control. Internal control – appearance, behaviour – and external control over the few things he could influence. And his influence now extended over the shopping centre offices, one of the consequences of which was anal attention to detail over office procedures. Normally this didn't affect Martin, his whole present and future plan being to follow all rules and avoid any form of conflict. And if only the guy didn't have such freaky non-eyes Martin might have been able to avoid being rankled by him right now.

"I know Simon, I understand the rules fine. But I honestly hadn't arranged for anything to be delivered to me here. No one even knows where I work to be honest."

"That's irrelevant Martin. No personal mail is allowed, full stop."

"Well it's not actually irrelevant because..."

Simon shook his head like a sad vulture, his tiny dot eyes staying fixed on Martin's.

"I don't want to fall out with you over this Martin. I expect you to abide by the rules just the same as everyone else who is contracted to work for Templeton-Bayer Services. Just because you are third party security doesn't mean you have any special privileges."

"I'm... well aware of that."

Simon handed over the package. It was unexpectedly heavy. Martin stiffened as he took it, mind racing, suddenly confused.

"I'm going to let this slide this once because of your exemplary record," he raised a finger and paused for effect, "but if it happens again I will be forced to implement our disciplinary procedures."

Simon quietly brought down his hand into his opposite palm in a chopping motion, dot eyes staring at him.

Martin didn't even notice. His pulse was rising, arms starting to tingle as he held the envelope out in front of him, away his chest. He took a deep breath to try to keep calm. He had suddenly lost all mental strength to argue his point further and, to his relief, the confrontation appeared to be reaching a natural end anyway. An escape point. So he took it.

"Of course Simon. Thank you. It won't happen again."

Simon gave a small nod, like a teacher having reluctantly scolded his favourite pupil, then walked off. The giant knot in Martin's chest slowly unravelled and he could feel his neck again. He looked down at the package in his shaking hand and kept it there.

Monica had been standing in the security room doorway, watching the scene with interest. She was part of the evening security shift and had taken over from Barney at two p.m. She was eagerly waiting to hand over to Martin to get home. Built like a comic book bouncer, she was a good ten inches taller than him with a neck just as thick. She had a face like a badly cut polystyrene rock and straw blonde hair violently pulled back into a ponytail. Her blue uniform shirt looked like it was in agony, stretched across her wide chest and bosom as, with her arms tightly crossed, she smiled at him.

"Well bugger me, he turned you inside out. He even gave you a chop! A downward chop. Can you imagine? That's one up from a finger wag you know. And I know a finger wag."

Martin didn't respond as he walked into the office, Monica stepping back to let him through.

"Seriously though, no-one knows you work here? You ashamed of us or something?"

He shook out his tingling fingers with his back to her and slid the package onto the table under the monitor wall. Relief. He guessed it was papers. Pamphlets or something from the feel of it.

"No… no, just you," he struggled to snipe back.

Monica laughed like a man, there was no getting away from it. A deep but genuine guffaw shook her body as she opened her arms and her startled breasts struggled to find a way out under the sudden pressure. She grasped the door frame, finished her laugh with a strained wheeze and took an exaggerated breath in.

"Love you too you shit!"

Martin hadn't really heard her. He was standing by the desk staring at the packet, fingers pushing it around, tapping at it like a strange sea creature found on the beach. For a moment he was twenty years ago.

Monica cocked her head to one side.

"How about I get you a shit coffee from the machine while you open your illegal mail. Deal?"

It took a while to register with him, but he turned and forced a smile.

"Yeah, deal."

Monica nodded deeply. "Good," she said, and disappeared into the corridor.

Martin stared at the empty doorway. The bright rectangle was so inviting. He could walk out now. Right now. Exit. Escape. He *needed* to walk out right now, his pulse was still racing, his forehead becoming tacky with the first seeping of sweat. He could already feel the relief of being outside this room, being outside the centre, being back in his flat with no-one around.

No. He mentally pulled himself away from the door and back into his body with a woozy shudder. The whirring of hard drives and the mutter of distant conversations were apparent to him again.

Martin looked back at the packet. He delicately brushed it with a finger and it spoke to him again.

"Martin, it's me, Vincent. It's important you open this right away."

An inanimate object infused with a psychic message. He remembered Vincent scaring the crap out of him with that trick many years ago. Paper was a good medium for it so he was told. Paper, card, wood and especially organic fabrics. Metals and plastics were much harder, although not impossible, depending on the type. Glass was pretty much a no no. Always best to go for objects that were touched frequently too – letters, notepads, door handles, pens. Not only that, you could tailor the message for a specific person. A great way to communicate secretly. This was something Vincent hadn't done in over eighteen years, since his last prank. This didn't feel like a prank and the knot was re-twisting itself in Martin's chest.

He could delay this forever and never know. He could take it round to Vincent's when he went this weekend and tell him his joke mail didn't work. He got a dark feeling he wouldn't get the chance and, in a fit of decision, picked up and ripped open the packet. He emptied the contents onto the desk. Several sheets of A4 paper and stapled booklets fanned out, along with some glossy coloured pamphlets and a black notebook. He picked out what looked like the covering letter and read:

"My dear friend Martin, I am sorry to say that if you are reading this I am dead. And unfortunately for me this is not the, 'comfortably in his sleep', version of this letter. I have been murdered. Unless this letter is telling you the name of the person who did it, then I either don't know who it was or was unable to psychically imprint it in time before they got me.

I have arranged for you to be the executor of my will because I know you better than anyone and I need you to find out who killed me. However much I hate placing you in danger, if I have been killed then there is much more than just my life at risk.

The question of why someone would want to kill me I believe is answered by the existence of my memoirs (enclosed). The other question you need to ask yourself is why I would write them in the first place.

The future hides everything from us, the past only what it doesn't want us to know.

Good luck my dear friend,

Vincent."

Martin felt light-headed as he stood trembling with the letter in his hands. The paper was telling him nothing, other than what was written on it.

"..if you are reading this I am dead."

He shook his head gently. No he thought, he was going to see him this weekend. He was going to get a bottle of whisky from Tesco tomorrow morning to take with him. It was all planned.

"..I am dead."

He was going to drive up there, park outside and when he was halfway up the path to the house Vincent would open the door.

"..dead."

The world was swimming. He grasped behind him for any part of the office chair and was barely able to turn it round in time before he collapsed into the seat.

He muttered, "No, but.." as his neck felt like it was shrinking, tightening around his carotid arteries, around his windpipe, his gullet. He started to choke as he could hear his ever loudening heartbeat in his ears.

He started to gasp little shallow breaths. The seat started to shrink around him, jamming itself between his ribs, crushing his lower back.

"Christ.."

Now his chest was falling in on itself, squeezing his heart and lungs. He tried to take a deep breath in but his ribs were straps being pulled tighter and tighter. He could feel his organs being forced up into his narrowing neck and tried to scream as the top of his body detached itself and floated up to the ceiling. The world was a blurry mess of colours, an angry vandalised painting that swung from horizontal to vertical as he slid to the floor and passed out.

***

People were murmuring around him. He could feel them close. Right next to his ear he could hear the bristling of hundreds of sharp carpet tile fibres as his head rolled over them. Thousands of tiny little electric sparks dancing across his cheek. He slowly opened his eyes to see several feet. One large pair of standard black shoes, a couple of pairs of brown leather gents shoes and a light beige pair of court shoes, all stepping and turning and shuffling around in some strange dance.

He took a long slow breath in. Much to his relief his body didn't resist it. There was movement and Monica's face suddenly dropped into view.

"Hey Martin, you OK down there? We did try to move you but it was like trying to shift a whale back into the sea."

Somebody, he thought it was Simon, said something about that not being appropriate.

"Relax, I know him better than you..." Monica stood up. The court shoes pushed their way through. He felt a tiny hand on his shoulder and was gently rolled back by Sandra, one of the senior office secretaries and assigned First Aider. She bent down to look at him.

"You're OK, you passed out. We put you in the recovery position until you came back round. You'll still be dizzy and disorientated, so don't rush to get up. Just in your own time, when you feel ready we'll get you up into a seat, all right?"

She was a thin woman with brushed back blonde hair and large glasses. The folds in her short sleeved shirt jutted out oddly in her bent over position. Her narrow grey skirt forced her to crouch in a particular way and her angular knees encased in her dark tights were close to his face. It was an odd perspective that made Martin feel like a small child again. Helpless and needing looking after.

He blinked a few times to test his vision and took another long breath.

"No, I think I'm good."

He put a hand next to his face and twisted round slowly, pushing himself up into a kneeling position. His cheeks and neck tingled as gravity pulled the blood out of them.

Simon appeared to be panicking, not having dealt with something like this before, and was trying to insist that an ambulance was called. Sandra reminded him of procedure, that they were only needed if there was actual injury or risk of injury. "He's only passed out." He heard another voice, the second pair of brown shoes, Henry Patterson, one of the shopping centre managers.

Martin felt extremely embarrassed as he knelt there with them talking over his head. He needed to let them all know he was fine and strong again. He grabbed the edge of the desk and pushed himself to his feet. A wobble and Monica grabbed his arm like a vice.

"Easy does it. 'The bigger they are' and I should know..."

Martin forced a chuckle and sat back down in the same office chair he fell out of.

Henry spoke up in his characteristic deep voice.

"Martin, you are fine to take some time off. We'll get extra cover from Ultimate Security while you sort things out. That's not a problem."

Simon seemed startled.

"What? But... OK, well you'll need to sign a leave form Martin, I'll get..."

Henry pressed a hand onto Simon's shoulder and spoke quietly but firmly in his ear.

"You sort that all out, I'll sign the forms, no need to come back in here."

Simon nodded, seeming to understand and left.

The room was starting to become pin sharp around Martin again as he shook his head and puffed out a few breaths.

"No no, I'm good Mr Patterson, like Sandra said I just passed out. Just need to go and splash my face."

He pressed his hands onto the top of the desk to push himself up.

"Martin, it's me, Vincent. It's..."

Martin yelped and dropped back down into the chair. He stared wide-eyed at the papers and pamphlets spread across the desk and the brown envelope he had just touched again. He couldn't believe he had forgotten. It all dropped into his guts again in a second and he felt sick.

Self-conscious he looked at the concerned faces around him.

"I'm so sorry buddy," said Monica.

Henry nodded.

"We didn't go through it, we just saw the covering letter from the solicitor. It happened to be on top. I'm sorry for the loss of your friend. Like I said, we can get cover no problem, take as much time as you need to sort his affairs. Sandra?"

He left the room.

"Solicitor's letter?" puzzled Martin. He looked down at the paper on the desk.

"Dear My Molloy,

My name is James Conrad and I am a senior partner of Conrad-Burnell solicitors. It is my sad duty to inform you of the recent passing of Mr Vincent Hayden-Philips..."

"What?" Martin picked up the letter and, as he tried to read further, the words slithered into different shapes before his eyes.

"My dear friend Martin, I am sorry to say that if you are reading this I am dead."

"You've just had a big shock and it will take you a while to recover. So just take things easy for the next few days", said Sandra. "Talking to the solicitors will help, they deal with this every day and I'm sure you'll find them really supportive."

"Right." Martin felt numb, but his breathing stayed normal. He put down the letter and the words reset themselves.

"Would you like some water?"

"No. Yes! Actually."

Sandra nodded, smiled at Monica and left the room.

Martin was relieved there was more space around him, although the second chair was too close and Monica took up a large part of the room.

She was looking at him with concern.

"You all right?"

He wasn't sure how he felt. He was just glad to not be on the floor walled in by shoes any more.

"Yeah. No. Not really."

He bent forward, put his head in his hands and pressed his cheeks and eyes back into his head until he was seeing coloured sparkles behind his eyelids. As he sat back up, blinking hard, he spotted two thin beige plastic cups on the desk.

"They'll be cold by now," said Monica, "Shit coffee anyway."

He felt a sudden uneasiness. He needed to be doing something. He needed to be doing something somewhere else. He needed to be in control again. He stood up, more slowly this time, opened the blue locker and grabbed his jacket and backpack.

"Are you sure you're OK to..."

"I'm good."

He hurriedly put on the jacket then brushed the papers on the desk into a pile and slipped them back into the envelope. "Martin, it's me, Vincent..." before shoving it into his backpack.

"I have to go."

"OK." Monica didn't seem sure what to do as she just watched him. "I'll tell Sandra and the others..."

"Thanks."

He left the room.

CHAPTER 6
FRIDAY 16TH APRIL 1993

"We need to find out who is controlling these people and fast!" calls Jack over the radio. "Any luck with the mob yet Maria?"

"I think I managed to change some of their moods to happy. Not worked. Instead of being pissed off and lashing out at everyone and everything, now they're loving it, like it's the time of their lives. Whoever is doing this has them deep under their will. I'm going to try something different, just need to find another safe place, I think they've worked out where we are."

"OK. Watch you don't get yourself surrounded, I can see quite a few starting to filter down the side roads."

"They are looking. Searching."

"Yeah, that helps Vincent... any proper leads Charles?"

"We've got a good vantage point over the city centre, just trying to get our more-mental-than-usual buddy to do his psychic compass trick for us."

"And?"

"Saliva, some gibbering and the foetal position. We'll keep on him."

Charles had taken Inna and Vincent to the top of Element Park, a five minute uphill climb to Hope Monument.

Below them, dark shifting shadows of trees and bushes confuse the eye. Staggered orange pricks of lamp light create galaxies of illuminated leaves around them as they show the safe paths through the foliage. At the bottom of the park and to their left, outside the gate, is the gathering of emergency vehicles at the incident centre. Civilians are still moving through here, but now only a trickle. It seems as if most unaffected people have managed to escape the square. They can see the chaos straight ahead of them. A throng of people run around like a flock of starlings on their dusk flight, smashing into the lines of police and hastily arranged barricades. The smoke of fires and tear gas grenades smothers the street and shop lights, draping a thick ghostly veil over the city. The monstrous, discordant roaring voice of the crowd is even louder up here.

Vincent grips onto an iron railing like a vomiting man on a violently rolling ship. Charles has him by both shoulders and is speaking softly into his ear, trying to focus his energies, but with little success.

"Damn it Vincent." He turns to face Inna. "I had thought it would be quieter for him up here, that it would allow him to pinpoint our psychic enemy, but it seems I just picked a nice romantic view for us all."

Inna had been standing quiet, looking around the city, seemingly oblivious to the noise from the streets below.

"You know, if I wanted to control all these people I would need good vantage point. Surely he can't be so strong to see through all eyes. So he need to have pretty nearly plan view of city centre yes?"

Charles walks up next to her.

"What are you thinking my princess?"

Inna points straight up at Burlington Towers, an exclusive city centre high-rise complex that dominates the skyline of the city. Its sleek black tower dotted with the dark orange window lights of curious and frightened residents. "I would be in there. Best view apart from where we are, and he's not here."

"Vincent?"

Vincent sways and bobs around, still holding onto the railing, his ship now lost on the open seas.

"Vincent, man!"

"There is intent. There is will."

"I know my friend", Charles takes him by the shoulders again and turns him to face the tower block, "but what do you make of that monolith? Is our nemesis to be found within?"

Vincent hardly seems to respond, but his mind is already scanning the building, floor by floor, each apartment, each room, each face pressed up against the glass, each couple holding on to each other barricaded in their bathrooms, each person standing in the dark, arms outstretched, motionless, concentrating...

"Ah. Something. Yes."

"Good man!" He slaps him on the back. "OK chaps, we've got a potential location for our usurper, we believe he is in Burlington Towers. Going to pop over there now with Vincent as our own portable psychic energy detector and flush the bugger out."

They start to move from the monument down to the nearer north-westward gate to the park.

There is no reply on the radio.

"Chaps?"

CHAPTER 7
THURSDAY 13TH SEPTEMBER 2012

By the time Martin arrived at Vincent's house it had started to sput with rain. The sky blanket was a puffy dark grey now, laced with violet, snagging on the rooftops. Vincent's house was in the suburbs to the north which was usually a fraught journey through the tight, busy streets of the smaller villages that had been engulfed by the encroaching city. However, at this time of the evening, most commuters had already made it home and Martin had only to contend with several slow buses and one aggressive taxi driver.

He knew this route off by heart. Vincent had bought this house with his and Maria's help shortly after he had been discharged from the secure psychiatric unit. It was a nice detached fifties place with big rooms, huge bay windows and small gardens at the front and back. It was also very quiet. Vincent had initially wanted a small farmhouse miles from anyone and their intruding thoughts. Maria convinced him that isolation was not what he needed as it would weaken his psychic defences. He picked this house from a shortlist they drew up and had been content there ever since.

Martin visited every two weeks and brought a bottle of whisky, which they sipped whilst talking about the good old days; the villains they had helped capture and the people they saved. They would keep each other updated about all the old Heroes and villains, what they were up to, who was getting married or divorced, what products they were advertising, who had died. Then they would spend hours putting the world right.

They would allow Hero teams to be fully independent again, scrap the Restriction of Innate Powers law, which they agreed was only brought in as a knee-jerk reaction to the London attacks. They would make sure that Heroes were seen, not as the police lapdogs and celebrity whores they were portrayed as now, but as people, people who would risk their lives to save others.

Then Martin would have to leave to get some sleep before his next night shift and, as he walked to his car, he would see Vincent sit back down in his armchair, pick up the whisky glass and raise him a toast.

His next visit was to have been on Sunday.

The bright yellow police tape cut a strange series of abstract lines against the maudlin background, as it sliced through bushes, entwined itself around a lamp post and criss-crossed the open front gate. He quickly turned his blue Ford Focus into a space about a hundred metres down the road on the opposite side to the house and turned off the engine.

Two forensic officers in their white plastic suits were chatting on the front lawn. One was wearing gloves and holding a bunch of clear bags with indistinguishable items inside, while the other tapped heavily and clumsily at a thick black tablet device, shaking his head. A third emerged from the open front door wearing his mask and with his hood up. He was carrying a bundle of the same square plastic bags containing what appeared to be books.

There was a large white tent erected on the lawn next to them and all the bags were taken there. Chunky plastic boxes with handles lay next to the tent. One officer was hunting through them for a spray bottle.

Two police vehicles sat half up on the pavement in front of the house. Bumper to bumper with them was a black unmarked car. On the opposite side of the road was a white box van decorated with blue stripes and a crest emblem. A fourth forensic officer was inside, leaning on a narrow shelf, dealing with some paperwork. Behind this van, almost blocking its small doorway, was another unmarked car, silver this time. Martin could just make out the silhouetted head and shoulders of two men sitting inside.

Next to the gate a plain clothes officer, most likely a detective, stood talking with urgency into his mobile phone. Martin then spotted another at the house next to Vincent's, talking to the neighbour, a nice elderly woman who looked after her disabled husband. Martin had spoken to her a few times. She seemed to be shaking her head a lot and pointing back at her house.

There were also four uniformed officers at the scene. One tall male officer standing on the pavement the other side of the gate to the detective, hands inside the chest of his protective vest looking up and down the road. A blonde female officer was further away with her back to him, talking to some people, probably other neighbours who were attempting to get a look and seemed visibly flustered they could not get any closer. The other two were making house-to-house enquiries, knocking on doors and interrupting late night suburban suppers.

Martin had thrown the solicitor's envelope on his passenger seat. He stared at it out of the corner of his eye. He had been growing increasingly restless as he drove here. Not another panic attack, but something gnawing at him. Something that didn't make sense.

He picked up the envelope, "Martin, it's me, Vincent...", by the sealed end and tipped the contents out onto the seat. There was the psychic cypher covering letter, (another little trick Vincent had told him about once), a glossy booklet introducing Conrad-Burnell solicitors, a pamphlet explaining the process and legal requirements of being an executor, several forms to fill in and return with identification and a black, B5 sized, hard cover notebook.

He touched the covering letter with a finger and read the altered text again.

"my memoirs (enclosed)"

"memoirs"

Martin muttered the word several times as he tapped the letter, its meaning alternately melting away and coalescing under his fingertips. Vincent was writing his memoirs. He couldn't understand it from any angle. Martin picked up the notebook and heard Vincent speak.

"I'm sorry my friend but, to prevent anyone trying to psychically force this open, you'll need a password to read it. Our old friends will help you out."

Despite knowing it would be pointless, he opened the notebook anyway. Blank. All the way through. Every page was psychically imprinted remotely by Vincent while the notebook had been held at the solicitors. He snapped it shut and placed it back down with the rest of the papers. His hands started trembling again so he closed his eyes and took some deep breaths in and out through his nostrils until it stopped.

A noise made him snap his eyes open. The two men had got out of the silver car. Plain clothes. Dark suits. They strode over to the gate and shook the hand of the detective, who immediately relaxed. Martin's brow furrowed. These guys were different. They weren't police. Probably PCA. Martin dropped his head back onto the headrest.

"Shit."

The unexplained death of any Hero was automatically flagged up to be investigated by the Powered Crime Agency. This posed a problem. Despite the anger of many Heroes at having to declare both their Hero and normal identities to a third party, and a number of cases taken to the European Court of Human Rights, all of The Pulse had registered eventually. Well,

Vincent was registered because of his psychiatric history, but the rest signed on voluntarily. All of them apart from him.

Martin swallowed. He felt a heaviness in his chest, in his guts, like he was sinking through the seat. Fortunately only Vincent knew he hadn't registered so, while they would find nothing about Martin in his house, Martin knew that PCA would be interviewing all his past powered acquaintances. Inevitably his name would come up and they would wonder why he wasn't on the database. So it was either go to the police voluntarily, and face up to five years in jail for not registering, or wait until PCA worked out he was Roadblock, pin him as suspect number one because he wasn't registered, then strap him in a Negation Harness before he could lie that he had been so busy with work he just forgot to sign up.

"Shit."

The PCA guys were in deep conversation with the two detectives, the other having finished talking to the elderly neighbour. The forensic officer from the van was leaning out the back and staring over at the meeting. The others agents on the lawn were glancing over nervously, still processing bags. Even the female uniformed officer was keeping her distance.

"Shit."

What was he doing here? Did he think he was going to get in his friend's house, search around for clues like some daytime TV detective? Stupid nonsense.

But he felt he needed to be here, to be close to his friend. He needed to speak to him. Face to face, not through recorded messages on paper. Ask him what he knew, what his concerns were.

Vincent had never mentioned being in fear of his life and Martin wasn't aware of any old villain with a grudge against him, they tended to focus on the more public facing members of the team anyway.

Then again, he had never mentioned he was writing his memoirs. That was a weird thing. He stared at the black notebook and wondered why the hell it even existed.

The agents were escorted inside the house and everyone outside visibly relaxed.

The officers doing the door-to-door were getting closer to where he was parked and he took that as a good time to go.

He took one last look at Vincent's house, his little oasis of calm. Martin needed his own oasis of calm to think properly and he headed back to his flat to find it.

CHAPTER 8
FRIDAY 16TH APRIL 1993

A black and gold painted iron bollard crashes through a window, gathering up a computer monitor, keyboard and mouse, a miscellaneous collection of stationery and a small silver photo frame as it scrapes across the top of a desk, then thuds onto the floor next to Maria. The shock makes her misstep and fall backwards.

"Fuck!"

"Maria, you OK?" I call to her.

"Yes, fine." She gathers herself back to reality and stands up, pieces of glass falling from her dress. "How the fuck they threw that two floors up I don't fucking know."

A hail of bricks crashes through the large windows next to me. They bounce off my shoulder and back and I shake the shards from my hair.

"We need to move. Now!"

We run with purpose through the empty offices. I feel my guts twisting in anxiety.

Inside is completely still. A dim blue light is lapping the room through the filtered windows. Sudden flickers of red and blue computer lights dazzle the eyes, fuzzy shadows melt details into static. The calm, surreal atmosphere of an empty workplace. Outside the crowd spits guttural roars of excitement. Projectiles smack off the outer walls, windows and drainpipes. The overlaid scuffle of so many footsteps sounds like waves crashing against the building, threatening to breach the walls any second and pull us out into the sea of rage.

We fling open the double doors at the other end of the room so hard they bounce off the walls.

"I think there's a fire escape into the alley the far side of us. If we get down there we can get to the Merlin Centre."

We head towards the "Exit" sign over a distant door to the stairwell, trying to be fast but quiet. We barrel into the stairwell and start downstairs, Maria's black dress flying behind her. A sudden loud crack of snapping metal and smashing glass stops us in our tracks. A cheer from below us. Several voices chant in unison, "Here!", then a crying scream as people start forcing their way in.

"Fuck!"

"Shit."

"Roof!"

Maria spins round and moves past me, leaping up the steps like a startled wild animal. I power my way up behind her.

I'm reckoning the crowd is already in most of the entrances down below and hunting us. Hopefully there isn't too much of a gap across to the next building, although if the psychic does have a good vantage point he might see us jump anyway. Still, if we can make a few rooftops we can get a head start on the crowd before they untangle their collective legs to move in the right direction.

I realise I'm still climbing stairs. Didn't think the building was this tall.

The stairwell echoes with screams and the rattling noise of the handrails being shaken. Footsteps like gunshots on the concrete stairs. And they are getting closer. This guy has several hundred people under his control, what does he care if he forces some of them past exhaustion, there are plenty more to carry on, trampling over their fallen bodies. He has an inexhaustible army. We, however, aren't inexhaustible.

Maria reaches the rooftop access before me, but it doesn't open, despite her violent efforts on the handle.

"Martin! Door!"

No time for finesse here. I turn the corner to the bottom of the short flight of steps up to the door. Maria presses herself into the wall out of the way as I gather my breath. Pump. Pump. Up the steps, two at a time, shoulder into the door above the handle. There is a satisfying gentle yielding of bending metal before it explodes open. I roll out onto the felted roof, half of a bent metal door frame and the latch bouncing away from me. Maria runs out behind me, spinning around to get her bearings.

"This way!"

I follow her, the screams and pounding of feet billowing out of the demolished doorway like a giant gust of wind behind us.

I have no idea where I am in relation to the rest of the city. Suddenly disorientated, a mild panic grips my chest. We run through a grid of rattling, shoulder high air-conditioning units and jump over meandering clumps of piping. The city is a blur of lights around me, all I know now is I need to follow Maria and hope she's right. She usually is.

I run out from behind a wooden sign to an open part of the rooftop and spot her near the edge. Beyond her is a jumble of roofs at all angles and heights, like crazy paving after an earthquake. In the middle however, jutting out from among the slate and felt and tiny loft windows, is a gleaming white and silver spire. Stretching up into the purple sky with its startling glowing blue tip as if trying to paint a new star, the Merlin Centre.

There is a sudden sound of metal giving way behind us, as bodies slam into the air-conditioning boxes and trip over pipes.

Maria moves back from the edge towards me and drapes her hands around my neck. A tiny moment of beauty and calm in this madness, like she had the power to stop time.

"We have to jump. Remember how?"

She gives a little hop up into my arms, and I cradle her. I allow myself a little smile as she keeps her head facing across my chest but twists her eyes to look up at me.

"How could I forget?"

I need a run up. I jog back to the edge of the billboard and start running as I hear a scream right by my ear. Legs tighten, each successive step denting the roof deeper. For the love of God just hold my weight for now.

I can sense outstretched arms clawing at the air behind me. Don't look back. Can't look back. I hear my pursuers' feet scraping on the felt at my heels as the side of the next building emerges, lengthens and narrows below me.

I hit the brick ledge with my right foot. It smashes beneath me but still gives me enough purchase to push away and I leap. Below me a vein of yellow light, a bellowing of voices. Behind me the screams of those who try unsuccessfully to follow me or are pushed to the street below as the momentum of the group fails to stop at the ledge.

Maria feels as light as a sparrow in my arms and I'm her wings. I feel like I can fly. I wish I could fly.

The ledge of the opposite roof whooshes up beneath me. The jump carries us further than planned. A triangular ceiling window looms close. Time for landing.

"Ah crap."

I hit the loose stones and moss only a few feet from the window, do a safety roll and crash through it backwards. I'm expecting butterflies in my stomach as we fall, but the ground seems to come up quicker than I anticipate. Oh. Not ground. It's the top shelf of a storage rack which quickly gives way under its unexpected load. Boxes explode around us as shelves concertina together under my back.

I squeeze Maria as close into my chest as possible as she pulls herself in for protection.

Ow.

That was harder. Proper ground. A hard concrete floor that forms a circular crater beneath us, cracks spidering away from its circumference. I roll onto my front, keeping Maria safely under me as, in the darkness, shelves collapse around and on top of us for what feels like hours. In my mind I picture an infinite room of shelves, all toppling into one another like an eccentric billionaire's game of domino rally. Eventually our world becomes still. With one arm, I push away the shelves and debris and stand up. I place Maria on her feet. She sways slightly, clinging to me.

"Are you OK? Sorry about that. Misjudged it a little."

"I'm fine." She breathes deeply, as if testing her lungs still work. "Adrenaline rush, that's all."

She lets go of me and, stumbling slightly over the wreckage, makes her way to a rectangle of light revealing an exit. She grabs the handle, opens it to a burst of light and jumps out.

I find myself smiling. That woman is completely unflappable.

I follow her into a narrow corridor. We jog down it towards a walnut brown door with a long rectangular strip of safety glass in it. On the other side we enter another corridor, almost exactly the same. More walnut, windowed doors line it at irregular intervals to our right. At the end is a solid looking door with no window and a punch button lock. I punch the lock through, the door swings open, and we find ourselves surrounded by racks of lingerie.

Above the bras and tights of the women's fashion section, banners advertise a mid-season sale. Most of the lights are on low and bounce off the many mirrors and polished metal surfaces, giving the sales floor an eerie glow as if lit from within.

Maria's head flicks around.

"This is Corbys!"

"So?"

"There is a flyover that crosses the street into the Merlin Centre. Two floors down!"

"Right."

I think better of asking her how she recognises the lingerie section of Corbys so quickly. Not really the right time.

We bound down the dark and motionless escalators which rattle noisily underfoot. I feel queasy on the first few steps until my brain realises they are switched off. For some weird reason I'm bringing my knees up and almost doing a tip-toe step down. They're just like normal steps now, come on you idiot!

I'm glad to get off them.

We run through the kitchen and glassware section to reach the flyover. It has large windows on either side facing up and down the street below. It's also well lit.

"They're going to see us." I say out loud.

"We've no choice."

We sprint across the flyover to a chorus of cries from the street below, along with a hail of missiles spakking off the glass.

The Merlin Centre is lit up the same as Corbys. Hidden lights cast unexpected shadows across the tiled walls and floors which confuse the eye into seeing the world upside down. There is no other noise apart from our echoing footsteps. We jog along the first level of shops, scanning for doors.

"I'm guessing roof access is through the management or employees only section", mutters Maria, half to herself.

"Can't see anything here. Let's try over by the fountain."

The Centre is split into two large atria, with a passage between them where the main stairs and lifts are situated. As we pass the top of the staircase, I look down into the second atrium and see the fountain is turned off. The metal sword held aloft by a white marble hand no longer has water gushing out from around the base of it like a sinking ship. Instead it stands in a tranquil pool, casting reflections into the water which scatter and bounce back around the empty space. I think it looks better like this.

A massive crash of glass and rending metal makes us stop and spin round. The whooshing sound of a hundred footsteps comes from behind. We turn and flee.

Maria suddenly straightens her arm, pointing at a nondescript double door in an alcove between a children's clothes shop and a leather bag store. Another security door. I punch at the lock and the button casing shatters, but the door remains closed. The mob cries, "I hear you", in unison and starts making chimpanzee noises while banging on the shop windows as they pass.

I tense my arm and thrust it forwards at the lock. This time it surrenders.

By now footsteps are at the stairs and coming up to our level.

We go through and push the doors closed behind us. Inside the doorway are several empty, damaged filing cabinets. I quickly fling them into a pile across the doors. Should buy us some time.

There's a grid-like maze of corridors back here, linking identical offices that are only differentiated by the names on the doors. Another moment of panic as I briefly wonder if we might be in the wrong place and have trapped ourselves in here.

We split up, going opposite ways down the nearest corridor. I find a small open area with a water cooler, the photocopier room and a tiny kitchen.

There is a piercing scraping noise. The filing cabinets are being pushed sideways along the floor as people pile into the doors.

I run back to the junction to see Maria coming back and shaking her head.

We don't look back towards the doors, even when the mob chants, "I see you!"

At the next junction I spot a door on the right with a square safety glass panel, through which I see a white painted staircase.

"Here!"

We follow the stairs up two flights.

A new type of panic now. A slowly creeping dread filling my lungs like an incoming tide. How can we secure the roof, and is there another way down if we can't?

Up here there are several small rooms dedicated to maintenance and a large one housing some busy air-conditioning equipment. An easy ramp leads up to a heavy, latched door with "ROOF ACCESS – KEEP LOCKED" stencil sprayed on it. Thankfully it's unlocked. I give a brief moment of thanks to the security guy who overlooked that one as we step out onto the roof.

The sudden chill catches me by surprise, mostly because I can actually feel it. I must be sweating buckets.

I close the door and twist the metal frame around the handle to secure it. Out here the darkness shrouds our eyeballs. We stumble towards the side of the roof facing the main square. My eyes slowly adjust to the gloom, allowing me to pick a safe path over trails of wires and pipes.

Gingerly we look down over the edge. The wall of the Merlin Centre curves out below us then disappears under itself. Below that, the crowd lurches around uncontrollably. They are carrying around a car like a piece of flotsam bobbing on the tide, and they repeatedly smash it into an abandoned bus.

The taste of ash reminds me of cold winters by a wood fire. Many of the buildings around the square are alight, the post office is almost completely engulfed. As my eyes track up I see the huge monolith of Burlington Towers, a glittering slab of black, darker than the night sky. At this angle it looks as if it's leaning back, trying to keep away from the heat below.

"Right. I fucking hope this does something." Maria closes her eyes and concentrates. Her arms drift forwards and up from her sides. "Sleep. You are all sleepy. So very... aw fuck...". She drops her arms and bends over, coughing. "So... fucking tired. Can't do this..."

She is panting, out of breath, shuddering from the adrenaline forcing its way through her burning muscles.

I place my hands on her shoulders and help her straighten up, to face the crowd. I'm holding her steady when we hear a dull banging from behind us.

"You can. You have to. We don't know how long it's going to take the others to find the bastard. Deep breaths. Focus."

I hear the door rattling and wails escaping from within.

Maria's breathing settles. Her head is turned slightly round, but not quite enough to look at me. She lightly places a hand on mine.

"Better watch that door, give me time."

I squeeze her shoulders.

"Right on it."

I leave her and run back to the agitated doors. I dig my feet in and lean forwards, one hand on each side, forcing it to remain shut. Roars of disapproval are followed by jarring thuds up my arms. I lock my elbows and look over my arm towards Maria.

She is facing the crowd, a black doll outlined in orange as her hair billows in the updraught from the fires. Her arms fall to her sides, then slowly rise in front of her again.

"Time. To. Sleep."

CHAPTER 9
THURSDAY 13TH SEPTEMBER 2012

Martin couldn't sleep.

He had felt the desire come on gradually as he sat on the sofa, but the usually comforting heavy veil behind his eyes didn't drop. His normally docile mind was buzzing with unfocused thoughts. He also kept scratching the side of his knee. There was no itch.

After an hour or so of trying, the tiredness gave up and slunk off to curl up by itself at the base of his brain.

He had been sitting up all night drinking coffee, stretching his legs, taking a piss, getting himself some biscuits, but each time he returned to the sofa nothing had changed. The solicitor's documents were still on the coffee table. Vincent had still died.

He was never usually in his flat during the night. The odd sounds he heard were magnified a hundred times; voices outside puncturing the stillness, the snap of floorboards settling in the flat above him, someone dropping a bottle, a screaming fox. "What did they mean?" he wondered. He felt like there had to be a meaning to it. All these noises must have some significance.

His stung mind tried to fit the pieces together into something coherent, even though it knew full well they were junk.

He centred the coffee cup on the coaster again.

He scratched his knee.

The beer can from last night was still there, balancing on the corner of the table. His mind made a sudden link: dropping bottle – recycle can! He jumped up, grabbing the can and took it into the kitchen.

The flats didn't get recycling boxes as they had limited room, so he had a hessian carrier bag hanging on the inside of a unit door which he used for paper, card, cans and bottles. When it was full he would take it down to the refuse room and sort its contents into the large communal recycling bins. He crushed the can flat between his palms and slid it into the bag.

Relief washed over his brain as he closed the unit door. Something made sense again. The feeling made his emotions well up so much he had to blink hard and sniff.

He couldn't go back in the living room. He leant on the work surface. He scratched a fingernail at a long-dried drop of something, watching it turn to dust. He tried to find a pattern in the granite effect worktop but couldn't see one.

He opened the fridge for something to do and found himself eating one of his yoghurts a moment later.

He fancied another coffee, but the cup was in the living room so he had a glass of tap water instead.

Healthier he guessed. Better to hydrate yourself with. A lot of people didn't drink enough fluid and were chronically dehydrated apparently. He guessed he must have read that somewhere.

His buzzing thoughts became louder. He started pacing.

Toilet? No, not long been. Can't do the vacuuming, it's night time. Recycling? Somebody might hear him, don't want to upset the neighbours.

Pacing.

Damn it. There must be something.

The buzzing thoughts had found their way into his arms, making them tremble like a confused conductor.

Must be something. Damn it!

If he could just point to something, the thoughts would fly out through his fingertips and everything would be clear again. Point at the solution and it would be fixed.

He scratched his knee. He was breathing harder.

Pacing.

Must be something!

"SHIT!"

He still had the glass in his hand when he made a fist and kept squeezing. The sharp, cracking sounds turned into scraping, crunching sounds, that turned into squealing, grinding sounds.

The thoughts were gone.

He slowly opened his hand to reveal a pyramid of pip sized chunks and a layer of glass dust. He poked at it with a finger before tipping it in the bin in the corner. He brushed the dust off in the sink and washed his hands with the cracked bar of soap, drying them on the tea towel by accident.

There was no solution. Nothing had presented itself to him. So in the absence of decision, he would carry on as normal.

He could hear the noise of morning traffic outside. Engines signalling the start of the morning commute. That meant time for bed.

He went into his bedroom, avoiding eye contact with the doorway to the living room. He undressed and for a moment wasn't sure where his pyjamas were, he used this room so infrequently. After a minor search he found them in the chest of drawers and put them on. He closed the curtains to give him some darkness and slid between the sheets.

He wasn't sure whether it was because of the letter or the unfamiliarity of being here but he was still awake some hours later, his brain picking up every sound and analysing it.

"For the love of God," he sighed.

"Look," he told himself, "there is nothing I can do about anything. He's… dead. Can't change it. So back to normal. Just get on with things. Work tonight."

His mind settled and he fell asleep minutes later.

He woke up a few hours before his next shift was to supposed to start with vague memories of a dream where he was on fire.

CHAPTER 10
SATURDAY 17TH APRIL 1993

Vincent becomes more and more agitated as the lift ascends. Charles stands next to him, hand on his shoulder, Inna stands in front of the door. A tinny jingle version of a Motown hit plays in the background.

"You'd think they'd have better lift muzak in an exclusive place like this." says Charles.

No-one replies.

Floor by floor.

Number by number.

Up and up.

"Always fancied a pad here. I wonder what their rates..."

Vincent suddenly cries out and presses himself into the corner of the metal box. Inna jabs the next floor button and lights herself up.

"Love it when you do that darling. Come on Vincent my buddy..." he says, pulling the shivering figure to his unsteady feet, "...we still need you, time is of the essence."

"Ting."

Inna jumps out through the doors and spins around, checking every corner, doorway and alcove in line of sight.

"Clear."

The two men join her in the lift lobby. This is decorated the same as the rest of the building, a strange fusion of art deco and asymmetric, geometric brushed aluminium panels and light fittings. All the lights are on. It's quiet. Nothing looks disturbed. Just a normal lobby.

Vincent's knees buckle and he tries to slide to hug the safe, cool marble floor. Charles pulls him up.

Inna jogs ahead. "He will be in one of the apartments overlooking the city, this side of building."

Apartment 1807 is directly ahead, facing the central lobby, with the corridor running left to right, each direction a mirror image of the other.

"Which way Vincent? Where is his lair?"

Vincent whimpers, grabbing on to Charles so hard his nails dig in to his flesh.

"No... it's too hard... I can't..."

Charles presses his face close to his friend's. "I know, I know dear friend. You're doing so well keeping us all in mind-link and making sure he doesn't turn us into his puppets too. I know how much of a strain that must be on you my dear Vincent, but we almost have him!"

Vincent starts crying.

"Tell us where he is, we'll roger the bastard to death and then you can relax again. It's almost over.

Just tell us where! Where... where..." he repeats the last word over and over.

Vincent writhes in his arms like an unhappy cat, clutching at the side of his head with one hand, trying to pull his skull open to let the pain out. He barely responds apart from sobbing a string of repeated, "No".

"Where Vincent, please! We're running out of time!"

Vincent cries out and tries to push him away. "He wants us all. He's too strong... I'm lost..."

Charles slaps him across the face with the back of his hand so hard the noise makes Inna look round. In a flash Vincent's hands are on Charles, one tight on his neck, the other pulling at his hair. He is rigid in a strangely twisted pose and locks eyes with him.

"Listen..."

All three of them stand silent. A wall light ticks as it expands with the heat. The dull roar of distant voices slips in through the walls.

"He knows we're here."

"Oh I'm certain of that my friend."

They stay this way, caught in a terrified embrace for another moment.

"1811."

"My good man, you've saved the day." He pats him solidly on his shoulder as his grip loosens around his neck. Charles rubs his throat muscles. "Although that is going to bruise..."

Inna heads right, glowing fully, tendrils of light sliding up her arms.

"This is Ignite to team. We have him. Room 1811 Burlington Towers. Probably going to lose the mind-link shortly so Vincent can cover us mentally. Wish us the best."

Charles and Vincent follow Inna, the identical decoration lending every section of corridor another odd moment of deja-vu. Despite the changing door numbers and occasional different piece of art on the wall they feel like they are walking through a cheaply produced 3D videogame. Vincent has an arm round Charles's shoulders but is now walking almost unaided, if unsteadily.

"OK buddy, full psychic shield on us."

"Already done."

Inna now stands facing door 1811, her light slowly bending around the front of her and flying away over her shoulders and hips.

"So how do we do this Mr Charles?"

He props Vincent up against a wall and stands next to her.

"Hard and now."

"Flashbang!"

She clenches her fists as her whole ribcage and torso glow so brightly that her body and the light around it become indistinguishable from one another.

Then a painfully loud crashing noise, like two trains colliding, makes her lose focus and her light fades. The walls either side of door 1811 shudder and crack, bowing outwards. The pole of a standard light punches through the plaster and tiny pieces of debris force themselves through the gaps around the door. Charles instinctively holds up an arm to protect himself.

"What the... get in there now!"

Inna grimaces and finally lets rip, a beam of light bursting from her chest that punches the door and a circular section of wall out. As her light fades they both see the door gracefully tumble out of a huge gash in the building where most of an apartment should be, before dropping out of sight.

"Jesus..." Charles's hands burn red hot and he runs through the opening looking for trouble, Inna close behind. She spots a door near her and touches it. Her light dissolves it to dust, but the bathroom beyond is empty.

Charles stands slightly bemused, surveying the damage. What furniture is still recognisable is forced up against the near walls in odd positions. The other end of the light pole hangs out of the wall, vibrating. The apartment has only about twenty feet of floor left in front of them, jutting into the tarry sky like a roughly torn piece of card. Chunks of concrete, steel rods and wiring reach down from the ceiling like witches fingers. Shredded wallpaper and a magazines flap in the cold gust buffeting them.

A sharp tearing noise makes them jump. On the far right of what remains of the apartment, a now dangling built-in oven and wall unit rip away from their fittings and drop out of sight.

"Shit." Inna slaps her forehead, "Should have got that. Hope it not land on someone."

"No-one we know or care about at least."

She sighs heavily. "Not much left to search."

"I know what you mean darling. I knew these places were open-plan, but this is a bit avant-garde even for my tastes."

It is then they notice the voices of the crowd have changed. What was once a primeval roaring in unison is now a cacophony of cries of pain and horror, people urgently calling names and the harrowing wails of those with the creeping realisation that the last few hours hadn't been a terrible dream they would wake up from in the safety of their beds.

A turquoise blue glow lights up the shredded ceiling as Jack floats up into view on the other side of the scar.

"Did I get the cunt?"

CHAPTER 11
FRIDAY 14TH SEPTEMBER 2012

"What do you mean?"

"I mean I've come to start my shift."

Martin stood in the corridor outside the security room. Barney was standing in the doorway, both arms up in a huge shrug.

"*I'm* doing your shift you big bastard! Got a call-in to say you had to take bereavement leave or summat. Monica did a double to cover you last night and she's doing tonight as well. Go home you twat!"

Martin didn't want to argue, didn't want to have to phone up the security company and explain things. He just wanted to work, be left alone to do his night shift.

"I can't not work Barney, I need to do my shift."

"No you don't, not unless you're fuckin' weird. Go home! Get all your shit seen to…", he leant forward at an angle and whispered, "…take a chance to have a bit of time off on the free…", he leant back, "…then come back when you're ready. Come on, let's go."

Barney stepped out of the room, put an arm on Martin's shoulder and moved to push him down the corridor. He couldn't move Martin of course and looked shocked when he found himself moving backwards instead.

"Fuck me mate, you a Terminator?"

He was a good guy and he meant well, but Martin could feel the anxiety trying to punch its way out of his chest.

"It's OK, I'll call them, tell them to stop her from coming in. I'll do it. It's not a problem, really."

"Martin?"

Sandra had come out of the office up the corridor on her way to leave.

"Oh, hi Sandra. I'm just about to call Ultimate to let them know I'll be on shift tonight…"

"But it's all sorted Martin, Monica's looking after tonight."

"Fuckin' told him."

Simon rushed out of the office from behind her with his jacket on. He didn't notice the commotion and in a fluster ran past them down the corridor, disappearing round the corner and down the stairs.

"Ultimate has given you leave for as long as you need. It's all been taken care of so you don't need to worry about a thing."

Martin started trembling. Why were these people so damned nice? He just wanted to work.

"I just want to work."

"It's like she said pal, it's sorted. Now get yourself home, get some pies down your neck and don't worry about this place."

"Martin?"

Monica walked up the corridor from the other end in a dark blue fleece jacket, a large black bag over her shoulder.

"What are you doing? I'm covering your shift tonight. You get yourself home."

"That's what we've been trying to tell the bastard but it looks like he's planted himself here."

Sandra put a hand on his shoulder.

"Martin, if you want to talk about anything we can pop into the office and have a chat? The others are going shortly so it will be quiet."

"I'm OK. I'm OK. You... you didn't need to come in Monica. Thanks for covering last night, but I'm OK now."

"Don't be daft, you've just lost your friend, you need to get yourself sorted out."

She looked concerned for him.

"The last thing you want to be thinking about is work. Come on Arnie, let's get your ass back home."

Martin felt like he was back at school, standing on the middle of the playground, cemented to the spot, determined not to give way. If he could just stay for a bit longer they might let him do the shift anyway.

A distant conversation echoed up the stairs along with multiple footsteps.

"Guys! Look... thanks, really. You're really nice for thinking of me like this but I never asked to go on bereavement leave. I mean thanks, Sandra, for thinking about that and sorting it all, but I hadn't planned on taking any. I mean I haven't got anything else to do so work is a good distraction, yeah?"

They all looked concerned now. Sandra lowered her hand from his shoulder and patted him in the middle of his back.

"Come on Martin, let's grab a seat in the office and get you a coffee. Monica will do tonight but we'll work out a schedule that works for you, all right?"

Defeat, tinged with victory. At least he could stay here longer. If he could get to the mosaic and just stand there for a few minutes he would be happy enough.

"Yeah. OK, sure."

He nodded to Barney and Monica.

The other conversation was almost at their floor. He could hear Simon, agitated, and another voice he didn't recognise.

He turned with Sandra and headed to the office. He didn't notice her look back over her shoulder to the other security guards and give them a reassuring smile that said she would take care of him. Barney shook his head and Monica leaned on the door frame as they watched him go, shoulders and head drooping.

"Mr Mol-LOY!" cut a cheery cry from the far end of the corridor.

They all turned, puzzled.

"It *is* Mr Molloy isn't it? Why yes it is! Or should I say Roadblock from The Pulse? So *this* is where you've been hiding!"

Martin wasn't religious, but he guessed what he felt right now was his soul dropping through the floor.

Coming up the corridor were the two PCA agents he had seen at Vincent's house. Simon was scurrying about behind them, unable to get past, muttering something about getting a call, that they had to get in the building urgently. But Martin's eyes were focused on the two men wearing black suits and ties.

Blocking Simon was a pale round faced man wearing sunglasses and a loose fitting suit. He had short dark hair, slightly spiked on top, sideburns down to the bottom of his ears. His purplish, flat oval lips were pursed tight, wide nostrils slightly flared, bag shadows just dropping out from under his frames. The Detector. He walked completely straight-backed, lifting his knees higher than he seemed to need to, palms facing backwards as his arms swayed slightly.

The man at the front, radiant with a huge smile, was striding towards him, arm outstretched as if to shake his hand. His suit jacket, fastened tightly by a single button in the middle, flared out from it, fold lines scattering to the jutting shoulders and pockets. His face was creased like an elephant's thigh, his smile a wound to the bone. Two granite grey irises sat inside his tiny dark rectangular eyes, fixing Martin's like lasers. His hands were huge, thick bones that had been deep fried and battered in skin.

The man stopped a metre short of where Martin was standing, Sandra still holding onto him, looking perplexed. Martin didn't take his hand. Sandra looked like she was going to take it for a second, but instead regained her composure.

"Can I help you gentlemen?"

The man finally dropped his hand. He clasped them both in front of his crotch and rubbed them as if he was standing in the cold. He was bent forwards, still looking at Martin.

"No Miss…"

"Sandra Clarke, office administrator."

"And the very helpful young man who let us in is Simon, oh I *do* enjoy introductions, and the two by the door are?"

"Minding my own business."

"Erm, Monica. Treadwell."

Simon tried to pass his hand around the Detector to shake but gave up.

"Simon Harris, Assistant Office Man…"

"Excellent!"

He was still staring at Martin when he gestured behind him.

"Well this is Agent Barclay and I am Agent Morris of the Powered Crime Agency, and this…", he gestured towards Martin, "… is a person of interest in the murder of one Mr Vincent Hayden-Phillips aka The Seeker. And as Mr Hayden-Phillips was a powered individual, a psychic no less, that means his death falls under our jurisdiction. And Mr Molloy here, who is also powered by the way…"

"What?"

"Martin, is this…?"

"Bullshit."

"…super strength, super athleticism, super dense body tissue conferring a significant degree of invulnerability, was an old teammate of Mr Hayden-Phillips back in the day."

"The Pulse? Shit, I remember them… no way?" Monica shook her head.

Martin's ears were full of the roar of blood. His earlier confusion had vanished. He was now a rock, immovable, muscles ready for anything against this threat. For eighteen years he had been anonymous, eighteen years not giving away his abilities, remembering never to refer to his Hero days in casual conversation, being normal, and here, right now, it was all being torn down. He had to protect himself somehow, stop the attack, but he didn't know what to do, so he just stood there, staring.

"And we need to ask you some questions Mr Molloy... or Roadblock, whichever you prefer?" Agent Morris smiled.

Martin didn't reply. He stood firm, ready to move. Barney and Monica sensed this and instinctively changed stance, expecting trouble. Sandra took a step sideways away from him, hand gingerly touching his shoulder.

"Martin, this can't be true, surely? Ultimate wouldn't have taken you on if you'd told them..." she brought the hand to her face, "oh, no, Martin."

The future chain of events carefully unfolded themselves at the front of Martin's brain like an origami figure sat in a saucer of water. He would be fired from Ultimate Security for not admitting he was powered. He would lose his only other connection to the real world after Vincent. PCA would interrogate him knowing he hadn't registered. He would go to prison for either not registering or because PCA would lay Vincent's death on him. Everyone would now know he was powered, whether in prison or out. He would never be normal again.

Martin felt a deep sadness and relaxed, resigned to his fate.

"It's true. And I prefer Mr Molloy."

"Marvellous!" exclaimed Agent Morris, suddenly bending backwards, now, please come with us."

He stepped forward, taking the space between Sandra and Martin, putting a hand round his back as she had, ushering him towards Agent Barclay.

Martin took a step forward, glancing back at Sandra who stood paralysed with shock. Barclay turned one eighty on his heels and walked away. Martin followed.

He passed Barney and Monica. He could barely find the energy to look at them, but he did. Horror. Disgust. Fear. A mix of all three.

"All this fuckin' time…" said Barney, backing off and disappearing into the security office.

Monica looked like a toddler about to cry. Martin turned his head away, he couldn't watch them looking at him like this.

His muscles trembled as he walked the corridor, sandwiched between the two agents.

This was it. This was the end of it all. He didn't know what else to do but go with them.

CHAPTER 12
SATURDAY 17TH APRIL 1993

"Roadblock, time to make haste my friend!"

Charles climbs into the second passenger seat upfront, next to a visibly shaking Vincent, as Jack starts up the engine.

I nod. I make sure the police officer has a good hold of the woman we have been helping over to the medical triage area and jog over to join the team. With noticeably much less energy than I had earlier, I make the step up into the back of the van, slam the door closed behind me and fasten myself in next to Maria. Mitchell sits opposite me, asleep, Inna next to him, covered in brick dust.

I'm so drained I can't hold my arms forward and end up laying an elbow across Maria's chest. Her eyes are narrow and grey. She doesn't even seem to notice.

While the riot was like a war zone, the aftermath was like an earthquake had struck the city. Structural and human devastation clung to the ground for comfort. The claws of broken windows reach out from the shattered façades of shops and buildings. Overturned burning cars litter the streets next to bent lamp posts and scattered barricades. The rest of the ground is layered with unrecognisable pieces of glass and concrete, metal and flesh. Darkening smears of blood lead the eye to twisted, torn bodies laying on the tarmac and paving slabs.

We had spent the night helping to put out fires and clearing debris for the emergency services. Afterwards we helped search for the injured and lost, solemnly lining up the bodies of the fallen on the plaza.

Our work done, we move off from the police enclosure and slowly pick our way through the narrowed roads. For a while we stop. The delay just about breaches my shortened limit of patience before we jerkily move off again. Out of the back window I see two police officers lifting some barricades to close off the road again.

It's early morning but I can't tell what time. It's that strange hour when the sun isn't visible above you but everything is hazy with light, detail obscured by a white fuzz, like the world isn't quite sure how much of it exists yet.

We drive back across the bridge. The queue of vehicles is still there, but they all are empty now. A few owners are here, sitting on the central barrier or getting things from their boot. They walk between the cars, wondering when they will be able to get free, where they'll get breakfast.

And with that thought I'm suddenly hungry for a fry up, but I don't know if I have the energy to eat. Oh I don't care. Hunger or sleep, you guys can fight it out between you, just let me know who wins.

I relax and let the turns and bumps of the van jog my head about.

Nobody speaks the whole way back.

The van jerks to a stop at the side of our HQ, jolting me from a start of a deep snooze. I cough some concrete dust out of my lungs and take a deep breath, my leaden ribs resisting me.

After the bollards drop into the road we turn down the ramp to the car park under the building. The shutter starts opening with a rattle. The top of the van almost scrapes it as we drive in. Either Jack is tired or anxious to get back. I decide I don't care either way.

The van pulls into its space next to the lift and Jack turns off the engine. Nobody moves. For a while we just sit there, each one of us waiting for one of the others to be the first to move.

The shutter slams down. Seems as good a cue as any. I unclick my straps and I hear someone in the front follow suit. Maria shakes her head and unfastens herself next.

I get up, hunching slightly to avoid tangling myself in the roof cabling, and tap Mitchell on his sleepy shoulder.

"Come on buddy."

The lad looks at me with glassy eyes, nods with a wobbly head and grasps the clasp to free himself.

I open the door and jump out. My knees give a little, like soft plasticine, and it takes me a few steps to straighten out to a normal walking movement.

As everyone gets out I notice Jack is sitting forward, forearms resting on the top of the wheel, head dropped down. Feels strange. I've never seen him look tired, or defeated, whichever it is. I'm kind of glad to have seen him caught in a human moment.

I give Charles a hand unloading the almost empty medical support trolleys from the rear as the others go up in the lift. Inna has to give Vincent a hand, he's so unsteady.

By the time the lift comes back down Jack has joined us and we're waiting with the equipment. We load it in and send ourselves up.

Charles thumps himself on his chest and coughs, clearing soot from his lungs he says. I lean back on the lift door, slumber a slow waterfall behind my eyes, trying to pull me down the river of sleep.

The quiet, enclosed space feels odd after the noise and expanse of devastation. I imagine the lift stopping and the door opening onto the main square, people stumbling about covered in blood, that crying woman with the burnt legs. I run out to help them but it seems to get dustier and darker the further out I go. Then I hear the chanting again.

The sharp bang of yielding metal snaps me to attention.

We both stare at Jack. His fist is embedded, planted down through two shelves of a trolley, fixings rolling around our feet.

"FUCKER!"

Jack pulls out his fist, glowing blue with a concentrated pulse.

I look over to Charles, briefly making concerned eye contact.

Jack has his head down, shakes it from side to side. He is hunched over, leaning on the broken trolley, impatiently shifting from foot to foot like a disturbed zoo animal, muttering under his breath.

"Jack my friend, we did all we..." ventures Charles.

"FUCKER!"

Jack kicks the trolley into the top corner of the lift. The shelves separate sending empty packaging, syringes and four determined wheels pinging around the small box we are in. I bring my arms up for cover. A shelf hits my shoulder and a wheel smacks off Charles's ankle.

"Christ Jack, what the devil..."

Jack spins round, glowing blue, looking ready to fly off through the walls at any moment. He squares up to Charles, inches from his face.

"He fucking got away didn't he? The fucker. Got. AWAY!"

Charles looks ready to wrestle him to the ground, then his body relaxes as he no doubt thinks better of it. He raises his arms to the side, in a gesture of surrender and tilts his head, speaking softly.

"Jack, this is not the end. He will get cocky and try again, but we will be ready for the sick son of an unmarried mother, and we will get him. It is not over."

Jack seems calmer, but still shakes his head vigorously.

"He was there. Unless Vincent fucked up..."

"He never does." I say.

Jack looks at me. His eyes are bloodshot, spittle coats his lips.

"Then he *was* there, but we missed him somehow. He was fucking playing us. In another room. Probably fucking next door for all we...!"

The fatigue kicks in as the adrenaline fades and Jack puts both palms to his eyes and squeezes them into his head, arms shaking as he walks a confused circle around a twisted metal shelf.

"Yes," said Charles, "he probably was, but like I said, next time he is ours."

"MINE!" Jack rounds on Charles again, neck stretched out in anger, a forceful finger embedded into his own chest. "He's fucking MINE! No-one makes me look like a fucking FOOL." He pulls the finger out of his lungs and steps backwards. "I blasted open the front of one of the most expensive properties in the city in full view of every TV camera this side of Birmingham to get to him and he wasn't fucking there. That'll be in every fucking paper tomorrow with the headline: 'MISSED!'"

"No it won't Jack," I tell him, "what will be on the front of every paper is the fact that we just saved the city. We stopped a mad psychic attack and helped rescue dozens of people."

Jack stares at me again. His eyes are swollen. I don't know if he can even see me.

"Martin is right my old friend, if we hadn't been there to contain the situation it could have turned out much, much worse than it did. Who knows how long he could have gone on for, or what he would have ended up doing to all those people. He could have sent them all into the river to drown! We did good Jack."

The lift stops and the doors open on the other side. Beyond is a wide corridor with three large storage rooms on either side, lit by powerful lights on the wall spaces between them. At the far end an open staircase flanked by two smaller lifts ascends to the balconies and floors above.

The shutters to storage rooms one and three are still wide open from when we hastily gathered equipment many hours earlier. Vincent is standing halfway up the steps, staring back at the lift. Maria is in the middle of the space and turns to look at us as the door opens onto what must be an interesting little diorama.

"But we lost!"

Jack flicks his head back and forth between us, eyes wide with disbelief.

"We fucking LOST! Don't you fucking GET IT?"

Neither Charles nor I know what to say any more, with Jack in whatever place he's locked himself. Maria warily steps towards the open lift door, hands clasped together at her thighs.

"Jack, is everything...?"

"FUCK'S SAKE!" Jack throws a hand up over his head, unable to bear looking at us any longer and storms out of the lift, a blue pulse shield covering his whole body so all of us know he is done with the conversation. He sweeps past Maria as she gingerly puts her hand out. The shield doesn't drop. We watch him go up the stairs at the far end of the corridor, past Vincent, who visibly cringes into the railings, turn left on the first balcony and head towards the gym.

The clanging of metal makes us turn to see Charles failing to quietly place pieces of the damaged trolley on top of the intact one. Both of us freeze in place.

"Witchy, look...", tiptoes Charles, "...you know Jack, and... well we're all fatigued and emotional, and I'm sure...he…"

Maria looks at him, expressionless. Keeping her hands together she makes her way to the stairs and climbs them slowly until she's out of our sight.

Me and Charles sigh with relief. He runs his hand through his hair, tugging his forehead up to stretch out the tension, and looks at me.

"Let's just get these in the right rooms for now and we can sort them properly tomorrow yes?"

I just nod and wheel the trolley out of the lift as he fumbles around for pieces on the floor.

I look over towards the stairs again, but Vincent is gone.

CHAPTER 13
FRIDAY 14TH SEPTEMBER 2012

"Well, looks like we found you at last."

Martin was sitting in an uncomfortably small, perfectly square room with no windows. He was sat on a hard chair, black square metal frame, pale wood seat and back. He relaxed his hands into his lap, trying to stay calm, willing each minute away.

A solid rectangular wooden table pushed end up against the wall opposite the door took up most of the central space, leaving only a few feet around it. On the right end of the table next to the wall, a small electronic machine was diligently recording audio. There were two CCTV cameras, also recording, one above the door to his left and a tiny one huddled like a cautious spider in the opposite right corner, pointing directly at him. He scrunched his eyelids closer together against the relentless heating of the overhead strip light. It wasn't flickering but seemed to be radiating pure migraine instead. Even though the walls were plain magnolia, the light gave them an oil slick green colour that seemed to slowly move around the room, making him feel even more queasy.

Opposite him, to his right, sat the grey haired PCA agent, Agent Morris, with the Detector, Agent Barclay, on his left. Agent Morris was tapping on a small tablet device, grinning widely. Agent Barclay was sitting at a slight angle around the corner of the desk opposite him to his left, as if waiting for Martin to make a break for the door. Behind them both was a black glass panel, behind which, he assumed, were the local detectives.

Martin had felt sick ever since they left the shopping centre. Sick about being found out, sick that everybody now knew, sick that had never told those he was closest to and had now lost them as friends, sick at (very likely) losing his job, sick with the anticipation of what he was going to be questioned about. And they had kept him waiting. He had been sat in this box room for at least an hour before the two agents joined him, started the recorder and introduced themselves. Morris briefly went over his rights, told him he wasn't under arrest but, "given the circumstances", it was in his best interest to help them. He had then pulled out the tablet from some cavernous inside pocket and had said nothing since.

That was another half hour ago.

Martin could feel his heart fluttering in his chest. He thought he might have been sweating but didn't want to wipe his forehead in case that gave some body language signal of guilt.

He tried guessing the distance between the charcoal carpeted floor and the plastic power cable housing that encircled the room at his shoulder height. About three feet? He stared at the recorder, its little red light the brightest thing in the room.

Should he say something? What should he say? He had thought about apologising for not registering, but doubt and fear had delayed him saying it for so long it would now seem odd to suddenly rupture the silence. Anyway, he was sure Morris would finish doing whatever he was doing and get round to him soon.

About ten minutes later Morris looked up at Martin and turned the tablet to show him the screen. Despite the woozy glare from the light he clearly recognised a very old publicity photograph of himself dressed as Roadblock. Aligned to the right of the picture were some general biographical notes about his abilities, political orientation, relationships, abilities, and a red mark denoting no real life alias. Martin tried to look nonplussed while nursing the beginnings of a headache.

"Wow. Now that's an old photo," he said, trying to start the dialogue off on a conversational level.

Agent Morris took the tablet back, stabbed at it with his finger a few more times, held it up vertically and turned it so that the flat shiny black rear was facing Martin, then tapped it again. There was an electronic shutter sound and a little red LED flashed briefly.

"Not any more." Agent Morris kept his eyes fixed on the tablet as he laid it down on the table. The screen wasn't easily visible from this angle but he could see the old photo being swapped for the new one. "Bastard," thought Martin.

"Martin Molloy isn't it?"

"That's correct."

Tap. Tap. Tap.

"And your address?"

Martin stared at the agent silently for a moment, but he didn't look up, so he gave his address.

Tap. Tap. Tap.

He then had to give his previous addresses since leaving the team, details of all employment in that time, driver's licence, passport and National Insurance numbers, (he didn't know any of these offhand and would have to bring them to the station within five days), details of his family, their names, ages, addresses, marital status, children etc., etc. The whole questioning process took about forty minutes and all the while Martin's patience was draining. Finally the agent held the tablet up in front of him, his grinning face shining from the reflected light like a shrivelled fruit.

He laid the tablet back down, turned it round and pushed it towards Martin.

"Fingerprints please."

Wearily, Martin pressed each finger onto the glass inside the confines of a small box as instructions came up on the screen. When he had done both hands there was a quiet chime and Morris quickly whipped the device back.

"That's much better."

He carefully placed his elbows on the table and slowly clasped his hands together, interlocking two fingers at a time.

"You'll have to forgive me Mr Molloy, I simply can't stand it when things aren't complete you see. There are so many old Heroes who are missing from the database you know. Very powerful ones who never registered, seemingly vanished off the face of the earth. Gaps." He looked at Martin for the first time since they arrived at the police station, a tight frown between his eyes. "I don't like gaps."

"Well I guess I could say I forgot or never found the time, but the truth is I figured it was nobody's business who I used to be, especially if I was never going to use my powers again."

Agent Morris's eyes widened, his knuckles whitened then he suddenly burst out laughing. A huge manic laugh that startled Agent Barclay as much as it did Martin. The Detector glanced nervously back and forth between Martin and his colleague. Martin guessed that this scenario wasn't covered in his training. After some time Agent Morris managed to control himself, bringing a hand across his chest to flatten his lapels and tie back into place before clasping his hands together again.

"Well, Mr Molloy, I sincerely appreciate the honesty. I would also appreciate it if you could tell me why you killed Mr Vincent Hayden-Phillips last night."

Martin felt a flash of anger that quelled the sickness in his stomach. He had been expecting this question, but wasn't ready for it right now.

"I didn't kill him."

"Of course."

"Look, you know I didn't kill him. I'm at work all night, shift records and CCTV footage will prove that, then I'm at home during the day, sleeping. I only go out to go shopping. The first I knew he was dead was the package from his solicitors that arrived a few hours ago at work."

"He made you executor?" asked Morris.

"Yes, yes he did."

"Why you?"

"Because I'm his closest friend I guess."

"Was. He is dead now."

"Well, yes, of course," Martin stumbled.

"It was brutal you know."

The agent's face filled with concern. Was it genuine?

"Really brutal," he said in a quiet, pained voice.

"OK." Martin tried not to imagine the scene with Vincent's body in it. "Thank you for that information..."

"Disembowelled from stomach to chest, brutal."

The sickness returned. This wasn't helping. He stared the agent in the eye.

"I believe you," he said tersely.

The agent stared back.

"For someone to do that, you see Mr Molloy, from the distance we believe they were standing, with no apparent resistance on the part of Mr Hayden-Phillips, that will have required a certain intimacy with the victim, someone known to him, a close friend."

Martin had assumed there would have been some kind of fight, a struggle.

"Like I said, you know I didn't..."

"Who else did he keep in contact with from the team?"

Martin was tripped again by the sudden change in questioning. He could feel a shake in his hands. "No, no, not here!" He huffed in and out a couple of breaths.

"No-one really. There was just me and Maria..."

"Who?"

"Erm, Professor Maria Gionchetta."

"The Black Witch." Martin and Morris both looked surprised as Barclay spoke for the first time. Morris immediately tapped at the tablet again and a picture of Maria appeared on the screen with her register details.

"Ah yes. Yes." Morris stared at the screen with his grin again, then shook his head and placed the tablet back down.

"But no. She is only an emotional affector, she couldn't have done what we witnessed."

"Absolutely not! But there were support staff from the local health authority who still visited regularly..."

"...who we are checking out as a matter of course, but you were his closest friend. Hmm." He clasped his hands again and rested his chin on them.

Martin grimaced and sat forward. His arms were still trembling and he needed to be anywhere else but here.

"Look, I know you pretty much have to do this..." he waved his hands around, "...interview routine as standard, you know, prodding people to see how they react. But I want to find out who killed Vincent even more than you do."

"Oh I severely doubt that." Morris looked shocked.

"No, seriously. This is just a job for you guys, for me it's personal. I worked with Vincent for years in the team and he's been a great friend... probably my only friend, ever since."

"And it's personal for me also." Morris grinned again. "Gaps you see. So many gaps with The Pulse. I've often wondered about your team. The horrific battles against The Controller. Miss Nesvyaschenko's death. Then, not long after you finally defeat him, the team suddenly splits up, and you all scatter to the winds. Very unusual for any team split. Typically, half would either try and form or join another team, even for a year or so. But not you lot. You all bowed out completely and no-one ever knew why."

Martin felt like Morris was burrowing through his skull, trying to scoop the very memories from his grey matter.

"And now one of you is killed, brutally I might add, by someone he must have known closely and all for no immediately apparent reason. Except of course there must be a reason, we...", he motioned between himself and Barclay, "...just aren't aware of it. Yet. Then we find you..." he grinned again, "...Roadblock, the day after he dies, vowing to find his killer. And you were unregistered I might add, which can still carry a fixed custodial penalty were we to press for it. We most definitely have gaps here Mr Molloy. Gaps that I am certain you will fill for us."

Martin clenched his teeth.

"Of course I will gladly help you in any way I can to find out who did this, but I am the executor of his will, which I have no idea how to go about doing. I've got stuff to do."

"Are you sad?"

Martin stared at Morris, puzzled.

"I'm... what?"

"Are you sad at his passing?" Morris opened his hands, elbows still rigidly fixed to the table, until his palms faced the ceiling and gave an exaggerated shrug.

"Of course I am. He was a good friend of mine. We went through a lot together. Of course I'm sad, it's just hard to take in what's happened." Martin saw little sparks drifting over his eyeballs.

"Who would do this to him Mr Molloy? Who would do such a brutal thing to your dear friend Vincent? Who that he knew would do such a thing, and why?" The agent leant forward.

Martin remembered the black memoir notebook and Vincent's psychic message. For a brief rebellious moment he fancied saying, "All of us," and challenging the agents to dig the rest out of him. Instead he said, "I don't know."

Morris's face dropped and became tense, his eyes narrowing on Martin.

"That is not the degree of information we were expecting from you Mr Molloy. We were hoping for something with a little more... detail than that." He tapped at his tablet again. "We will arrange for a psychic scrape within the next few days to..."

"No!" Martin started and pushed himself away from the table. "No way. I will help you in any way I can..."

"...by submitting to a psychic scrape so we can get the information we require to solve this urgent case before any more of your old friends, or you, are murdered in their own homes!"

"I can only tell you what I know!"

"...and the psychic scrape will tell us what you don't know you have forgotten, then *we* will determine whether what you know is of use to us."

"No. I'm sorry, I'm not having that done."

The two agents looked at him solemnly.

"You do realise that in a murder case refusing to submit to a psychic scrape can be construed as obstructing the course of justice."

"You can construe it as whatever the hell you like. I didn't kill Vincent. I don't know who did and I don't know why. But I am going to find out and..."

"...inform the relevant authorities of your information so that they can take that person into custody to be tried in a court of law? Did I finish your sentence correctly Mr Molloy?"

Martin ground his teeth as his breath grew shallower. Morris leaned forward and tilted his head at a slight angle.

"These aren't the old days any more you know. You can't just fly around the city using your powers to solve crimes for the cheering masses..." He bent his head back under him to look at the tablet and tapped something. "Well, you can't fly at all but you get the point I'm trying to make. We watch everyone on the register very closely Mr Molloy, especially those who have avoided being on it."

He now leaned back in his chair so far that Barclay turned to see where he was going. Morris finally settled, bum at the front of the seat, reclining right back with his palms face down on the edge of the table. He tucked his chin in so that his eyes lined up with Martin.

"So, this package that you got from his solicitors, what was in it?"

Martin felt a dizziness start rocking his head. He breathed deeper and forced it down his neck to his chest. He couldn't refuse to answer, but he couldn't tell them either.

"Papers."

"What sort of papers? Describe them."

"Look I only just got them a few hours ago and went straight home. I haven't had time to look through them properly and I didn't understand the ones I *did* have time to look at."

"Do you have them on you."

He pictured them scattered on his coffee table.

"No." His head cleared suddenly. "But they're confidential anyway. Private documents."

"This is a murder investigation Mr Molloy, nothing is private. What solicitor was he with?"

"I can't remember."

"Oh please."

"Out of everything that's happened since yesterday, trying to remember the name of some random bloody solicitors isn't my top priority."

"For someone who says they want to help us... you aren't."

"I just don't know what you want to know, OK?"

Morris was shaking his head from side to side.

"What are you hiding in there Mr Molloy?"

Martin looked him in the eyes again. Cold.

"You know, we can force you to submit to a psychic scrape if we have sufficient grounds."

A slight smile crept across the agent's face.

Martin swallowed and felt the hairs stand up on the back of his neck. He absolutely could not have that happen. None of the team could. But right now he was the one facing two determined agents who weren't allowing him any reasons to refuse. And he was losing the feeling in his arms.

Barclay suddenly turned to face the door. Martin and Morris looked at him. As the sound of voices outside the room grew louder, the Detector stood up and put a hand on Morris's shoulder, a split second before the door was swung open vigorously.

The man in the plum coloured suit stood triumphantly in the doorway. He scanned the faces of all the men in the room before alighting on Martin.

"My dear friend Martin, I believe it is time for us to make haste," said Charles.

CHAPTER 14
FRIDAY 23RD APRIL 1993

I can't remember when I first started calling the HQ "home", but it hadn't taken as long as I thought it would.

Moving from my terraced family house to an open plan apartment right in the centre of the city was a huge wrench at first. I'd spent my whole life so far in that house. I'd grown up there with my family, been there with my older brother to look after Mum when Dad died, been there to find Mum collapsed on the living room floor from a stroke, been there on my own for five years using it as my base of operations until I agreed to join The Pulse and they gave me an apartment inside Pullman Tower.

Weirdly, it never felt like I'd "arrived" or "made it" as they say. Straight off it felt like a workplace, a workplace I also happened to live in. This was a job after all, and I didn't take anything for granted. But that did mean that I started to feel oddly anxious around the third week, like I was overstaying in an expensive hotel. I had dreams of being called into a meeting with the others and the conversation always starting with: "Now Martin, it's been lovely having you here but…" That feeling *did* go, eventually.

At the time I guessed that living alongside the team was like sharing a student flat, which I'd never done, so that in itself was novel. It was strange being so close to other people that weren't family, observing how they interacted with each other, picking up on their individual personalities, their own likes and dislikes. It was fascinating in a way, like learning a new language.

The others helped me fit in very quickly. They always had time to make sure I knew what I was doing, keeping me up to speed with their operations, showing me the facilities.

I got quickly involved with them all in the training room exercises. I think the first session was only four days in, and I soon learned why they didn't delay. Fighting as a team is *not* the same as fighting on your own. Sounds damned obvious of course, but those first training experiences were big eye-openers for me. Coordination of attacks and awareness of team positions are the two most important factors of Hero teamwork, and I was terrible at both. I could see Jack getting more and more irritated with me as the sessions went on, but he never chastised me or removed me from the team, we just plodded on with more and more practice. It took months for me to become competent, and it was only then that I was allowed out on a mission for the first time.

Of course it didn't help that Vincent, our psychic link, couldn't get inside my head.

After the first practice session, where I knocked over Maria, got in the way of Jack's pulse blast and twisted my back, Vincent took me to one side in the kitchen.

He was suspicious at first. He had thought I must be a psychic of some sort, deliberately blocking him, but I guess my utterly clueless expression was all he needed to know that I wasn't. Apparently I was a "passive blocker", and a damned good one, which meant I lacked the functioning part of the brain that allowed psychics to hook into another person's consciousness. I was actually quite glad to just be lacking *one* part of my brain after such a poor performance. Anyway, I was quite rare, and for Vincent that was enough for us to become instant friends.

We worked out a system where he would prepare me for the training session in advance and give me verbal hints during it. At the same time I worked hard to study the team's movements and interactions so I could fit in and pretend to be connected to his link. It worked surprisingly well, nobody suspected a thing, other than that I was a bit slow to catch on.

Now, fighting as a team is second nature, and I can barely recall life on my own.

"Shitting little bastard!"

Mitchell bursts electricity down the controller and the Mega Drive fries, the TV screen image going diagonal for a second, then filling with static.

He throws the pad onto the floor, drops his head, sighs, then goes to the corner of the room and picks up a sealed box from the pile. As he comes back he looks up at me and gives an embarrassed smile.

I left the kitchen with a cup of coffee to find him playing some fighting game featuring a mix of classic and contemporary Heroes and villains. I don't know what it's called, but I've seen him playing it before. More often than not it ends with another knackered console. At least we got him some backups.

"It's that eighties bastard Blast Zone, always blocks me with his seismic barrier before juggling me in the air for like ten seconds, you know? Fuckin' rock hard."

"I think he was quite a bastard in real life too. Looks like they programmed him right then."

Mitchell blows out his cheeks, shaking his head again as he drops the box on the sofa and starts ripping it open.

"I'll leave you to it. Let me know when you've saved the world."

He laughs.

"It'll be next month at this rate, you know?"

I walk through a short corridor onto the balcony of the atrium and take in the view. The central section of the skyscraper has been hollowed out on five floors with balconies surrounding the large central space. It stretches the whole width of the building, the windows either side allowing natural light to flood in and bounce around the glass and metal surfaces inside.

The bottom floor is where the large service elevator ends; the six storage rooms and some maintenance stuff take up most of the space there. The next floor up has the gym, small pool, sauna and such at the front, and the training room at the back. This floor has the lounge and kitchen behind me and the meeting and communications rooms across the atrium. Above me are our apartments, split either side of the building, and the top floor has the "garden" at the front, getting all the sunlight, with the lab hidden away at the rear. Stairs go up to all floors either side, front and back, but there is also a central, open staircase on the other side of the atrium opposite me, that opens onto each balcony and goes up just five floors from the storage area to the lab entrance.

There is an incredible sense of space and light in here and even now it still looks amazing to me, like a giant cube of the outdoors has been carved out of the air and dropped into the middle of the building.

Walking around the balcony, it widens out at the sides by the windows, with display cabinets, tables and chairs sparsely arranged. TV screens showing various national and local channels hang from the ceiling, three on each side. I was told these were "chill-out" areas where you could read a paper or watch the news with a coffee, but most of us either watch the big screen in the lounge, when Mitchell isn't playing some game, or the TVs in our rooms. They don't get much use.

As I reach the other side and turn the corner to head to the open staircase I look down and spot Charles striding along the opposite balcony with a towel flung over his shoulder. He's in a spandex leotard and has just come from the gym by the looks of it. He doesn't look up and I don't shout down to him as I can tell he's in a mood about something or other.

It's not him I'm concerned about though, I want to speak to Jack. He's been unusually quiet since the riots and we haven't seen much of him apart from training and our daily "Hero and criminal activity" update meetings.

Sipping my coffee I climb the staircase up to the top balcony.

Here, the staircase goes up another single flight before ending at a large pair of plain brown doors with flat handles. The doors open into the lab corridor. It's wide, about fifty metres long, and unlike any other corridor in the building. The floor and ceiling are a dark grey colour, the walls brushed steel all the way down and which oddly bend in towards the middle, narrowing the passageway by a foot either side. It is lit only by small flush ceiling lights along its length and by a glow like the sun from the other end.

From here, all that can be seen at the far end are two giant bronze coloured dragons, curling in the air. It's only as you walk down the corridor, past the narrow middle, that your view widens and you see they are part of a sculpted pair of doors, a good fourteen feet high. The dragons are a peculiar mix of Western and Chinese style, with large bat wings, dinosaur-like heads and serpentine, reptilian bodies. One dragon on each door, they curl across its pale bronze surface, their flame breath licking the edges of the panels, feet resting on two oversized round knobs.

To the left of the doors are an iris scanning machine and a microphone with control panel.

Then you walk further down the corridor and you see that the walls either side of the door are made of toughened glass bricks, a foot deep, that gently curve away roughly fifty metres in both directions to the outer walls of the building. The blocks are so dense it's a struggle to make out the room beyond as they warp the light passing through them. The glass glows a light yellowish green from the sunlight, the doors a soothing orange.

I was told the whole arrangement was designed to induce a sense of awe, a feeling that you shouldn't be here unless you need to be. Works on me; this is only the third time I've ever visited.

I line my eyes up with the scanner. There is a quiet confirmation beep followed by an electronic voice,

"Vocal recognition required."

I press the red button under the microphone.

"Martin."

Another quiet beep and I hear a click. With no sound at all, the dragons part, and the lab is revealed.

I spot Jack at a long workbench. He is cloaked in a pulse shield, using his powers on some sheets of metal to bend and cut them into shapes I can't really figure out.

There are four metal benches at the bottom of the stairs in front of me. The stairs stretch about ten metres each side of the doors. The walls on both sides are made up of glass cabinets filled with mannequins dressed in some of our old costumes. I see my original one on the right and cringe. It looks like a party costume the fat kid stretched so they couldn't return it.

Around the sides of the room are small sections partitioned off, either containing odd looking machines for a very specific use, smaller work areas with gadgets and soldering irons, or filled with stacks of boxes and equipment yet to be used.

At the back it's mostly storage for oversized items, a small generator, some compressed gas canisters, a pile of scrap. The roof has a system of rails and pulleys arranged in a square around the sides. On these hang several large chunks of machinery, their black power cables twisting around them. Jack has brought over a green laser cutting machine and it dangles next to him, illuminated by his pulse bursts.

The centre of the room is taken up by a glass walled cube with a solid steel floor and with an ugly air extraction and filtration system on its roof. It sits on stilts off the ground with a single narrow set of steps up to a security door with a pin code lock. That one I don't have access to. The walls are completely clear and inside I can see some expensive white lab machinery, several computers, and some smaller glass boxes with tiny machines moving around inside them.

Jack once explained it all to me, but the only words I recognised were "radioactive materials" and "exotic energy studies", so, as far as I was concerned, that was one room I never intended to set foot in.

As I walk down the steps Jack sees me and raises a palm up. He turns off his pulse shield and flicks some switches on the laser cutter.

"Sorry."

"No no, safety first, that's all. Don't want one of my pulse beams bouncing off the worktop at you. Doubt even you could withstand that one."

He meets me halfway between the benches and the stairs. I get the feeling this is as far in as I'm going. He was like this the last time I was here. I wasn't offended then, and I'm not now. I can tell he likes to work, and when he works he likes to do so until he's done. I decide to keep this short and sweet.

"Not going to bother you too long, just wondering how things were going in here?"

He looks at the floor behind and to the right of me, head at an angle, nodding.

"Yes. Good. Good."

I stay silent for a few seconds and he realises he's going to have to explain himself a bit.

"I've been working on developing something that might detect The Controller's psychic powers. Something a bit more reliable and accurate than Vincent."

"You mean like a triangulator?"

He makes a face.

"Not really. You see, Vincent keeps saying that all psychic Heroes have a 'signature', that he can tell straight away whether a psychic event is caused by somebody he knows or not. Thing is…"

He looks at me for the first time.

"…no psychic detection equipment has ever been able to identify any individuals. So he's either bullshitting us, or it's something we haven't yet worked out how to measure. So I've designed a much more sensitive detector based on a few theories I have. I need to test it on Vincent as a control, then when... and I say 'when', The Controller gets bored and decides he wants to fuck with us again, I'll be able to compare the readings, see if there is any difference, and if there is we should be able to pinpoint his *actual* location."

"Wow. That would save so much time if he attacks again..."

"When," he points a finger at me, "When. He will have enjoyed his little riot puppet show far too much to not try it on again. He's probably recuperating right now, but he'll be back. I know his type."

Jack turns away from me and walks to the workbench.

"Anyway..." Crap, I'm losing him. "Yeah, anyway, I just came up to ask if you wanted to come to our special Italian dinner tonight? I mean it's all of us, not just you and me, that would be weird!"

I laugh. He doesn't.

"Erm... Maria and Charles are doing the honours, so it should be good food *and* theatrics. Starts at eight in the kitchen, soo..." He's shuffling around bits of metal, glancing at a pile of circuit boards off to the side. "...see you there? I mean this is obviously important, really cool stuff, but I think you're due a bit of a break yeah?"

He nods to himself.

"Yes, important work."

He pulls one of the boards right up to his face, scrutinises it and looks disgusted with himself. Then he strides away with it over to the partitioned work area where he hops onto a stool, swivels a magnifying glass down from the wall, clamps the board into some rubber grips and grabs the soldering iron.

Well I guess that's that done. We'll be lucky if we see him until after the weekend.

I walk back up the stairs and turn around when I reach the doors. Thin strips of smoke rise up over Jack's head, somewhere behind the partition, somewhere behind the laser cutter and its cables, somewhere behind all the little flashing lights and worktops. I know he'd kill me if I described it as a playground, but with a mind like his you could disappear in here forever.

CHAPTER 15
SATURDAY 15TH SEPTEMBER 2012

"I can't believe he's gone."

Charles's finger tapped the sculpted leather steering wheel as they sat at a red light. His right elbow rested on the driver's side door frame, as he stroked his ginger goatee. He tugged on his silver and blue cravat, tucking it down into his suit.

"Can't believe it."

He shook his head, tutting, seemingly disappointed with the whole world as he stared forward through the rain smeared windscreen.

Martin said nothing. He and Charles had barely shared a word since leaving the station. The two PCA agents were very interested in talking to Charles. Well, Agent Morris outwardly so, he couldn't tell what Agent Barclay was feeling. In fact Morris's behaviour was quite bizarre, like an over eager fan trying to steal the signature of his favourite Hero, dodging around in front of them as they tried to leave, trying to make out they were best buddies who hadn't talked in ages. When

Martin looked back at the police station doors as he went to get in the car, Morris was standing completely still on the threshold, staring right at him, expressionless once more. Creepy bastard.

Tutting and a sigh. Martin wasn't bothered by the silence, not feeling entirely in the mood for conversation after his ordeal. He was glad to be out of the station, thankful for Charles for that at least, but desperate for his own space.

He shrunk his chunky frame into the passenger side of a car with interior space larger than his bathroom, and wished the journey away. Having given up trying to sit upright on the slippery champagne coloured leather seat, he allowed himself to slide down and tried to place himself somewhere else. His eyes involuntarily darted between the pedestrians crossing in front of them. A woman with a bright orange raincoat and clear umbrella with white and orange circles printed on it, three young boys soaked to the skin in their t-shirts and hoodies, a tall woman wearing a blue sweater and black skirt, clutching a black handbag close to her as her umbrella was buffeted above her head.

The lights changed and Charles pulled away quietly. As they drove alongside the river, past the New Merlin Centre, Martin tried to focus. He closed his eyes and let the soft purr of the engine reverberate through his brain, lightening his body, pulling him up through the roof...

A sharp trill from just below the radio on the dashboard was a cold water shower to his brain.

Charles spoke the word "Answer" and his secretary Carol replied.

Something about Derek Torra, the hugely influential and popular talk show host, wanting him to be a speaker at a charity fundraiser dinner in a few months. He replied, telling the girl to clear his calendar for that day while making a wide sweeping gesture with one hand, name-dropping half a dozen other pop, television and Hero stars and signing off by telling her that his great friend and stylist to the stars, Chris Sheer, had been approached by Modern Heroism magazine for a photo shoot; she should pre-empt a phone call from his people by getting the full details from Grace, the magazine's editor who was, naturally, another great personal friend.

Martin didn't know if this was how Charles always spoke on the phone or whether it was all for his benefit. In any case he wasn't impressed. Those kinds of people existed in another reality far away from his own life. The same was true even when the team existed. He never considered himself a celebrity. He had no choice but to do what he did to help people, it was never for his own benefit, never to get himself known and invited to celebrity parties. Never to get him a book or TV contract. To him, Heroism was about sacrifice, selflessness, giving up your chance of a normal life to use your abilities to help those in trouble because you could. So when the rise of the "Hero celebrity" happened, towards the end of their run in the nineties, he was completely against it.

Heroes started giving up their anonymity in exclusive interviews in the papers and on TV. Actual Heroes appeared in guest slots on sitcoms and soap operas. They were in the entertainment pages, wearing designer suits and dresses at the latest film première while promoting their new book or album. New Heroes appeared on the scene, having never brought down a villain, but featuring in a multi-page "scoop" in the newly launched, glossy "My Hero!" magazine. The private lives of Heroes became fair game, and the game was played by both sides. Being good at your chosen vocation was no longer enough. It was Heroism as an end unto itself, and Martin had no respect for those that chased that goal. So whenever there was any press interest in the team, after they had stopped a crime or helped the emergency services, he made sure he was elsewhere.

In any case, Jack controlled communications and personal comments to the press were not allowed without permission. He was the official voice of the group if anything needed to be said and, as one of the biggest teams in the city, they gradually started to generate increasing interest from the press and TV. The media wanted interviews, photo shoots, a tour of their base. This was such a huge shift from the anonymity and secrecy of the early years that it took a great deal of adjustment for the team, except for Charles who kept pushing for it. Jack reluctantly started to allow some heavily scripted interviews with himself and Maria or Charles and one brief photo shoot featuring the whole team for a Heroism Today article, but Martin was glad that Jack shared his view about the changing media focus.

By the time they split up Charles was already courting the press heavily on his own and being snapped at numerous red carpet events. Within the year he would have a newspaper column and be a regular on the chat show circuit. Within two years he would have his own prime time entertainment show, making him one of the most well recognised celebrity Heroes in the UK. Within five years he had moulded his own little media empire.

Despite not wanting to ruin the calming silence, a simple, nagging question finally got the better of Martin.

"Why are you here?"

Charles jumped as much as Martin had earlier when the phone rang.

"I'm sorry my friend? Whatever do you mean?"

"I mean, why are you here, rescuing me from the station, taking me back home?"

"Well, we heard you had been taken in for questioning. Maria mentioned that the agents who had spoken to her had noted you weren't on the database. We figured you might need a saviour. You weren't under arrest after all. You could have stood up and walked out at any time, but I know you too well Martin. You always want to be helpful, even if it puts you in a bind."

"You heard?"

"Contacts, my dear friend, contacts."

Martin promised himself he would open the door and bail out if Charles called him "friend" again.

"Maria. Right."

He felt a pain in his chest saying that name after so long.

"Yes, Maria. She told everyone what had happened. I came up from London as soon as I had a break in filming to see if there was anything I could do and, as it turns out, there was. You were up to your eyeballs in 'Pokes'! Haven't even been home yet myself."

"Well thanks."

"Don't mention it."

Charles gave a long nod, silently acknowledging the gratitude had been time delayed.

"But why do you care anyway?"

Charles put a hand to his chest and leant back theatrically.

"Martin, how can you ask such a thing? You are my friend. A teammate. What we went through together..."

"...was almost eighteen years ago. When we *were* in a team. And we haven't spoken once since. So, why do you care?"

Charles sighed expressively.

"It may have been eighteen years ago," he continued, "but we are all still bound by what happened. We still need to look out for each other. The team *always* looks out for each other. Particularly when something like this happens to one of us," he looked over to Martin, "and the PCA start asking questions."

Martin nodded grimly.

"Of course. Yes."

He turned away and looked out of the passenger window, marbled as it was by raindrops.

"You think I'm being disrespectfully objective about this situation don't you?"

Martin rubbed a thumb along the wood panelling on the passenger door.

"Would I be wrong if I said yes?"

"Of course you would. Of course you would. Of course!" Charles's voice got louder. "You really think I cared so little about our Vincent?"

When Martin didn't reply he continued speaking.

"Look, I know he went through some tough times with his own mental state after we disbanded but what could I have done? Maria was best placed with her institute to take over his care from those disgraceful state run... hovels. Hovels they were, where sick Heroes were treated like dangerous zoo animals, to be caged and poked from a distance. Maria got him out of there and got him proper help. I always made sure I knew how he was doing and if there was anything I could do for him, but there was nothing he needed from me. But I was there, I was always there and available if he had."

Raindrops slammed the glass, trying to penetrate it, but instead burst open and were dragged away to the edges of the bodywork. A bus whipped past in the opposite direction, only a low rumble reaching the inside as a vibration through the chassis. They were in a little time capsule of glass and metal passing through the world.

"But when we were in the team, I was always the one to make sure he was clear-headed, knew what was going on. I was always on the lookout for signs he might be slipping away from us. Now why would I do that if I didn't care about the man?"

"Because he was a useful tool."

"Oh that's unfair."

"Is it? Really?" Martin turned in the seat to face Charles. He had been growing steadily impatient with Charles's revision through omission. "Tell me, how many times did you have a conversation with him outside of an engagement?"

Charles turned his head to look at Martin.

"What? Plenty of times." Charles chuckled with surprised shock.

"About what?"

He spluttered half formed words at the glass as he turned off the main road towards Martin's estate.

"I... come on, you can't expect me to remember every chat I had with him. It *was* eighteen years ago as you said yourself." The last few words were hammered home individually.

"You never talked, I know you never talked."

Charles was shaking his head, interjecting repeatedly with a definitive "No."

"I know because he *told* me you never talked."

Charles fell silent as they stopped to let an oncoming vehicle through a section of road narrowed by parked cars.

"Actually I might be being unfair, I think you asked him to hand something to you once. Was it a magazine? I can't quite remember. And neither could Vincent." Martin was growling with a slow burning anger. "He did remember all the times you hit him though, yeah, slapped him about, to make sure he was 'clear-headed'. And you never, ever apologised."

The car came to an abrupt halt. Martin wondered if he had hit a raw nerve and momentarily felt his fight-or-flight response kicking in. It was only when he looked outside that he noticed they had stopped across from his flat. When he looked back at Charles, he had turned in his seat and was staring straight at him.

"You want to know why I'm here?"

"Yes."

"Fine." Charles gritted his teeth. "What did you tell the PCA?"

Martin snorted and looked away. He unbuckled his seat belt and reached for the door handle only for the sound of an automatic lock to snap like a gunshot next to his ear. He dropped his raised hand to his lap and reached round the back of his neck to rub it with the other. Charles knew he could take the door off in seconds, and for a long while he was tempted.

"What. Did. You..."

"Everything." Martin couldn't stomach making eye contact again, so he stared at Charles's initials embossed on the glove compartment. "I told them everything about the jobs I'd had, where I'd been living, family…"

"About the fucking past! About what happened!"

Martin felt weary, as if the last eighteen years had just wrapped themselves round his shoulders.

"If you even have to ask, you don't know me at all."

Charles moved back slightly and slowly, like a surprised feline trying to sit down nonchalantly after being discovered somewhere it shouldn't be. He ran his eyes up and down Martin's profile, waiting for him to look but, when he didn't, he tapped a depressed button on the dashboard and the doors unlocked.

Martin immediately got out. Outside the car the clouds were a flat hand pressing a dirty duvet into his face. He dipped his head, pulled his jacket up over it and ran round the front of the long pastel blue bonnet and across the road to the shelter of the dark doorway. He stood there and waited for Charles to go. He didn't want to be watched going in.

The sleek blue machine, lit orange from inside, seemed to sit there for ages. Martin could just about see him staring over for a while, then he looked down and fiddled with the dashboard before pulling away, the warm glow leaving him behind in the dark grey colour of the reflected rain.

CHAPTER 16
SATURDAY 15TH SEPTEMBER 2012

He put his wet shoes on yesterday's free newspaper in the hall and hung his coat over one of the wobbly chairs in the kitchen to drip safely over the lino. He went into the bathroom and rubbed his head dry with a hand towel until he felt warmth from his short hair. He stared into each of his eyes in turn in the mirror. It looked like the same him from this morning, but it didn't feel like it. He was an impostor in his own body, unsure why he was there.

Everything seemed muddled. Events and people were stirring up silt that had been long left to settle at the back of his mind. But there was something badly wrong and he needed to fix it. Except he couldn't. There was nothing he could do now but follow the least painful path ahead of him.

He wished he could be at work, standing under that glass ceiling, trying to forget.

Those two agents had shifted him off his alignment completely. He was set adrift, buffeted by waves of memories and had almost been dragged under by their leading questions. Then with Charles turning up deus ex machina, it was like the past had finally collided hard with the present and he was trying to crawl out of the wreckage.

Not to mention he had been forcibly registered. His anonymity was gone. He was on the database. He was known. The cloak of invisibility that had allowed him to walk around the streets with a light chest had been pulled away and he was now exposed for the world to see. Nobody's business but his own was now everybody's business. He felt like everyone would know when they looked at him, they would see who he really was. He felt acutely aware of how many eyes there were in the large world outside.

And Charles was both a surprise and not. His descent from the celebrity heavens to pluck him to safety was a surprise, given their mutual animosity and time spent apart. The cover story questioning was not.

They had made a pact all those years ago to never tell anyone what happened. They had created a story to explain all the strange events and they would stick to it until death. Yet Charles still hadn't trusted him to keep to the script, still thought he was weak, still had to make sure.

And. Of course. Vincent.

He stepped out from the bathroom into the hallway and into the living room, soaked in moonlight. He looked at the envelope on the coffee table. In his mind it was a dangerous relic that, when touched, would transport him back in time to a terrible past and leave him trapped. But he had to go there, to the last place he wanted to be. It was the only path he had left.

"Martin, it's me, Vincent. It's important you open this right away," spoke the envelope to him as he picked it up again.

"I know buddy. There's nothing else I can do," he said out loud as he opened it.

CHAPTER 17
TUESDAY 4TH MAY 1993

There is nothing else I can do but lie like this.

I lie on my side, she is tucked right in to me, our legs forming a snuggled seventy seven. My arms curl around her, covering her breasts. She bends her arms so her hands lightly grip my wrists and we lie there, the soft pillows tingling my cheek as the passion slowly throbs itself out of our bodies.

Her hair is in my face like a flower scented spider's web. I'm tangled and I don't want to get free.

I want to stay here forever.

I nuzzle Maria at the back of her ear and she giggles like a schoolgirl, gripping my wrists a bit tighter.

From my apartment in the HQ the muffled sounds of the city seem so far away. All our apartments are on the fourth floor of the atrium section. It was a no-brainer, as well as a requirement for joining the team, that you moved in to the building. "Understated luxury", Charles commented once.

It's an odd mix of a home and a workplace. It took ages to get used to, to relax. Now it feels like I've been here all my life. I can't imagine living any other way. I can't imagine not being here with her.

I look down and see her beautiful shoulder rising out of her long hair draped over it. I lean forward and kiss it. The only thing that exists is us, right now, right here.

As our breathing returns to normal and the sweat dries on my back, Maria huddles in closer. She isn't usually this quiet.

"You OK?"

She hesitates.

"It's Jack."

"Oh."

Within seconds I go from feeling safe to feeling guilty. Our safe place from the world is now our safe place from reality. I tuck my nose into the back of her hair and lie quietly, waiting for her to go on. She feels smaller in my arms, like I've lost a piece of her.

"He's... virtually locked himself away in the lab. He's obsessed with The Controller, trying to find a way to stop him. I've tried to speak to him but everything I say is a distraction that makes him angry. Everything I do just upsets him. I mean, you know Jack as well as I do, but this time... I don't know what I can do."

"Yeah I know Jack. He'll eventually find some way we can get him. Some technology we can use to stop him or track him down. Until he does however, he is just, well, best left on his own I guess."

I can feel her heartbeat through her back pressed against my chest. She moves her top leg so that it lays over mine.

"I guess."

We've been together for nearly ten months now.

No, be honest with yourself.

We've been having an *affair* for nearly ten months.

She married Jack just over two years ago. They got together only a short while after she joined the team in 1990. She told me she liked the fact he was so sure of himself. This confident older man was intoxicating to a young intelligent mind just leaving university. He was her strength and she was his heart.

In the early days we just flirted. But then she flirted with all the men, including Charles, who would always flirt back outrageously, acting like some dapper Victorian gent being seduced by a siren. It was harmless. We were a close knit team who trained together and fought together, almost like a military unit. There was a lot of banter between us and, while we weren't all best buddies, we got on with each other, gave each other as much space as we needed. The flirting and dark humour was all part of that. It worked, basically.

Then a couple of years ago things changed. As the profile of the group increased, Jack became more concerned about our identity, how we looked to the outside world. When Michael and Tessa left he became even more determined to create the "perfect" line up, the proper mix of powers and personalities. He started to spend time away from the team in his office and lab, drawing up media plans, tinkering with gadgets, designing updates to our costumes.

I could tell Maria was becoming restless and unhappy. I could see that Jack was no longer noticing her arm round his waist and was ignoring her attempts to hold hands. His head was always years away in the future.

To be honest, even before he changed, I've never been quite sure how to approach him. He's a businesslike, stoic leader. Even after the years we've worked together we've never spoken of anything other than tactics and training. Yes, brief chats about my background and Hero history, but I always took those to be data gathering talks as opposed to proper conversations, and he never volunteered any personal information of his own.

So instead, I focused on helping Maria. I'd make coffee and we'd chat in the kitchen with Vincent or we'd train in the gym together. I hated seeing her sad and at the time I figured I was being a good teammate, helping cheer her up and making sure whatever relationship problems they had didn't affect the functioning of the team. I never planned on falling for her.

She hadn't planned on falling for me either, but over the months the marriage worsened.

Jack became cold and irritable, even more so than usual. His outbursts became more frequent and public. He became more controlling and refused to talk with her about his work. It was, "his responsibility", things had to be, "done properly or not at all", and of course, "these things took time". The physical side of their relationship pretty much died and, as he pulled away from her, she became frustrated.

After all, she was a young, energetic woman who wasn't shy about her body and here she was being locked out. Even when out of her girlish, Gothic costume she wore tight tops and leggings that hugged her slight figure.

In many ways she was the opposite of Inna. The Ukrainian, with her taller, more curvaceous and muscular build, wore a shapely costume in action and skintight jeans and low cut tops when out of it, but it was never done to show off her body. Those clothes just fitted her so she wore them. For Maria the clothes were always to show herself off. The flirting, and the attention it got her, made her happy, made her know she was still wanted.

As Maria and I spent more time together she started to become attracted to a person different to the men she usually went for. I wasn't anything like Jack and the men she had been with at university, the alpha males swaggering about stuffed with self-belief. She said she thought that if she worked hard enough, became more like them, she would get them to include her in the core of their world, not realising there was only ever room for them. At the time she considered all other guys to be socially awkward and lacking in confidence, but I didn't fit either group.

Apparently I was, "caring without being meek, confident with humility and without the cockiness, and

I was never quick to judge". I told her my Mum brought me up well and she laughed.

She started to confide in me about Jack. She started telling me how unhappy she was. She started to find out about what I wanted from life, about my family and she told me she started to fall in love. Then one evening, after another blazing row with Jack, who was too busy designing a range of matching encrypted communications devices to even notice the negligee she was wearing, ran crying to my apartment and we spent the rest of the night together.

Maria always joked, (as much as you could joke about cheating on your husband I guess), that she was the one to blame. She came to me dressed in almost nothing and made the first move. But the truth is, no matter how happy I know we are in each other's arms, we both felt guilty. If anyone found out, it wouldn't be just her marriage, it would be the team that would be destroyed.

"Thank you Martin."

I had started to doze off to the low hum of the central heating.

"What for?"

"At the riot. Holding me, helping me concentrate on the roof. I managed to get a lot of them sleepy. I think it helped calm things down a bit."

"Hey," I said, squeezing her tightly, "it's OK. It was messed up that night. We were all stressed out. And I had just dropped you through a roof."

Maria laughs.

"I'm still picking fucking glass out of my costume."

We lie silently for a moment, breathing in time with each other.

"No, really Martin, thank you. Just... being with you relaxes me. Centres me. I needed that back there."

"I'll always be there for you."

"I know."

A distant helicopter whups through the air. The conversation stops until we can no longer hear it.

"He'll be back won't he? The Controller. What the fuck he'll do next time I... don't even want to think about."

"Then don't."

"But we need to plan something otherwise we'll be on the defensive again, and we might not get so lucky the next time."

"Don't worry, like I say, Jack will come up with something."

"Well he'd better be doing something fucking useful in there."

I feel uneasy getting in the middle of one of their arguments. I always try and deflect the conversation away, not take sides, work out a compromise so they can end the row. My little way of making up for what we are doing I suppose. In reality I should be trying to prise them apart by encouraging their disagreements, forcing a split between them. That's what some guys would do, and why not? We're happy. I know we're both happy and they aren't. What's to save? But I can never bring myself to do it, even when the perfect plan pops into my head. I just can't take the thought of Maria getting upset.

And even with what we feel for each other, neither of us wants the marriage to break up. The team would never survive. People would take sides. Trust would be lost forever. And what any team needs to survive is trust.

With that thought I kiss Maria on the back of the neck as she settles her head in the pillow to fall asleep. A few minutes later, she is.

I lie awake. My body is calm, my mind is churning.

Pushing myself and Maria to the back of my head I go back to thinking about the riots. Whenever I'm alone, whenever it's quiet, they come back to me, unwanted.

I see the bodies lying across the plaza, faces caked in blood and soot. I feel the fear running through me as I try to outrun the crowd up the staircase and across the rooftops. I'm there again. It's real again.

There is a new fear though. A bigger fear. The Controller is too powerful. There were several hundred people under his will at once, for hours, and he didn't seem to be stopping or slowing down.

It's been almost a month since the psychic riot and there has been no word on him. He hasn't attacked again, and nobody has any leads. The apartment they think he was using belonged to a couple who were away on holiday. Police background checks came back clean, they didn't even know any powered individuals let alone socialise with any. None of the affected civilians had any knowledge of him, it was purely a remote control attack.

The police tried to trace him using CCTV footage, but almost all cameras were deliberately located and destroyed by small groups before the main riot started, so there was paltry coverage. Naturally, nobody involved remembered seeing anyone suspicious. Burlington Towers itself held no clues. With his power he could walk through a crowd of police, shouting at the top of his voice and firing off a machine gun completely undetected. Jack was right, he had won.

What would he do next? What would be enough for him? Was this riot just a test of how far he could stretch himself?

I hope Jack does have some sort of plan because I don't know if Vincent can withstand a concentrated attack from him, and then we'll all be vulnerable.

Seven of us, some of the most powerful Heroes in the city, and only Vincent stands in the way.

I feel a deep-rooted anger in my belly. Nobody seems to truly appreciate how much he does for us, the strain it puts him under. Even Maria is casually dismissive of him as if he's a tool to be used. I've never broached the subject with her of course.

Vincent has been locked in his room most of the time since the riot. His usual "self-righting procedure" as he calls it. Isolation and meditation is required after any strenuous psychic activity. I'll catch up with him when he's balanced again; have one of our kitchen chats over a giant bowl of nachos with salsa and cheese. Yeah. I need that right now. A simpler relationship.

A slow shudder of tiredness passes behind my eyes and I bury my head behind Maria's.

How long would this relationship play out? Who would leave the team first or what would happen if the team ended? Would the other one follow? Would she leave Jack? Would our affair last that long? It might fizzle out naturally, or one of us might end it; Maria because she wants to support Jack, or me because this gathering guilt becomes too much?

As usual, no answers come.

Got to live in the present Martin. Got to stop worrying so much about the past and the future, concentrate on the now.

As my mind finally calms down for the night, all I wish is for things to stay the same as they are right now.

CHAPTER 18
SATURDAY 15TH SEPTEMBER 2012

Maria tapped daintily and efficiently at the screen of her phone, completely ignoring him. She sat opposite, eyes looking down. Martin couldn't help but watch her.

She must have known he was staring, but she didn't look up. Tap, tap, tap. This was stranger than seeing Charles again. He shivered with nervousness and wondered if this had been a good idea.

After re-reading Vincent's letter several times and hearing the message from the memoirs again: "...you'll need a password to read it. Our old friends will help you out", he had realised that was all he could do. And the only number he had was Maria's.

Vincent had given it to him on a scrap of paper, several times in fact, always telling him he should call her. "It *had* been years after all", "she's divorced now", "time is a great healer", "things are different", he had said. Martin always said he would think about it and Vincent would always shake his head with a rueful smile, knowing full well that he wouldn't, as

Martin shoved the piece of paper into a pocket. He had a small pile of them gently compressed under his empty address book by the phone.

The only thing that would have caused him more anxiety than calling her, was having to reveal his Hero identity. Well that one was already scratched off the list, so what was there to lose by going for number two as well?

His bravado was brief. In the end it took him almost three hours of sitting on the sofa staring at all those scraps of paper before he had been able to make the call. It was as if picking the wrong piece would lead him to a dead end, a locked room, and he would never be able to choose again. His chest felt like it was filled with concrete as he picked up the phone and dialled. His heart faltered when he heard the ring tone and nearly exploded when he heard her voice. If he had closed his eyes, he could have been lying next to her in a warm bed. Eighteen years gone in a heartbeat.

It turned out she had been waiting for him to call. "It's about Vincent isn't it?" He didn't press her as to why or how she knew. He assumed that the others had received letters from him too, although perhaps not containing the same cover letter, and no memoirs. It was a very brief call. She had said they should meet. She would book somewhere for lunch. She called him back a few minutes later to confirm the where and when, and that was it.

Martin had felt exhausted when he put the receiver down, drained of emotion yet strangely elated. By the time the call was over it was past ten in the morning.

He would normally have been asleep by then, on the sofa again probably. He had changed out of his work clothes, putting them in a neat pile on the spare chair in the bedroom. He read the embroidered logo: "Ultimate Security", and wondered if he'd ever get to wear them again. After putting on one of his two sets of casual clothes he made himself a strong coffee, grabbed some biscuits from the tin and finished them off before making his way to the Metro.

Sitting next to the train window, with the hard glare of the sun scorching his eyes, he still felt not quite right. It was like he was in a scene from a movie, a camera filming him. This is the, "Martin on the Metro to meet Maria", scene, just look out of the window and we'll catch shots of you as you pass us. When he worked his way through the people at the stop and emerged onto the riverside street, they were all unknowing members of the public caught on film. When he stepped through the door and told the maître d' he was here to see Ms Gionchetta, the polite gentleman was an extra given the role of his life, as he saw him to the corner table, tucked out of the way. And when he saw her sitting in the silvery light of the restaurant, and she got up and shook hands very formally, he could almost hear the director shouting instructions from behind the bar.

Martin found himself still staring at her. Tap, tap, tap.

The strange surroundings didn't help ground him. Le Sauveur was a chic restaurant in the West End, just off the river. He had heard of it in conversation with some of the office staff who had gone there after a night at the nearby theatre. "Expensive with lovely décor and very relaxing", had been their overall impression of the place.

It was just at the tail end of lunch but the restaurant was still three quarters full. Glasses and cutlery clattered and shrieked. Waiters' shoes scuffled on the wooden floor. Notes of conversations clashed and formed a din that pressed against his face. A line of mirrors above the back of the seats stretched around the length of all the walls, reflecting glass, silverware, and faces into his eyes. He was anything but relaxed. It felt like he was in twenty rooms at once.

"Expensive."

"I said I'd pay."

Martin was startled. He hadn't meant to talk out loud.

"We'll split it, it's fine."

Maria hadn't looked up from her phone. She had barely looked at him after they shook hands. He felt like he was here for an interview, or to pitch some business venture and this was a test.

She hadn't looked at the menu either, probably knew it off by heart, thought Martin. She had ordered a glass of wine when they sat. The waiter assumed sir would like a beer, but he went for water instead. His body was feeling wobbly from lack of sleep and the start of the slow process of adjusting to being awake during daylight again; he had figured alcohol wasn't going to help. He took a long gulp, trying not to consume the unwanted slice of lemon, concentrating on the cold feeling slipping down into his stomach. The sensation was welcome.

He put the glass down and waited. Some minutes later Maria stopped tapping, held a side button until the screen went dark and placed the black phone down on the intense white tablecloth. Then she looked at him.

Her eyes were the same. Large, dark, mysterious. The make-up was similar, but more subtle, not as theatrical as The Black Witch. Bluer he thought. The eye shadow was still expansive and almost circular, but it no longer highlighted her eyes, it made them appear to sink deep into her skull. The dark purple lipstick no longer emphasised her sharply delineated lips, but instead concealed tight vertical wrinkles. Her hair wasn't long and hypnotically flowing now, but a severe black bob that ended at chin height. Of course the doll-like costume was gone, but so were the tight jeans and tops. Instead she wore a black suit jacket with a thin blue striped blouse underneath, a long, straight black skirt and court shoes. Plain, yet classy. The only decoration was an expensive looking watch, silver strap and round blue face, and a black necklace, half hidden under her collar.

She looked so different, and yet was the same. He had a strange sensation of intense disappointment that he couldn't trace to its source. He hoped it wasn't because he was incredibly shallow, because he could see how much she had aged. No, it wasn't that. It was more profound. A feeling of something lost.

There was a sliver of silence and Martin couldn't keep eye contact.

"I'm sorry about that, I was replying to an email from The London College of Psycho-Psychiatry. They want me to work with them on creating a new course for the 2016 intake. It was quite urgent."

Martin nodded.

"That's OK."

He turned his glass clockwise, anticlockwise, clockwise, between fingers and thumb.

"So, your research is going well then."

"Is it? How do you know?"

"Well, I mean I see you on TV often..."

"So from the number of talking-head interviews I do you can work out how well my research is going?"

"Well, not directly, I just meant that your work is obviously respected well enough for you to be asked to go on to these programmes."

"So I'm like an actor turning up on a chat show just coincidentally at the same time as their new film is being released?"

Martin shook his head.

"No, that's not what I meant, I was just interested in what work you were doing..."

"We're trying to determine the difference in effects of passive and active aggressive psychic incursion on long term memory formation."

She took a sip of wine.

"Right..."

"We theorise that they can permanently alter long-term recollection even after the psychic incursion is fully withdrawn. Also, I'm currently mentoring a group of students, one of whom is doing his final dissertation on some joint research we are doing with Edinburgh University, to try to ascertain whether specific types of memory are more at risk of dissolution after a psychic incursion, that is, whether you are more likely to forget your name or whether you loved someone."

She stared at Martin for a moment with her dark eyes. The recollection of a passionate embrace with chest tearing sobbing flashed across Martin's mind. He let it go. She looked down at the table.

"But you're not here to talk about my work. Are you?" her lips tightened, "Martin?"

Saying his name seemed like an effort to her. She sighed gently, her shoulders dropping.

"It's about Vincent. What happened to him."

Maria nodded.

"I know what happened to him. I heard from his solicitor. We all did."

Well that answered how she knew.

"I assumed so."

"And then I went to the police station and, because I was his legally assigned next of kin, I had to identify his body."

Martin hadn't realised. He swallowed hard.

"Ah hell. I didn't know."

She took another sip and looked over to where the baristas were working hard at their coffee machines.

"Well..."

Martin gave up. He was never good at talking about himself. Had never worked out the point of it. Instead he took another gulp of cold water, the lemon batting against his upper lip, then placed the glass down.

"Maria, I think we're in danger."

"We?"

"The team."

"That stopped existing a long time ago..."

"You know what I mean."

"Why does Vincent dying endanger the rest of us?"

"He was murdered."

"I know, it said in his letter to me. Said I should help the police and the PCA as much as I could. He even apologised for putting this burden on me. Silly man."

"And he was writing a memoir. About the team."

"I know, he told me. Charles wrote one too. Actually he wrote several and they sold very well by all accounts."

He leaned forward.

"Not a *real* memoir though. Not one that told everything that happened."

"I know," she said more forcefully this time, "he said it was a cathartic thing, getting it all out of his head and onto paper. He said it would help him come to terms with it. I agreed. I had been trying to get him to something similar for years but he always avoided doing it."

"Well I bet he didn't tell you he was going to publish it."

Her head stayed turned towards the baristas, but her eyes turned and fixed his gaze.

"Yep. He was going to publish it online, whatever that means. It was to be released for free."

She was facing him directly now, unable to disguise the horror on her face.

"He... never told me that."

"Yeah, well I only found out when I got the letter through, and I'm pissed off about it too."

"No. I'm not 'pissed off' Martin. You don't just get 'pissed off' about that."

Maria was rising in the chair, spine extending, hands flat on the table, her eyes incredibly becoming even larger and staring him down.

"None of us will tell anyone else. NONE of us. That was what we agreed. We don't write it all down to tell the world. Why the fuck would he even *think* about doing that?"

Her voice was getting louder and Martin was slowly sitting back.

"I have no idea, all I know is he was psychically writing everything down and was going to release it. He didn't say why."

Maria was shaking her head jerkily.

"No no no no no. Impossible. There is no way he would do that. How dare he. How dare he! The shit!"

Her eyes were darting around the table as if the painful memories were before her, waiting to pounce.

Martin's buddy defence kicked in.

"Hey steady on. Don't speak about him like that. Not right now. He must have had his reasons."

She stared at him again.

"He knew what we all went through. So do you. How can you defend what he was going to do? Well of course," she snorted, "you were lucky in comparison to the rest of us."

"Lucky?" He didn't mean sound quite so angry but that's how it came out.

"Yes, you weren't violated! You don't have to live with the memories of the things he made you do. You don't have to spend your life trying to forget them, but unable to because he didn't want you to. No, only *you* get to be our untouchable saviour, only *you* are graced enough to just get 'pissed off' about it, because it didn't fucking destroy you from the inside out!"

She was a shaking statue, rigid and terrified. Martin felt her gaze as he had never before. That look had always been reserved for the most violent scum they fought, for Jack and his indiscretions, but never for him.

Her eyes darted around, suddenly conscious that they may have been overheard. But they were sheltered in the corner, and the other diners too lost in their own conversations to notice. She pulled her hands back from the table towards her chest and wrung them. They were squeezed white and seemed faintly arthritic. Were they all really that old now?

She had no idea, thought Martin. It had genuinely never crossed her mind to consider how he felt. Sure, he hadn't been affected like the rest of them, but he had gone through his own private hell and this hadn't crossed her mind. He felt angry that she thought he had got off lightly. He felt pain too. He had suffered and wanted to tell her how much. But then he looked at her sitting opposite him. She was collapsed in the chair now, slouched like a discarded doll, staring idly into her lap, arms crossed, hugging her slight chest. She may have aged like him, but she was still trapped back in the past. He pushed his anger away with deep breaths.

"I'm, sorry. Shit, that doesn't mean anything does it."

"Sometimes it means everything and nothing at the same time."

A waitress came over and asked if they wanted to order from the menu. Martin said "no" straight away, but Maria asked for another glass of wine.

Martin sat back and the restaurant chatter flowed around their bubble of silence.

"So..." she said weakly, "when was he going to publish them?"

Martin cleared his throat.

"When he was done, or in the event of his death. Problem is, I can't read them."

"You've... got them?" She was suddenly alert, as if she had heard a gunshot.

"Yeah, he left them with his solicitor and they sent them to me. He was writing them psychically from a distance. I think that's why he was killed, somebody found out about them. But they're password protected in any case, and he didn't tell me what it was."

"So you don't know what's in them then..."

"No. Did he ever mention anything to you about a password, something he might have used?"

Maria shook her head, eyes darting over the table as she racked her brain.

"No, he... never mentioned anything about that."

"Damn. Out of all of us I thought you'd have the best idea."

"Nothing."

She looked up at him, anxious.

"Writing them from a distance… so they weren't even at his house? He died for no reason."

"No, he did. He let us know someone dangerous knows what happened back then. They are after the memoirs and aren't afraid to kill to get them, for whatever reason they want them. Probably blackmail I was thinking." Martin delayed saying the obvious. "I mean, some of us are pretty well off now, and would pay anything to stop that information getting out. And if not for money, they could have a Hero they could get to do anything they wanted."

"Or it's one of us," said Maria straight out, calmly.

They shared a tense look.

"That thought had crossed my mind, but I don't want to think it, do you?"

Maria's wine arrived and was poured, but she didn't move to drink it.

"You want to know what he looked like don't you? His body. Whether I know someone who could have done what they did to him?"

The thought had been bouncing around in his head since she mentioned identifying the body. He was glad she brought it up on her own as he hadn't yet worked out any way to broach the subject.

"I guess that could help figure out who it did it, yes. I mean, did you recognise…?"

"No. I didn't."

She picked up her drink and sipped, distracted now. Martin felt like a bastard for dredging up that memory.

"Sorry, I just thought it might... well, yeah."

He started to feel more uncomfortable.

"I guess I'd better go."

"Why?" said Maria, looking puzzled.

"This is... difficult."

Every muscle in Martin's heart was straining for what used to be. Their relationship seemed unbalanced now. They used to be equals. They used to be lovers. They understood each other. Now here he was finding it hard to even talk to her, like he was hopping through a minefield.

He decided not to go yet. As long as Maria wanted to continue the conversation, he'd stay.

"He made me executor of his will, you know?" he said, avoiding the obvious topic. "I have no idea what that entails. Guess I've got to go see the solicitors next week."

"Didn't they send you any information?"

"Yeah, pages of the crap. I haven't looked at it yet."

"I'm surprised he made you executor and not me." She looked him up and down, the first time she had really taken notice of him. "But that's Vincent I suppose. If you need any help with it all, let me know."

"Thanks, I could do with the..."

"I know a good solicitor, better than the ones he used."

"Right."

Martin finished off his water in one last gulp. Gone warm.

"He wants me to meet up with everyone again. Everyone on the team. It was one of his last requests."

"They won't want to see you, you know."

Martin felt cold.

"Yeah, I'd kind of expected that. Thing is, apart from you and Jack, I don't know how to get in touch with the others."

Maria sat at a slight angle, watching him.

"I know Mitchell's address. You got a…?"

"Nope, no pen."

"I was going to say a smartphone, so you can tag the location and get the GPS to guide you there."

"I don't know most of what you just said."

She looked at him sadly.

"I suppose you think mobile phones are still the size of bricks…"

"Pens and paper never run out of batteries. Uh, when you have them."

She reached into her small black handbag hanging over the back of her chair. She pulled out a thin black pen, grabbed her unused napkin and wrote on it, before handing it to Martin. She had written the address of Davies' Self Defence Centre and a phone number.

"Oh cool, I always wondered what he got up to."

"Prison mostly."

"Really? Oh… wow. Not so good."

"But now he runs that," she pointed at the napkin with the end of the pen before slipping it back in her handbag. "It's in Nellbourne, not far from the cinema complex. He also knows where Andrea is, but good luck getting him to tell you. He's never told me. I've lost track of her entirely."

"So he knows where she is but isn't telling? How come?"

Maria tilted her head, one side of her short bob swinging out.

"Apparently it's quite 'complicated' between them. I never asked for the full details."

Martin folded the napkin over and slipped it into his back pocket.

"As for Jack, that number is a direct line to his secretary. Tell her you got it from me before she bars your landline. You won't get an appointment though. Charles has been trying to get to see him for years."

"Great. But thanks. I appreciate that."

The waiter came over and asked what they wanted to eat. Maria ordered a salad while Martin declined, saying he wasn't hungry. Maria tutted and ordered him some bread thing with olives.

"So..." started Maria with purpose.

Martin winced. Was this it? The chat he both desired and dreaded having?

"...where are the memoirs now?"

Ah, it wasn't.

"They're safe."

"Safe where?"

"It's best you don't know. They're safe, that's..."

"So you don't trust me, is that it?"

"No, it's just that the fewer the people who know the better. The last thing I want is to put your life in danger. Any more danger."

Maria was looking at the table thoughtfully, lips tight.

"He talked about you a lot. Did you know that?"

Martin had never really wondered what Vincent thought of him. They were just old friends wasting air now and again. "No, I didn't. What did he talk about?"

"Your chats. He enjoyed those. He found some peace in these last few years. I know you helped him a great deal."

"I only visited him now and again, I didn't help him like you did."

"It was what he needed," she said, leaning slightly forward to look at him. "That contact, that friendship. I gave him psycho-psychiatric help, you gave him what I couldn't. He always appreciated that, you know."

"Yeah, I just wish I could have gotten up to his house more often, but shift patterns you know – they kill your social life. We talked a lot on the phone."

Maria nodded.

"He liked that. Often said you were the only one he was really comfortable talking to. Said you understood him. He used to say you were trapped."

The noise of the restaurant had faded during their conversation but it suddenly rushed back into his ears.

"What… what did he mean by that?"

"Don't know. He wouldn't elaborate, just said he had to help you. I suppose you both needed each other in a way."

Trapped? Martin tumbled that one around in his head but nothing stuck to it.

"Strange that it takes someone to be murdered for us to see each other again."

She was calmer now, her face had relaxed and her eyes were more open. "Yeah. It's good to see you again."

That was as far as the conversation went in that direction, as the food arrived. His bread was an elaborately woven thing, salty and chewier than he had expected, but the olives were nice.

They chatted about Charles coming to his rescue at the police station and, much to his relief, she didn't quiz him about what he had said under questioning. Most likely Charles had already passed it on.

They talked briefly about work and then her phone made a pleasant chiming noise to remind her of a meeting back at the Institute. She dropped thirty Euros on the table and stood up, swinging her bag on to her shoulder. Martin followed her to the door.

There was an awkward moment when a handshake seemed too formal but a kiss was out of the question. It ended with neither.

"Good to see you again Martin."

"You too. Really."

Was there a faint smile on her lips?

"Don't do anything stupid. Leave this to the police. I know you want to avenge Vincent, but the person that did this is… powerful. You don't know what you might uncover. Some things are best left in the past."

"I'm just going to talk to everyone. That's all. Can't be that hard. That's what he wanted."

Maria nodded and left. Martin waited a polite moment before leaving too.

As he stepped out of the restaurant into the street, the sun seemed to be trying to strain itself through the mucky cotton wool layer above him. He noticed Maria had already disappeared and that the street was busy.

It was a Saturday and it was heavy with people hovering around the many restaurant doorways up and down the street. A hunch of students brushed past him, their backpacks swinging into oncoming pedestrians, talking excitedly about some Hero fight in central London the previous week. A bus squeezed through the agitated cars and made a slow, tight turn into the stop near him. Noises of cars, noises of people. A woman's oversized handbag hit him in the back. A small dog on a leash strained to sniff at his feet as its owner walked past. A young girl with a nose ring taped a poster about a Hero religious group to a railing around a tree, one of several attached to every other tree along this side of the road. A low riding car coughed throatily as it lurched along, only a few metres at a time, in the busy traffic. The array of colours started to dart around in front of Martin's eyes and all the sounds merged into one as his neck started to pulse hard.

He backed up until he could feel the cool wooden frame of the restaurant door behind him. He had to concentrate. Not let it get too deep. Breathe it away. Gripping the frame tightly with both hands he closed his eyes and took a deep breath in through his nose. He got the mixed scent of restaurant lunches and the sharp scent of wet, rotting leaves. He imagined he was at work, standing on the mosaic of the sailing ship, grey silence hanging off his clothes and he was floating above the city, away from all the rabble and confusion. He was being lifted up and he was safe again.

A sharp pain behind his left eye brought him back down to the pavement with a rush. He opened his eyes. Immediately they came to rest on the other side of the street where, parked up outside a clothing boutique, was a police car. Inside he saw one officer, a young woman with blonde hair, staring across at him. She flinched and looked away.

"Great", thought Martin, "they've got uniform following me now."

He kept watching the car. The woman seemed to be looking at some notes next to her, then in the rear-view mirror and then over to him again. He caught her gaze. This was obviously too much contact for her as she quickly started the car and pulled straight out into the traffic in front of a black cab.

He watched the car drive away, eventually losing it when it turned at a junction.

He took a second to think over what Maria had said about the others. "They won't want to see you, you know." But he had to speak to them all. Vincent had wanted him to. One of them might know of someone who could have killed him. Or one of them *had* killed him.

At least he knew where Mitchell was. He had got on well with the lad, looked out for him during his time on the team, so that meeting shouldn't be too difficult. But

Jack was going to be interesting, if he ever got to see him.

Maria had lied when she told him she didn't recognise the perpetrator from the damage done to Vincent's body. They had been too intimate for too long for him not to know when she was lying. But he didn't blame her. At least he knew now that the killer was somebody known to them all, not a stranger. It had been good to see her. Time had changed a lot about both of them, but they still seemed to recognise each other in the end.

Martin yawned and felt a surge of sick tiredness soak down through his muscles. When did he last sleep? A quick bit of mental arithmetic told him he had now been up for over twenty hours. His sense of time was completely out of whack. He had a system for "coming down" off the night work but he had totally ignored it. Home. That's where he needed to be right now. He would make a call to Pullman Enterprises to try and get a meeting with Jack, get some sleep, and see Mitchell in the morning. Daylight morning.

He lifted himself away from the wall. The strip of wooden frame he had been gripping came away with him. There was a dirty grey gap where it had been. He quickly glanced around but luckily everyone was too wrapped up in themselves or their phones to have noticed. Embarrassed, he placed it back in position giving it a little double tap to secure it, then walked back to the Metro stop.

CHAPTER 19
SATURDAY 15TH SEPTEMBER 2012

"I'm sorry, Mr Pullman doesn't take calls from individuals. That's because I don't take calls from individuals. Mr Pullman only deals with high ranking managers of major corporations or their liaisons, and that is not you. How did you get this number?"

Martin stood at the Metro station payphone with Maria's napkin hanging over the top of it.

"From his... ah, Maria? Professor Gionchetta? Look, I apologise for calling this number but I need to see him. Tell him it's Martin, he'll know who I am."

"*I* don't know who you are sir, therefore I sincerely doubt Mr Pullman will."

"He did have a life before Pullman Enterprises you realise? I'm an old friend from back in the day."

"Oh... you are powered?" she said, sounding amused, "well Mr Pullman doesn't engage with any powered individuals any more. It's a very strictly enforced rule. We employ Detectors and Nullers to ensure no powered individuals can enter any property owned by the Pullman Group. You cannot enter any property owned by the Pullman Group. If you do you will be detected, nulled and arrested. Or neutralised. Whatever gives the most expedient outcome based on your powers. Good day sir..."

"Please, just tell him Martin called. It's about Vincent's death. We need to talk."

The phone went silent for so long that Martin thought he had been dropped into a holding line. He was about to give a tentative 'Hello?' when she spoke again more quietly.

"I know of the passing of Mr Hayden-Phillips. I will put your message in with the hundreds of other unsolicited messages I have for Mr Pullman. I can't say when he will become aware of it. Good day."

CHAPTER 20
SATURDAY 22ND MAY 1993

"Well, looks like everyone got the message."

Me and Charles are on a walkway overlooking the large foyer at the front of the HQ. Usually quiet with only the concierge robot buzzing around, it's now a mass of people trying to make their way to a row of tables below us. They come through the revolving door in a steady stream of ones and twos and, unsure where to go, gravitate to the large queue in front of them, hoping it leads somewhere.

From above they look like loose clothing, swirling and collecting at the side of a river as the current brings them in. Occasionally a face looks up from the throng and breaks the illusion.

"Didn't know there were this many Heroes in the city."

"Well my dear fellow, approximately one quarter of these will be sent home when our hard-working admin staff below work out they have come from outside the country."

"Really? That many?"

"Why of course!" said Charles, "it is once in the proverbial blue moon that a Hero team holds open auditions for a new member. They will come from far and wide for such an opportunity. Those two for instance..."

He points out two oriental girls in bright primary coloured costumes, heads twisting around, eyes wide open as they inch forwards.

"Probably Japanese. Korean maybe. Flight tags still on their backpacks, see?"

"Christ."

I had naively thought around forty, maybe fifty tops, would come from the city and surrounding boroughs. It was closer to two hundred and it was still only half nine in the morning. Registration closed at eleven.

Had I lost that much perspective on how big a deal we are? Oddly, I guess I've been sheltered from it by being part of it; too close to see what people think of us.

But this is no popularity contest for me. I'm not doing it to become famous. In fact I don't care what people think of me, as long as I'm doing good work and we don't cause too much damage to public property. I just assume I'm tolerated at best. If people get that we're helping them, great, if not, no skin off my nose. I'm doing it because I have to, because I have to do something useful with my abilities.

It was never my goal to be part of a Hero team anyway, it was more or less by accident I joined The Pulse.

Three years was it now? Yeah, I remember seeing the news reports of the The Pulse being founded, their first big fight against the villain team Bad Justice, and their ongoing work in trying to rid the city of organised crime. That's how I came to their attention in the end. I hadn't gone looking to join up, I had my own neighbourhood to protect. The people there knew me well and I was quite content with that. Then one of the smaller local drug pushers got a super strength powered heavy, some distant relative I think, to help him out and they proceeded to ruthlessly wipe out the competition. Seventeen bodies in one month on a single estate. These guys were dangerous, recruiting, and on their way to being a major gang. I couldn't let things go any further.

I first met Jack, Maria, Vincent and Paul and Tessa when I smashed through a seventh floor flat wall, my arm round the neck of that powered bodyguard and landed, him first, at their feet. Turned out they had come to take the gang out themselves after hearing of the mounting body count. But I had the local knowledge and beat them to it. I remember getting to my feet, one foot on the big guy's back as he lay there groaning, and said,

"Oh, hello."

I did wonder later whether I should have said something a bit more memorable, puffed out my chest and proclaimed my latest victory, but that wasn't me. No wonder I ended up getting the nickname Captain Understatement. The first memory I have of them was Jack looking bewildered when I explained I had taken them all out by myself and they just needed to call the police in to round them up. I remember Maria smiling at me as I shook the brick dust out of my hair then Vincent said, "I like this one" while squinting at me with a puzzled expression.

A couple of weeks later I was doing a routine patrol when Jack and Paul flew down from the sky to invite me to an informal meet and greet at their HQ. Nothing serious, no guarantees Jack kept saying. I was almost certain that it hadn't been his idea. The two guys hooked me under my arms and flew me into the city there and then.

I had never really wondered about other Heroes, how they felt about their abilities. I'd kept himself quite distant from others like myself, in my own small world: my neighbourhood, Mum, my day job at the plastics factory. I figured they were much like me, whatever they could do and wherever they came from. But then, soaring over the neighbourhood, crossing the southern bend of the river towards the centre of the city, I began to see things in a new way. I felt jealous of those able to fly, to be able to see the world from such a perspective. They had such a vista, such a view into different lives, distant, yet all seeing. Such a privileged position. I wondered how they coped with having such a power.

I failed in trying to remain cool and instead spent the whole flight twisting my head this way and that, spotting landmarks and following the trail of an ambulance rushing noisily through the late evening traffic. Then they suddenly slipped between office blocks, turning sharp angles as I swung around locked in their elbows, square chunks of window lights whizzing past me. A man staring at a screen with his head on his chin. Two women walking towards the lifts, laughing. One spotted us and tapped her friend on the shoulder, but we were gone before she turned. I smiled as I imagined her spending the rest of her life never being believed for what she saw.

This was incredible.

It became even more incredible when we swooped upwards in front of a skyscraper and came over the edge of a balcony a few floors from the top. The windows here were set back about sixty metres or so, with a large set of double doors leading inside. This appeared to be a landing pad of sorts, but there was no aircraft, just Maria. I was floored.

When we all met at the housing estate I was so wrapped up in tidying things up for the police I didn't take that much notice of any of them. My eyes clung to her like screws to a magnet. She was in her trademark black doll-like dress, face as pale as the moon, hair softly moving in the wind. We landed just in front of her. Paul rolled his shoulder. It made a crunching noise and he joked about not looking forward to taking me back. I apologised as Jack pointedly said his wife would look after him for now and we would all meet in the lounge in an hour. He bent over, gave her a kiss on the lips and went inside with Paul.

I remember standing completely still like an idiot, staring at Maria. She just smiled, took me by the arm and gave me a guided tour of the main areas of the HQ. After that, and the friendly chat with the team that followed, a short nod from Maria to Jack finally made him officially invite me to become a member. For a trial period of course, he hastily added, to see how things went. Part time, so I could still attend to my duties in my own neighbourhood. But should I get a permanent place they would give full protection status to my area, under my experienced stewardship.

I hadn't known if I was supposed to hesitate and say I'd get back to them, but they all looked at me as if waiting for an immediate answer. No pressure. And yet strangely there wasn't any. Something about the place, the team, just felt right. Maybe it was because I had cleared out the drugs gang and felt like it was time for something bigger. Maybe I realised I could help more people this way. Or maybe it was something in her eyes. Was she affecting me? Using her power to relax me, drop my guard and become friendlier? No, that wasn't the done thing, I knew that much. Whatever the reason, I said yes there and then and never looked back.

A few months later Paul had to leave when he was severely injured. Tessa and Michael, who joined as his replacement, left to start a family together a year ago after she got pregnant. Charles joined us after the team he was in broke up acrimoniously. Jack was no friend of the old team leader and Charles liked him even less, so both men spotted an opportunity to annoy him and benefit each other. Inna started at the end of last year after failing to find work in electrical engineering, despite getting a first in her degree and coming to our attention after outing herself during a vicious bank robbery she got caught up in. Mitchell was Charles's choice from an advert he had cockily plastered over boarded up windows and lamp posts after Jack suggested they lacked a power with crowd control abilities. He had only been with us a few weeks before The Controller started his attacks.

But we have been fairly stable as a team, growing in confidence and experience with each encounter. We all have our defined roles and support the others as needed. We work. Which leads to my next question.

"Tell me again why we're recruiting?"

Charles sighs, uncertain of the words coming out of his own mouth.

"Our esteemed leader thinks he has spotted a gap in our array of powers, after the riots you know."

He looks sideways at me.

"Right. Because hiring one more member will even the odds when we face another mob of six hundred. Good idea."

Charles murmurs, "mmm", and looks back down at the crowds.

"Wouldn't a closed interview have been better though? Pick the type of power we needed and approach them directly?"

"Well we have positive buzz apparently! Now is the time to take advantage of it and see if we can't find ourselves someone special who has been hiding in the shadows. So it seems."

"Well, I'm just glad I'm not having to organise this. It's madness down there. Looks like we've got all sorts too. Not sure how much use *he* would be."

I nod towards an old guy, must be in his late sixties, showing off his plasma sculptures to a group of young kids. They are very impressive and I know I wouldn't like to feel the blast of that power directed against me in anger, but all the same, most of these people are not going to be a good fit for us.

"You never know. In fact I can see it now: he dazzles the enemy with a sculpture of the Eiffel Tower so magnificent his foe simply gives himself up without struggle. After all, what is any weapon against such beauty."

We share a chuckle.

"Anyway, time is passing, our throng is gathering and I must join the others ready to await their interrogations."

"See you later."

Charles heads into the back offices.

I feel myself getting a headache from all the babble out here. I'm thankful Jack hasn't asked me to help with the interviews. There are times when Jack's preconception of my level of intelligence comes in handy. Think I'll have some time to myself in the gym.

I hop in the lift up to the third floor of the atrium and head across to the kitchen. As I grab a bottle of water from the fridge Vincent comes in looking for a yoghurt.

"Hey?"

"Hey."

"How're the headaches?"

He grimaces.

"Still there, but easier than they were. I knew it was bad but I didn't think it had been such a strain on me. I usually recover faster than this."

"Well you said it yourself, he was the most powerful psychic you've come across yet and you had to cover all our minds. That's going to be tough mentally."

Vincent nods. He picks strawberry.

"Sleeping better though?"

Vincent stops moving and holds the carton steady in his left hand.

"I get this..."

His eyes seem to be searching for the right word.

"'S'up buddy?"

"He's still around you know. Like... in the background, scanning... but nothing I can get more than a hunch on you know? Like something isn't right. Nothing concrete. Nothing Jack would be interested in."

He moves again, grabs a spoon from the cutlery drawer and sits down at the long cream oblong dining table. I join him, watching him carefully peel back the lid, scrape the underside of it clean, fold it in quarters and place it beside the pot.

"How do you reckon Jack is? I mean he's been pretty invisible until last week, and then this."

"Auditions. Yes... strange one that."

Vincent spoons the same volume of yoghurt each time, swallows it and licks the spoon clean, front then back.

"He's been..."

He stops moving again, spoon hovering inches above its goal, then dives in.

"...quiet. Very quiet."

I take a gulp of water from the bottle.

"Yeah, back to his 'I will fix everything' mode. Which is normal, especially after his tantrum in the lift, so I guess he's OK!"

"Normal..."

Spoon, swallow, lick.

"And you? You 'normal'?"

"You already asked me that."

"Nope. I asked you how your headache was, not how you were."

Vincent smiles and points the spoon at me.

"You... damn. Anyone else and I would have gotten that meaning from their minds. Still can't get you. Heh. Still not told anyone by the way."

"Thanks. Appreciate that."

"But useful, given how strong The Controller is. Might not be able to keep that one quiet for much longer."

I spin the bottle on its end between my hands.

"Would prefer you to. Don't want to be Jack's next science experiment. You know how rare multiple powers are, even if one of them is passive."

"Even so... interesting."

"I don't like interesting."

Vincent smiles and carefully scrapes the rest of the yoghurt from the awkward corners.

"Anyway, I asked how you were."

Vincent laughs then starts shaking. He glances towards the door, then back at me. All joking is gone.

"He's too strong Martin. If he attacks again I don't know if I can hold him off. I mean if he concentrates that amount of will again, but just on us, I don't know what I can do. I'm still weak from last time, I don't..."

Vincent closes his eyes and breathes deeply to stop himself shaking. His knuckles turn white around the spoon.

I knew there had been something on his mind, the way he had been so distracted lately. I'm glad he's finally confide in me.

"You need to tell Jack. He can figure out something to help you back to normal or boost you up, some method or drug that..."

Vincent's back goes rigid.

"NO DRUGS! I'm fucking done with them."

I push the water bottle to the side and slap a palm on my forehead.

"Sorry, I know... shit, I shouldn't have said that pal, it just came out. I know what you've been through OK..."

Vincent relaxes.

"...but there might be something else he can do to get you fighting fit again."

"I'm done with ECT too, I get confused for weeks after. I just need time. I hope I get time."

"OK, look, get some rest yeah? If he's going to be back you need to be at your best. Don't worry buddy, I'll look out for you. And if the worst comes to the worst," I shrug, "I guess I'll have to look out for all of us. But I'm sure it won't come to that anyway "

I'm aware what I just said doesn't sound convincing. Vincent puts the spoon down alongside the pot.

"You're right. Once they hire the new guy we'll be safe from harm."

"You never know, we might find another psychic you can combine powers with."

"Nah..." Vincent looks towards the door. "...only three out there, and they're rubbish."

I laugh and Vincent breaks another smile. As I get up and head to the door I call back to him.

"Say, want to join me in the gym? Got a machine set up for you with polystyrene weights!"

"Piss off."

"That's better. See you later, hopefully once all this shit has calmed down."

"Yeah, will be nice to have mostly my own thoughts again."

He looks down at the empty pot, his face turning serious again. I know he will sit there now for about ten minutes, barely moving. Then he'll leave everything on the table and go to his room for the rest of the day, leaving Maria (usually) to find the mess and curse his name as she tidies up.

I'm worried for him. He's suffering a lot more than after the previous incidents. Definitely a lot more stressed. And I think he's right about The Controller too, which makes me even more worried for all of us.

As I leave to get changed for the gym to pound my anxieties away, he has his hands flat on the table and is concentrating intently, forehead scrunched up in wrinkles. He looks like he's searching for something, something he knows is out of place.

CHAPTER 21
SATURDAY 15TH SEPTEMBER 2012

Home.

Safety.

Martin walked through the door and it clicked shut behind him with a satisfying double thunk of the magnetic lock.

Seeing Maria again had been so strange for him, another unsettling event. But he was home again now, the only safe haven he had left.

He took off his soaked jacket and hung it up. Keys on the top of the shoe store. He emptied his pockets out too – a receipt from the restaurant and some spare change. An old mint.

He gazed at himself in the mirror in the darkness. He could only see the pale blue outline of his face from the faint light coming through from the living room. He flicked the hallway light switch and it didn't come on. He was two steps away and into the kitchen before he realised.

"Damn it, only bought a bulb the other day. I'm sure these things are designed to die after a few months."

Shaking his head he flicked the kitchen light switch. The light didn't come on.

Martin stopped still. Fridge clock gone. No red light on the cooker switch. Then he heard movement through the wall in his bedroom. Instantly he was hyper aware. He could almost hear silence itself as a background hiss, and there was a person sized gap in it less than ten metres away in the living room. He turned silently to face out towards the hallway. As his eyes acclimatised he spotted all the drawers and cupboards were open, contents shifted, spilt out onto the tops and floor.

He stood completely still, knees slightly bent ready to move. He could feel the other person was doing the same. If this was the same guy who took out Vincent he could be gutted in seconds. He reached over and carefully picked up a long kitchen knife that had been left dangling half over the side of a drawer. He might not have much time to get to him so anything that increased his reach was useful.

Movement. A shift of weight trying to pass through the doorway. Another shift. Soft huff of compressing carpet.

Now!

Martin stayed low and ran, twisting left round the door frame. He clocked the person's silhouette and dived at it, knife first. A blue flash ripped the knife from his hands, shredded the front of his jacket and shirt and crushed his breastbone in so hard he heard it crack as it hurled him straight back down the hallway. The specially strengthened front door buckled and split as he slammed into it, slivers of light from the communal corridor breaking in around the frame. Some very old training came back to him and, as he landed, he used the rebound off the door to roll forwards. A second blast passed over him, ripping the walls open and splitting the top half of the door away. The corridor light momentarily blinded the intruder as Martin rolled to his feet and ran at him again. Head down, he hooked his right arm round his waist, stepped past him on his left then flung him like a giant discus. He hit the bookshelf hard and cried out. He wasn't expecting that. Martin had the advantage. He ran forward again, upper cutting into the bastard's stomach, lifting him off his feet and cracking his head on the ceiling. Smashed plaster and shredded shelves tumbled around them. Martin quickly pulled his hand away, it was stinging. He squinted at it in the dim light. Was it burned? Shit, concentrate on the enemy. He looked up in time to see a glowing fist accelerating towards his face from the left. It caught him full side on. More stinging. Martin spun round and lost his footing, crashing down onto the coffee table chest first, obliterating it.

The man was quickly over him. The room glowed and a fist ploughed into the back of his head. His face broke the floorboards under him and his head and shoulders dipped into the new dent in the carpet. Martin could feel hot blood filling up his nostrils. That was a feeling he hadn't had in a while. It scared him.

Adrenaline kicked in and he managed to twist himself onto his side, grabbing a long piece of the dead table and whipping it into the side of the intruder's head. The piece of chipboard shredded itself into nothing, centimetres from his ear. The man was standing tensely above him, outlined in a blue glow that illuminated the cloud of wood dust. Martin couldn't make out his face, but he knew who it was.

"You fucker."

A blast of energy hit Martin's chest and his whole body was forced into the under floor space, cracking the ceiling of the apartment below. All the air was forced from his lungs and he had to gasp in before he could cry out in pain. The edges of what clothes remained on him were singed and smoldering. The exposed skin on his belly and chest felt hot and raw.

He could smell the air heating up around him, the pungent aroma of melting carpet. The glow blinded him.

"No!"

He tried to pull himself out, reaching with one arm to try to grab his attacker, but he knew he couldn't reach. He knew he was dead.

***

Then there was a strange noise like a deep breath in and the TV disappeared.

It immediately reappeared at ceiling height above them, screen facing down. It hung there for an improbable second, Martin could see the top of his attacker's head reflected in it, then it dropped.

His head disappeared through the screen and ended up buried in the electrics and tube of the old fat television. Even with his body shield on that had to have hurt.

The attacker swore as the weight pulled his body forwards. Martin dragged himself out of his self shaped hole as the man hit the floor, TV head first, just to the side of him.

Moments later there was a scream of rage and a blinding flash as TV, floor, wall and windows exploded outwards and into the street.

For a second the shield would be down.

The attacker shook himself to regain composure and turned just in time to see the sofa collect him in the chest as Martin swung it at him. It split in half with the force as he was sent flying out the opening head first into the night sky. His blue shield came on and he made an awkward landing across two cars before bouncing onto the street.

Ignoring the pain wracking his body, Martin tensed his legs and jumped the three floors down, forming a crater in the lawn below.

He had remembered how to land from a height. This was all coming back too quickly. He looked up to see the attacker shakily getting to his feet. The man was glancing around frantically, no doubt expecting TVs to start pissing down with the rain. The ground started to tremble, nearby parked cars shifting away in a circle around him, and he blasted off on a trail of blue into the sky.

"Come back you bastard!" shouted Martin.

But he was sure he wouldn't. Whatever happened with the TV wasn't part of his plan. In any case, Martin didn't want him to come back. He was pretty much done. He hadn't taken a beating like that in almost twenty years and he felt every day of it.

A huff of air again and a small figure wearing a dark hooded top and jeans materialised under a nearby lamp post. Their face was literally shrouded in shadow.

They looked at each other in silence, the stranger nervously shifting their feet. Martin gulped to get his breath back.

"Hey there, you..."

The figure tensed, stepped away and vanished.

"No, wait... thanks!"

Martin coughed and felt a rib snap.

"Ow... thanks, really..."

He looked around and saw his destroyed possessions scattered across the street. One of the cars the attacker had landed on was his. As he stood in his little crater in the rain the reflected sounds of approaching sirens reached him.

He let out a sigh.

"Ah shit."

CHAPTER 22
WEDNESDAY 9TH JUNE 1993

"Shit, we're too late."

The police cordon closes up behind us and, as we creep towards the smashed doors of the Merlin Centre, we see the first body. It's a young woman lying face down just inside. Her curly auburn hair is matted together in clumps of blood, which soaks through her t-shirt from her neck down. There are ruddy brown smears of blood on the glass, a crazy swirl where her face had smashed into it and a long, thick track going down to where her head now lay at an awkward angle.

We got the call from CI Pace less than fifteen minutes ago. Shoppers had started attacking each other, they were feral, uncontrollable. The security staff and some officers who were nearby were attacked as soon as they tried to intervene. All bar one was now dead. The only people affected were those inside the centre. They weren't coming out and were stopping anyone getting in to help.

Pace was convinced it was The Controller. So was Jack, who was in his costume and flying to the scene within minutes. Of course he had to wait until the rest of the team arrived with Vincent before anyone could go in, otherwise they would all be at risk. He had been pacing about impatiently when we arrived.

An armed response unit is on its way but would wait until The Pulse gave the all clear. CI Pace actively wants our help this time, not to mention he is very wary of sending highly trained armed officers in to an area where a psychic could gain control of them.

Jack has a plan. He flies Maria to the roof and will come down through the offices. Charles and Mitchell take the main plaza entrance. Vincent and me come in from the Vortex Street entrance, underneath the flyover which had been shuttered off. Finally, Inna and our new recruit Andrea, take the far doors that lead out onto Emerald Road as it stretches south down to the river. We are to keep in open radio contact at all times with Vincent keeping us all psychically shielded and safe from any intrusion.

As Charles and Mitchell approach the front doors, the young lad stares at the woman's body.

"Now, now boy. Hold yourself. We've only just arrived," affirms Charles, despite the silence and stillness putting him on edge.

They step forward, crunching over tiny cubes of glass. Charles grabs the handle of a door and dramatically pulls it open. Sparks course over Mitchell's hands as he goes in first, head twisting around. Charles follows, glancing down at the girl. He moves sideways and, still facing forwards, kneels down to press two fingers to the side of her neck.

"Not long dead this one."

"There's more."

The early morning sunlight bouncing off the glass had stopped them seeing much of the interior. Now they have a clear view of the foyer and the main concourse as it curves away from us. It's full of bodies. The walls and floors are spattered in blood, dark pools slowly creep around lifeless corpses.

Three women shoppers, dressed fashionably, lie near each other. The stiletto heel of one is embedded in the eye socket of another. Rough clumps of hair have been torn out by the roots, leaving patches of seeping scalp. All of their faces are bloodied, eyes gouged, all of their nails broken, all of their fingers covered in each other's blood and skin. Across from them lie a woman and three young children. They can't be sure from this distance, but it looks like their necks have been broken. Over there, a large bellied man is impaled in the chest by a broken light fixture. A thin young lad, possibly a student, lies on his back, gasping, one arm up on its elbow, fingers twitching.

Two people run out from a cosmetics store, one chasing the other. Charles puts his hand out to stop Mitchell intervening, but they don't seem to notice them anyway. One guy is a businessman in his fifties. Blood streams from a wound in his stomach. The other is a middle aged black woman in a one piece, multicoloured summer dress. Clutching a blood soaked metal pole, part of an expanding security barrier, she spins round to face the older man. He is holding a collapsible A-frame advertising board which he swings at her. The board smashes into the side of her head with a shuddering crack and all the tension leaves her muscles as she slumps to the ground. The man loses his balance from the attack, twists himself round and falls onto his back.

"Holy fuck! They're all mental!" Mitchell backs away.

"With me boy, with me."

Charles waves him to follow. He weighs his options for a second. It wouldn't look good if he ended up running out of the place and back to the police line, so he gulps hard, increases the electric power to his fists and tracks Charles a few metres behind him.

The businessman with the board struggles to get to his feet as they approach him.

"Sir?", says Charles, "You're hurt. Don't try and get up, medical help will be..."

The man is now on his feet in a wide, wobbling stance facing away from them. His head twists round and fixes Charles in the eyes.

"Kill. You. All."

"Sir, please." Charles holds up a hand.

The man grimaces in pain as he clutches his stomach, then seems to forget the pain.

"KILL!"

The gentleman turns round and runs at them, arms out, fingers stretched like claws, tense and layered in blood. Charles hesitates. He couldn't set the man on fire, he's a threat, but he is also not in control of his actions. He prepares to grapple him to the floor when a burst of electricity passes by the side of him. Three barbs of lightning stretch out and pierce the man's body. He convulses violently, pulling his arms in, his muscles in spasm, and he slams sideways onto the floor, his momentum carrying him sliding up to Charles's feet.

As he lies there shaking, Charles turns to see Mitchell staring wide-eyed at him. The boy looks up at him, looking worried.

"He's just knocked out! Did the same at the riots. Same thing. That's all."

Charles nods supportively.

"No, no, nice work. Let's move on."

"But, but… the guy's bleeding?"

"We can't stop to help him or that lad," he thumbs to the student on his back, "until we've got the guy who is controlling them. The medics can't get in until he's dealt with, and the time we would waste dragging them outside is time we lose stopping the bastard and getting help to everybody else."

Mitchell's forehead twists in agonised uncertainty. He looks deflated and puzzled.

"It's difficult I know, but we have to prioritise. You'll understand in time. Come."

Charles taps him on his shoulder and gets a mild shock.

"Guys?" says Maria over the radio, "We're seeing lots of bodies and severely injured up here. Looks like all the staff attacked each other with whatever they could lay their hands on. All sorts of injuries."

"Same here," confirms Charles.

"People everywhere, even children," calls Inna.

"This is nasty. And Vincent's going crazy, I think he's very near."

"OK team," Jack says, "Andrea, do your flitting around, give me a quick sit-rep of the place. If you see anyone looking suspicious DO NOT approach them. Tell us where they are and we'll join you."

"Right you are boss."

Andrea nods at Inna and within a blur is gone. All the team hears for the next ten seconds is wind whipping noises through their earpieces and some garbled speech.

"What was that? We can't make you out at that speed."

The swooshing stops.

"Five people still going at each other on the upper level food court and there's one guy holding a gun to his head, same level at the big windows to the front. Lots of really badly hurt people."

"Everyone, upper level, front!"

We race up escalators, down stairs and soon converge there.

The observation windows are four giant vertical panes of glass that stretch from above the front doors to the top curve of the roof two floors up. At the moment they all have huge semi-transparent stickers over the centre of them, forming one giant advert. The ad has large overlapping balloons of blue, purple, red, orange, yellow and green with store names written inside. The low hazy sunlight scatters as it passes through these, pushing giant blobs of soft colour through the air inside. The whole top level feels fit to bursting with a bubbling rainbow.

There are more bodies here too. One girl, still alive, is slumped against a wall next to a bin, panting. She clutches her left hand where several fingers are missing, blood oozing through her fist.

"Watch her," warns Jack as we walk past.

The floor splits into two balconies running either side of a view down towards the front doors. Behind us, the escalators churn, endlessly getting nowhere.

We split up, four either side of the gap, slowly walking towards the windows.

Ahead of us is a man, a blurry edged silhouette against the colours flowing past him. He is large, wearing a bulky jacket, but the sun seems to melt pieces of his outline, threatening to dissolve him completely. His right arm is bent up, holding something against the side of his head.

We reach the platform in front of the windows and join to form a single line again. Blinking against the sun we all see the gun in his hand, a sharp silver light burning through the flowery air.

"Flit?" calls Jack.

"Yep?"

"Hold off for now, but I may need you to grab that gun if this doesn't work out."

"Gotcha boss."

"Witch?"

Maria steps forward, almost sideways, knees bent, and regards the man with an intense expression.

"Confused, scared, helpless. Desperately helpless. Having trouble trying to affect him though, like I'm being blocked. I'll keep trying."

"Yeah, you keep fucking trying!"

The man shifts position and presses the gun more firmly into his temple. We all stop moving. "Keep fucking trying. It won't do you any fucking good!"

Maria faces him, palms out. "Please sir, stay calm, we want to help you."

"Put the gun down," says Jack firmly.

"Why are we trying to help him? I bet he's the fucker who started this! He's playing with us," shouts Mitchell, sparks jumping off his arms.

Jack silently curses the boy. "Even if he is, we don't want him dead."

"It's me! And it isn't me! It's him. And it's... me!"

Spittle flies out of the man's lips as he sniffs tears back in.

"Barry?"

***

Charles catches all of us off-guard.

"You know this guy?" I say to him.

"Barry Mason, Vigilance. You helped us out with the Metallurgist, what, four years ago?"

The tension drops a few notches.

"It's not him. No. Not him," babbles Vincent, who hangs back slightly.

"Barry? Jesus. It's me, Jack!" he steps forward, now recognising the old Hero.

Barry stiffens, steps back and holds the gun horizontally, eyes wide.

"I'll use it! I know how to use it. He'll use it. He will. He doesn't care. Doesn't fucking care!"

Barry screams at the disembodied will of The Controller. His cry echoes around the silent centre.

"OK, OK." Jack stops moving.

"What happened here old bean?"

Barry looks uncomfortable. He rolls his lips in, presses them tight together, trying to find his thoughts.

"Was outside!" he spits, "just shopping...", rivulets of sweat drop in his eyes, he blinks hard to clear them. "...heard screams 'n' shit. Saw people going mad. Pulling each others' skins off. Man killed his own kids, just... twisted their necks like that!"

No-one says a word.

"Knew some bad power shit was going on, so I ran in. To help. To try and keep them apart until it stopped," he squeezes his neck muscles tight and lets out a whimper.

"As any of us would do my friend. Any of us would."

"But I couldn't!" he screams again as his gun arm shakes, "I couldn't! Before I knew it I was crushing people with chairs. I put a girl through a window. Threw a security guy over the balcony. I was rampaging. I couldn't stop. Nothing could stop me. Got this gun off some fucking brick shit house of a guy. Shot people. In the face."

"It's not your fault Barry," says Jack, "it's a powerful psychic who's doing this. The same one from the riots."

"I KNOW! He's inside my head now!"

No-one says a word. Vincent backs off slowly.

"He wants chaos. He likes fucking things over."

"But you're stopping him right now," says Maria, "You're not letting him pull the trigger."

I look around at Vincent who is still stepping back slowly.

"Vincent buddy!" I whisper, "cover Barry with your psychic link."

Vincent just shakes his head.

"Too much... too much..."

"Vincent!"

Charles tries to get through to Barry again. "Maria's right my old buddy, you're strong enough to stop him. Now put down the weapon, let's get the heck out of here and grab a nice cuppa. What do you say?"

I watch Vincent grab the barrier behind him and slowly slide to the floor.

"Vincent, cover Barry now. You've already got us, he's just one more. Quick!"

"Too late. All too late. Oh God."

"One bullet left! He knows this!"

"What's one bullet between friends Barry?" says a very relaxed Jack, "come on, just drop it and we'll all be fine."

"NO!"

No-one says a word.

My gut is twisting itself in knots. This is bad. Vincent is no help and everyone else seems to have stalled. I lean forward to try and catch Andrea's eye, past Mitchell on my right.

"Flit! I think Jack might need you about now."

Vincent starts crying.

"Oh God, oh God..."

"It's OK Martin, everything's fine," says Maria.

"What? Oh, you mean you've got him? Cool, keep him calm and I'll get the gun off him."

Maria laughs.

"Relax you fool," she says, "it's all a bit of fun."

"What the... fun?"

Barry suddenly relaxes and stands up straight, lifting his chin. He looks at each of us in turn, stopping to stare right into my eyes.

"Oh, but it has been fun hasn't it guys?"

My throat feels very dry. No-one says anything.

"Is this you or him? Are you The Controller?"

Barry laughs. In fact he shakes so hard he can't keep his gun arm up and has to support himself on his thighs as he bends over, bawling at the ground.

Jack sputters. I look over and see him trying hard to keep a straight face but then he cracks and is soon laughing hard too. He reaches over and puts a hand on Maria's shoulder as she giggles to herself. They are all laughing now. Mitchell is firing off short little bolts of electricity into the air as Andrea whoops with delight at each one. Inna glows brightly, the tiles beneath her feet starting to turn to dust and blow away. I've never seen her laugh, she clutches both arms across her stomach and trembles as she forces out deep guffaws I didn't know she had. It's a very odd thing at a very odd moment.

I feel the colours in the air start to suffocate me. I sweat as I feel them slipping down my throat, twisting themselves around my lungs and heart. It feels like my eyes are bulging, expanding into bubbles, oily colours slipping around their surface as they threaten to go free and float to the ceiling. I look down to see my hands and for a moment I see two realities overlaid: my fat ham hands in their gloves with the beige tiles beneath me, and another pair of paler, slimmer hands emerging from black sleeves, blue carpet underneath. I'm falling upwards now.

So easy to fall. It feels good. I want to give in but something doesn't feel right, like I'm falling asleep at the wheel, blissful slumber trying to take me at the worst possible moment. I instinctively know this is wrong. I can't do this. I can't.

I drop to one knee and bring a fist down into the floor.

Tiles shatter in circular waves. I hear the cracking, the splitting, just about feel the sharp edges jutting into my skin. Adrenaline kicks in. My eyes pop as they come back into focus. Deep breath and the colours blow away.

Silence.

Barry looks at me, watching me with interest as I stand up.

"Well, aren't *you* exciting?"

"This stops now."

"Oh?" he looks around, swinging the gun barrel along the line of us, "how exactly?"

"Doesn't matter how. I just know I'm going to do it."

Barry sighs deeply, looks sad.

"You know. While this has been fun, I think you're right. About stopping I mean."

What's his next move? The others are immobilised, standing like statues. I can hear Vincent scrabbling around on the floor behind me, barely able to protect himself.

"Seriously Martin, where does one go from here? A whole city? The country? How many times can you take over a bunch of plebs and make them fight each other before it gets boring. Repetitive."

"You tell me you twisted bastard."

"Heh. The answer is… not many, as it turns out."

He looks down at the gun.

"Lucky find this. A weapon that can be used at any time, in so many ways."

"Like you said, if it's boring for you now, then stop."

He looks up at me, nodding.

"You're a good man Martin. Brave, confident, powerful. I guess it's as they say," he shrugs, "all good things must come to an end."

He brings the gun up to his head.

"Flit! Now! Grab it!"

No-one says a word.

"Damn it!"

I leap forward towards him and manage to get a quarter of the way there before he pulls the trigger.

I've never seen anyone shot in the head before, except in the films. It isn't like it is in the films.

As the side of Barry's head spews a dark crimson tendril of flesh, he crumples to the floor, the empty gun pattering away over the tiles.

"Oh shit."

I stand over the body, panting anxiously. Nothing I can do.

"Guys?"

As the gunshot echo dies, the others seem to snap out of their reverie. Jack immediately becomes extremely agitated, swearing repeatedly, aiming his insults at both The Controller and Vincent. Maria turns away from the scene and covers her face. Charles stands still, looking at his old friend and just says, "You bastard." Andrea starts crying, Maria takes her in her arms to comfort her. Mitchell looks like he's in shock and about to faint, while Inna stands bewildered, staring at her own hands, unable to believe someone had control over her.

Jack blasts the front of a clothes shop open. Twists of ripped fabric curl through the air. He rounds on Vincent, pointing a finger at him.

"Much fucking use you were!"

Vincent is on his side, shrunk into the angle between the glass barrier and the floor, trying to make himself ninety degree shaped to escape their eyes.

"Too late... too late..." is all he says as Jack screams at him.

I can't intervene, not when Jack's like this. I'll wait until he has emptied all his anger then I'll get Vincent to his feet and walk him back to the van while the rest help the medics and the police secure the place.

Charles calls in CI Pace to confirm the situation is over and walks away from us, giving detailed instructions as to where to find the most critically injured. Maria wipes tears from her eyes as she tries to shed the pain and fear of those hurt in the building.

I go over to Mitchell and take him by the shoulders. The boy looks miserable, all his sparks are gone.

"You okay there?"

He shakes his head.

"No."

He's honest. That's one step along the road to trying to take this all in I guess. That's good. I tell him to go and get the girl with the missing fingers and take her to the ambulances outside. Give him something to do. Inna must have overheard as she follows him, wringing her hands.

I hope someone that young can get over this kind of thing. Christ, I hope *I* can get over this.

I try not to look at Barry again, even though my eyes are being drawn to him. Instead I look out of the window as the sun brightens, cutting through the fuzzy edges of colour and making everything more distinct, more real. Worse.

Jack blasts away part of the railings and drops through the gap to the floor below. Maria helps Andrea walk round to the escalators and they leave Vincent blubbing like a baby, tiny, clutching at himself, snot dripping onto the floor.

I need to get out of here.

CHAPTER 23
SUNDAY 16TH SEPTEMBER 2012

Martin couldn't wait to get out of there.

After spending an excruciating seven hours at Accident and Emergency, mostly sitting on a trolley waiting for X-ray machines to become free, he was released and driven back to his apartment in a police car.

A forensic officer had taken his clothes from him at the hospital, as evidence. They were so shredded and burnt he didn't care. His top clothes had almost fallen to pieces as the nurse had removed them. He was able to wriggle out of his jeans with the help of the gloved officer.

He watched impassively as the man folded them and stuffed them into cellophane bags. He wrote on the labels and scanned their barcodes into a small tablet device which he tapped at. Only when the man picked up Martin's shoes from under his trolley did he think about saying something, but in the end he kept quiet while they too were sealed away. The forensic officer thanked him and left, leaving Martin lying in pain in only his underpants and socks.

One of the doctors, a small Indian girl had been kind enough to bring him some disposable theatre clothes to cover himself before he left. They were pale blue, thin, creased like paper and rode up his crotch like the edge of a metal ruler.

As he left, a police officer was waiting for him, to take him back to his flat. Martin said he would get a cab but the look from the officer said he wouldn't be doing that.

Nothing was said on the way there. As they drove up his road the officer gave a quick squawk of the siren to clear the road of onlookers and a couple of kids kicking a ball around. Like he needed more attention drawn to himself.

Getting out of the car was far more painful than getting in. He had to steady himself on the open door and the roof, until he was sure of his balance, before putting his full weight on his feet. Even swinging the door shut gently sent a spike of pain round his chest.

Somehow the damage looked worse than he remembered. A huge area had been cordoned off encompassing his block of flats, the identical one next to it, three terraced houses the other side of him and all the buildings opposite. There was one fire engine parked in the middle of the street outside the tape, lights flashing, and he could see several firemen over by the flats. Two were looking up at the hole in the building, pointing at things while deep in a serious conversation. Another two came out of the communal doorway. One shook his head as he approached the other men and joined in their pointing exercises.

Three police cars sat behind the fire engine. An officer sat in the driver's seat of one, on the radio. The other officers were guarding the scene, standing in front of the tape stretched across the road.

Windows were lit up along the street with concerned faces pressed close to the glass. Couples were chattering and pointing, their rooms bathed in orange, framed by the brickwork. Kids were out with their parents, some dozing as they were held in arms, some hyper and running around their gardens, screaming at the novelty of being awake and allowed out at such a time. Most people were still in their pyjamas, having just thrown a coat on over the top, and were standing there shivering, desperate to burn into their memories this momentous event on their street.

Martin walked through the small crowd standing along the pavements. Those that noticed the car arrive and saw Martin getting out, moved out of the way as he approached the tape. Others did a quick double take as he walked past, and eyed him intently.

He walked past the police cars and along the side of the fire engine. He could now see another police car on the other side of the blockaded street and a white box van marked simply, "Forensics".

The street was littered with bricks, most of them shattered into fist sized chunks. The glass from the blown out windows of parked cars sparkled on the road. Martin's car was near the middle. The blast from his attacker's take-off had bent in the passenger side so it was completely concave. Martin hadn't noticed that earlier. This night was just getting better all the time.

He looked up at his flat. It was as if a giant hand had scooped away the front of the building on the middle floor. He could see the half of the sofa he had been left holding sitting uncomfortably close to the open edge. Wires and insulating foam dangled out from the space between floors and the bright flashing light of the fire engine highlighted the exposed brick edges. That was going to take more than one trip to B&Q to fix.

Martin walked towards one of the officers guarding the scene. He stopped about a foot from the line and wondered what was the best thing to say. In the end he thumbed over to the wrecked flats and said:

"I was in that."

He heard a ripple of whispers going through the gathering behind him. The officer just nodded.

"PCA will be wanting to speak to you. You sure you're OK to be up on your feet already sir?"

Martin just nodded grimly.

"If you could wait here a moment please," said the officer as he walked to a group of three men standing on the pavement opposite the flats. Martin saw a tall man in a light beige raincoat, whom he assumed was a detective, talking to two men dressed in black.

"Oh, not them," he thought to himself.

The officer stepped carefully through the strewn bricks and interrupted their conversation. As he pointed back towards where Martin was standing, all three turned to follow his finger. Martin could see

Morris's grin as he waved him over. The officer returned and lifted the tape up.

"You can go over now sir."

Martin bent down only slightly, awkwardly, to go under the tape, which caused him to groan. The officer pulled the tape up higher and he managed to get under just by dipping his head and shoulders.

"Thanks."

Morris was grinning from ear to ear, stretching his lower face out like a pelmet hanging across the top of a window. Barclay was as impassive as before. The third man gave him a nod of acknowledgement then left the group and went over to the fire officers standing on the lawn.

"Mr Mol-loy! How good to see you again. I do hope you are well and that isn't an impromptu form of superhero outfit, as that would be a criminal offence. Ha ha, I'm only joking of course, and glad to see that you are indeed not dead. My apologies for making you surrender your clothing to us as evidence, but we believe you may have been involved in an incident involving the public use of innate powers that resulted in considerable damage to property and injuries to an innocent member of the public."

Martin wasn't going to engage in any kind of shouting match, as the smallest inhalation of breath was sending muscle twisting jolts through to his back, but this was news to him.

"Injuries?"

Agent Morris's face elongated even further, a look of frozen horror scraped across it. He looked at Barclay then back at Martin.

"Why yes! Didn't you know?"

He really wasn't in the mood for these annoying theatrics.

"Of course not. I was taken away by the medics almost as soon as they arrived and I've only just got back now."

"A little girl..." Morris stared at him, looking like he was in pain, "a little girl, across the street. Part of your wall entered her bedroom through her window. Injuries. Bricks and glass." He was shaking his head sorrowfully. "Cuts to her face. A little girl. Cuts to her face and arms. She'll be fine." He made a face like it was no big deal.

Martin was almost ready to explode at him.

"But will *you* be Mr Molloy? You look like you've been crushed."

Again the sudden switch. Martin should have been ready for it, but it still caught his tongue for a second of two.

"I've had worse."

Morris's face lit up.

"Yes, yes you have."

They stood looking at each other as the nearby street light lit up the drizzle like puffs of flour.

"I've been reading up about you Mr Molloy. You seem to me to have been a good man. You worked hard, looked after the vulnerable, always seemed to do the right thing. Loyal to your team. A good Hero."

Martin didn't like where this was going.

"Then something happened and the team disbanded and you never used your abilities to help again. Why was that?"

"I would like permission to enter my flat to get some clothes and..."

"Abandoned everybody. Abandoned the city."

Martin started shaking. He clenched his teeth together hard.

"...and get my wallet so I can pay for somewhere to stay tonight."

Morris leaned in closer.

"As if you had lost the will to help anyone again."

Martin felt hot inside.

"As if something so terrible had happened that none of you could face it. As if using your abilities was a reminder of what you had done."

He's digging again, thought Martin. This is what he does. Blank it out and don't let him goad you into revealing anything.

"Now, we have Mr Hayden-Phillips dead and you severely beaten by a fellow Hero. Roadblock and The Seeker? Something you did that they don't want anyone to find out about?"

"I don't know what you're talking about Agent Morris. I just want some clothes, please."

Martin could feel his will dissolving as the agent refused to acknowledge him.

"Something The Seeker was going to do or say that would reveal a secret?"

Martin felt a cold shiver in his chest. Little did Morris know how close he was to the truth.

"You can't go in, by the way. None of us can until the fire service have deemed the building to be structurally safe. So... something his killer was looking for at his house, and then was looking for at your flat, before you interrupted him?"

The two agents had stared straight at him the whole time. Martin felt pinned to the spot. He felt exhausted and sore. He felt like telling them to piss off, then going inside, putting his mattress in the bathtub and falling asleep like a baby. He sighed carefully.

"I was attacked. In my flat by someone who was searching the place."

Morris watched him intently.

"They beat the crap out of me, destroyed the place and flew off."

"Agent Barclay, note that, they had the power of flight."

Barclay nodded slightly but made no move to take out a pen, paper or tablet to write anything down.

"Then... the police and ambulance arrived and I was taken to hospital." Martin shrugged and felt pain.

Morris brought his hand up to his throat. He made a fist with his fingers, pressed his thumb in under his jaw and with his index finger bent tightly, pulled his chin flesh down.

"Hmm. I see. There are some missing elements in this scenario. Such as what you said to each other, exactly what powers were used by whom and when, and the, not insignificant, matter of who your assailant was."

"I don't know who it was," he lied.

"I don't believe you," Morris replied.

Martin stepped forward and leaned in to the agent, tensing his muscles to control his shaking.

"Right now, I don't particularly care. I just want to get some clothes, my wallet and find somewhere to sleep. If you want a statement I will give you one tomorrow. Now if you don't mind..."

Martin turned to go towards the fire officers. In a flash, Morris was in front of him.

"Actually we do. This is a crime scene and you are not allowed to be here any longer."

He wasn't looking at Martin any more. His eyes were darting around the scene, distracted, and he spoke as if he was reading from a procedural list: they would retrieve his valuables as soon as they were allowed and would assess if they were evidence; at ten a.m. an officer would collect him from wherever he was staying to take him to the station, where he would be required to give a full statement; he would not be permitted to leave the city until the investigation into the death of Mr Hayden-Phillips was concluded. At the conclusion of his list, Morris barely registered Martin's presence and wandered off towards the lawn to speak to the detective. Barclay stared at Martin silently before following his boss.

Martin was too tired to care about this behaviour and slowly trudged back towards the police tape where the officer lifted it up again for him, over his head this time. He had no idea how long this would take. The building seemed fine, it was just one part of the wall after all, couldn't take that long to assess, he reasoned.

Then again, he knew nothing about that sort of thing, it could take days.

While he waited, a police car pulled up next to the forensic van and two officers, a man and a woman, stepped out. They walked towards another pair of officers behind the tape and started chatting. It looked like they were on patrol and had stopped by, rather than being here on duty. Martin squinted in the half darkness of the encroaching dawn and was sure he recognised the female officer. It was only when she looked over and saw him that he recognised her. She had been sat opposite La Sauveur after his meeting with Maria. Her eyes widened and she started looking around the scene.

Just then the two agents came back over towards him. Morris was waving and calling, "Mr Molloy?"

Martin watched the female officer hurrying back to her car, beckoning her partner to join her as she hopped into the driver's seat and started the engine. He shrugged, seemingly unaware of the need to rush, and reluctantly returned to the car. He waved to his colleagues as she did a rather violent three-point turn between the parked cars and onlookers and drove off.

"Mr Molloy!" shouted Morris, right in his ear.

He paused, making Martin turn to see his grinning face.

"What?"

"I just have one more question while you are here. I know you are going to give us a very full and detailed statement later on this morning, but one thing is bothering me: why did your attacker leave without killing you?"

Martin wasn't ready to talk about floating TVs.

"I don't know."

"I mean, he is obviously very powerful. We have your estimated strength and skin density on our database and, given what he did to the building, he *could* have killed you if he had carried on."

Morris was nodding vigorously to himself. He turned to Barclay, who nodded along with him.

"And yet..." he gestured up and down the length of Martin's body.

"I don't know. I guess I got the upper hand. Maybe the sirens spooked him. It wasn't something I worried about at the time."

"No. He should have killed you." He was nodding again.

Martin wondered if this was a game the agent liked playing. A real life game of Trumps in which he was desperate to win the hand each time they spoke. In truth, Martin knew that Morris was far more intelligent and cunning than his odd behaviour suggested, and that made him dangerous.

"Thanks."

Morris burst out laughing. Even Barclay made a lopsided smile.

"No, no, of *course* I'm glad you are alive Mr Molloy, it makes you far more fruitful to question." And with that he walked back to the flats.

As he continued to wait, the dawn light slowly felt its way down the street, crawling across the tops of the cars like a friendly sloth come to hug him back to slumber. Most of the onlookers, suddenly realising the time, drifted back indoors. A few were in animated discussions with officers, wondering how they were going to get to work that day with their cars on the inside of the tape line. Agent Morris was gazing at the crater in the lawn where Martin had landed, his hand under his chin again. Agent Barclay was standing a few feet away from Martin, as he had been when they came over. He was staring intently straight down the road and didn't move.

CHAPTER 24
WEDNESDAY 9TH JUNE 1993

I stare at myself in the mirror.

My face is a tight, shrunken husk, my body drained of energy. Each blink is a heavy curtain coming down and it takes a huge effort raise it again.

The image of Barry pulling the trigger plays over and over in my mind. The bullet escaping the side of his head in a burst of red, the pink froth of brain following it. I shut my eyes to hide from myself.

I failed. I should have realised that Vincent wasn't going to be able to get himself together quickly enough to help. I should have realised Andrea was under his thrall and wasn't going to be able to whisk the weapon out of his tightening fingers. I should have moved faster, sooner, and maybe, maybe... nonsense. I could have got halfway to him instead. Still dead. Nonsense.

I splash my face with freezing cold water and strip off my bloodied costume, leaving it in a heap on the wet room floor.

It had taken the police armed response unit minutes to secure the shopping centre and get the medical teams in. We had offered to help move the injured but were told firmly our help was no longer required. A medic took the fingerless girl from Mitchell and Inna, leaving them standing, confused amid the carnage. Between us we counted over sixty dead bodies and dozens more injured. CI Pace met us outside. Jack told him we thought The Controller was gone, bored of his games and wouldn't bother the city again. He told him that it was almost all over before we went in. He told him the psychic had made a friend of ours kill himself before we could intervene. He didn't tell him that we had been taken over. The CI just nodded, our thousand yard stares telling a thousand words. Then we slowly climbed back into the van, Vincent crumpled up against my side as I helped him get aboard. He shrunk in to the seat like a piece of dried fruit.

When we arrived back at HQ this time there were no supportive pats on the back, no attempts to embellish our achievements. Wordlessly we put the equipment away. Charles, frustrated and angry, stripped off his bloodstained costume and threw it to the back of one of the storage rooms. The others scattered, leaving me to silently take Vincent to his apartment and drop him on his bed, where he curled up into a tight ball and fell asleep. Then I went to my own apartment and into the shower room, and I have been standing here ever since.

I twist the knob on the wall until the water is hot, very hot, then step under. Anything less than seventy degrees doesn't even feel warm to my touch. With little enthusiasm I scrub at the dark mottled patches of blood that have soaked through my costume and stained my skin. My arms and stomach are covered. It into a gritty paint that drops bright blotches into the thin pool of water around my feet. I hold one arm up under the current, leaning on the wall. The rivulets of water snake urgently around the curve of my skin before meeting up underneath and falling away in a dribbling liquid sheet.

Now I see an image of the fingerless girl, clinging close to Mitchell. She was holding her hands up in front of her, blood oozing through the rough cloth he had wrapped around them. She was shrugging tearful gasps of air, legs trembling as she put them down, as if each time was her first step.

I blink hard.

I desperately hope The Controller keeps to his word, whatever that means to a sick manipulator like him. He had demonstrated that he could disrupt Vincent's protection and take the others over any time he wanted. There is literally nothing the team can do to prevent or stop another attack. We are just as vulnerable as the citizens we are trying to protect.

I put my head under the spray and watch the fine steaming mist scatter around the sides of my face.

Except The Controller hadn't taken over all of us. He hadn't taken over me. I stood there and watched all of them laughing, doing nothing while Vincent shrunk away powerless to help them. He wasn't involved in stopping me do anything. I knew it was wrong as it happened. I had full control over myself. I was pretty sure I had. There was that moment I saw another pair of hands, through someone else's eyes. He was trying, but couldn't do it. No, everything I did and didn't do was on me alone.

One thing I don't know is whether the others realised I was unaffected. It wasn't the time to ask on the way back. Maybe Jack will pull me aside later and ask about it. If they even noticed. They may have been too far under his control, too confused. I could always say he deliberately didn't take me over, that it wouldn't have been half as much sick fun for him if he had us all, that he needed one of us to think we had a chance to save Barry.

I rub the top of my scalp. It's starting to become warm.

That was for my benefit. He could have left the others fully aware, just frozen to the spot leaving them helpless spectators to the unfolding horror, but no. He took them completely, laughing for him.

I shake my head hard. Why is this going round in my mind anyway? It's over. I don't need to think about it any more. No more thoughts of Barry's brain or the fingerless girl. Just a shower and some rest, that's all I need.

"I can't stop thinking about it either."

I nod in agreement. It's hard to stop thinking about something like that. You can't just... wait, what?

I pull my head out from under the spray, push myself away from the wall and rub the water off my face. Standing just outside the shower, pale bare feet poking out from under a light pink silk dressing gown, is Inna. She seems unsteady on her feet, rocking from side to side, arms crossed under her chest. She looks at me with a frown.

"Can't stop. Just see the bodies."

I'm not at all sure she's actually there. This is doubly strange. Ignoring the fact she's in my room with me, standing naked in the shower, she has never even initiated a conversation with me before.

She seems genuinely disturbed though. Her hands are clasping her opposite sides tightly, her mouth tight as she chews her lips.

"The riot... that was bad, but today... I wasn't myself. I was him, and he made me do nothing. Nothing at all."

Her head is trembling. Anger? Shock? Her neck keeps tensing, still biting her lips.

"Inna, I... this isn't really the best... give me a minute, OK?"

I'm flustered, not sure what to do first: cover myself or turn off the shower. She needs to talk and I need not to be naked any more.

She lifts her chin up and shakes her hair out.

"You think I don't feel anything."

I feel a full confessional coming on. One I am uniquely ill-equipped to deal with right now.

"No, not at all."

"You all do. 'Ice Queen'. That what you think of me, yes?"

"Inna no, of course we don't. Look, just let me get something on and we'll have a chat, yeah?"

"I feel things. I see the pain of those people. I hear the screams. I feel HIM scratch inside my head." She screws up her face in anger as she starts to glow with her light.

"I know. We've just been through a really messed up moment..."

"Oh you do?" she looks at me in surprised anger "You know how I feel?"

This proves my theory that I could never be a counsellor. My mind stumbles over what to say next.

"You feel... afraid. In shock. And part of you doesn't know what to feel. Like me. You're not immune to feeling like that. You're not a robot."

She tilts her head down and looks at me now with a curious expression I can't make out. Somewhere between sadness and amusement. It's then I realise that was probably the first time anyone in the team had told her what they thought of her. Had any of us actually, *really* tried to have a conversation with her? Charles bantered with her, but that left her more confused than anything, thanks to his fondness for flowery language. I think she just smiled to make him go away sometimes. The rest of us... nope, can't recall any time we tried to chat with her. How could I have not realised? Here was me, vilifying the others for ignoring Vincent when all of us, including me, were ignoring her.

"You are right. I'm not robot."

She slowly uncrosses her arms.

"Look, grab a seat, I'll get us a... coffee or something, yeah?"

"I need to feel too. Like you."

She looks lost.

"Come on, let me grab my dressing gown and..."

As she opens her arms I notice she has the ends of the silk belt in her hands. She pulls on them and the loose knot flops open. The gown parts and in one imperceptible moment she lets it slip off her round shoulders onto the tiled floor. She stands naked, vulnerable and truly beautiful in front of me.

"I need to feel, Martin."

I'm feeling something for sure. My heart is racing and I can't stop my eyes scanning every detail of her flesh. Something about her saying my name, for the first time, feels exciting.

She walks around the glass partition slowly, legs crossing, thighs squeezing past each other as she approaches.

A primitive part of my brain wants this. A newer part tells me this moment is wrong. I don't know how to resolve the argument in my head, so I do nothing but slowly back away until I'm under the shower again.

"Look, Inna..."

She reaches round the side of my head to test the water, pulls her hand back with an "Ooh" and smiles.

"You like it hot yes? Me too."

Her whole body glows as she steps under the water with me. The already hot water vaporises before touching her skin and within seconds the room is full of steam. She presses herself up against me, her breasts moulding themselves across the top of my collarbones, forcing me back against the wall.

My God she's beautiful A blonde angel burning away the very water around us. An angel ready to burn away my pain.

My excitement starts to get the better of me. She feels it and giggles as she gazes into my soul. My brain is still stuck in neutral, coasting down its mental hill as she wraps her right leg around the back of my thighs, embraces me and kisses me passionately. She is burning hot to touch but nothing I can't withstand, unlike my own desire.

Come on, stop this! She is vulnerable, unable to process what happened earlier. She needs help. But so am I, and so do I. Thoughts of Barry and the fingerless girl are still circling around in my head. I'm taking advantage of her, whether she made the advance or not. But isn't she taking as much advantage of me? Am I not vulnerable too?

Her red hot skin stings against my lips, her tongue dances around mine.

In a second of profound despair I lose all resolve.

I put my arms around her and bring her closer to me. As I return her kiss I feel tears welling up in my eyes, which then fizz away into the air. I need this and she needs this. We're both lost.

Barry and the fingerless girl.

Her hands are all over my head and back, pulling at my tense muscles, scraping at my neck.

I was the only one unaffected, deliberately allowed some semblance of control before it was taken from me.

The steam fills my nostrils, intoxicating me.

We're all vulnerable, he proved he can take us any time we want.

She grasps my buttocks and groans as our hips meet. She pushes herself back and forth onto me, arching away, fingers digging into my shoulder blades. I can feel myself inside her. I can actually feel it. That's a new sensation.

One problem no-one considers about having super tough skin is that it applies to the whole body. Every somatic sense is dulled to such an extent that a knife digging in me feels like a finger prod would to someone else. I rarely ever feel the wind on my face, let alone the touch of someone else, and hardly at all the feeling of sex. But Inna is glowing with her light from within and her touch bites into every part of my flesh like nothing I've experienced before.

She clasps the side of my head, face screwed up in determination, fixing my gaze, grunting like an animal. I can feel every movement, and so can she, since I'm able to withstand her touch.

Does she always light up when she's aroused? Had she burned someone before this way? Someone she loved? Killed them even? Was that why she was so distant and cold, because she was afraid of what she might do should she get too close to someone again? The tears start pouring from my eyes as my heart gives way. Poor Inna. We never even try to talk to her. We don't know her at all. But I think I know now how much she needs this.

I lift her under her buttocks and hold her as she moves up and down on me, sliding across my body, a layer of steam hissing between us. She looks like she's crying too as she holds my head, kissing me again. Beautiful. This is just beautiful. Pour your heart out Inna. Pour it out on me. I'm here for you.

The biting gets more intense. I feel like I'm on fire, ready to explode.

Oh God. This is nothing like when I'm with Maria. That's slow. Tender. And I never let on to her that I don't feel a thing...

A cold blue shock shoots down my spine.

Maria! Christ! What the hell am I doing? This just isn't right in so many ways. I can't do this.

I push Inna away in a panic. Too hard. She has to twist and put her arms out to stop herself bouncing off the far wall of the shower.

"Inna, I'm sorry. I didn't mean..."

She's angry, confused, breathing heavily, standing in front of me, tendrils of light starting to twist around her forearms. I shuffle forward, waving my arms about.

"We shouldn't be... I mean this is wrong. You need to *talk* to someone, not... this. I'm sorry. Oh God I'm so sorry. You've been through hell. Please, Inna, we can still talk. Please?"

Her face relaxes. She takes a deep breath in, lifts her chin up and her glow disappears.

"You get one chance only. Then it's gone."

She leaves the cubicle, picking up her gown as she goes, slips it back on and walks out of the bathroom. Seconds later I hear my room door click shut.

My head is a mess. I can't think straight. I step back and lean against the shower wall. As the hot water pours over my face, I feel nothing at all.

CHAPTER 25
SUNDAY 16TH SEPTEMBER 2012

Martin cried in pain as he woke himself up rolling onto his crushed ribs. He gently pushed himself back until it stopped feeling like he was lying on a hundred shards of glass.

A flutter of panic flitted through his body. The sheets weren't right. That wasn't his lampshade! He felt like a battered barrel rolling around on the deck of a roiling ship. Quickly enough his memories caught up with what he was seeing.

"Oh crap."

He was in room 210 of a cheap motel on the A-road to the west of the city centre, the nearest and cheapest lodgings he could get at six on a Sunday morning.

In the end he had to wait another hour and a half before the building was declared safe and a group of officers, CSIs and Morris and Barclay went inside. He had expected them to ignore his requests but was happy to see an officer come out ten minutes later holding the two halves of his wallet. As he handed it over he apologised, saying they were going through room by room and it would be much later by the time they gathered any clothes for him. He handed him a small blue information card saying he was to call the station and tell them where he was staying and someone would drop them off for him.

The corner of his credit card had turned dark caramel and bent slightly, but the magnetic strip was intact. He hoped it would still work and thankfully it did, much to the amusement of the night receptionist at the motel.

Martin stared at the ceiling. Aside from his heartbeat there was a new throbbing sensation in his body, the sensation of blood being forced through bruised tissue as it tried to knit itself back together.

Heartbeat. Followed by twitch of muscle.

Heartbeat. The rhythm became hypnotic after a while, his flesh willing him for a few more moments of sleep to fix things before he got up and started ripping apart its few hours of hard work. So, as he always did on his days off, he allowed his body to have its own way and dozed several times. Either the third or fourth time, he awoke to a sharp cramp in his lower back and carefully shifted over a few inches to the right until it eased off. He lay there breathing deliberately, testing how deeply he could inhale before his ribcage creaked a warning at him.

He knew he was lucky to be alive. This wasn't the first time in his life he had nearly died, it was just the most recent. And yes, he had been frightened. This time and all the others. Terrified in fact, and he wasn't ashamed of it. As a Hero you soon learned to respect that feeling. It kept you grounded in reality. Reminded you that, despite the fame and praise and that incredible feeling of making a difference to other people's lives, you weren't immortal. You were just a bit stronger and tougher than average. He had heard stories over the years of Heroes overestimating their abilities, ignoring their fear and getting killed by their complacency. Last night he had felt how powerful those blasts were and was sure that, given time, he would have been ripped open, just like Vincent. But he knew and understood his limitations. When you were part of a team you learned to never put yourself in danger if it would end up with someone else having to risk their life to pull your arse out of the fire. No, fear was good. Being alive was good too. And using his powers to stay alive, well it was just what he did.

"Just what he did?"

Martin turned that over in his mind a few times. He hadn't thought that one since he was in The Pulse. Just what he did? What he did now was spend his nights patrolling an empty shopping centre for twenty minutes out of every one of the eight hours he was on shift. What he did now was run out of the supermarket with his shopping, panting, so that he wouldn't be around too many people. What he did now was fall asleep on the sofa in front of the TV and wake up just in time for a quick shower and breakfast before starting the whole cycle again. That's what he did now, a routine that guided his life.

Well, that *was* his life.

And that fight last night, that was something he *used* to do. Thinking on his feet, reading his opponent, not knowing what was going to happen next. It was everything he hated, everything he had wanted to escape from. So why was it that, despite almost getting his skull caved in, he suddenly felt so alive. The first pain for years, the first action. It was as if he had been watching the past eighteen years through a blur and he could now see the smallest imperfections in the coat of paint above him. If he stepped out of the door right now and it turned out he was back in their old HQ with another mission waiting for them he would be the first to reach the van, pulling his costume on. No hesitation. None.

"Stop dreaming you wanker."

This was the here and now, he told himself. All that was gone. Torn away from him. Right here and now was all that mattered. And right here and now he was homeless. His apartment had more floor space than on the original blueprint and it was going to take forever to get any possessions back from the police, especially with the PCA involved. Oh yes, and he was probably jobless too. Ultimate Security would no doubt be calling him tomorrow to tell him he was fired. Calling his destroyed phone anyway.

"Bloody brilliant," he thought to himself, as all the different permutations of hassle slowly unravelled in his head.

Even with Vincent dead, his home destroyed, his own body burnt and swollen and with no clothes or uniform he just wanted a little piece of how things used to be. Just enough to remind him that the world could go on normally with him as an insignificant part of it. A tiny cog spinning away, not connected to anything of much importance.

He screwed up his eyes as the vibrations from passing heavy traffic thrummed through his bones. He turned his head to look at the alarm clock. Eight forty seven a.m. He'd had less than two hours sleep but his body was telling him he wasn't going to get any more.

After a careful set of movements involving spinning on his buttocks and sliding and falling out onto his knees, he was on his feet and stumbling the wrong way towards the bathroom. A change of trajectory later and he was gazing at his face in the painful electric light.

Yep, that was a beating all right. He had the beginning of panda eyes and his left eyeball had a blood clot surrounding the iris. He had dried trickles of blood down his upper lip from his nose bleeding during the night, (on the sheets too no doubt, the maids would hate him), and the left side of his lower lip was swollen. In fact his whole face and neck were slightly puffed out.

Taking his top off took him three full minutes, the longest he had ever spent removing an item of clothing. Arm stretched up, attempting to pull the top up and over. Pain. Elbow in, trying to pull the armpit over it. Agony. End of sleeve between teeth, trying to slide straight, then bent arm out as he rotated the top away from it. Crunch. Eventually the top dropped onto the tiles, defeated. The knife crotch trousers soon fell next to them.

He leaned forward towards the mirror as he poked his chest. The skin was shiny but had dulled somewhat since last night and crinkled under his finger like a plastic bag over a wet leg of ham. He hadn't had a burn like that for a long time. He shook the memory of that incident out of his head, another near death experience, and stepped into what he would soon come to call the "disappointing shower". Realising there was no way he would be able to scrub himself before it turned lunchtime, he just stood there hunched over and motionless like a statue of a defeated barbarian in the pissing rain.

Afterwards, not so much refreshed as a bit cleaner, he applied the burn cream he had got from A&E to as many areas as he could reach and the crinkles became shinier again. After putting back on the seepage soaked theatre clothes, (which proved easier than removing them), he headed downstairs to see what passed for a breakfast here and whether anyone had dropped off some proper clothes yet.

As he shuffled by reception the elderly man behind the desk waved to get his attention. He had been on the desk earlier when Martin arrived and hadn't even blinked at his attire. Either they got a lot of hospital staff staying over or he had been working motels for years and had seen much stranger sights in his time. The man, who introduced himself as Peter, had short silver grey hair, thin and stuck together with what smelt like some kind of 1950s hair lacquer. He had a fixed half smile and when he nodded his head tilted to one side.

He reached below the curved wooden reception desk and handed Martin a large brown evidence bag and a small pale yellow envelope. An officer had come by about an hour ago. The bag contained a random looking mix of clothes. He didn't open the bag out on the reception desk, but a rummage around identified at least one of each type. Finally he could burn these nasty blue disposables.

"Perfect!" said Martin out loud.

Peter half smiled in understanding and nodded sideways. Martin put the bag down on the desk, and tore open the envelope along the top. He pulled out a similarly pale yellow piece of writing paper. It had been folded over multiple times until it was only a couple of centimetres square. He unfolded it like an ancient document and read the inscription inside:

"BLACKFORGE CONSTRUCTION SITE, BROAD STREET, BY TRAIN STATION, 10PM TONIGHT."

The writing was in awkwardly drawn capitals, as if made by someone's wrong hand. Martin's memory went back to the teleporter who saved his life only hours ago. As a team they'd had dealings with teleporters, but the ones they had known were either dead or had long since left the city. People with that power often felt little attachment to a place and, with only a small degree of irony, moved around a lot.

Certainly none had been involved with the team around the time of The Controller, so this had to be someone else. Apart from being a Good Samaritan, who were they and what did they know? Was it someone Vincent knew? Perhaps a friend he had met when he was institutionalised or getting treatment at Maria's clinic? No, Martin would have known. Vincent told him everything about his life. There were no secrets between them, not after what happened. Well, except the memoirs. He still had to admit that was a doozy.

Anyway, this was nothing anyone else needed to worry about for now. He folded up the note again and slipped it into his pocket. With the packet tucked under his arm he thanked Peter and went over to the lifts.

Back in his room he got changed slowly and carefully.

CHAPTER 26
SUNDAY 16TH SEPTEMBER 2012

After a large breakfast and coffee, at the pub opposite the New Merlin Centre, he made his way to the police station.

It was a rectangular building on four floors set on a side road a few minutes' walk from the pedestrianised area by the Centre. It looked like an abstract version of a castle wall; a concrete grille with lots of narrow windows pressed close together horizontally, hidden in deep vertical channels. A blue sign saying "Element City Police Department" hung over the dark wooden double doors.

Martin hated hearing about local authorities spending millions on superfluous office moves but he would be happy for the police here to get a new residence. Not only was this place depressing, he couldn't fathom how the building could hold all the police needed for the entire city. At least this time he was going to use the main entrance, rather than being driven in underneath it by Morris and Barclay.

He was about ten minutes early and wanted to leave already. Inside there was a small reception desk on the left, a toughened glass partition separating the bored looking policeman from the waiting area. Two rows of six plastic chairs sat opposite, bolted together and to the floor. The floor was made up of whitish marble rectangles with black flecks in them and was polished enough that he could make out fuzzy reflections of the ceiling strip lights in it.

After he introduced himself to the officer on the desk, Martin took a seat. He did not want to see, let alone speak to, Agent Morris today, although he was sure he would be doing the questioning. His body was a throbbing mass of tissue and crunching bone. Having to force himself to sit and relive the incident, having to concentrate enough to not let slip anything that might identify his attacker was going to be exhausting. And an odd smell, a combination of fruity air freshener and stale disinfectant, made him wish he hadn't had such a full breakfast.

After a few minutes he had to get up and walk around, the pain in his back had started to spread out to merge with the pains in his chest wall, making breathing hard. As he idly flicked through a windowsill display of leaflets on car safety, police budgets and innate ability equality laws, a secure door beeped open and a tall man appeared from the corridor to the side of the reception office.

"Mr Molloy? Detective Chief Inspector Forrester."

The DCI was a tall, pale, shrivelled stick of a man with an extraordinarily narrow nose that jutted out like a sail. There was a rough tuft of light brown hair on his scalp that grew straight up and had been harshly brushed down and across to create a serviceable fringe. His face was red with tiny visible veins on his cheeks, chin and tip of his nose. Eyes were buried in deep pits of sockets, skin darkened to charcoal around them. He looked like he was haunted.

Martin thought he must be ill, yet the handshake was firm and brisk and the guy seemed livelier than his appearance indicated.

"Ah yes, you were at my apartment last night."

"Yes, sorry I couldn't speak to you then, the PCA had taken control of the scene."

The door scraped as an old lady in a salt and pepper woollen jacket came in. Forrester followed her movements intently.

"That's fine. Thanks for getting my wallet for me by the way, I would have been on the street last night otherwise," smiled Martin, wanting to keep things light.

Forrester looked mildly agitated and keen to leave as he continued to watch the old woman approach the desk.

"Yes. No, no, of course, we couldn't have that. This way please."

He led Martin round the side of reception as the woman spoke to the officer about having come in last week about "it" and wondering when something was going to be done.

The DCI opened the push button door lock and Martin followed him into a series of narrow, white corridors. It was labyrinthine, much worse than the shopping centre offices. Seemingly randomly placed dark brown doors led into small rooms on each side. Muffled phone rings and conversations. A whiff of coffee. An electrician on a small stepladder doing some work in the ceiling space, tiles lying against the wall; probably asbestos given the age of the place. Into a wider corridor that seemed to stretch the length of the building. Some glass walls here. He could see into larger office spaces filled with desks and people, some in uniform, others in shirts and trousers or skirts. Always phones ringing. The noise of drilling.

"Sorry about the mess Mr Molloy, we're finishing off some renovations, long overdue I might add."

"This was the place *after* work has been done?" thought Martin.

"That's OK, I work in the New Merlin Centre, there's always some electrical or plumbing work being done behind the scenes, I'm used to it."

"Uh-huh."

Forrester seemed distracted. He opened a door into one of the larger offices, and ushered Martin into a smaller, simple room just off it.

"I'll be with you in just a moment Mr Molloy, please take a seat. Would you like a tea or coffee?"

"I've not long had something, but thanks."

Forrester smiled and closed the door as Martin sat down. He could hear phones, conversations and clattering keyboards through the thin separating wall.

Looking around, this room seemed nicer than the other one, perhaps this had already been done up? It also adjoined another office. The wall behind him was half partition, half glass window, a set of thin horizontal blinds drawn tightly closed in the next room. Again, there was no exterior window. They didn't seem to like natural light in here.

Martin's leg started trembling. He didn't know why he was nervous. He already knew what to say, had been practising it all morning. "Some kind of energy blast", not, "blue pulses", "too dark to make him out" which was true but ignored his gut feeling, and no mention of the teleporter. That would just confuse things, and in any case he wanted to find out who that was for himself, before the police got involved.

Laughter from outside. It rankled him for a moment, but then he figured you must need gallows humour in this job, especially on the homicide or sexual assault teams, otherwise it would get to you too much. He was in their workplace after all, it wasn't public.

He jumped when Forrester burst through the door with a clear plastic folder full of papers, a laptop and a small cup of water.

"Sorry to keep you."

"No problem."

He gestured the cup of water towards Martin.

"Throat always gets dry doing these," he said as he put it on the table with the folder.

Martin just smiled as he wondered if it was typical for a DCI to be taking a statement. Wouldn't that be a more junior officer?

Forrester interrupted his train of thought as he asked how he was, and did he have enhanced healing.

"I wish."

A shared chuckle.

Forrester opened the laptop and tapped at it. The DCI apologised for having him come in so soon with his injuries, but then said the shorter the time between an incident and making a statement the better, otherwise important details could be forgotten or mixed up, and of course it helped the investigation proceed faster. He then explained the procedure, telling him he could have a break at any time if it became too distressing or if he was in pain from sitting.

Over the course of the next two hours Martin was taken through the previous night in minute by minute detail. What had he seen, heard, felt? Where were both of them in relation to each other? Who hit who in what order, and where did they end up? He dropped in his pre-prepared details and although he was pressed as to whether he could remember more, he wasn't grilled on it. He relaxed as he realised this was just information gathering, not an inquisition.

As he answered each question the DCI tapped with two fingers at the keyboard. Every now and again he would glance up to the glass panel behind Martin, looking pensive, but then always looked back at him, gently nodding his answers out.

When they were done, Forrester clicked something a few times then left the room. He came back in with three printed pages. Martin was to check for any errors or omissions then sign and date at the bottom of every page. If anything was wrong he was not to feel nervous about bringing it up; it had to be as accurate as possible and he would rather he had to do any changes now rather than continue the investigation with the wrong info.

Martin nodded in agreement and started to read. Forrester excused himself while Martin was halfway down the second page.

It all seemed to be here. Detailed yet generic. This could have been any energy powered Hero from reading it.

There was a heated conversation outside for a minute. Martin expected Charles to fling the door open again, but nothing came of it in the end and he heard people walking away.

He finished all three pages, signed and dated them and sat back in the chair. That had been relatively painless. And his leg had stopped trembling a few minutes in.

Forrester was a long time coming back. It was quiet outside now.

Martin looked around and noticed that the blinds in the next room had been opened, not fully, but enough to see inside. He guessed there must have been a meeting or something going on. But without the DCI?

The other room was just over twice as big as his, with a larger table in the middle and nine chairs around it. There was a large whiteboard at the far end of the room. It was covered in sticky notes, photographs, pieces of printed paper he couldn't read from this distance and arrows and notes written in thick black marker pen. It was like some student art project.

Martin realised he probably shouldn't be looking at it and turned around. He turned back when he realised he had just seen a photo of himself.

He looked more intently this time and saw the picture Morris took of him yesterday. There were six other mug shots of all the members of The Pulse spread out in a column down the left hand side of the board. Vincent was at the top.

They were all colour coded. He was brown. His line stretched across a time line period of three days. They had him confirmed as being on night shift the night Vincent was killed, the day before he got the solicitor's letter. A note the day after simply said "work package (Solicitors)". At the end of the time line, they had marked "Powered fight at apartment. Target #2?"

He looked at the time lines for the others on the Thursday: Professor Maria Gionchetta (home, unconfirmed), Charles Heathcote (Dorchester London, confirmed), Jack Pullman (unknown), Mitchell Davies (home, unconfirmed), Flit (?alias?, unknown).

Interesting. He had thought he was the only one not registered. Looks like Andrea had wanted to stay off the database too for some reason. He could certainly think of a few.

In the middle of the board was a column headed "Interviews". His meeting with Morris was ticked and dated. Underneath were Maria and Mitchell, also ticked and dated to yesterday. Below Maria was Charles dated to sometime next week. Jack and Andrea were blank with an arrow pointing to a red box on the right with a list of bullet points.

Martin's heart started to flutter and skip beats as the heat rose up his neck. He knew deep down it had to be one of the team who took Vincent's life, but he had been trying to bury that thought somewhere deep. The time line made it crystal clear that the police and PCA were working along exactly that train of thought.

He nervously looked to the door, aware now he definitely should not be seeing this, but Forrester didn't seem to be coming back.

OK Vincent, he thought to himself, you want me to find out who killed you? No better place to be right now. Time to make some mental notes.

On the far right of the board were handwritten lines. His eyes darted across the information: "Energy signatures inconclusive", "Five sets of prints confirmed", "Concentrated energy blast", "No struggle", "Mr Molloy unregistered".

And on the board, in amongst all the writing and lines there were pictures, scene of crime photographs. Martin had been avoiding looking at them. Out of the corners of his eyes he could just make out dark red meat. Cupboards and drawers open, contents scattered. A pair of legs sat on an old chair. A glass of whisky sat on the small table next to it.

Martin was breathing quickly and heavily from the top of his lungs now. The world was starting to shrink around him. He had to look. He couldn't look. He had to know what this bastard had done to him. He didn't need to know, Morris had told him enough detail. This was his friend Vincent. He had to look, had to see if he recognised the damage done to him, see if he knew who it could have been.

Martin blinked rapidly, focusing on the bottom left corner of the largest of the photographs, sitting in the centre of the time line. He tried to calm his breathing, steel himself. Maybe he would know straight away who it was. Maybe this was all that was needed to catch him?

He looked.

He couldn't make it out. It was a straight on shot of a large soft chair, Vincent's favourite. Martin had sat opposite that many times, sharing a drink. There was a pair of legs in dark blue sweatpants ending in thin ankles in white socks disappearing into an oversized pair of dark brown velour slippers, the light beige fur lining poking out from around the edges. Something strange about the legs, the tops of them at the hips seemed to be further apart than they should, and they were turned oddly, uncomfortably. The chest area was mostly dark. Dark reds and blacks. Nothing could be identified as human. Either side of the chest the shoulders sat far lower than they should be. The arms of Vincent's light blue cardigan were untouched. His hands on their thin wrists snuck out from the wide ends. His right hand was clutching the end of the arm rest, left hand hanging over the side of it. There was no head to be seen.

Martin felt vaguely annoyed that he didn't recognise this as his old friend. It was as if a photo of him sitting in his chair had been vandalised, an open flame taken to the middle of it until it shrivelled and melted away. He stood up and moved closer to the partition window, dipping his head slightly to get a clear view through the blinds.

"This just doesn't..." he said aloud.

"Mr Molloy?"

Martin didn't hear the detective call his name. He needed confirmation. That photo was useless. It was like a bad horror movie prop, so obviously unreal. He needed to know. There was another photo to the right. It looked like a cut of meat hanging in a butcher's window. He had no perspective on it, no frame of reference. Another photo was Vincent's face, eyes wide open staring intently out of shot, face frozen by the camera flash. Martin was confused. This was like a puzzle with no instructions. This was ridiculous! He looked back at the previous photo. There had to be something here.

"Mr Molloy."

If Martin had been listening he would have noticed the detective was speaking quieter this time.

As he stared at the first picture he spotted an ear. It was almost hidden by the harsh shadow of the flash, towards the back of the picture. From there his mind quickly pieced together the underneath of the chin, the head hanging over the back of the chair. The neck stripped of flesh, shiny white vertebrae curving over the top of the soft material. The completely empty chest and stomach cavity, just a rack of rent open ribs dropping down to those twisted legs. Suddenly the puzzle made sense.

Martin screamed and covered his mouth. He stumbled backwards in shock, hitting the chair which struck the desk with a scrape. He put his arm back and steadied himself, knives of pain digging along his ribs. He stood there panting screams.

"Mr Molloy…"

DCI Forrester came over to him from the door and tried to take him by the arm. Martin yanked his arm out of his reach. He could still see the picture. Maybe from here it would devolve back to a random butcher's cut. It didn't. Maybe here he wouldn't be able to make out the twisted neck any more. No. Like finding a face in patterned wallpaper, this could never be unseen, he couldn't stop seeing it. Vincent opened like a piece of meat. Who could have even thought about doing this to him? Martin was going to crack their chest open and tear out their heart for this.

Forrester moved in front of him, hands on hips, blocking his view. For a moment Martin stared through him, then his shirt came into focus and he looked at him.

"Mr Molloy, I'm… I'm really very sorry you had to see that."

"*You're* sorry? He was torn apart!"

His neck felt tight and the blood pulsed behind his ears.

"I shouldn't have…"

The detective looked uncomfortable.

"Please be assured that this wasn't our idea and I didn't agree to it, none of the team did but…"

"Morris!" Martin hissed.

The blood drained from his head but he kept his balance. He was shaking with anger. He had to control himself. The time line. He had to remember that. Locations. He couldn't lose those either.

"…I was overruled. I'm not happy about that. I knew how much distress it would cause you and I can't apologise enough."

Martin could tell from his face that Forrester was being genuine. The man looked ill with concern.

"For your information we do have a robust complaints procedure that includes external agencies should you wish to make use of it, and I would corroborate any complaint you made. It wouldn't make me 'flavour of the month' with the PCA, but this…" he pointed to the glass behind him "…was absolutely not the right thing to have done."

Martin stepped away from the desk and had to tip his head back to look Forrester in the face.

"Agreed."

"Mr Molloy, I am sorry for your loss. If there is anything I or any of my team can do to help right now, let me know."

"Yes, yes there is actually. Find the bastard that did this, before I do."

The detective watched as Martin turned and rushed out of the room. When he was gone, Forrester looked through the blinds and stared at the board next door, shaking his head.

"Well I hope it was worth it Morris."

***

"Martin?"

He didn't hear her call his name. His mind was still an angry blur as he came round the side of the reception, the security door clicking shut behind him.

"Martin!"

He was in the lobby of the police station now, striding and half running towards the exit. This time he heard the voice and saw Maria stand up from the front row of plastic seats and walk towards him. She put a hand out and touched his arm. Her face twisted in shock at the marks on his face.

"Oh God! Are you all right? I heard you were attacked."

"You heard? Heard where, how?" Martin was unsteady on his feet, buffeted by unwanted emotions. "First Charles and now you! Have you got some direct line to the cops I don't know about?"

Maria looked concerned. But more than that she was looking *at* him. At the restaurant she had barely wanted to acknowledge his presence, she was too busy, distracted. Now she was worried about him as she held his arm. Martin felt a sadness slide through his gut and up through his chest. This was the first time anyone had touched him in years, and it had to be Maria. The sadness filled his neck and welled up behind his eyes.

"Martin, be calm, please. I thought you would still be in hospital..."

As she spoke she saw a tear tumble from his eye down his cheek.

"Oh Martin."

He was usually so good at hiding his feelings. He had so much practice over the years. As little human contact as possible, as routine a life as he could make it, hiding away from anything that he felt could come too close. But now he felt the tears surge out and, shaking, knew he had no power to stop them.

He held Maria in his arms, head over her shoulder as she put hers arms round his back, head sideways on his collar bone and they stood there as the last eighteen years poured from his heart.

CHAPTER 27
THURSDAY 17TH JUNE 1993

Maria has her head on his chest, arms wrapped round him as we all cheer and clap for them. Mitchell puts his fingers in his mouth and gives a loud whistle. Andrea hits him on the arm for nearly deafening her. Charles laughs and puts his hand on Jack's shoulder. Inna stands next to me smiling and clapping while Vincent is sat at the back of the room staring at us all.

We are gathered in the lounge. I don't think we have ever all stood in here at the same time before. It feels crowded with us standing between the cream sofas and the dark wood coffee table. The two diamond shaped mirrors on the wall multiply us dozens of times over. The room is full of us.

The reason for the jubilation? Jack and Maria have just announced that they are going to renew their wedding vows. In a few weeks it will be their fourth wedding anniversary and, having finally seen off The Controller, Jack decided that it would be the perfect time to hold a celebration. There has been too much death and sadness, he said, such that there is plenty of room for a little happiness for a change.

"Oh, and I promise..." he holds a finger up to Maria "...not to bury myself in lab work quite so much. I think if nothing else, we've discovered this year that to be a team you need to be there to support each other as much as you can."

"Well said dear leader, well said."

Charles keeps clapping forcefully, beaming at the renewing couple, standing right next to them. He doesn't need to be quite that close. This is Maria and Jack's moment, not a time for him to be trying to grasp some reflected limelight for himself.

Oh and what a moment it is for Maria and Jack. They both look happy and relaxed with each other. He has just promised to spend more time with her, Maria's main complaint about their marriage for the last year. And not to mention the fantastic media coverage we will get from this. We are already the toast of the city, bar a handful of swiftly ignored commentators, critical of what happened at the Merlin Centre last week. Jack says this will surely cement our place in the top ten Hero teams of the country; big challengers to the London teams for sure. It's all good.

Pity Maria hadn't told me.

I feel like shit.

Here I am clapping with a tense, fake smile, as part of my world collapses around me.

Of course I'm happy for Maria. After all, she has her husband back, which she had wanted for so long. I know how much sadness his behaviour had caused her, and knowing that this sadness has been lifted gives me some comfort. Yet that feeling is tiny next to the giant, screaming, hollowed out void that is my body right now. I can almost feel my own clapping echoing around inside me. My mouth is dry. I realise I'm clapping now just to keep my balance as I feel the room start to spin. I put one hand on the back of the sofa to steady myself and make sure to smile more to compensate.

It was only a week ago that Inna came to me in the shower and I still haven't worked out what that was all about. She was back to her usual self and had been avoiding all attempts at conversation. I could either never find her or, when I did, she was always in a room with someone else. All I know is that I had taken advantage of an emotionally vulnerable woman and had cheated on the woman I loved, who herself was cheating on her husband to be with me. All that was needed now was for Jack to be cheating on Maria with Inna and it would be a full circle.

I almost laugh at that rather glib thought. Then all I think about is me and Maria lying next to each other, holding each other, supporting each other. And all I can see in the future is that not happening any more.

Maria and Jack look around at us all, smiling. Maria catches my eye, grins deeply and squeezes Jack closer to her. I can feel my face harden. I just nod towards her.

"We will of course be inviting all the Heroes of the city to take part in our happy day right here in the building. You guys, naturally, are the guests of honour."

Mitchell whoops loudly.

"And I would be more than honoured, my friend, to take care of the flower arrangements."

Everyone bursts out laughing as Charles recoils in mock indignation.

"Oh you laugh my Heroic fellows but my floral skills are widely respected throughout the powered community and there is many a fiend that fears my gerbera dome bearing down on them."

Andrea is laughing so hard Mitchell has to help her stand up. Inna turns to me.

"I am happy for them. They make good couple. You need to be together with someone to get through difficult times."

I stare at her blankly, aware my smile has gone.

"Yeah, I guess that's right."

"Of course it is!"

She grins and slaps me on the back before going over and hugging Maria. Mitchell is shaking Jack's hand. Not wanting to stand out by not getting involved I force a grin and move over to congratulate them.

"...should have done it sooner really, but was lost up to my neck in details and plans and had lost sight of the full picture. At least now with that psychic shit out of our hair we can get back to how we used to be. And you know, this doesn't just have to be a ceremony for one couple?"

Jack widens his eyes and turns his head back and forth between Mitchell and Andrea until she becomes embarrassed and looks away. Mitchell just grins at her.

"Oh come on guys..."

"No, no, you never know what might happen in the close confines of this building. It's its own little world in here, and you two do seem to be getting on rather well."

Andrea rolls her eyes, then looks at Mitchell while trying to hold back a cheeky grin. "I guess you never know, but you know me, I don't like to rush things."

All three laugh.

I put out my hand.

"Congratulations Jack, I'm really happy for the two of you."

Jack turns to face me, takes my hand, gives three good shakes, then keeps his grip tight.

"Martin. Thank you. You know..." he studies me carefully, looking into each of my eyes, "...I never really say how much I appreciate what you do for the team."

"I... just do my best."

"No really. You are quiet and unassuming but reliable to a fault. I almost forget you are there sometimes, yet we couldn't do without you."

Inna and Maria are having a giggling chat a few metres away. They are discussing dresses. Maria is trying to describe what she wore for her wedding. Mitchell and Andrea are hand in hand next to the sofa, looking into each other's eyes. Charles says something about ordering florist foam and walks out of the room with purpose.

"But that's what it's all about isn't it Martin, being part of a team? It's not about glory or thinking only about yourself, it's about that unspoken trust with those around you, isn't it?"

"Absolutely."

Jack still has me in his grip.

"And I do trust you Martin. Completely."

"Well, thank you."

"And I know Maria does too. She has spoken a lot about how you helped her, looked after her emotionally, all the while I was being a terrible husband."

My neck feels like it's shrivelling from the inside as my brain flip flops like a metronome. Should I admit to having been her confidante, or attempt a deliberately modest denial to protect the lady's honour? Jack laughs.

"No need to say anything Martin. I... I know I made things difficult for her over the last year, TWO years to be accurate. I should have done so much more for her."

Jack's smile drops and he looks genuinely sad.

"I should have been there for her. I shouldn't have put you in a position where you had to become marriage counsellor for the both of us. That wasn't fair on you, let alone her."

The smile returns.

"Thank you for all you've done for our marriage Martin. I can't tell you how much that means to me."

"That's..." I swallow dry, "that's OK Jack. I'm glad you are both happy again."

"Strange isn't it? Strange that it takes such huge and terrible events for us to see what is right in front of us."

"Yes, it is."

Jack shakes my hand twice more then lets go and walks over to the two ladies. Maria immediately slips her arm around him and gives him a kiss on the lips.

I feel hot and sick. The room is being pierced by thousands of tiny pricks of light from inside my eyeballs as my pulse slams against my eardrums. I leave the lounge and head towards the kitchen. It's empty, thank Christ. I turn on the cold tap full, let it run for a few seconds then cup a large handful and douse my face. Again. Again. The heat slowly flushes away through my feet. I turn the tap off and grip the sides of the sink, water dripping from my nose and chin down the plughole. The white dots in my eyes fade away. I feel the tough plastic of the sink bending in my hands and I relax. I grab a handful of kitchen roll and scour the water off my face, dropping the sodden wad in the swing bin.

I need to speak to Maria. I need to find out why. Is this the end of us or could we carry on? How hard am I kidding myself, of course it's over! It was always a stolen love anyway, but for me it *was* love. But what was it for her, a distraction, a temporary replacement until the real one was fixed? No, it was more than that. I had been there for every emotional pounding she had taken. We had shared so much of each other, things neither of us had told anyone else, things she had never even told Jack. I'd had visions of a future where she was divorced and the two of us, having left the team, were now living happily in a nice mid-terraced place in the city. She was back doing the studies she told me she missed and I was doing security work to support us both. Vigilante Heroism didn't pay after all.

What a stupid dream. How naive had I been? I'd never even asked her what she wanted, and now it turned out she had just wanted her husband back.

"Everyone reacts to stress differently don't they?"

I nearly jump through the ceiling panels. It's Vincent. He slowly wanders through the doorway and sits down at the dining table.

"Stress? Yeah, I guess they do."

I hear laughter and chatter still flowing down the corridor. I guess Vincent had had enough of the atmosphere too. Vincent stares straight ahead at a large square painting of an array of tins of soup painted in different sets of colours. Charles had bought it from a struggling artist acquaintance some months back and felt it fitted the dining room. I thought it looked like a bus shelter advert but fell short of saying it out loud. Vincent's eyes study it deliberately, each square of colour at a time, row by row, up and down.

"Some people retreat into themselves, try to resolve it internally. Like you."

I lean back on the sink and watch him.

"Some people explode outward, unable to work things through. Others go through a process. They feel the need to form new bonds or re-establish old ones to put themselves back into a state when things were more stable and predictable, then from that base they can give themselves a new start. A network of support for all those involved to help them all through it."

"Like Maria."

Vincent's eyes stop scanning the painting and look down at an angle towards my feet.

"I didn't say that."

"Yeah I know, but *I* did."

I walk slowly over to the table and sit opposite him. He's wearing a grey hooded top that hangs in giant bulging wrinkles. His long narrow head and thin fingers poke out of the gaping openings. His grey eyes are shrouded by dark skin, his messy hair falling onto his forehead and the sides of his head where it's closely shaven. He looks shattered. His problems with insomnia are well known, mostly thanks to unbidden voices piercing his psychic barriers in the night. Psychic barriers that unfortunately only exist while he is awake. The recent strain brought on by trying, and ultimately failing, to protect us from The Controller must have made things far worse.

"And you Vincent? How are you dealing with it?"

His eyes drop.

"I can't begin to."

"You will in time."

"Will I?"

Vincent presses himself against the upright back of the chair.

"Like you say buddy, we all deal with it in our own way. And I'd like to think that if any of us was having trouble dealing with it we could share that. Get help. You know?"

"And do you need help Martin?"

For a moment I freeze. Has he suddenly found a way to read me? Now would be a very bad time for that to happen. Maybe it's obvious. Maybe he can see it on my face.

"No. I'm fine right now."

"Are you sure? I mean I could tell with the others, but you're more... evasive."

"Hey. I share stuff with you all the time. You know me better than anyone in here."

An unfortunate lie, but I value Vincent's friendship, especially now he's probably going to be the only person I can confide in.

"Yes, but there are different ways of being evasive?"

OK, this is puzzling now. What's he getting at? I'm sure he doesn't know about me and Maria, he must have something else on his mind.

"What do you mean?"

"I mean, you know *I* can't read you or talk to you telepathically like with the others."

"Well, you can do your psychic paper trick on me. Bloody freaks me out every time..."

"Yes, mustn't do that too often though... but I mean, *I* can't affect you, but someone like The Controller, that must have been bad right? Unable to help Barry."

Yep, he's definitely fishing.

"Under his control like that. I mean the stress you must be going through, like the others. Terrible."

He's leaning forward, head at a tiny angle to one side staring at me.

"You can ask me straight out you know."

Vincent seems puzzled by this comment, so I decide to put him out of his torment.

"He didn't."

"Didn't what?"

"Take control of me. He didn't stop me moving or stop me thinking straight. Took me too bloody long to realise he'd done it to everyone else though. All that wasted time I could have..."

Vincent becomes agitated. He is sitting up straight bouncing up and down, fingers clutching at the loose material around his wrists.

"You didn't? I mean you weren't? All the time?"

"All the time. I was the only one of us who was any use for anything and I still waited to the last minute to try..."

"So he never? I mean, not ever..." he points a finger at my head with a shaking hand.

It's no use trying to tell him what's bothering me when he's obsessed by something. I just sit back and sigh.

"No. He tried, I could feel that much, but he never controlled me or spoke to me telepathically. Just like with you. And just like with you, I haven't told any of the others. You told me not to, remember? When you discovered that? Said it wouldn't go down well."

Vincent gives a pained smile, seems much calmer and relaxed.

"I had hoped...I did wonder, because he was so powerful, whether he could get through your barrier, but... thank God... I couldn't have protected you anyway. I couldn't protect any of us, no matter how hard I concentrated, the pain was just..."

He looks down at the table, forehead tensed in a tight bundle of wrinkles.

You selfish moron Martin. Here I am tormenting myself about not being able to save one man while Vincent has been feeling the weight of hundreds of the dead on his shoulders for weeks.

"Vincent. It wasn't your fault. None of it was. You said it before that The Controller was stronger than you thought. At the riots he took over hundreds. At the Merlin Centre there were only seven of us. Eight including Barry. All that concentrated psychic power on such a small number, there was nothing you could have done."

"And now there is nothing I can do and I am silently blamed for all their deaths and for letting The Controller take over your minds."

"Aw Vincent come on, you know that's not true."

"Because he's a manipulator Martin!"

Vincent is oddly twisted in his chair, looking at me again.

"He is *more* than powerful. If he was just powerful, that would be easier to deal with. But he knows, *knows*, how to hurt people. He knows how much control to give to a person, when to give it, when to take it away, what to make them do to cause them the most anguish. He's a torturer. A torturer, even for those he can't control. Even when he's not in your head."

"Yeah I... I guessed the last bit of that stunt at the Merlin Centre was for my benefit. He didn't need to get in my head to mess it up. You're right. A bastard." I nod.

"Even when he's not in your head..."

"Dear Lord, I wondered where you two miserable fuckers had eloped to!"

Charles drifts through the doorway and after a handful of swift footsteps is opening the tall white fridge-freezer. Vincent shrinks back into his seat.

"We... were just saying how much of a bastard The Controller is." I say.

Charles has his head buried inside the chilling machine as he rummages around at the back. His voice is muffled.

"Oh, what a great topic of conversation at such a glorious moment of celebration. That will keep the party spirit alive... here it is!"

He pulls out a dark green bottle with a gold foil collar and brandishes it in triumph, brushing off some frost with a thumb. Muttering something like "chilled not fucking frozen" he pushes the fridge door closed and turns to look at the two of us. I can only imagine our expressions. He shakes his head.

"Chaps, there are times for ruminating over dire horrors in our history, for great horrors they are. Now I am not denigrating their importance, but this moment..." he spreads his hands "...is not one of them. Our two most favourite teammates are renewing their wedding vows and everyone, even Inna, has the first smile on their faces that I recall seeing for a long while. Apart from you two glum buggers that is."

I hold up my palms in surrender. I should at least make the effort to appear outwardly happy.

"Yes. OK. You're right. As long as we realise though that as a team we will need to discuss what's happened to us sometime... then yes, for now, time to forget and enjoy the moment."

I notice Vincent glance at me.

"That's the spirit my man! Come now, let's leave this shrivelled carcass in his self-imposed gloom, because for us there are fine crystal glasses in the cabinet next door and I'm certain there is another magnum of these lovely fellows down in storage five," he says, waving the bottle at me.

It takes me a moment to calm my raised hackles at the casual abuse of Vincent. I had chided Charles before, but right now is not the time nor the place for this argument. Vincent would understand, I'm sure. I stand up and push the chair under the table.

"Sounds good to me."

Charles is already striding to the exit when, on reaching the doorway, he spins round.

"Oh and fantastic news, Jack has requested my good self to be his best man at the wonderful occasion."

I think I manage a pretty decent half smile despite myself.

"Great. That's really great Charles."

"And..." Charles makes a large gesture of looking around for anyone overhearing before continuing in a stage whisper "...don't tell her I told you, but Maria said she wants you to give her away."

I feel my lungs shrink wrap my heart. No words come.

"I guess because she's estranged from her family." He taps the side of his nose, "But keep it to yourself for now. See you back in there!" he beams and exits the room.

I can't move. My breathing is tightening up and the under cabinet lighting begins to bloom in the corner of my vision.

Vincent stands up without moving the chair. Hunched over, he glances across the table at me.

"Even when he's not in your head," he says, before slipping out the doorway.

CHAPTER 28
SUNDAY 16TH SEPTEMBER 2012

"I still remember how it felt to have him in my head you know?"

Martin nodded.

"The way he allowed us to coordinate our thoughts, passing on important info that others in the team had found, keeping us protected. He was the glue that held the team together, although none of us really recognised that at the time of course. I think we took him for granted. No, we definitely did."

They were sitting in a coffee shop window seat, a few streets down from the police station. Maria had a small glass of white wine and Martin a large black coffee. He was having trouble drinking it over his increasingly fat lip.

"I'm not trying to make excuses you know, but psychics were even more distrusted back then than they are now. People were so suspicious of them, thought they were always inside your head, reading your thoughts. They didn't realise how broad a range of abilities or self-control a psychic could have. And I guess we were afraid too, as a team. I mean I was never nasty towards him, not like the others, but there were times I didn't talk to him when I should have because I believed I didn't know how to. I could talk to anyone but him. I didn't really understand."

There was a steady chatter around them as shoppers started sitting themselves down for lunch.

"I think it was difficult for all of us, including me sometimes. He did have a habit of being able to avoid speaking the obvious."

"But you tried Martin, that's the point. You were his saviour. All the work I did with him since then... it was genuine of course, but I do wonder how much of it was me trying to make it up to myself."

"We were all young. None of us were... psycho-psychiatrists, we were kids in a superhero team. We have to stop blaming ourselves at some point. We helped him. In the end, we helped him. He was pretty much back to normal the last few years. Medicated and isolated yes, but you know, at least he was more himself again."

Maria stared at her wine.

"Thanks to treatments you pioneered... Professor." He emphasised her title.

She looked at him, slightly exasperated, but with a playful smile

"Don't call me that."

They tried to keep each other buoyant amid the sea of missed opportunities. They sat and sipped their drinks as the shadows of large stencilled lettering on the window slowly crept across their table.

They talked about the times Vincent had saved them, solved crimes and of course the many quirky things he did that they had to get used to. Like the times he would make them jump out of their skin when they would turn on the light in some room to find him huddled in the corner asleep, or the time he tried to make a cheese toastie actually in the toaster and nearly set the kitchen on fire.

Then they silently wondered how many of those times were when he was seriously disturbed by the voices, his control wavering and were cries for help.

Martin finished his coffee. He asked Maria if she wanted another wine, but she said she had to go back to work soon. He caught the attention of a waitress by raising his hand and regretted it immediately as the twist to his chest tugged all his ribs apart like an accordion of agony. Another coffee arrived in due course.

"By the way, the police are releasing some of your items from the surviving portion of your flat and we've arranged movers to take them to Charles's place out by Hislington."

"Oh, right."

"He's got more rooms than TV contracts you know, one of his spare ones would probably cover the same footprint as your old place."

That pissed Martin off.

"Oh great, that's nice."

Maria hadn't noticed.

"Why you lived in such a tiny place I don't understand. Working as a night guard? You didn't gamble away your split did you? That should have lasted you the rest of your life..."

Martin had been relaxed, if sombre, but now he felt the magma rising up through his guts.

"Well I guess I just figured some more deserving people needed that. That and I didn't appreciate being paid off by people who want to run my bloody life for me."

She noticed that.

"Martin, we're trying to help."

"No, you're taking over. I've managed fine on my own all these years and I don't particularly like it when other people start messing with my stuff, however many pieces it's in. I can sort myself out."

Maria's voice became hard.

"Look, we happen to have contacts within the police who told us they were releasing your possessions. OK, fine, they hadn't told you yet. But where else were you going to put them? The motel? You have nowhere for your stuff to go, and Charles has space. He's not even there most of the time. It makes perfect sense."

Martin's anger fizzled away. He was too tired to keep it boiling.

"You could have asked, that's all I'm saying. None of you speak to me in over eighteen years and suddenly you're moving my furniture for me."

"Communication works both ways Martin."

"Like I said, it was difficult. You know why."

Maria looked away, uncomfortable, and sipped her wine.

"And anyway, I suppose none of this has anything to do with any memoirs floating around."

Maria's brow furrowed and her mouth dropped as her face slackened.

"That's... that's not fair. You're right Martin, we don't have to help you at all. We could abandon you to your cheap motel, hoping that this... person doesn't try and kill you again, but you're in danger, and none of us want to see you hurt."

Martin was ready to snap back with a comment about them not being able to find the memoirs if he was dead, but something about her expression made him halt. Of course they were trying to protect the memoirs. He couldn't be blind to that, as he was party to all the presumed contents and shared their feelings to a large extent. But how much of his frustration was from seeing them trying to hide the past and how much from his own reluctance to let anyone in? He remembered Vincent saying something about stress once, about some people retreating into themselves.

He closed his eyes and took a deep breath. He wondered if he was ready to start allowing himself to remember, let alone start sharing it with anyone else. He breathed out and opened his eyes. Maria was looking concerned. Even if Charles was being as self-serving as always, he could trust Maria, couldn't he? Damn it. If it made life a bit easier for a while he would bite.

"OK. I'm sorry. I'm... not used to people doing things for me. I don't cope well with it. I'll take up the offer. Thanks."

He took another gulp of coffee and gazed out the window. So many people out in the world nowadays. Everything always seemed busier.

"What's happened to you Martin? Seeing you like this..."

Their eyes met. A sliver of a memory cut into Martin's consciousness. They were sitting on his bed, she was telling him how Jack ignored her so much she felt he despised her. She couldn't fathom what she had done wrong. He told her she had done nothing wrong. It was *him* who was doing wrong. It must be deliberate, surely he couldn't be blind to how much he was hurting her? She started crying, telling him she was so happy he understood. He took her by the shoulders and said he would always be there for her. She looked up at him, leaned forward and... a raw, penetrating phone ring tone burst into life behind him. The owner let it ring just a little too long, staring at the screen all the while, before starting a loud conversation with a distant person about their life today.

Maria was looking through her document holder and pulled out some papers.

"This is Charles's address details and alarm code. Obviously, don't lose that anywhere. And this is my address and number. Just in case, you know, you might have lost it in the damage done."

Martin was planted back into the present day.

"Er, thanks. Yeah, it's all so much hamster bedding now."

Maria laughed. "Do you remember that rabbit we had for a while? I was convinced I could manage animal emotions and thought it would be a good mascot?"

It took a few seconds, but Martin did recall a black and white lop-eared rabbit in one of the common rooms. That and the little bum raisins it left scattered over the furniture. Maria cleared her throat, looked embarrassed at her lapse of composure.

"Anyway…"

As he folded up the papers he remembered there was something he needed.

"Hey, is there any way at all you can get me in to see Jack?"

Maria looked at him oddly.

"I've already spoken to his secretary, who wasn't happy I had that number you gave me by the way. She is obviously programmed to brush off anyone not work related and I've gone on 'the pile'."

"Hah! That's where all my fucking messages end up, takes days for him to get any of them. I've never even tried to get an appointment, but I wouldn't give you much chance before next summer."

"Crap. Surprised she even takes your messages the number of times you and him have argued against each other on the news."

"However we may disagree on a professional level doesn't change who we were, or what we were part of. The team sticks together, whatever happens."

"Yeah, Charles said much the same."

"Well I'm sorry, but I can't help you with Jack. Mitchell's a good bet though, you can probably just turn up whenever you like, he practically lives there. Listen, I've got to get back. I'm giving a lecture this afternoon, then a meeting with one of our research sponsors…"

"Sound like a fun afternoon."

Maria stood up, grabbing her bag around the zip and shook her head. "I would much rather be in the lab. Got data to get through on our last project and need to finish the schedule on our next one."

"Ah. Not so fun."

Maria leaned on the back of the chair and looked down towards him, the tips of her sharp bob swinging down by her chin.

"Look. Your things won't be at Charles's for a good few hours. Go back to the motel, get some rest, heal up."

Martin felt an ache across his forehead as she said that. Then he remembered the message he picked up this morning with his clothes.

"Yeah, I guess I've got nowhere else to be."

CHAPTER 29
SUNDAY 16TH SEPTEMBER 2012

"BLACKFORGE CONSTRUCTION SITE, BROAD STREET, BY TRAIN STATION, 10PM TONIGHT."

The building site was dark, lit only by a three quarter moon in the sky. Surrounded by high wooden panel fencing all the way around, it was even quieter than the ghostly Broad Street outside. They were building student flats here and the skeletons of two large complexes carved up the night sky. One had a skirt of a single floor of brick wall around it, the other was still only foundations, concrete floor and steel beams. A dark yellow generator sat next to him. It was covered in a blue tarpaulin tied at the corners to any available loop or handle, a small pile of bricks on top to weight it down. The wind got under it and made it puff out and crackle. A freight train dragged itself past the back of the site, the sound of its squealing wheels slicing through the air until their echoes vanished.

Martin had forced his way easily through the cobbled together plywood front gate. He made sure there were no security cameras to catch him and that the few people out on the pavement weren't paying him any attention.

He had become nervous of being followed recently. He didn't want to call it paranoia because it wasn't. He knew the police had been watching him and no doubt PCA were tracking him somehow. Nervous, that's all. And pissed off. It was now seven minutes past ten. He had been standing near the sleeping generator for eleven minutes and was now beginning to feel the cold. He was also tempted to tie the flapping tarp down. He had already called out several greetings at varying volumes, based on how confident he felt that he couldn't be heard, but there had been no reply and now the cold was sapping his strength.

At Maria's suggestion he had gone back to the motel and slept in his clothes for hours. When he woke up he seemed to hurt even more than before. He wasted some time walking around the area to keep his body moving. He had thought about going to see Mitchell, but wasn't sure if his place would be closed or busy. He didn't know how these martial arts schools operated.

A nice local pub dinner and a bus ride later he found himself here. Now his bruised bones and muscles were in need of another rest. His eyes were sliding back into his skull. He was pissed off. He let his mind wander back to the building site battles he had taken part in. Classic place for a fight; few civilians, lots of cover and hiding spaces, not many eyes on you as they tended to be fenced or boarded in and you could do a considerable amount of damage without risking lives or lawyers' fees.

A shiver of cold rattled his loose ribs. Christ. Two more minutes and he was out of here.

He knew the teleporter had arrived when he heard an odd echo. An interrupted gasping sound started to bounce around the enclosed space from all directions until so many became overlaid it sounded like a steam engine gone berserk. Then, just as suddenly, they stopped. Standing a few feet ahead of him was the stranger, clad in the same jeans and dark hoodie as the night his flat was destroyed.

Hero greets were always a tricky social dance to choreograph, always skirting around exactly how much each party knew of the other and what the point of the meeting was, until both were satisfied of the identity and trustworthiness of the other. This Hero was clearly a very competent teleporter, they could take objects with them when they jumped and had a knack for improvisation. Martin had to assume they knew about him and his abilities, although he wondered how long they had been observing before deciding to get involved. That by itself would tell him a lot about the person.

However, he didn't know what they wanted. This put him at an uncomfortable disadvantage. They had remained mute and distant so far, not uncommon of course, but Martin had been out of the Hero scene for years and had no idea what modern Heroes were about, having to hide their use of abilities for fear of arrest. It was a different world now that powered people were forced to register, hide their abilities or go underground. Much more dangerous and unpredictable, which was ironically the complete opposite of what the legislation intended.

The figure shuffled about. They're feeling the cold too. Well they're human at least. Martin decided to tread carefully all the same. He swallowed back the tension in his neck and took a deep breath.

"My name is Roadblock, but you probably already know me as Martin. I didn't have the opportunity before, back at my apartment, but I just wanted to thank you for..."

As the figure jogged forwards quickly towards him, Martin stepped back and clenched his fists. They were almost in his face as they flipped their hood back and a mess of blonde hair escaped.

"I fucking knew it was you! You haven't changed at all, well apart from the hair, or lack of, no offence I mean..."

The girl's green eyes stared into his.

"Er... none..."

"Had your poster on my wall you know, as a kid, The Pulse!"

She made a wide poster flattening gesture with her hands in front of Martin's face.

"You guys were fuckin' awesome, Pulse with his, well, pulse weren't it and Sunlight dissolving shit to dust like 'whoomph!'..."

She made a chest thrust gesture, flinging her arms back.

"...and The Black Witch calming people down or making them trust her. I mean, all the girls I knew always wanted to be Sunlight because she was 'so pretty' and all that shit, but I always wanted to be The Witch, mysterious and intelligent and all that you know? Not that Sunlight wasn't bright or anything, I mean she had a degree didn't she?"

"Electrical engineering but..."

"Yeah, how cool would that have been, a Hero engineer! And of course Buzz and Ignite and the mysterious Seeker and of course... you. You know, I always liked you, bit of a crush I'm embarrassed to say really. Quiet, strong, dependable, did your shit and didn't go on about it you know and I respected that, even as a kid. You guys were the best line up definitely. I'm so stoked to actually talk to you instead of staring from a distance, that's always a bit stalkerish isn't it?"

"I... guess..."

"Oh yeah, I checked all around the site by the way, it's clear. Nobody followed you. No suspicious people or vehicles hanging around the nearby streets. And I'm sorry for being late and everything you know?"

Martin shrugged, throwing up his palms.

"Hey, no worries."

"Aw thanks, that's the funny thing about being a teleporter, you always think you have more time than you actually do to get to places so you always end up being late even though you can get there in seconds! Funny innit?"

Martin couldn't help but smile at the fast talking, blonde Brummie girl stood in front of him. She was hopping up and down with delight, hands now tucked in the front pouch pocket of her hoodie. She wasn't what he had been expecting at all. He had been expecting a guy for a start, don't know why, probably the TV dropping thing. She seemed honest, guileless and bright, and not too unfamiliar either.

"Hang on, you... you're the police officer who was watching me at the restaurant."

Her face dropped. Martin's brain was pinging with bouncing ball bearing thoughts.

"Yeah, pretty badly 'n' all." She looked concerned and started to wave her arms around before placing them across her chest. "Oh, nothing official, you're not under observation. Honest! Well at least not by us, I can't speak for the PCA and I'm not close enough to the main investigative team to know much more at the moment. But I can find out for you! I've been trying to wheedle my way in. Gary, one of the officers, I used to go out with him a while back, could be a bit of a twat but he's all right really, been chatting to him, you know 'bumping into him' in the corridors and all that. They're all pretty tight-lipped though, I think PCA has got them spooked."

"You're a police officer."

"Wow you do time travel too? That bit was your life two minutes ago. It was a fun time but things have moved on you know?"

"Yeah, yeah, what I mean is you're powered... but you're a police officer too. That's..."

"Illegal."

She just nodded and looked at him. They stood quiet for a while as that piece of information fully sunk in.

"I'm illegal. And it pisses me off, all the things I could have done, all the crimes I could have stopped or people I could have caught if I'd been able to slip right up to them on duty. But... not allowed. Got to hide it all the time. It's so tempting to just use it you know? But I've got to be careful, otherwise I'd lose everything. My dad would..."

She was chewing her lip now and looking at the crackling tarpaulin, her eyes narrow and sad. Then she became aware of her expression and gave Martin a coy smile as she turned back to him.

"But still, when I'm not on duty, I'm everywhere! I'm all over the city, making muggers trip over traffic cones that suddenly find themselves at their feet, slamming doors shut on shoplifters and whipping knives right out of the hands of kids trying to 'teach each other lessons'. I fuckin' love it! Got to watch for cameras though, especially the new high def ones, but thanks to a bit of insider knowledge I know where most of them are."

"Were you at my flat the other night?"

"Time travel again..."

"I mean afterwards, the car that turned up?"

"Oh shit yeah, my partner wanted to stop off at the scene to chat to a friend of his and as soon as I saw the PCA I had to bail. That Detector they have scares the crap out of me."

"I'm not his biggest fan either. Looks like Roy Orbison at his own funeral."

"Who?"

"Uh, never mind."

"I was at The Seeker's place too, I was doing some overtime when the call came in. I saw PCA there too. I was terrified, they could have sniffed me out but seemed too busy. Kept as far away as I could though. Got lucky. Checked afterwards why they were there and discovered who had lived there. After you got interviewed by them I kind of accessed the database from someone else's computer to find out your address and sort of... followed you."

"Not stalkerish at all."

"But I'm glad I did, otherwise you'd be dead now!" she beamed, eyes squashed into narrow smiling lines by her high round cheeks.

They were silent again.

Martin slowly assembled in his head how much of a risk she had taken to be here right now. Not only had she lied to get into the force in the first place, she was using her powers illegally to fight crime. She had hacked into a police computer to find him, followed him when on duty and then risked her exposure to drop a TV on his attacker. And she had told him all of this, someone she only knew from posters and the TV back in the nineties. She had trusted him that much. It had been years since he had last felt that kind of implicit trust from someone. The feeling that all those around you respected you for what you were and what you did for them. He had forgotten how deeply reassuring that felt and it dug up dozens of forgotten good memories in an instant.

"Bit cold innit! Fancy a bite?"

"Sounds good to me. Burger King?"

"Nah, too many cameras and not enough fat, I know somewhere that does the meanest chicken burger for less than four euros and more than six hundred calories! Oh and yeah, my name's Hayley."

CHAPTER 30
SUNDAY 16TH SEPTEMBER 2012

They were sat in a small takeaway, five minutes walk from the city centre. A small, rectangular, harshly lit shop with four square white plastic tables pressed tight up against one wall and with a metal counter at the far end. Behind the counter three Asian men seemed to be getting very frustrated with each other while preparing even the most basic orders for the small number of punters trickling in.

The chairs had thin, hollow metal frames painted white with tiny circular seats covered in dark maroon crocodile skin patterned PVC. One of the protective feet had come off Martin's chair some time ago and the metal end tapped on the pale wood panel floor. The chair was so small he could barely fit a single buttock on it.

Hayley sat opposite him, her back to the counter, hood up. She had slipped in behind him and grabbed the table by the window while he ordered; furthest from the camera behind the counter and the most shaded spot with the light behind her. She had eaten two chicken burgers, a portion of onion rings and onion bhajis and was currently draining a huge cardboard cup of banana milkshake while polishing off her portion of thick cut chips. Martin's chicken burger was decent but he'd had better, a little too oily even for his junk food palate and stuffed with very dead lettuce that tasted like shredded bank statements. The chips were all right though.

A bell tinged as two loud talking young men came in and went up to the counter to stare at the plastic menu board. The "cooks" went into an immediate mild panic.

Hayley noticed Martin staring at the empty food wrappers and boxes on the table.

"Sorry, I kind of eat a lot. Jumping makes me hungry. The more I do it the more I need to eat. It's like the ultimate body workout, although the DVD would be shit."

Martin laughed. Hayley looked bemused.

"What?" she smiled.

"Nothing."

One of the owners repeatedly pointed at a pie in the glass cabinet on the counter and barked at the man next to him as the two lads stared at their smartphones, hunched over like high board divers.

Martin didn't mind this place. It was small, out of the way, quiet, and nobody cared who you were. Probably the same reasons Hayley liked it. He shook a stray shred of lettuce from his index finger and wiped off some salad cream with a shiny paper napkin. She sucked up the dregs of the shake and mulched the last chips in her mouth with it. As he took a sip of his coffee she sat back and gave an audible sigh while patting her stomach.

"Well, that's another ten miles or so in the tank, but I've still got a lasagne and some garlic bread in the freezer before bed. Thank God I've got three rest days coming up."

She looked up at him from under her hood, a huge smile slowly growing across her face. He could see her better now in this light. The smile alone was disarming, wide and genuine, but those big cheeks, slightly oversized nose and chin and those narrow, happy green eyes made her look like some handmade doll from a children's TV show. Her straw blonde hair just peeped out from under the lip of her hood.

"You know, I really can't believe it's you? Here, sat right in front of me in Sunny Food Palace. This is really weird you know."

"You and me both."

She scanned his outline.

"You're bigger than you look on TV."

"Too much of this crap," he pointed at the sagging, grease grey box in front of him. "I don't have your fitness routine unfortunately."

"So you not done much Heroics since you guys split up?"

She looked disappointed. She was probably expecting to hear tales of his midnight crime fighting, secret teams trawling the streets for drug dealers and pimps and a hidden underworld of Heroes and villains battling on the rooftops while the people slept, unawares.

"Nope. Nothing. Bought my flat and settled into the quiet life. Then the Innate Power Registration Act came into force anyway. Wasn't going to register for that..."

"I know, you just vanished!"

"Went quiet for a good few years. Had enough cash to survive. Just kept to myself really. Grew a beard, a rubbish one, but it did the job. Then after I was looking older and fatter and, well, after the money went, I looked into security work. Night work, fewer eyes to recognise you. I'm with an agency now. Done all sorts, but at the moment..." he paused.

Here he was revealing intimate details of his life to a complete stranger. He should be being guarded, doing a tit for tat information trade at best, but something about her unconditional trust in him made him comfortable. Unlike his earlier conversations with Maria, there was no apprehension here, no filtering of his thoughts. This was like his chats with Vincent.

"...I'm doing nights at the New Merlin Centre. Well, I hope I still am."

Her eyes lit up.

"No fucking way! Do you know Monica, Barney?"

"Yeah, I do." Martin was surprised.

"Oh I've met them loads! Always shoplifters for us to pick up and kids pissing around in the Centre, you know, giving them loads of grief? All that time you were doing the night shift there! Small fuckin' world eh?"

"I guess."

Hayley tried to hide a sudden, low rumbling burp but couldn't quite.

"Sorry."

"Don't mention it. So what about you? Why a police officer of all things?"

She looked at him seriously.

"I got frustrated you know? I could have gone underground, carried on working in clothes shops in the day and done the Heroism at nights, but I wanted to help people all the time, not just in my spare time you know? And yeah... I know how big a risk it is, especially as I've got loads of friends in the force now. Makes it hard sometimes, can't properly open up to them no matter how close I get. Worst is when I have to arrest other people like me... us. If they are causing a disturbance I don't mind, but it's the ones that were trying to help that get me the most. I remember one woman who tried to stop a mugger and sucked all the heat out his body. Turned out she didn't know she could do that. Most people find out as kids, but she just never knew. We found her crying on the pavement next to his frozen body, everybody giving her a wide berth, even her two kids, they wouldn't come to her any more. She just kept saying how sorry she was, she didn't mean it, that she didn't want to lose the kids. We had to arrest her. 'Manifesting innate powers in public', murder of course. That got dropped to voluntary manslaughter in court but she still got jail and lost the kids to her partner. Lost all her friends, her job, her life really... so... yeah, it's difficult sometimes."

The now sweating owner handed over two brown paper bags to the lads. When they asked for curry sauce, he hurriedly threw far too many plastic tubs into the packets to placate what had been a fairly innocent query. The door tinged as they left and the owners started a protracted disagreement about the glass cabinet and its contents.

"So," stated Martin.

"So," stated Hayley as she leant forward on the table, pulling the ends of her sleeves over her hands.

"Why the hell are you following me anyway?"

"To save your life from Jack of course."

That caught him unawares.

"Don't look so surprised. Like I said, you guys were my favourite superhero team. I know exactly how all your powers work and what they look like. That was Jack. Those were his pulses. He was trying to kill you, I'm guessing because he reckons you worked out he killed Vincent?"

Martin almost forgot to breathe in for a moment. She got it. She's good.

"You're quick. Well yeah, that's what I reckon too."

But the memoirs, what happened to them all, what they did, nobody must know.

"But, why would Jack kill him in the first place? Vincent's been in and out of institutions all his life. I bet he could barely register his *own* thoughts let alone anyone else's with all the suppressants he was probably taking. He was completely vulnerable, no threat at all. Jack is, well, he's the head of Pullman Enterprises, head of one of the richest and most innovative tech companies in the country. He like, lives in a totally different world to Erskine Drive. Why would he even risk doing what he did? It just doesn't make sense."

"I know."

"I mean, the one thing I *do* know from the investigation, courtesy of Gary, is that they haven't yet worked out who it is. That means only you and me and Vincent saw him and his powers and none of *us* are telling for obvious reasons."

"Right."

"Well, at least Vincent and *me* have obvious reasons." Hayley looked coyly at him. "Why haven't *you* told them?"

"Why haven't I?" Martin struggled to think himself out of the memoir exposure nightmare in his head. "Well, even if I did, what good would it do? He is who he is. He's pretty much untouchable, and what evidence do I have other than saying I think it was him who tried to kill me? Yeah, why would he kill Vincent in the first place like you said... you guys just wouldn't believe me."

"Hey! Don't you 'you guys' me! I hate that shit."

Martin shrunk away.

"Sorry I didn't mean it like that."

"I know, it just gets my back up when people make sweeping statements about us like that, like we're stupid We're not! We do understand and we investigate everything, it's just probabilities; what's most likely to be the case often is."

"I said I'm sorry OK?"

"Don't be. Damn it, I can't get mad at you. It's *you*!"

She was smiling again.

"Anyway, they have a list of suspects and things have picked up speed since you got attacked. They are worried the killer is on a revenge trip or is mentally ill. Those scenarios always tend to end badly so they're trying to get on things quickly while the PCA bring in more agents."

"More?"

"Yeah, everybody's pissed at that, but they can't really complain, given what's happening."

"Well, they'll be following me for real from now on I guess. That's going to make seeing everyone else a bit harder."

"Seeing everyone?"

A slip. Martin needed to be more careful.

"Ah, one of Vincent's last requests. In his will. He asked me to meet up with the old team for one final time. Much to my regret, but there you go."

"Right. Gotcha. OK, so you're going to meet your old team to find out what they know, I'll keep my foot in the door of the investigation, see how many excuses I can make to 'drop in' and take a quick scan of the board. I'll start following Jack to work out his routine. When will we reconvene to compare notes?"

"Whoa... what?"

"Oh come on Roadblock... sorry, Martin – still feels odd calling you by your first name – you didn't think you were going to get away with a 'Thanks, now piss off' meeting did you?"

Martin felt shocked and a little guilty. That's exactly what he had hoped for. Sure, he had warmed to the girl over the course of their chat, but he was still expecting it to be temporary. He had expected this meeting to be stressful. Most of him hadn't wanted to go to the building site in the first place. Too much extra knowledge, too much hassle dealing with someone else in the middle of all this. An extra person to think about, another set of opinions to pick at his quickly unravelling pattern of life. A stranger who wanted to get to know him, someone he owed for saving his life, maybe even knew his secrets and would use that to get what they wanted. He had expected there to be demands, blackmail even, but it seemed that all this trusting young woman asked for was to be allowed to help him.

"I want to help, all right? You've got to meet up with everyone again and sort Vincent's affairs and all the while you're not having the easiest few days as it is. You need an extra body to check up on Jack and anyone else you want watched to see what your digging stirs up. In any case I'm single at the moment and I don't think my Sex and the City box set can take any more punishment. Or my rabbit…"

"Your what?"

"Never mind," she said rapidly, fiddling with the plastic sealed ends of her hood strings.

Martin smiled.

"Fine, but be,,,"

"…be careful. Yes dad!" she leaned forward. "I'm a police constable in case you'd forgotten, I don't need to be careful when I can taze people in the neck."

"OK, tomorrow, here, same time?"

"The Sunny Food Palace HQ. Those three guys are our highly trained ninja guards and the secret entrance is behind the wall fridge; turn the third battered sausage from the left anti-clockwise to open it."

Martin couldn't stop himself laughing out loud.

"What's your number so I can send you info?"

Martin shrugged.

"I don't own a mobile phone…"

"Destroyed in the flat? Shit, feels like you've lost a leg doesn't it?"

"Sure does," Martin assumed.

"Well let me know when you get a new one yeah? So you heading back to the luxury motel tonight?"

"No I'm... crap, I'd forgotten! I'm staying with a friend of, well... an old acquaintance of mine. My stuff is in one of his rooms until I've sorted myself out. Which reminds me of something else, going to have to track down the number of my house insurance company. That's going to be an interesting conversation."

Hayley raised an eyebrow. "*One* of his rooms? How many rooms does this friend have?"

Martin sighed. "It's Charles, you know, Ignite?"

"'Course I fucking know, who doesn't? I watch all his shows. Camper than a bunch of tents in a field but fuckin' funny. He's your knight in shining armour you lucky bastard."

"Yeah, well I just need to be able to stand him for a few weeks until I get sorted again. Might not even see him if he's busy enough. I'd better sort myself a taxi."

"No, I'll give you a jump!"

"What? No there's..."

"Nothing to be afraid of, exactly. I'll jump you over there. Been past it a few times on patrol so I know the location in my head. I need that by the way, can't just jump anywhere, need to have seen it in person, know the location, where stuff is, so I don't appear half inside a chair or whatever. Come on, there are a few nice quiet alleyways around here and the rapists shouldn't be out yet."

"I don't... well thanks. But I've never..."

"I know, not many people have, obviously! You've flown though? I remember Paul and Jack giving you a lift into places before."

"You remember well."

"Well it's just like that, except it isn't! And it doesn't hurt."

Hayley stood up and, keeping her back to the camera, moved away from the table, grabbing Martin's arm. He stood up warily.

"Doesn't hurt?"

"No. Well it doesn't hurt me. People I've rescued usually tend to projectile vom for a few minutes then curl up on the ground in pain until they pass out, but they're OK after that. Well, probably, I'm usually gone by then. But I don't see any mention of their deaths in the paper so I guess they turn out fine."

305

"You're not exactly filling me with confidence you know."

The door tinged as she turned him round and pushed him out onto the cold street. The owners chorused 'Bye!' as they left.

"I'm only kidding you twat. Well, apart from the vomiting."

They walked across the quiet street, draped in a shiny coating of rain, and slipped into an alleyway between a bookshop and a nail bar. Martin hit every wheelie bin with his knees and elbows, their dark corners sending shivers of pain along his slowly knitting ribs.

"This should be fine."

Hayley stopped and they faced each other in the darkness.

"OK, so how does this work?" he whispered. "Do I have to hold my breath or something? Do you need me to be quiet?"

She shook her head.

"Nope, we just do it."

"But what if you..."

She slipped her arms around him and looked up into his face with smiling moonlight eyes.

"This is fuckin' awesome."

Then they jumped.

CHAPTER 31
MONDAY 12TH JULY 1993

"Fuckin'... just... jump! Jump, dickhead!"

"Nuh, it's too high Dave..."

Gaz teeters on the edge of the red brick building, some seven storeys up. Dave can see his face scrunched up in fear as he gazes down into the wide alleyway underneath him. There were only three of them left and he wasn't going to let the bastards get them.

***

Bill and Skids had been blasted apart at the car park. They were just chatting, planning who would do that day's drops, ripping the shit out of Big Mal in their safe place where they knew no-one would hear and send Ripper after them. Then this huge white beam tore them apart as they kicked a half empty bottle of water around.

Then the panic. Dave had never felt anything like it. Even when the police raided the flats a few months ago he had kept his head, gathered the gear, grabbed Middle and remembered the routes out that got them to safety. But this time, his thoughts wouldn't let him sort them out, and they collided inside his brain as he heard his mates calling out in fear around him. He remembered stumbling forwards to where his friend's ashes lay streaked across the concrete and sending one of the biggest rushes of air he had ever made in the direction of the attackers. Cars flipped over sideways and tumbled away from them, as if someone had flipped gravity to the west. He saw some more blasts of light, heard shouts and, as suddenly as it had begun, the panic went.

That's when they started running.

He, Gaz, Sticks and Harry ran straight up the ramp from the lower level, leapt the barrier and headed across the street outside into the market. Max must have stayed behind – he heard his sonic blasts going off until a huge sound of smashing, tearing metal stopped them.

He thought they'd be safe going through the market. It was busy with early shoppers. Stacks of boxes and wrapping were pushed up against the stalls as the stall holders finished setting up. He ran through the meat stalls, pushing a fat man carrying a plastic tray of something out of the way, sending him tumbling to the floor. Slipping between two stalls, the rough tarp scratching his face, he saw a blue flash and Sticks, who was running along the row parallel to him, came flying past surrounded by brick and dust. He landed heavily on the cobbles, winding himself. Dave heaved him to his feet and pushed him on.

Suddenly a voice commanded them to stop. Sticks ran on, but Dave turned round to see a man dressed in white and blue, floating in the air. He clapped his hands and sent a tight air burst towards him. The man brought up some kind of transparent blue bubble but it didn't seem to help him as he cried out in surprise and went tumbling away out of sight.

"Fuck you!" cried someone close and lightning erupted from behind the stall to his left. Flecks of ripped, melted tarp and burning veg stung him as he barely managed to duck in time. He looked to where it had come from and saw a terrified man hiding under the smoking wooden table. He saw a pair of blue boots running along behind the stall. He looked ahead to see Gaz nipping up the steps out of the market to the ring road. He hadn't seen Harry since they entered the market and he didn't know where Sticks had gone until he heard a scream.

He jumped up and ran to the T-junction ahead. To his right he saw Sticks writhing on the floor. Next to him was a young kid in a helmet and goggles, all in dark blue. Electricity was dancing around his arms and he was clutching his head. One eye of the goggles was broken, with blood dripping out. Looks like Sticks had managed to get one in.

"Guys, what the hell?"

That sounded near, as did the footsteps following it The flying one would be back soon too. They needed to get to some proper cover, but had to lose sight of these guys first.

Dave shouted a warning to the people near him to get down and sent a wide, high blast in the direction of the running feet. The electricity guy was blown back into a fruit stall, collapsing the table top around him. Covers and cloths ripped off their fastenings, bags of potatoes tore open and their contents fired off like mini cannonballs.

He heard angry curses and warnings and smiled as the mash of fruit and veg covered and obscured the view ahead of him. Then there was a flash of orange and the debris lit up as bright as the sun. He had to cover his face as a wall of fire devoured everything that entered it.

"Oh fuck."

Out of nowhere, Harry appeared and grabbed Sticks.

"We've got to move, split up and head for the mills."

Dave nodded and ran for the steps as Harry took Sticks behind the stalls and underneath the overpass.

At the top of the steps, he could see Gaz on the other side of the road, disappearing down some stairs opposite towards the huge red brick buildings dominating the skyline. Without waiting for a gap, Dave ran straight across the six lanes of traffic, creating a blast of air either side to protect him. A white van braked hard, beeping. Then it leapt like a startled horse into the air as the gust caught it, before gravity brought it back down with a thud. He could hear cars hitting each other behind him as he jumped over the wall of the steps, fell twelve feet down and landed gently with a cushion of air underneath.

The old mills were condemned and boarded up. They were due for demolition as they didn't fit the "regeneration" theme of the city. The sharp broken windows revealed darkness within. Perfect, thought Dave.

A tight gust blew in the doors and he was soon losing himself in the dank corridors and rooms. Rotting, snapping detritus on the floor gave away his location so he took to slower and quieter steps instead. The quiet seemed as intense as the fight he had just survived. He imagined he could hear everything for miles. What he did hear was Gaz scurrying across the floors above him.

Once they got through here and came out the other side they would lose those bastards in the alleyways of Old Town and hunker down at one of Big Mal's safe houses. The man was going to be so insane about this that Dave was hoping he wouldn't have to meet him face to face to give him the details.

He passed by an old mattress leaning on the wall, green with mould and piss and went through a doorway into a huge empty room. It was the height of four storeys inside the building and was lined with walkways attached to the walls. Several large rectangular pits were punched out of the floor. The place had been stripped bare. Large windows took up the ground floor walls. On three sides they were covered in rotting panels of wood. The fourth side was open and reflected light was seeping in through the many gaps in the glass and frames.

Dave headed for a thin gap of light on that wall, a narrow doorway at the far end. The doors were heavy and rusted in a slightly open position. He pulled himself through into a small courtyard. There was a thin tree growing out of a large crack in the concrete ground and moss clung to every surface.

He heard scuffing steps and a panicking voice above him. He turned round to see a shadow skimming the ledge of the roof of the building and followed it down a passage that led off the courtyard, down some steps into a low alleyway. It stank of damp down here and rank water pooled against the walls.

Dave heard Gaz sobbing above him.

"Gaz?" He tried to whisper loudly.

"Gaz?" He tried louder and his pal's face peered over the edge.

"Dave! I'm fucking stuck!"

"Fucking quiet! You need to get down, the flyer will spot you up there. Come on, jump. I've got you mate."

Gaz stepped forward.

"I... can't mate. Shit, they're gonna kill us!"

"Fuckin'... just... jump! Jump dickhead!"

"Uuuh, it's too high Dave..."

***

Gaz turns round. He must have heard something.

"Gaz?"

Dave can hear his pal mumbling, muttering, but can't make it out.

"Jump!"

There's a tiny scream as the sliver of grey sky between the buildings turns a fierce white.

"Gaz?" he whispers as flakes of ash gently twirl down around him.

"Found you."

Whipping round he sees a small girl in a reflective gold and silver costume standing next to him. She's wearing a pair of wide safety goggles that cover both eyes and a gold cap with the sides cut out to let her hair fall freely.

"You fucking..."

Dave goes to blast her but she is suddenly gone again in a blur.

"Jesus Christ guys, what are you doing?" says another voice.

"Found them!" he hears the girl shout from somewhere else.

Dave runs.

He finds an open door into the next building and barrels through a series of small empty rooms, their walls hacked apart. He can hear bursts of energy going off nearby. One lands nearby and blows through the wall into the room behind him.

He can hear screaming. It's Sticks. He can't help himself and runs to help his mate. Up a staircase and above him somewhere.

As he flings open the door to the next floor, he primes a blast of air just in case. It's quiet again though.

Then a ceiling collapses in front of him and smashes on the floor. Sticks is on top of the pile of rubble, bleeding and broken.

"He's all yours," says a voice.

"Fucking hit me in the face will you? Fucking hit me!"

A shard of electricity comes from the gap above and hits Sticks in the face so hard he is pushed back across the floor, striking the wall.

Dave should run. Instead he creates a vertical blast of air that rips straight up through the ceiling and out the roof. Then he runs. Back down the stairs, more rooms. Where is he? Is he nearly at the other side? Blackstock Road must be near. Just need to find another door.

He almost falls into a dark room. It has smaller windows high up the wall. They aren't boarded up but have bars over them. He jumps up, grabbing the bars to hold himself there and looks out. Another courtyard. He must have been running along the whole site instead of through it.

"Shit!"

He drops to the floor and turns to leave when he hears footsteps outside. As the door opens he prepares a blast.

"Dave, what the fuck you doing here? We need to head for the Old Town side."

It's Harry.

"Where the hell have you been? The others are dead."

"I know, they're fucking monsters these guys. Come on, I think I know the way out of..."

His next word turns into a scream as he is engulfed in flames that explode through the doorway behind him.

Dave falls back and lands hard on the dirty, wet floor. As he watches his friend stumble about on fire he slowly pushes himself back, dragging wet muck with him. Harry is still screaming as he falls onto his face. Dave presses himself against the wall under the tiny windows. Harry coughs, gargles, tries to lift himself up but flops back down and stops moving. As the flames sizzle against the damp mould on the floor they come into the room. Six figures, all in costume, stand in a line behind Harry's spitting corpse, and stare at him. Dave is in awe, he's terrified, he's OK with this, all at the same time.

"That's good, keep him docile so he doesn't throw another fucking tornado at us."

"Little runt nearly killed us."

"Yes, he's a feisty one isn't he?"

"Glad we got the other one, nearly took my fucking eye out back there!"

A seventh figure in costume appears at the doorway.

"Oh God. Guys, this is... what the heck? We can't do this..."

"Roadblock, we are trying to track down one of the biggest, most vile drug dealers in the city. Remember those dead girls in the canal? Those kids knifed by the railway? That reporter found dead in her burnt out flat? These aren't nice people, and you don't find scum like this by being nice."

"But these guys are just runners, don't blame them for the shit their boss does!"

"They have a choice! They could go to school, get a fucking job, but instead they work for him. That makes them just as bad. In any case they attacked us first."

"What?"

"Yep, I saw them – threw a bunch of cars at us in a public car park."

"Only after..."

"Not to mention endangering dozens of lives by ripping apart a market."

"And that shit who did some sort of energy punch on me."

"And him."

"Not to mention *this* one attacked me..."

The tall man in the white and blue all-in-one costume, the flyer, steps forward.

"His blasts can get through my pulse shield. Interesting. Yes, we can't let that exist, but not before we've found out what we need to know."

He kneels down in front of Dave. Dave's tongue starts buzzing with a strange taste.

"You my windy friend are going to tell us where Big Mal is. And even if you don't know exactly where he is you are going to tell us the location of every crack house, every prostitute lock-up, the make and registration of every car he owns, and you are going to tell us this willingly, otherwise you'll end up like all your crispy, crushed and disintegrated friends."

"Jesus, Pulse, this is wrong!"

"Then fuck off and let us do our job!"

The man at the door hovers for a moment before cursing and leaving the room. The flyer looks deep into Dave's eyes and he has the oddest feeling of someone experiencing his life with him. The man smiles and whispers:

"There we are. That's all I wanted really. I could have got this out of your dim skull from miles away to be honest, but well, what fun would that have been?"

Dave struggles to hang on to a single thought long enough to do anything and can only manage to come up with, "Fuck! You! Shit!"

All six Heroes burst into laughter at the same time. The flyer walks to the door behind them.

"Well he's not going to tell us anything willingly. Make sure you get it out of him will you guys? Try not to be too messy."

Dave watches in confusion as the five remaining Heroes approach him.

"OK, so who wants to go first?"

Dave screams.

CHAPTER 32
SUNDAY 16TH SEPTEMBER 2012

Martin screamed.

At least he thought he did, but no sound came out. Instead he felt an intense cold slip into his lungs, down through his gut and into his pelvis, all of which seemed to be shrinking back into his spine. He was falling fast, but also rising, also slipping forwards, back and all versions of sideways he could imagine as the strongest waves of wind pulled at him. He could only keep his eyes half open and through the thin slits he could see strange geometric ghost shapes flashing by against a dark maroon backdrop. Or it was purple, or dark green, or jet black? It either kept changing or his brain couldn't work it out. Then there was a sonic boom of a noise as his body expanded back into shape. There was ground under his feet and a tree in his face. Hayley unwrapped herself from him and stepped back.

"See, that wasn't so bad?"

Then he vomited. He clung to the tree trunk and wretched in painful spasms as his burger and chips returned to the world. With each squeeze he could feel his raw ribs sharpening themselves against the inside of his skin. He was gasping air in between throes as the dizziness started. He hung on for dear life as his inner ear slowly learned how to function again. More vomiting. Bile too. He was on his knees now, one arm wrapped round his bark friend, staring at the dark fronds of grass soaking their night damp wetness through his jeans. His breathing became less desperate as the waves of queasiness subsided. He looked up and could see a crushed pink granite driveway through the trees. It was lit up by two rows of lights either side and led up to a large country house illuminated pale orange against the sky. This must be Charles's. A couple of windows were lit up and there was a small light on by the door, but it otherwise seemed quiet.

There was an amazing chill wind against his face. It seemed to quell his guts and he pulled himself up unsteadily. Hayley was looking at him thoughtfully.

"Hmm, you have it quite bad. You'll probably get the diarrhoea too."

"Great."

"Sorry. Anyway, see you tomorrow. Good luck with him," she thumbed towards the house.

"Thanks Hayley. I really appreciate your help you know."

He hadn't thought her smile could get any bigger.

"Anything you need boss!"

She jumped away quietly. The sonic boom he heard when he arrived must have been in his head.

He stepped out from the trees, shaking out his remaining dizziness and crunched his way up the drive. It expanded into a large circular area in front of the main house. A three-door garage sat off to one side.

Immaculately trimmed bushes and two large stone bird baths lined the grass opposite the front door and the garden and trees behind them stretched back past Martin into darkness. Only the silhouette of a pair of dark gates at the road could be seen down there.

The house itself was twice as big as the block of apartments where he had been living. Red brick, two floors, two wings extending either side of a jet black doorway recessed in a white porch with cream marble pillars. It was lit from outside by several large rectangular uplighters hidden behind what he could just make out as a long series of flowerbeds below the windows. As he stepped up to the door a tiny camera above the lintel beeped and an electronic voice spoke.

"Welcome to Heathcote House, Mr Heathcote will be with you shortly."

There was a distorted clattering noise and then a human voice.

"Martin, is that you? Oh yes..."

The magnetic lock buzzed and clicked and the automatic doors opened inwards to reveal Charles standing in the hallway. He was alarmingly casually dressed, wearing designer jeans, a black polo neck jumper and a pair of beige moccasins. Martin had never seen him wearing jeans, it was always trousers, chinos. It was strange that this was the biggest shock he'd had tonight.

"Martin, my dear friend... good God! I'd hate to see the other guy... assuming he's still alive?"

He opened his arms out and, when Martin didn't move, slapped them down on his thighs.

"Come in, come in to my humble abode."

Martin stepped across the threshold and was hit by a scent wall of wood polish and lavender. The entrance hallway had a cream marble floor that stretched about fifteen feet ahead until it reached the bottom of a wide T-shaped staircase that led up to the U-shaped balcony above. The walls had dark wood panelling up to a high roof with large wooden beams and a large brass and frosted glass chandelier. Several doors lead off to various corridors and rooms. The only one open was to his right, and he spotted some nice furniture bathed in the fidgeting orange reflections of a fireplace that was out of sight.

This entrance hallway would probably have covered the floor plan of his entire flat. It was actually quite understated despite being exceptionally grand; tasteful, like something you'd see on TV, not garish as he had expected. However, the one thing that caught his eye was straight ahead at the top of the staircase where it split. A large painting of Charles in a dark suit gazed down over all who entered. Charles followed his line of sight and laughed, shaking his head.

"Well, yes, please forgive me one moment of hubris. I had that commissioned when I got my contract with BSkyB four years ago. It *is* quite dominating isn't it? I'm not sure it suits the place but can't quite bring myself to get rid of it."

Martin's stomach churned audibly as he felt nauseous again. The overpowering scent of flowers wasn't helping.

"I am of course assuming you got the message about your belongings from Maria? Damn hard to get hold of you without a mobile."

"I don't see the point in them."

"Don't see the point?" Charles looked startled "Mine is my lifeline! I couldn't live without it I have so many things happening simultaneously. So much to keep track of. Although…"

He looked Martin up and down as a look of pity crossed his face.

"Yes, I suppose that makes sense. Well there *is* a point now, here..."

Charles pulled out a black phone from his back pocket and handed it to Martin. It was disconcertingly warm.

"It's all set up with a couple of hundred in credit and the number has been passed around to everyone so we can get in touch with you."

"Oh. Perfect."

Martin stared at his reflection in the black mirror. Might as well be a chunk of rock for all he knew how to operate it.

"You know I didn't actually expect you to be at home. I got some code or other from Maria and was just going to let myself in…"

"Oh I wasn't going to let you arrive to an empty house, no matter how long I had to wait in the end…" He tailed off slightly but Martin made no move to apologise. "What sort of host would that make me? All your things arrived earlier by the way."

Charles started walking towards the staircase and Martin followed as the front doors closed and clicked shut behind him.

"Maria arranged the movers while she was at the police station. They dropped what there was of it in the middle of the room I've cleared for you. Of course it's going to need some proper sorting out before you can comfortably call it 'home' for now, but you can do that in your own time."

They climbed the stairs and went left, Martin staring into the eyes of the painting as he passed.

"How did you... get past the gate by the way? I have some quite expensive security here."

"Jumped the wall."

In his battered state? Not the best cover. Charles looked back at him, staring at the bruised eye and red swelling blotches on his face.

"Of course."

The balcony was carpeted in a deep maroon and brown pattern. Soft and expensive. There were glass cabinets up against the walls here, filled with medals and awards. Some of them Martin recognised at a glance, the Freedom of the City medallion was one. He had gotten one too although he wasn't sure where it was any more. Others seemed to be from later on, media awards. Was that a BAFTA?

The long balcony overlooking the doorway had larger cabinets in it. Although he didn't get a good look, he spotted a series of mannequins wearing several variations of Charles's old team uniform and some pieces of equipment that looked familiar.

They walked straight ahead at the top of the steps down a corridor lined with photographs. Dozens of photographs. Martin tried to look at as many as he could until he got dizzy from cricking his neck from side to side. They were all of The Pulse in various incarnations over the years. Even from before Charles joined. Those nearest the balcony were magazine photographs in 1993, shot after they helped stop the psychic riot. Martin winced at seeing his younger self smiling awkwardly. As he carried on it felt as if the corridor was narrowing on him as he was taken back in time. Dramatic shots of them taking down Patient 23 on Hammer Bridge, another bunch of promo shots for a kids' Hero magazine, some individual photos of their old late eighties costumes which looked embarrassingly dated today, and all the way back to the original line-up and hairdos from 1986.

Charles was marching forwards, ignoring them. They were decoration to him probably, barely looked at now. To Martin this was like being submerged in fear. There was a shot of Barry as Vigilance shaking hands with Jack, the rest of them in the background. Here was a glossy group shot for the press after ridding the city of Big Mal. Martin could feel his body shivering from the memories.

Charles suddenly broke to the right and disappeared into a room. Martin gladly followed him. There was all his stuff. One large taped up box marked "Fellowes Removals and Storage". Smaller cardboard boxes with cut out handles had blue stickers saying "Property of Element City Police Department" with "Released" stamped over them in black ink. Some were closed, others had been opened, presumably by Charles, and he saw they were stuffed with random jumbles of items. Clothing was in large clear plastic bags on the floor and the bed. There wasn't that much else. A lot of furniture had been destroyed during the fight but he recognised the sideboard from his bedroom, sitting next to a large wardrobe and bookcase that already belonged in the room. Opposite was a large white dressing table with a huge mirror. The walls had expensive looking cream and light green stripe wallpaper with gold leaf floral patterns. A door led off to what he could see was a grey marble tiled en suite.

"Like I said, you'll need to sort it out yourself. I made a start, but I don't know where you'll want everything to go, so I left the rest. Now, you can stay here for as long as you need and my whole house is yours. I only ask you keep out of my bedroom and the study. This is the largest guest room, mine and Mawar's room is at the other side of the house. In case you're wondering, she had to go back to Malaysia to look after her sick grandparents, so you're free to rattle around in here during the day without disturbing anyone."

"Oh, I'm sorry to hear that about that, my best wishes to them. Look, thanks Charles, I... really do appreciate this you know."

He grinned.

"Well, couldn't have you staying in amongst all those sweaty business travellers and cheap family holidaymakers could we? You deserve better than that, you're one of us after all."

Martin wondered when that started being true again.

"Do check that everything is here though. I believe the police and those damned PCA people are holding some items still. For 'processing', whatever that means. I hope it's nothing sensitive to you. Or us."

He looked at Martin.

"I hope everything that needs to be safe, *is* safe, shall we say. Don't want the Pokes poking around in our private matters and..."

"It's safe," sighed Martin.

He walked over to the nearest open box. Bathroom stuff.

"You do know what I am talking about don't you."

"Yes. It's safe."

"So the police don't have it?"

"No."

He wasn't entirely sure to be honest, he would have to look through the boxes. But he couldn't be bothered with that right now, or having to deal with a Charles hissy fit if he told the truth.

"The fewer people who know where it is the better. And right now the only person who knows where it is, is me," he turned to look at Charles "and that is the way it shall stay."

"Martin, I have multiple contacts in the Hero world. I know people who can secure it *very* safely indeed, or even destroy it completely if need be, reduce it to atoms."

"I don't think that will be nec..."

"Martin! Somebody killed Vincent for it. The same person attacked you because they assumed you had it. You're safe here now, this whole building is rigged with defence mechanisms and cameras. Look, this button," he moved over and pointed to a recessed silver circle underneath a wall light "turns this into a safe room if you hold it for three seconds, but..."

He held up a finger and walked towards Martin again.

"...who else is he going to go after if he can't get to you? Who else does he think will have what he wants? Don't forget you're the only one of us that could survive a beating like that should he get too close. If you tell me where it is, I can have it secured or destroyed within hours, get the word out under the radar and this whole disastrous episode will be over. Might even catch the bastard into the bargain."

Martin felt weary. His body was telling him that he had done too much today, his stomach was still confused about where it was and he had just survived the corridor of buried memories. He didn't need this right now.

"I'm guessing Maria told you I had them."

Charles nodded. "We all keep in touch."

"So I gather. Look, Vincent entrusted me with his memoirs. Only me. They are to be handled by nobody else. I'm going to sort this out for him, because he wanted me to. It was in his bloody will, it's my responsibility."

Charles did his nonchalant cat movement again, peering sideways at him.

"Of course. No, of course. It's only right that his best friend should shoulder his burden. But all I'm saying is you're not out in the cold. The team are here should you need us and we're all willing to help, to do what we can. He was one of us and we are all responsible for finding out who took his life. After all, the team always sticks together."

They stood looking at each other for a while until Martin started to feel his knees give way.

"I need to..." he motioned towards the bed.

"Of course!" Charles suddenly straightened up and smiled. "My apologies dear friend, you need time alone to recover from your injuries and sort your possessions out. I shall take my leave of you."

He headed towards the door.

"You have your phone by the way?"

Martin held up the mobile and waved it.

"Good, good. I'm actually heading back down to London now. I'm staying at the Dorchester if you can't get me by my mobile, although you will, obviously. I only came up to ensure the movers didn't steal or damage anything and that you got here safely. I have a week of meetings and filming ahead of me so," he spread his arms wide "avail yourself of my hospitality. My house is yours, my food is yours, my cars are yours… except the ones in the second garage, they are rare collectibles."

His eyes narrowed slightly.

"Jumped the wall..."

Martin's stomach churned again.

"Yep."

"Fucking 'Hero-proof' security my arse eh?" He shrugged and left the room laughing to himself.

Martin closed the door. He had a look inside the en suite. Very modern with a boiling hot towel rail. After the pantomime this morning he didn't feel like another shower. He took his jacket off, dropped it on top of the pile of clothes bags, kicked his shoes off under the bed, cursing when one tumbled too far, and carefully lay himself down.

He stared at the mobile for a while, turning it over in his hands until he found what he guessed was the power button. The screen lit up brightly with a clock and something that looked like a sliding power switch.

Was that the time? Christ. He put the phone down on the bedside cabinet and vaguely considered looking for something to eat in the kitchen. Within moments he was asleep.

CHAPTER 33
FRIDAY 16TH JULY 1993

Big Mal's HQ was a few blocks away from the old red brick mills. He had taken over a square, 1970s derelict office building some years ago. It was four floors tall and sat awkwardly behind a row of flats above some small, local shops.

The area is notorious for drugs and prostitution, yet low in violent crime. Big Mal controls what happens here, and what happens here only happens because Big Mal wants it to.

Jack had decided to wait before taking them on. Give them time to stew, get worried, call in backup and fortify the place.

"Wait until they are all in one place. More scum to take down in one hit!" he had said.

I'm still reeling from the other day. I haven't slept yet and have been trying to distract my mind through coffee and exercise, but even the gym gave me no respite.

The plan for that day had been for Maria to calm and befriend them in the car park and then Vincent would get the info we needed. That had been the plan. I suspected things weren't going to follow that plan when we all piled in the van without Vincent. When I asked where he was, I was told he wasn't feeling well and not to worry, we would improvise. That we did, by murdering eight young lads. We could have neutralised them easily. Those guys were young, inexperienced and spooked. Instead I was left chasing after the team in panic as they churned their way through bodies like a runaway combine harvester.

I know the guys well enough to know how any of them would react to different situations and what I would be expected to do next. We are a good team together. This though, this was different. I had no idea what was going to happen next. There was no communication and they acted like they had an agenda I was unaware of. I'm worried about them. I read something about soldiers suffering from post-traumatic stress disorder when they return from war. What they had experienced was too much for their brains to process and it kept being triggered, kept coming back to them in flashbacks. It changed them. Was this happening to the others? They had turned callous, unconcerned about collateral damage in their pursuit of Big Mal. Jack hadn't got The Controller but he was damn sure he would get this guy, and everyone seemed to be following suit. Whatever it took.

But that couldn't be right. Not all of them, exactly the same? Maria would never have agreed to this level of violence yet she is deliberately confusing and angering people. Inna has lost her self-control, using her powers directly against people and with such strength too. Mitchell and Andrea have turned into a cruel duo, openly using their powers to cause pain. Charles is nonchalantly setting people on fire as if flicking open a cigarette lighter. And Jack... to be honest he hasn't changed much. He has always had the least amount of empathy and restraint when it comes to his powers and his goals, but now he seems to be encouraging the team to follow his lead.

No. This couldn't be PTSD, not affecting all of them like this. This has to be something else. As I stand here, surrounded by rubble and bodies there is only one possible explanation, and it chills me.

***

I was still reeling from the other day when, this morning, Jack instructed us all to suit up and hit the van, they were going for Big Mal. Vincent (who wasn't going to be with us again) had detected that the man himself and all his lieutenants were at the office block having some big meeting.

In the van I learned the plan of attack. We would pair off and take all the entrances including the roof and work our way through the building, subduing anyone who went for us. The gang would be trapped inside and we would force them onto the middle floor and hold them there until they surrendered themselves to the police.

I was reassured. The other day was just a blip, a moment of madness where they let out the wretched anger they had bottled in for weeks. This operation was going to be done properly. I even let myself smile. This was the old team, back together. We were in good spirits in the van, adjusting our costumes, following our usual routines, chatting normally. Someone had even fixed whatever it was that had been squeaking for months.

The drone had been hovering over the building for about twenty minutes before we got there and had identified lookouts in the surrounding streets and on the roof. As we parked up a couple of blocks away Maria sent them to sleep. Using the alleyways and dim light of dawn as cover, we took up our positions and waited for the radio signal.

The signal was given. We breached and went in. Mitchell and me tag teamed our way along the ground floor, Inna and Andrea were parallel to us on the other side of the building. We kept both the exits covered behind us and forced the gang up the stairs. After the element of surprise wore off, bullets started pinging around like balls in a tombola. I kept Mitchell covered and Inna vaporised them mid-air before they reached Maria. We could hear Jack's pulse blasts shaking the building from above us.

The gang was shouting to each other chaotically as they went up to the second floor. This was where we met Big Mal's powered bodyguard, a tall black guy called Ripper, who turned his skin to metal on sight. He was mine. As the others fought around us we traded blows. I could instantly tell I was up against a fighter who knew some good moves and we were evenly matched. Fortunately it was only his skin he could change to metal. My dense body could take the repeated punishment, but after five minutes I could tell he was hurting inside and it wasn't long before he collapsed to the ground, done.

The remainder of the gang, including Big Mal, were now trapped on the third floor. We surrounded the centre of the building, two offices and a corridor around a large meeting room. We took shelter as bullets tore through old walls and windows until we heard a loud voice shouting. The shooting stopped. Big Mal and Jack traded insults. All his powered bodyguards were down. He had sent the rest upstairs and Jack had taken care of them. Despite this he wasn't going to come out for anyone.

"Now we wait for the police I guess, unless you fancy putting them to sleep Maria?" I said.

Maria looked at me and smiled.

"I don't think that's the kind of language these people understand," she replied.

"Sorry?"

The answer to that question came in the form of Jack. A pale blue wall of pulse energy surrounded the offices. There was gunfire as some people panicked and shot at it before Big Mal got them to stop again. He started shouting that he wasn't going to be intimidated, he was untouchable, we would have to kill him. Jack laughed loudly then said something I couldn't quite make out. There was a loud rumbling now. Dust and ceiling tiles fell down as a massive cracking noise split the air.

I shouted out to ask what he was doing but could hardly hear myself. I took a couple of steps back and gasped as the corridor ripped in a giant circle around the meeting rooms. It twisted round one way, shrieking reinforcing bars banging as they snapped, then the other, grinding concrete pillars apart. Then the third floor slipped down past my eyes, the fourth floor and roof after it, as the building was cored open. I could hear the screams of those trapped in the room as they fell. Then the rubble hit the ground floor, exploding out through the windows, and they went silent. In the middle of this central hole floated Big Mal in a pulse ball. He was staring down at the carnage below him muttering "You're fucking mad, what have you fucking done?"

"Not so big when you're all on your own are you... Mal?"

Big Mal turned to Jack and let forth a stream of obscenities, cut short only when Jack seemed to get bored and nodded to Maria to send him to sleep. He slid down and curled up in the bottom of the sphere, snoring loudly.

I desperately tried to ask why she couldn't have done that with everyone else, but they all walked past me.

Jack tapped me on the shoulder. "These old seventies blocks, prefab shit. Structurally unsafe I hear."

I could hear cries and groans coming from the hole and I pushed past my teammates to get down there.

The police arrived as I was still lifting chunks of concrete and plaster to reach the injured. Jack handed over Big Mal and, with Maria's help, explained to the detective what had happened. I worked with the fire brigade and medics to free people. Jack said I would stay on the scene to help them and they got in the van and drove off.

It was hours before I was satisfied I had gotten everyone out that was still alive. I got handshakes from the firemen as they emptied the building, parts of which were still falling in. "Structurally unsafe" was the phrase I heard on all the lips around me, already ingrained into their consciousness and no doubt already being written into the official report.

***

As I stand in the rubble, surrounded by bodies, I realise this isn't PTSD. This isn't any temporary madness or laser focused desire to take down a drug gang at all costs. The team has been taken. The whole team has been taken by The Controller and he is going to make them do whatever he wants.

I feel a sudden pain in my chest. Concentrated panic. I look down at my scuffed, concrete grey hands and I realise I have no idea what to do.

CHAPTER 34
MONDAY 17TH SEPTEMBER 2012

Martin awoke with another mild panic like the day before. Two strange beds in as many mornings. It was early, about half eight. He had slept fitfully and was heavy eyed and aching. He was also still dressed in yesterday's clothes, which he only realised when he saw himself in the en suite mirror. His panda eyes were completely formed now and he watched himself lick the swollen side of his lips. Shiny, warm and slightly tender. His face wasn't as puffy as yesterday though and the general redness had faded. So, small mercies he guessed.

Taking his clothes off was just as bad as the day before. His burnt skin had crusted over in a thin toffee apple like layer that crinkled and split as he contorted himself free of his top. Something else he hadn't felt for a while, an itch over the burn. With his chest exposed he went to put on his cream then cursed, realising it was still at the motel. He should have used it last night too he thought, as he poked at his skin, making it crackle like sugar icing on cling film. How long would it take to heal properly now? He never was a very good patient.

He had to rip open three plastic bags of clothes before he found one with a vest in it. A plain blue shirt went over the top. Then his comfy jeans went on. They were a bit creased but they would do.

As he crushed the empty plastic bags into a ball he glanced at the small pile of boxes at the foot of the bed. That was it then. All that was left of his his old life. He felt lighter. He peeled one strand of tape off the topmost large box and flipped one side of the lid open. He had expected to find everything intact, forgetting that only his clothes had been safe inside the bedroom. Instead he found little shreds of his life. The battered picture frame fell apart as he picked it up, the perspex sliding out and disappearing inside the box with a dull plunk. He took out his family picture, the Polaroid was curled from the heat and one corner of the film had changed colour, radiating out a mixture of beiges and dark browns towards the middle like a dirty rainbow. The outer edge obliterated his mother's face and most of him cradled in her arms.

He looked around and spotted a silver framed picture of generic flowers on the bookcase. He swapped out the pictures. The Polaroid looked odd, floating in the middle of the glass, slightly askew, but he was just glad it still existed.

He pulled his three books from the same box. They had fared worse than the picture and were flash burnt and shredded. Amusingly, Charles's autobiography was the most fire damaged and Martin didn't hesitate to drop it in the bin. He wasn't too worried about his book on sixties Heroes, he could always get a new copy, but it joined the other book in the bin with some regret. The book from his mother was the most intact. The hard cover had taken the brunt of the heat and only the exposed page edges had browned. He was glad he still had that little something of hers that kept him calm, and he put it on the bookcase with the picture.

A phone ringing made him spin round. It was loud, like one of the really old turn dial models. The mobile on the bedside cabinet had lit up like a spotlight and was busily vibrating itself towards the edge. Martin picked it up gingerly, worried he might not be able to work it. Luckily there was an obvious green phone symbol at the bottom of the screen. He tapped it and said hello. A woman answered.

Charles had been trying to get a meeting with Jack for years with no luck, so Martin was more than surprised to be speaking to Lucy, Jack's secretary, calling to say that Mr Pullman had a free period between meetings from twelve twenty five to twelve forty today, and he would look forward to seeing him then. He had to be there fifteen minutes beforehand to get registered for a visitor's pass and if the meeting overran "which was very likely" she said, slightly too eagerly Martin felt, it would have to be reconvened. The phone beeped the end of the call and Martin slipped it into his pocket.

He had a busy day ahead. First back to the motel to grab what little he had left there and check out. Then he had to track down Mitchell from Maria's napkin note, which was thankfully still legible despite him sleeping on it all night. Most importantly he was going to meet Jack, the man who killed Vincent and almost killed him. He was going to find out why and avenge his friend's death in whatever way he could.

He had a curious sense of purpose. The first he had felt in a long, long time. It felt good, if a little frightening, to be so sure of something in the middle of this chaos.

CHAPTER 35
SUNDAY 18TH JULY 1993

I am only sure of one thing in this chaos, he has to die.

I sit in the kitchen, at the long oblong table, hugging a fresh cup of coffee. I let the bitter aroma waft around my face and up my nostrils. I can only feel the barest of warmth on my palms, but the smell stings the back of my nose like I want it to.

I could have left the moment I realised what was happening. I should have left.

This atmosphere is so sickening I dread waking up each day to breathe it in. Every room, no matter how big, is now too small. The walls squeeze in, trying to push me out like a splinter stuck in a festering wound. The HQ, our building, has become poisoned from the inside and I just want to run, to escape and let the sickness run its course.

I would have to go back to my old neighbourhood. Sort myself out with a flat and then...

Nobody would believe me, and if they did it would ruin the team. And in any case, what could anyone else do?

I couldn't tell anyone what was happening. They had come up with perfectly plausible explanations for every event, done more public appearances in the last month than they had in the previous six. They were the darlings of the Hero world, the saviours of the city. They could do no wrong.

And what would happen if somebody did believe me, what could they do? Assault the HQ? The Controller would take them over and make them kill each other. If it became public knowledge it wouldn't matter, he was so powerful only the strongest psychics in the world coming together at the same time would have a chance at stopping him. That would mean conscripting some of the biggest superteams from around the world. And The Controller would fight them, with the team, with the police and any passing civilian. He would fight them all and relish every second. It would be war in the city. Who knows how many would die, and how many more Heroes he would take over. And then he would be unstoppable. No, I couldn't run. I couldn't live with myself if I left them here alone to be his puppets. I had to help them. I had to find The Controller and stop him. If only I could find him.

I know he's here. He would want to be close where he could see everything happening. I had spent my downtime between missions searching the building floor by floor. I had swept every storage cupboard and sleeping area, even breaking into the others' apartments to make sure, but I found no trace, no evidence of him. The only room I can't access is the lab, which has a very conspicuous new voice ID and iris scanner at its doorway. Through the translucent, toughened glass the nearby machinery and computer equipment look the same as always, but I can't see further in, it's just a dark mist. He has to be in there, sitting in the darkness surrounded by half finished gadgets and blinking lights, scanning the city around him, working out how next to move his chess pieces around the board.

I have to kill him. I have to kill a man to stop the deaths around me, to bring everyone back to their senses. It's the only logical option. The Controller has shown no compassion or understanding of what he is doing. He is a psychopath who uses his powers thoughtlessly to relieve his personal boredom. It's all a game. Nothing would ever convince him otherwise.

I have to kill him. But I have sworn never to kill, to never take a life, and I have kept true to that all through my time as a Hero. It has been incredibly difficult at times. Sometimes the person I fought was much more powerful than me. Striking the right balance, to take them down quickly but without killing them, was very tricky to judge. Sometimes they wanted to go down fighting and were willing to die in an attempt to stop me. And sometimes the people I came up against were so objectionable in personality or worldview it made me smile to think of a well timed blow to the head caving in their skull. But no, I have sworn to myself, like the old Heroes that believed in upholding justice, that those kinds of people will pay for what they do within their lifetimes. That means knocking them out or capturing them, rendering them safe for the police or Special Forces to take away.

The problem is you can't render a psychic safe. There is no material or drug that can stop their power stretching out from their minds if that is what they want to do. Even if you render them unconscious there have been instances of psychics reaching out from within their locked minds, most famously Mindbender, back in the seventies. That angry psychic, locked in a drug induced coma, had worked out what was going on and had used the patients and staff of an entire hospital as human shields against the police and Heroes who eventually managed to stop him for good. They did what they had to, and so must I. Yes, the only way to stop him is to kill him.

Of course I would have to take on the whole team first to get to him. And not only are they all powerful, they are all psychically linked to each other through him. Not to mention he has access to the building security systems from within the lab, which means every camera, door and lift lock in the place is under his control too. The only advantage I have is that he can't read my mind. Which might only give me a few minutes advantage, but it's something. Of course he won't hesitate to throw my teammates at me, even if it means to their deaths. That means having to hold back just enough so I don't kill or injure them, judging the balance of attack. Tricky.

I can't feel any heat from the coffee now and the smell has lost its potency. I take a sip and let the taste slip down my throat.

Warm.

It's now or never.

CHAPTER 36
MONDAY 17TH SEPTEMBER 2012

Davies' Self Defence Centre was on the second floor above a dance studio and a small supermarket in the Nellbourne area of the city. It was just before nine in the morning and the narrow street was busy with cars stuck behind slow buses. Around him hurried people hoping not to be late to work, school kids moseying along with sausage rolls and pasties in brown paper bags and elderly shoppers out to catch the Monday bargains in the charity shops.

Martin stood near the pavement edge, looking up at the windows. They were large square windows with metal frames and one was ajar. He looked back down at the battered white doorway, recessed with two small concrete steps leading up to it. It had recently been repainted white straight over the old paint and was scarred like a chickenpox face. The glass panel was mottled with metal wiring inside it.

He waited for a gap in the foot traffic, crossed the pavement and opened the door in one swift move. As he closed it behind him the bustle faded and he quickly relaxed. Strangely he hadn't noticed he was tense at all, it hadn't bothered him much. Perhaps because he wasn't dreading this meeting as much as the one with Jack.

There was a short entrance corridor that led straight up a flight of vinyl covered steps with metal strips along the edges. There were several cork boards covered with posters, flyers and private ads and, where there wasn't any more room on the boards, people had stuck them to the walls with tape and Blu-Tack.

As he went up the stairs he saw the walls had framed posters and photos of dance shows and pupils standing in rows, some with medals and certificates. They were all smiling faces of young girls with one or two older women, who he guessed were their teachers. He did spot a single boy looking glum in a couple of shots and smiled to himself.

He remembered a girl at school, his first crush, who used to go to ballet class in the local church hall. He had toyed with the idea of going to class with her but unfortunately the school P.E. teacher had spotted his unusual physical strength and enrolled him in the under-10s rugby team without even telling him. Of course, practice fell on the same day as her ballet lessons. He was devastated. Now, he couldn't even remember her name. Rebecca? Louisa? Something ending in "a" anyway.

On the first floor landing he passed a doorway leading into a large dance studio surrounded by mirrors. It was empty.

The second flight of stairs changed tone. Here were framed photos of boys and girls wearing martial arts outfits, holding medals and trophies. One caught his eye, a cut out page from the local newspaper dated 2005, a feature on the club with a photo. The only photo that had Mitchell in it. He was standing at the end of a row of four youngsters wearing a collection of their medals, trophies at their feet. A large woman stood at the other end of the row. From the subtitle he read she was the local councillor.

"Retired Hero defends city by teaching kids to defend themselves"

He could tell Mitchell looked uncomfortable to be in the shot. He had that tense distracted smile he used to have himself back in the day. The photos continued up to the top landing where they parted for a modestly sized blue sign with white lettering: "Davies' Self Defence Centre".

The door was open. It led right into a vinyl floored studio. There were a couple of wall height mirrors at the far end and two large kick bags hanging from the ceiling to his right. A small gust came through the opened window and the noise of the traffic returned. At the far end of the room there were three doors. One was obviously a small storage cupboard, the other probably a toilet. The third led into what looked like a small office with a light on inside.

Martin had walked halfway across the studio when Mitchell appeared in the office doorway and leant on the frame. Martin stopped and gave a slight smile.

Mitchell stared at him, running his eyes over his bruises and cuts.

"Hey," said Martin, trying to feel out the situation.

Mitchell looked at him wearily.

"You're out of shape. You here to sign up for some classes?"

Martin laughed.

"I hope that's not your sales pitch."

Mitchell grunted. Didn't smile. He pushed himself away from the door frame and went over to the closed window. Tugging on the metal handle he opened it. The sound of cars got louder.

He turned round, wiping dust off his hands, and stared at Martin again, expressionless.

"She said you'd be round, you know?"

"Erm, Maria I guess?"

"Who else?"

He walked over to the storage room door, opened it with a key, and went inside. Martin could hear scraping and rummaging.

This was more difficult than he had anticipated. Mitchell continued to move things around in there for an increasingly awkward length of time.

"Yeah, I've discovered she likes to keep in touch with everybody. She even gave me a mobile phone..." he took it out of his pocket and showed it to the open doorway "...first one I've ever had and no idea how it works. Don't tell her that, she'll probably get me lessons."

No response. Moments later Mitchell came back out of the room carrying an armful of plastic coated gym mats which he slapped down on the floor.

"Need a hand?" he stepped forward.

"I got it."

Martin stepped back. Mitchell went back inside the storeroom. Martin breathed deeply. Christ this was tough. This wasn't the cheery, upbeat kid he remembered. He had thought that being the youngest he would bounce back the best from what had happened. Maybe he had just caught him on a bad day.

"So... 'Davies' Self Defence Centre' eh? Been going a good few years from the looks of all those photos. It's a good thing you're doing here."

Rummage. Bump.

"Was this the first thing you went into after we split?"

"No," said the doorway.

Mitchell came out with another, bigger armful of mats, which he splat on top of the others. He gave a big sigh and looked at the pile, hands on his waist.

"After registration, I couldn't use my powers any more, you know? Did all sorts of shit. Would have joined the RAF like my brother but not allowed. Trained as an electrician – irony, yeah – and did that for a bit. Couldn't settle. Removals. Bit of labouring for my uncle. All sorts, you know?"

He turned to face Martin, wringing his wrists, tight forearm muscles twitching.

"Then, you probably know, I got busted for shocking some guys who tried to jump me and my girlfriend at the time."

"No, I didn't hear about that."

Mitchell looked surprised, then shrugged.

"Well, got two years in the Scarry..."

"They sent you to Scarrington? Maria did mention you spent some time in prison but... Jesus."

"Yeah."

Scarrington had been a maximum security prison for powered offenders. It had powered prison officers and twelve inch thick steel walled isolation rooms for the more excitable inmates. It was the testing ground for the first generation power dampening drugs. You typically only went in there if you killed someone or really went to town with your abilities in public. Martin had heard of some harsh sentences for Heroes in the years after registration, a show of intent if you will. He guessed Mitchell had got on the wrong end of that era.

Mitchell turned to the office doorway and hovered for a moment.

"Survived that by learning self-defence. Came out and did it proper. Got my training certificates and..."

He lifted his hands up.

"Shit. You've come through a lot."

Mitchell studied him sideways.

"You too by the looks of it."

"Hmm? Oh this?" Martin prodded his puffy eyes. "Should have seen the other guy, you know? And my apartment."

Mitchell just nodded, then went into the office out of sight.

Martin hesitated to go in after him.

Damn it! This should have been easy, but it was harder than with Maria. In the end he made himself almost fall forwards onto his foot to get him moving to the office.

It was a small rectangular room with an old desk pushed up against the wall, a shelf above it filled with large box files. Opposite was a narrow kitchen surface with a sink and two cupboards above and below. A coffee machine was slowly bubbling in the corner, a half drunk cup sat on the desk on top of several scattershot piles of papers: sports page clippings, invoices, half made flyers. The walls were just as chaotic: year planners, charts, certificates, pinned up invoices and cheques, posters, more photos of smiling kids in outfits, a calendar buried in large marker pen scribbles. There were some older floor mats rolled up against the wall nearest him, along with some long thick bamboo poles and a small broken punch bag.

Mitchell picked up the cup and took a long gulp until it was empty.

"Martial arts and coffee, the only way I get my buzz now, you know?"

He picked up a bundle of wooden poles wrapped in insulating foam and walked out of the office as Martin stepped aside.

"No no, you managed to find something constructive to do. That's good. That's really good. I'm just a night guard, only people I have to worry about are the mannequins in the..."

"Why are you here man?"

355

Mitchell dropped the poles at the bottom of the wall opposite the windows. He was shaking his head as he went back to the pile of mats and started to drop them out on the floor in a line.

Martin looked down at his hands and was suddenly taken aback at how bruised they were. Three fingers on his left hand were swollen and skin was flaking off across his palms and wrists. Must have been the light in here that made them look so bad.

Mitchell carried on, ignoring him. He moved on to a second line of mats, stopped, counted out the back line twice until he seemed happy, then dropped another mat lining it up with the gap between the two behind it. He finished the line and went along both of them, kicking the odd corner so they were lined up square.

He looked at Martin. "I said why the fuck are you here man? I haven't seen you in, what...?"

"Eighteen years."

Mitchell shook his head again.

"Eighteen fucking years man. And here you are, just... fucking... here."

"Yeah it's... been a long time when you think about it. I've been finding the memories come flooding back though, seeing everyone again."

"Look, Maria said you'd be coming over, you know? The fuck why?" Mitchell shrugged.

"Vincent... he..."

"Was fucking ripped open, yeah?"

"Yep."

"So... you think I did it? That why you're here?"

"No, what? No, he said I had to visit everyone in the team."

356

"Because one of us killed him, and you need to figure out who before the Pokes do because the dick went and wrote some... diary telling everything about what happened and we don't want them to get it. Cover it?"

"I, yep I... guess that covers it."

"OK."

Mitchell walked around the nearest mat, wringing his wrists.

"Well I didn't kill him and I don't have his diary or know what the password is. That everything you needed?"

"Look Mitchell, I never said you killed him, I'm just trying to do right by Vincent. This was his last request to me."

"Ah 'course. Why else would you be here. Why else?"

Mitchell flung his arms out then slapped them back down on his thighs. He rolled his eyes, bit his lower lip and looked out the window, head wobbling.

Martin wanted to tell him he hadn't been avoiding him, that he'd hidden away from everyone, that he could barely look at *himself* in the mirror for years let alone face any of them. But none of it came out.

"Well sorry Martin, this was another one you were too late to save. Ain't nothing you can do for a dead guy now."

That one took the wind out of his lungs and Martin swayed on his heels as Mitchell walked past him, muttering under his breath, and went back into the office.

He couldn't leave it like this. He had to set things straight. He got on with the lad back when they were in the team, looked after him, felt responsible for him. How could he have not known he went to prison? All this time.

"Look..." he went back to the office, stepping inside this time. Mitchell had clicked a button on the coffee maker.

"Someone dangerous is out to get us because they want Vincent's memoirs, his... diary. It *could* be one of us, I don't know. They killed Vincent. They went after me..."

He pointed to his face. Mitchell was leaning on the tabletop, looking back over his shoulder at him.

"I don't know who they are going to come after next. It could be any one of us. I got lucky, *really* lucky. The next person might not be."

"Oh yeah."

Mitchell nodded deeply, like he was appreciating the words of a wise man.

"So you're here to save me, yeah? Here to protect me from whoever wants to let the past lie. Well *I* want to let the past lie, you know? I've spent years, YEARS picking myself up from different fucking gutters, and after all that time this is all I have. This place. Oh yeah, and a seven year old boy who I can only see because of a court order 'cause his mother convinced them I wasn't the sort of person to bring up his own child."

He turned to face Martin.

"So, you know what, I don't need you fucking around with my life thanks. In fact, if this guy did come after me I'd probably shake his hand and ask if he needs any help, you know, 'cause I'm done being fucked about with by shit that happened eighteen years ago!"

"Mitchell we need to look after each other. I'm just trying to make sure everyone is aware of the danger. Vincent is dead!"

"Fuck you and the fucking horse you rode in on. Who made you our saviour, eh? Especially after you royally fucked it up the last time."

"What... I didn't..."

Martin suddenly felt a tightness in his chest as the noise of the traffic faded away.

"This isn't going to bring either of them back so why don't you piss off back to your..." he flapped his hand at him, searching for the right word "...security guard hut and leave the past alone."

Martin wished he could, but the past didn't seem to be done with him yet.

Mitchell turned back to the coffee machine and became angry at the slow speed of its heating element as Martin took deep breaths. Gradually the tunnel vision opened out and he could hear the thrum of car engines again.

"Fine. OK. Fine. I didn't expect us to be best mates Mitchell," although secretly, he had. "That's fine. But at least can you tell me where Andrea is. Nobody knows, and if the killer finds out that means none of us can protect her."

"Only person who knows is me, and I'm not going to tell you."

"Look, ignore the fact it's me here, this was Vincent's last request."

"Fucking nutter was never any use..."

Martin's indignation gave him a second wind of confidence.

"Now that's not fair and you know it! He kept us alive more times than we can count."

There was a moment of silence as the coffee machine hissed.

"She wanted out of the Hero shit, away from it. I didn't, but I respected her decision. Eventually. I don't want her dragged back into this crap, not with someone after us. The fewer people who know where she is the better."

"She needs to be put under protection."

Mitchell turned round again.

"Oh and who is going to do that? The police don't give a fuck, the more of us are dead the better as far as they're concerned. You? You gonna watch over us all Martin? Keep us safe in our beds at night? Or do we all pack up and go live in Charles's mansion like one big happy fucking family?"

"This isn't some joke Mitchell! Forget whatever beef you have with me and start thinking. Vincent was ripped open from head to toe and spread over his living room. His own home. I was nearly killed. In my own home. This person knows where we live and isn't afraid to take us on, *whatever* powers we have. If Andrea doesn't know, then she is vulnerable, however fast she still is. She needs to know."

Mitchell paced in front of the table top, wringing his wrists. Eventually he put his fists on the edge and leant on them, head down, eyes closed, thinking hard. The coffee machine light clicked off.

After a long pause, he finally spoke.

"Fine. I'll call her. Tell her to watch out for anything suspicious, but not to freak out. Even though she will."

"That's not going to be enough Mitchell."

"She'll think it's me trying to get more access to Patrick! If I go fucking wading in there I won't see him again until he's eighteen. That's all you get. Things aren't simple any more, we've all got our own shit to worry about."

Martin's brain caught up with the conversation.

"Your son, he's... yours and Andrea's?"

Mitchell shrugged and turned round. He picked up the glass jug of coffee and poured it straight into his cup.

"Didn't even fucking know that..."

"It seems I've missed a lot of things over the years."

"Look, just fuck off out of my place now. Where you came in? That's where you go out too. It's a nice feature, you know?"

Mitchell didn't turn round, but stood sipping his coffee, staring at the gap between the two cupboard doors.

Martin's body felt heavy. He kept his head down as he turned round and left the studio. He hurried to get outside.

***

After he left, Mitchell wandered out of the office across the studio, gently tapping the corner of one mat with his foot, turning it slightly.

He stood in front of one of the kick bags, breathed in deeply, placed a fist in his palm in front of him, elbows up and bowed. A series of kicks followed, slapping the front and sides of the bag, sending it wobbling and twisting at all angles. The more he kicked, the angrier he felt. This wasn't working. He kicked harder, swinging the bag more violently, more difficult to hit with subsequent kicks. He started shouting with each kick. Louder, longer. Kick. Kick. Kick. Then he stood in a wide stance, pressed his wrists together, palms forward and, screaming loudly, let go a huge burst of electricity. The whole studio lit up blue.

The bag hung defeated, split across the middle, only held together by the plastic coating at the back and a stretched out chunk of stuffing material. The stuffing was blackened, tiny wriggling gold threads of it burning across its surface. Smoke curled up around the thick support wire and out across the ceiling as Mitchell stared at his hands.

CHAPTER 37
SUNDAY 18TH JULY 1993

I stand up and walk out of the kitchen.

I intend to make it look like I'm going to the gym, but instead I'll go right through it, across the lower balcony then run up the open staircase to the lab floor, hoping the diversion will give me enough time to punch through the door or walls into the lab before the others arrive to stop me. I'm very aware it's not much of a plan, but it's the best I've come up with.

I couldn't tell if Vincent was under his control or going insane from trying to keep The Controller out of his head. Whatever the reason, he had been curled up in a ball in the corner of the lounge for three days now, babbling, and sometimes screaming nonsense at the invisible world assailing him. He didn't respond to me, would start wailing and pull away if I tried to help him up. I had to leave him there in the end, just taking him water and food which he never took.

As I walk into the lounge this time, Vincent is gone. Instead Maria is on the sofa, staring at the TV showing a repeat of an eighties comedy show. She is out of costume and wearing a dark plum silk night gown and large bunny slippers. I have a flashback to Inna in the shower until I spot the grey and red pyjamas she is wearing underneath. I relax.

Then a thought occurs to me, when had he taken them all? Was it at the shopping centre when he killed Barry, or did he arrive at the building later and gain entry then? Had he taken them one at a time or all together? The extra security on the lab doors didn't go up until a week after Barry died, so did that mean Inna was herself when she got into my room, or was that the start of his games, feeling around to find everyone's weaknesses? It was hard to tell. The riots and the shopping centre had taken it out of all of us mentally, nobody was quite themselves for weeks afterwards. Maria and Jack's vow renewal could have been him, but could have been a reaction to the stress they were under. I just couldn't work out the starting point of it all.

Hell, it didn't matter. It was all going to end soon enough.

"Penny for your thoughts?" she said.

"What?"

Maria is sitting at an angle facing me, legs crossed, wiggling the bunny slipper on her top foot so the insole slaps against her heel.

"Your thoughts. What goes on in that head of yours Martin? I do have trouble working it out sometimes."

I really don't feel like entering into conversation, especially if it's The Controller messing around.

"I guess I like to keep myself to myself."

"You do don't you my darling."

I feel a pain in my heart.

"And where are you going to keep yourself to yourself tonight?"

"Gym," I say, trying to end this. I should just leave the room now, but that might make him suspicious. Need to carry on the charade.

"Mmm."

Maria purses her lips and nods with a frown. Then she stands and slowly walks towards me.

"You know... I do so miss our nights together."

Inside my head I call The Controller every curse I can think of.

"We just seem to have drifted apart recently, don't we?"

"I suppose."

"Oh," she says, making a concerned face and placing her palm on my chest, "Martin, my sensitive lover, I've been ignoring you haven't I?"

Bastard. Bastard.

"You've just renewed your vows and it's your wedding anniversary in a couple of weeks, I imagine you've been busy sorting that out. Thought I'd best leave you to it."

"So thoughtful."

"And I figured that if you needed me for anything you'd tell me whenever it suited you, just like you did with your vows."

Maria takes her hand away.

"Ouch. Yes, you're right. I should have told you before we announced it, but it all happened so quickly. Jack changed after what happened to us, back to how he used to be, the man I fell in love with. We're just... right again."

I feel empty. I want to be smashing that lab door open right now.

"Well I'm glad you've got back what you really wanted."

Maria puts her hands on my shoulders and looks me in the eye.

"Oh Martin, if only you had Jack's personality, his drive, you would be perfect for me. As it is, you were the much needed physical part of my life when it wasn't happening any more. In all honesty I need a much more dominant man, strong minded, arguments and all, just as long as he takes care of me in the end."

She leans in towards my right ear.

"Daddy issues," she whispers and winks at me.

I take her wrists and pull her arms off me.

"I'm happy you're happy."

I let her go and she crosses her arms.

"Thank you Martin. Jack and I really appreciate your support, and I'm thrilled you've agreed to give me away. It means a lot to me."

I grind my teeth. My vision is beginning to swim and my fingers are tingling for some reason.

"It's... anything, anything I can do."

"Really?"

"Of course."

I back away to leave.

"In that case... take me now. Here, on the sofa."

The rage boils over.

"YOU... what? I mean... I don't understand..."

Surely he must know that I know it's him by now. But if he doesn't I can't lose that advantage. Need to stay calm, normal.

"I should have explained really. Sorry, again something I didn't tell you. Jack and I have agreed to have an open relationship. I told him about you and me you know, after he apologised for not giving me enough attention."

"You did what?"

Of course he would know, he's inside both their heads! Of course he would screw with them, he wouldn't be able to help himself.

"It's OK. He was upset at first, but then blamed himself in the end. He realised that we just weren't compatible sexually and that as long as we renewed our vows to each other I was free to have relationships outside of our marriage."

She walks towards me again, her hands dropping to the thin belt bow at her waist. Yeah, I've been here before you bastard, I'm not playing this game again.

"So you see Martin, everything is just like it was for the both of us and everyone is happy."

A shrill scream rushes down the stairs and around me. I twist round. Where the hell was that from? Upstairs?

"What?"

"Well, he *is* a dominant man."

I spin round to face her.

"What are you talking about?"

"An open relationship works both ways..." she smiles at me as she pulls open her gown.

Another scream, this time with the word "help" buried deep inside it. That was definitely from above us.

"Jesus Christ... Inna? INNA!"

I run to the bottom of the stairs leading up to the next floor. My heart flutters and skips so much I can barely keep my balance. I know something is very wrong.

"Inna?"

More panicked screams, men's voices shouting, laughter. I turn back to look at Maria who is casually unbuttoning her pyjama top.

"What the heck is going ON?"

"We're all friends in here Martin. We should all be allowed to have a little fun with each other, no?"

"Oh God. No, oh no..."

CHAPTER 38
MONDAY 17TH SEPTEMBER 2012

Martin didn't want to be here. He felt himself sinking into the past, chest becoming tight as the weight of memory pressed in on him from above. He stood outside the main entrance to Pullman Tower, their old HQ, gathering his thoughts for a few minutes before walking towards the doors. They slid open silently as he approached.

Barely was his foot inside before two tall security guards in black trousers and shirts were in front of him asking him to leave. Facial scanning software had done its thing in spite of his swellings, found a match on the Hero register and flagged him. He was actually quite glad of this for shocking him back into the present day. He explained he had an appointment to see Jack. The largest guard interrupted him and said that Mr Pullman didn't see powered people.

"He does today. Mr Molloy, twelve twenty five. You can confirm it with Lucy."

Martin enjoyed a moment of self-satisfaction at the man's slow confusion, followed by his hasty call upstairs while they made him step to the side, away from the doors.

He had a look around at the lobby while he waited. It had been gutted of any mention of The Pulse. Their logo on the walls and floor, team banners, all gone. It was now polished pale cream stone floor, glass frontage, white walls, blueish metal panels. The reception desk used to be central, but now it was in the right hand corner. The lifts were round to the left of it, on the far side of a row of body scanners and a small security station up against the left wall.

He was surprised at how busy it was. He hadn't seen this many people here since the recruitment day when they hired Andrea. The whole building had been converted since he was here last, not just the lobby; massive refurbishments into office space and laboratories for Jack's ever expanding empire. Even so, it felt weird being here. It looked different, it smelt different and the lighting had changed, yet it felt oddly familiar.

"This way."

The large guard waved him towards the nearest metal arch. The other guard stayed close. He dropped his wallet, keys and the new phone into a plastic tray then walked through. It went beep. Scanners always did.

They frisked him and swept him over with a small handheld machine, grabbing at his belt buckle each time. Martin supposed it *could* be used to kill someone, but if so it meant Marks & Spencers were selling weapons for a tenner. After they were satisfied the buckle wasn't an immediate threat to employee safety, they took him away from reception to a windowless room opposite the lifts. There he was questioned about his abilities and warned against using them inside the premises. If he did he would be immediately immobilised and restrained until the police arrived.

Eventually they gave him a visitor's pass, but kept hold of his belongings. He was to collect them on the way out. The smaller security guard accompanied him in the lift, in an uncomfortably silent journey, up to the forty second floor. The old five floor atrium had been floors twenty to twenty four. Martin couldn't see if they were available as the lift was voice activated and there was no floor number display. He didn't fancy attempting to shout out for a stop off on the way up either, as he didn't think his new friend would be too impressed.

The lift stopped with a female voice calling the floor number and the door opened. The lobby for the office was almost as large as the one for the whole building. Same cream polished stone floor, white walls, glass and brushed steel everywhere. Lucy sat at a long curved desk that was empty apart from two monitors, a keyboard and mouse. Opposite her were leather sofas, a coffee table and behind them an expensive looking drinks machine. Between them, straight ahead from the lift, was a pair of plain brown doors with flat handles.

His security friend went and stood in front of these doors while Martin introduced himself at the desk. Lucy scanned the barcode on his ID badge, all the while giving him the oddest of looks, then told him to take a seat until he was called in.

He fancied a coffee but didn't want to embarrass himself by conspicuously failing to operate the machine. Instead he just sat down on the very comfortable sofa and waited. After a few moments the whole entrance procedure faded from his mind and the past came back into focus. It felt wrong to be here. He felt nervous.

He hadn't realised he was tapping his foot until he noticed Lucy glaring at him. He put up a palm and mouthed "Sorry". She stared at him for a few more seconds then looked back at her monitor and started typing away again. She had been glancing across at him ever since he sat down. He guessed his purple eyes and fat lip were out of place in such a perfect room. He should have worn his trousers instead of his jeans too.

A flat screen monitor on the wall behind her played a looping promotional reel of Pullman Enterprises equipment and services, on mute. A super steel production factory. Some quick shots of sports cars ending with a Formula One car turning a corner in slow motion, followed by some technical graphics showing, he assumed, which parts the company were responsible for making. Now the Rainforest, a giant river, some exotic wildlife, some indigenous people in hard hats and t-shirts with words sliding across the screen: "responsible", "ethical", "revitalising". The word

"PROTECTION" in giant letters, then a picture of some odd looking machine in a CGI cutaway of an office building, circles spreading out from it like old pictures of radio waves, then an arrow and the figure "150m+". A man in shadow staring at the building, wavy lines wriggling from his head towards the building, then suddenly he stops and clutches his head, the words "Psychic feedback neutralisation and localisation" appear and the man in shadow is now being arrested. A new CGI cutaway shows a skyscraper with these machines installed every dozen or so floors, wiring stretching between them, to a mast on the roof, the words "Install and forget". Now some school children writing and painting, smiling to the camera, an educational fund.

Jack's been busy.

It was just past twelve thirty. If he was going to see Jack in this "window" he only had ten minutes left, and so many questions. "Did you find what you were looking for at my flat?" would be the ballsy opener, but that would show his hand too soon. They both knew what happened at the flat and what he had been looking for. What he needed was a confession, for Vincent, but that was going to be hard to get. Unless Jack had turned stupid over the last few years he would be just as sharp and prepared as he always was. Martin knew the only reason he had managed to get this meeting was because of the memoirs, and he had to use that to try and get under his skin.

Martin stopped tapping his foot again. He didn't even look over at Lucy this time.

He just wasn't a very good talker though. Jack was going to run rings around him, palm him off and he'd be out in five minutes before he'd had a chance to come up with a counterargument. "Fine. Just relax then and see what happens. Play it by ear," he told himself, wringing his hands to stop the tingling, huffing out a deep breath to stop his light head floating away.

Why was so he nervous? He wasn't this bad before he met up with Maria or Mitchell. He had no need to be nervous now. Apart from the fact Jack almost killed him two days ago. There was that. Anyway, what was Jack going to do? Murder him in his office? Make out Martin attacked him in anger and he pulped him in self-defence, then produce some forged security tape showing what happened?

Shit. He could probably do that.

Then Martin chuckled to himself. Charles was going to be so pissed off when he found out about this. Wonder what he'd been spending years trying to see Jack about anyway?

"You can go in now."

There hadn't been a buzzer or a phone call, she just spoke suddenly. Martin stood up in surprise and pointed at the door on his right. Security guy stepped to the side.

"Straight through please."

"Thanks."

He nodded a little overeagerly and headed for the door.

"Easy," he thought, 'this is going to be fine. Unless he murders me. But don't think about that and you'll be OK."

He touched the handle expecting to turn it when both doors opened inwards by themselves.

Then he saw what lay beyond.

His heart leapt up and jammed itself sideways in his neck. He twisted round, scanning the reception area and the lift door. This wasn't right. This can't be the same place, this was the forty second floor, much higher up. He stared at Lucy, bewildered and pointed through the doors.

"Is this..."

"Straight through sir," said the security guy sternly, forcing Martin to change focus to him so fast he had to pull his head back.

He was panting. He gulped painfully and looked back through the doors. Ahead of him was a brushed steel lined corridor that curved in slightly at its centre. At the end was a tall bronze coloured set of doors, either side of which was a wall made from thick translucent glass that reflected a green tinge back towards the waiting room.

This was the entrance to the lab.

He stepped forward slowly, creeping into one of his nightmares. He half expected the floor to turn to mist and to start falling uncontrollably. The door silently closed behind him but he didn't notice.

"It's just an office, that's all."

He walked faster. As he reached the narrowest part he felt his shoulders automatically pull in. The walls didn't touch him by any measure of distance but he could feel them slide across his muscles. Any second he expected to hear a speaker crackling into life. Pain shot down his ribs and back as he squeezed himself inward and he only relaxed when he got past it, breathing out deeply with an audible crack. He winced and approached the door.

The corridor opened out and he could see the glass wall curve away on both sides. He glanced at the wall to the left of the door but it was undamaged. There was also no iris scanner or voice recognition machine. He looked at the doors themselves. They were different. A pair of knights on horseback faced each other on opposing sides, decked out in full armour with one holding a large sword, the other a mace. Streamers of cloth curled through the air in the background. The horses were rearing up decoratively, their feet resting on two oversized round knobs.

It wasn't the same door. The old lab door had dragons. He felt a flash of anger at himself for being duped, then pulled on the knobs. There was no resistance and the doors swung open easily.

***

Jack's office was almost circular, like a square with three sides bowed out, only the back wall was flat. Behind Martin was the thick glass wall and giant doors and to the right, curving floor to ceiling windows with a commanding view out over the city. To the left was a huge dark wood and glass display cabinet. Ahead of him, on the wall, was a giant Pullman Enterprises logo and below it three large flat screens displaying lots of boxes filled with numbers and graphs. It was a marble floor again, but this time a deep green colour with random swirls of creamy white trying to bubble out from within. Offset to the back of the room, framed by the display screens, was a dark wood oval desk. On it sat two monitors, at least three small black tablet devices and a few papers in neat piles.

Jack was standing by the windows. He was wearing a dark grey suit, tailored to fit, white shirt collar just visible around the neck. His brown hair was slicked back as it always had been. His arms were crossed and he had the poise of a Hero watching proudly out over his city. The sunlight filtered light blue through the windows, making it look like he was covered in a pulse shield. But he wasn't of course, just a trick of the light. Martin couldn't see his face, just the turquoise outline of a cheek and eye socket.

"Did you like the entrance?" he said suddenly. "A lot of people don't know that The Metallurgist made two sets of those doors for his base. The dragons guarded his main laboratory, protecting his experiments, his dangerous work, keeping his secrets."

He turned to face Martin. He barely looked a day older.

"The knights guarded his chambers, protecting his library, his history, keeping their king safe from invaders. Before your time with us of course. We pretty much emptied the place before we called the police in to arrest him. We could afford to be a bit more brazen when we were less well known."

Martin didn't speak. Jack gave a vague smile and slowly wandered over to him.

"So, how are you Martin? Keeping yourself out of… or not, by the looks of things. I hope the other guy came off worse."

"Bastard broke my TV."

No reaction.

"And my sofa. And, well, my entire flat."

"Always were a bulldog weren't you? Never afraid of a bit of a scrap."

The smile widened, then disappeared as he looked thoughtful.

"I heard what happened to you."

The two men held eye contact. Martin was screaming "It was you, you bastard," in his head. "come on, just say it. We both know it."

Jack turned away and walked round to the other side of his desk.

"So it seems our killer is after these memoirs that you possess, which can't be read without a password nobody seems to know. I suppose then the first question, after the obvious 'Who did it?' is 'What do they want them for?' Are they going to publish them, perhaps blackmailing one or all of us into the bargain, or do they just want to destroy them, to make sure nothing ever gets out."

"Well that kind of ties into the obvious question doesn't it? I mean none of *us* are going to blackmail ourselves with that information, and no-one outside of the team knows about what happened, so…"

"...it must be the second option, destruction of the evidence by someone with a lot to lose."

Martin allowed himself a wry smile.

"Nice office you have here Jack."

Jack laughed and walked away from his desk to the left hand wall, the glass cabinets. They were filled with awards for business and gifts from other countries, a tribal shield and spears, a set of crystal glasses and a decanter, some abstract bronze sculpture. The central cabinet was full height and contained a black mannequin wearing the final version of his costume with his control bracelets and a pair of nineties high tech glasses on small plinths at the base.

"It's interesting isn't it, what we've all become over the years, all because of what happened. You know I had a plan, for every decade, what I would be doing. Right now I would have been a mentor to at least two Hero teams, living and training here. I wouldn't be active myself any more but would have given them guidance, protected them from any interfering judiciary and anti-Hero pressure groups which, if you remember, I predicted the rise of. I would have been an international spokesperson on Hero rights, contacts in the highest places in governments around the world. That was the plan."

He stared at the costumed mannequin, lost in thought.

"The latter is still true, to a degree but, ah... it's all business now. Heroics, I couldn't care much less about any more. I see teams Element City One and Two racing round the city when the authorities let them out of their kennels on a tight leash and…" he shrugged "I feel nothing."

Jack had his back to Martin, still looking at the cabinets.

"But, society still views us with such suspicion, still decides for us what we can and cannot do. Unless you are either so outwardly morally decent or happen to have saved the city from destruction at some point in your prior career, they just won't trust you. Do you know how much convincing it took the government to accept our contract over my competitors? It was clearly the best deal and the best technology, yet even with my unblemished history, my charitable work, everything I've done for this city, this whole fucking country… I was powered. The company was run by a Hero. Suspicion. Mistrust. This…" he suddenly jerked into motion, moving along the glass wall and pointing at a silver trophy of a caped figure in flight, "…this was my first business award. Four years it took me to get things together enough to focus on a single project. Locked away in here. Trapped."

Jack tilted his head as he looked at the award.

"Went a little stir crazy I must admit. You see I was never like you, someone who can exist on solitude. I needed a challenge, purpose. I was lost for a long while."

"We all lost ourselves."

Jack looked at him, searching his face. Martin was expecting him to bring up the "he had never been taken, so he wouldn't know" argument, but it didn't come.

"We did, didn't we."

He tapped the glass.

"For revitalising the steel production industry in the country, thanks to our Metallurgist friend's legacy. Took some time but I managed to recreate his super steel. Not exactly of course, I've no idea to this day how his abilities *actually* worked, but it's close enough."

Jack walked round the back of his desk, placing a hand on his chair.

"But plans... plans change. We all changed. The Controller had a profound impact on us and, like it or not, what we are doing now, the people we are now, is all because of what he did to us."

"Not me."

Jack looked surprised.

"Oh really?"

"Nothing I have done is related to him in any way, I've made a point of it."

"By locking yourself away from anything that could remind you of what happened. Yes, not related at all."

Martin felt anger in his stomach.

"But that all ended when Vincent died, and ever since you have been tearing through the past like that bulldog you are, dredging up bodies and clouding the present with our dirt. Some might say that it isn't the memoirs that need destroying, it's you."

He instinctively clenched his fists. Jack noticed and smiled.

"What I'm saying Martin, is that all of us, including you, have a lot to lose if those memoirs get out. PCA have been busy sniffing around the woods and it's not helping that you are leading them to all the shallow graves."

"I've already lost enough the last few days. Vincent, my job, my anonymity…"

"Oh, so you have nothing more to lose is that it? So you don't care about the rest of us?"

"No, what I mean is I can't afford to lose any more. There's not much more to give."

Jack looked concerned, then nodded.

"So even though you have no business, no academic career, no family and no TV shows, you understand that this has to end?"

"Damn it," thought Martin. "Didn't I know he would turn this around somehow?"

"Of course," continued Jack, "it should never have even started. Vincent should never have written… whatever it was he decided to write in the first place. The past is a shared delusion until it is given form, and we don't even know what form he gave it, do we? Thankfully he had enough insight to protect it from wandering eyes."

OK, here was an inroad. He could play this one.

"Actually, I managed to decipher the lock yesterday. Was trying different things he used to say, words and phrases he used, when one of them worked. I read it. It's… everything."

Jack was staring at him intently. Martin carried on.

"Everything about the team from when he joined, everything about each of us, nothing is sacred. Don't forget Jack, it wasn't just The Controller who knew the inside of our heads."

"I know. And what of The Controller?"

"Every damn second of every day he had us. It was like I was reliving it. I could barely sleep last night."

Jack just nodded.

"Yes, yes, I can imagine. And of after that?"

After?

"Er, just his time in the institutions. How he struggled to stay sane after what happened. Then what each of us went on to do."

Jack pointed at him, smiling.

"What we've built up over those rotten foundations. You see! You see what there is to lose?"

Martin had to focus on what Jack had to lose.

"So how is business lately?"

That seemed to throw him for a second.

"Good, good. We're just gearing up to roll out the Psy-Guard system to all major government buildings. Oh and Maria is in the final stages of publishing the results of a three year psychic research study, Charles is in talks with a US network that wants to buy his show for their new international channel and Mitchell just wants to keep his combat centre open and not lose access to his son. Your point being?"

This wasn't going as intended. Jack was unflappable. He shook his head, patted the back of his chair and walked over to the window again.

"You do realise Martin, that after Maria, you were the one on the team I trusted the most. I never said anything of course, I wasn't that type of leader. I just gave everyone the opportunity to do their best and I expected it of them, nothing less. And you never disappointed me."

"Never?"

Jack turned his head slightly.

"There was nothing I did that disappointed you?"

He had to try to get him emotional. Get him angry. Maybe he'll let something slip.

"You really want to talk about this do you? Pull up more weighted down sacks from the bottom of the lake?"

Martin walked over to the window, a few metres away from him. He remembered this view, out over the city, towards the river, the centre of town just beyond. It was covered in low cloud again. Murky.

"We all did bad things Jack. Some of us did them without anyone making us."

Jack sighed deeply.

"Cause and effect Martin, cause and effect. Nothing happens for no reason. Everything can be traced back to one moment when something important, some cog, some fact was changed. I would get obsessed with the details of some machine or idea I had. I would ignore her, a distraction was all she was when my mind was fixed like that, and you would be there to pick up the pieces."

This wasn't the reaction Martin had expected. He must have had a lot of time to mull things over and, unusually for him, had taken part of the blame on himself.

"All the same, there are boundaries, I… things that should never have happened."

"I know. And yet there is no apology necessary, The Controller already made you... us, pay for that affair in his own psychopathic way."

This was pointless, he was getting nothing. The grey city stared back at him, unmoved by his frustration. Vincent had entrusted him to find out who killed him and he had failed. How was he going to get Jack to admit to his murder when he couldn't even get him to admit to beating him up a few days ago? What the hell was he doing anyway? What was his plan here? With any of this? Just wander around visiting everyone, saying "Hi!" and hoping one of them would drop a clue that would lead to some evidence he was going to thrust in Jack's face to make him collapse to his knees, begging for forgiveness? What was it Jack always used to say? Oh yes: "No plan, no result." Well, no shit.

Martin dropped his head, looking down at the traffic threading its way through the streets. That was it then. He'd seen everyone he could and ended up nowhere. He would have to leave PCA to do their thing and hope that they didn't dig up too many skeletons before they were done. He was so deep in thought he nearly didn't hear Jack speak.

"Lucy says she can't read you. You... didn't by chance sneak some psychic power blocking gadget past security did you?"

So the secretary was psychic, that explained the strange glances at him.

"No, no, I only brought myself."

"Didn't think so. Security here is very thorough on that sort of thing."

They were.

"So it wasn't a fluke then. Hmm… You know Martin, all that time you were part of The Pulse and you never told me you were psychic immune."

"Well you can add that to the list I guess. Look, I should…"

"That's what I mean about trust Martin,"

They faced each other in front of the window.

"…you *were* the one I trusted the most. The one I trusted to do the right thing. Then I find out, in the most brutal way possible, you were fucking my wife. He told me. In my head. He showed me her memories of it, the pleasure she had. He made me know it was my fault. Then he made us play act getting back together, renewing our vows just to fuck with all three of us."

"Jack, I…"

"Then I find out that you never told us you were the best placed out of the whole team to go up against him. Even more so than Vincent! He couldn't affect you. He had no hold on you at all. And I discover this *after* everything that happened."

"No, he used you, all of you against me. I wish everyone would stop saying I somehow wasn't affected because he couldn't control me."

"But I know you suffered Martin. You suffered because you weren't the man I thought you were."

Jack's face went tight.

"You think you had to hide from society to avoid contact with us? Truth is, nobody wanted to talk to you anyway. Why? Because you failed us."

"Wh… what?"

"And that's the biggest breach of trust Martin. How on earth could you not have worked out sooner what was going on? I mean, we murder, and I say that word out loud because that is what we did, we murdered the gang, those drug runners and you did nothing. Even before that, when we were acting crazy... renewing our vows? And she didn't warn you? Seriously? With how close you were?"

Martin stammered his fragmented thoughts out.

"The riots! I thought you guys were traumatised, needed something to hold on to, someone to let your anger out on."

"We killed all those people and it just didn't twig. And then..."

Jack paused. Martin could see his eyes glaze over as the past played out inside his mind.

"... what we did."

His heart pounded in his chest. He didn't want to hear any of this.

"It's still painful, isn't it Martin? You know there isn't a day where I don't remember her. Inna."

Martin stood paralysed. He tried to control his breathing as the room began to spin.

"Every day I remember what we did. And I hate myself more. Even though we were all in his thrall, it doesn't absolve me of the guilt."

Martin swallowed hard against his suddenly dry throat, hands trembling.

"Every day I feel... shame. Anger of course, even now. But mostly shame. But..." Jack only moved his eyes, and looked at Martin, "...even though it doesn't and will not ever excuse what happened, we had due

387

reason to act the way we did. We were all screaming behind our eyes, trying to stop ourselves. Apart from you."

He pointed at Martin, his arm frozen in the air.

"In all those moments you were what was left of the team's identity, our values, our beliefs, our morals. You were the only one with control over themselves, and consequently over all of us."

He deliberately stepped towards him, arm still out, still pointing.

"You knew what we were doing was wrong. You knew."

He was a poised silhouette, slowly stalking a terrified prey.

"You stood there. You saw us. You heard her calling for help. You knew what was happening. And yet, despite the whole team being in our moment of greatest need, you did nothing." He hissed the last word out between his teeth, moving closer towards Martin. He finally dropped his arm.

"Nothing."

"I tried my best!"

Martin's voice was loud and wobbled.

"Too little and too late."

"I couldn't stop…"

"You know, I forgave you for Maria years ago Martin, but I have never forgiven you for *that*."

"Please, I…"

"In fact, I *am* right aren't I? Here you are going round each one of us trying to figure out which has the most to lose, the most reason to kill Vincent, when it turns out it's you after all. I mean who would want *anybody* to know how badly you failed? How badly you failed her?"

"I didn't…"

"You are a coward Martin. A fucking coward! You know, if there *is* anyone who needs to hide away from the world and never be heard from again, it is most definitely you."

The pressure of the room squeezed Martin's skull inward as he felt his whole body go light.

"Get the fuck out of my office," said Jack, spinning on his heels and walking back to the desk.

Martin no longer existed in this room for him. Martin shared the feeling. Carefully, he turned round and walked towards the door, thoughts churning like debris in a whirlwind. "That wasn't how it happened. That wasn't it at all. There was nothing I could do. Jack knew that. Surely they all knew that. Is that really what they all thought of me?" He thought he had been avoiding contact with them, but had they been avoiding him? Was the only reason anyone was speaking to him at all because he had the memoirs? Even Maria? The amount of information she had been passing round the team about him, it would make sense. It was all a ruse. That's all this was. Martin felt his lungs collapsing in as the edges of his vision clouded up. He went for the door handle and turned it.

"Although I *am* glad you and Maria are meeting up again."

He spun round to stare at Jack.

"What?"

Jack had sat himself back down and was tapping at a tablet device.

"Well, it's just nice to see old friends getting along. I'm sure you'll be screwing again in no time. Although, and I'll be honest with you here, she hasn't aged well has she?"

The handle suddenly snapped off in Martin's tight fist. His eyes darted around as he looked down at the mangled super steel fitting, then back up at Jack, now busying himself reading through paperwork, making notes on his tablet as he went.

"What... the hell are you?"

Martin was shaking. Jack didn't even look up.

"Lucy will show you out. Never come back."

Martin threw the handle to the floor and stormed out. The handle screamed across the marble until Jack jumped up from his desk and stopped it with his foot. He picked it up and turned it over in his hands, studying it like some strange sculpture.

"Lucy?"

The voice activated intercom lit up.

"Yes Mr Pullman?"

"Could you get Ms Gionchetta on the line please?"

CHAPTER 39
SUNDAY 18TH JULY 1993

I pound up the stairs, cries and shouts bouncing off the walls around me, tumbling down onto the lower floor.

I reach the living quarters. I hear a loud conversation between the men mixed in with Inna's screams and cries as I approach her apartment. The door is ajar. I hurl it open, shouting at them to stop. My shout peters out, throat going suddenly dry as the scene coalesces before my eyes.

Her room has the same open-plan layout as mine. I am standing in the lounge area inside the doorway. She has the same chairs and cupboard units as me, except for a display cabinet filled with awards and trophies in gold and silver. On top is a small round vase of yellow daisies. Inside there are statuettes of leaders I only vaguely recognise, a fist holding a sickle, a small photo of her standing between two men dressed in Eastern European military costume, a red star pin badge.

In the centre of the room is a low king-size bed with dark brown and cream covers. The brown sheet is scrunched up and pulled out from where it had been carefully tucked under the corner of the mattress. One cream pillow lies on the floor next to Jack's right foot as he kneels there. Mitchell stands at the other side of the bed, watching. Charles stands at the foot of the bed, back to me, dropping his trousers to the floor.

"Guys, what the hell are you doing?"

Charles whips down his underpants and moves towards Jack, to reveal Inna lying awkwardly on the sheets. Her knickers have been pulled off and lie trapped underneath her buttocks. Her top has been ripped open at the front, exposing her breasts. Jack has her legs apart, grasping the top of her thighs and is pulling her onto him. Her face turns to me. She stares right into my eyes and screams for help.

I stride across the room towards the men.

"This. Stops. Now!"

"Like fuck it does."

I push Charles out of the way. He stumbles and reaches to the wall for support. I reach out to grab Jack by his shoulders. There is barely a flick of a loose hand, and the next moment a pulse blast hits me in the chest, sending me flying backwards. My legs wrap over the back of a chair, flipping me upside down. The momentum carries me through a wooden coffee table and into the TV and its stand. I manage to get my arms out above me to stop myself landing on my head and I fall sideways to the floor, curling up in a pile of smashed wood and glass.

"Martin, I know you two had a very brief 'thing' but can't you see there is a queue? In any case, why don't you have my wife instead? I know we're married but it never stopped you before did it?"

He laughs. Inna screams my name, worried I'm hurt. I'm not. Blood pounds its way through my neck as I get to my feet, and shake glass out of my hair.

"Stop this. If you can hear me Jack, I'm sorry OK? And whatever 'you' want you bastard, just don't do this to her. Anything else but this!"

Mitchell laughs and unzips his jeans, pulling out his penis. Charles, naked and aroused, stares at him and grins from ear to ear.

"Yes, I know," he makes him say.

Jack is now on top of her, attacking her like an animal as she wails helplessly.

"STOP THIS!"

I barrel forward towards them. Jack looks up. He moves his right arm over Inna towards me. Something thuds into my side and I'm off my feet again. I see plaster, chunks of concrete and wiring as I pass through the wall into the bathroom. I see a brief reflection of myself in the mirror, then I crash through the shower screen and my right shoulder and arm embed themselves in the wall, tiles shattering.

I cough out concrete dust and rip my arm free. I've got to stop this. There is no plan for this. No training. Three versus one isn't good odds, especially when one of them is Jack. There is nothing I can do, but I have to do something, Inna is screaming for help. Through the hole in the wall I see it all. Inna pressed into the bed.

Jack on her. Charles walks round the other side as Mitchell masturbates by the dresser.

"I know a way to shut her wailing up..." I hear him make Mitchell say.

I step through the damaged screen and run for the bathroom door. On the left of me as I come out into the bedroom is the display cabinet. I pick it up and run towards Jack, holding it up in front of me like a long Roman shield. I barely get two steps before it bursts into flames that erupt into my face. I let go, blinded by the heat and kick the burning furniture away from me. It's shredded by Jack's pulse shield, trophies and medals scattered like shrapnel. I rub the flames from my face, blinking rapidly to get some moisture over my eyes. The left side of my torso suddenly contracts hard, trying to pull my buttock up to my armpit. I twist sideways as the pain rips through my body.

Mitchell hits me with another bolt of electricity, this time to my legs. My quads go into spasm. I try to keep standing but I fall backwards, and lie there trembling on the floor.

Need to get up. I need to get up. Inna is screaming again. Deep breaths. Get some oxygen back to the muscles. Get up!

"See Martin, your problem is you don't know about fun do you? You're one of these white knight hero sorts that think they always have to be so virtuous and just, and so fucking uptight, when sometimes you just have to... let go."

All the air is forced out of me as I am crushed flat onto the floor.

"You know, you should set yourself free and forget about things that need not concern you because, if I'm honest, there's not much I can do with you, you're so boring."

Another pulse field hits me. The floor under me creaks with that one. I suck in a breath of air.

"Just... stop this, guys... here, and we never need to say... anything more about it... OK?"

The three men ignore me and start to engage in a theatrically exaggerated discussion about how reasonable or not my request is. I don't care if it's fake, it gives me time to think. I tilt my eyes down, trying to lift my head. I see her legs dangling over the side of the bed. She is quiet. What has he done?

Maybe I can delay them by talking crap, or piss them off enough they just give up trying.

"We... we're a team right? We can find a way through this if we... stick together, yeah?"

The three men stop talking and look at me. Jack strokes his chin.

"Of course... *through* this... why didn't I think of that?"

He holds one arm out, fist clenched, then brings the other fist down on top of it.

My ears pop and I feel ten feet wide. I feel a sensation of falling, then realise I *am* as I see a roughly circular edge of a hole above me in the brightly lit kitchen ceiling. The piece of floor I'm lying on shatters the dining table and I feel pain as it hits the floor below and snaps in half under my pelvis. I cry out as my vertebrae crack and blood gushes from my nose.

I slowly roll myself over onto my forearms, covering them in concrete dust and bits of broken ceiling tile. Blood drips into the dust, forming little balls of red paste. On my knees, I lean backwards, carefully stretching out my back. A crack, some pain, but I can still move.

"Right bitch..." says a voice above me "...where were we..." followed by sounds of a scuffle and more garbled cries for help.

As I force myself to my feet, Maria comes in through the door. She stares up at the ceiling, eyes wide like an excited child.

"Oh wow! That hole is bigger than me, the whore I am!"

I shudder with rage.

"Stop this! This is madness, stop it NOW!"

I barge past her as she laughs at me, egging Jack and the others on from below. I run up the stairs. Back to Inna's room. I still have no plan.

Inna is on all fours. Men at both ends of her. Charles is touching and kissing Mitchell. They are nearest so I launch myself towards the two of them, toppling them both in one go. I quickly get up and round on Jack, only to see him drawing his right arm across him again. A pulse wave sends me sideways out of the open doorway.

I cross the corridor, smash through the door opposite and tumble across the floor of Charles's room. My left arm hurts. It caught that wave full on. It's bare now, clothing torn off it, and swollen pink. I can't feel two of my fingers.

I heave myself across the corridor. To her room. No plan. I'm crying.

I can't hear anything other than the blood rushing in my ears. I can't speak. I gasp out random vowels, breathe in hard sobs. Inna is crying too. He's making her do this, making her fully aware, but unable to stop herself.

I pick up a chair from the lounge area and throw it at Jack. He catches it in a pulse bubble.

I stand still waiting for the inevitable. I haven't the energy to try to dodge out of the way.

He takes his time.

"Fuck off will you? You're really trying my patience."

The chair hits me square in the chest with a crack and I fall back, smashing through the wall.

I lie on my back in the corridor.

Inna is screaming.

I get up. Into her room. No plan.

I smell burning. I'm on fire.

I stumble to the bathroom. Under the shower.

Inna is screaming.

Her room.

I'm wet. Mitchell shocks me. I spasm. I fall through the hole.

I'm in the kitchen. Ankle hurts.

I crawl up the stairs.

Blood smears on sharp concrete edges.

Corridor walls bend in on me.

Room.

Left ankle drags on carpet.

No plan.
I'm crying.
Everything is swimming.
Do I see fire?
Blue. Definitely blue.
I swing at something and miss.
I fall.
Carpet.
Laughter.
I'm crying.
On my knees.
I look up.
Inna's face.
Twisted in wretched, heaving despair.
"I'm sorry," I say.
"…please…" she says.
My heart squashes to the size of a berry as tears pour from me. I can barely breathe in to stay alive.

None of my muscle is any use.

I can't save her.

Charles picks me up gently, like a friend tending to a drunken buddy, and ushers me out of the room.

I walk groggily with him.

I want to throw him through the fucking wall.

I can't.

"Just close the door behind you and forget about it my dear chap. It's for the best."

He pats me on the back.

I want to break his.

I want to take him out, then Mitchell, then Jack. All of them.

Instead I just nod.

Why am I nodding?

I'm crying.

I shuffle out into the corridor as Inna screams my name. She begs me not to go.

My mind is mist.

I wipe snot from my face.

Can't do anything.

All I can do is nothing.

Just walk away and forget it. Blank it out. It's not happening, it never happened.

Somehow it will be fine. Somehow things will be fine. For now I just need to find somewhere to hide and wait for it to end.

Somewhere to hide.

Somewhere to hide...

My heart tightens. A surge of adrenaline sets my pummelled muscles on fire.

"That's it, run!" comes the shout from behind me as I hobble towards the atrium.

Along the balcony to the open stairs at the back.

I can hear them still. From here it sounds like a horror film playing on a TV turned up too loud. Doesn't seem real.

Up the stairs. Bloody ankle hurts.

Top of the stairs.

Through the doors. Brushed steel corridor.

The narrow bit in the middle tries to bend in to catch my shoulders, to stop me moving, but I'm not. I'm going to get there. Get this bastard.

I try the iris scanner, lining my eyes up with the narrow glass slit. There's a small pause then a harsh buzzer sound.

I speak into the microphone.

"Martin."

Buzzer.

"Roadblock."

Buzzer.

"The guy who's going to rip your THROAT out you SICK FUCK!"

Buzzer.

I smash the scanner then go for the door. My punches bounce off the metal like it's rubber.

I grab a handle and pull. There is no movement. Not even a noise, like a straining lock or twisting hinges. Nothing.

"Come on!"

I feel hope fading in me.

I kick at the door next to the knob. I may as well be trying to force open a cliff face.

I go round to the glass wall.

My fists are bleeding and I can feel my muscles scraping at my skin from the inside but I hit it. I punch and tear and bellow at it. Blood smears across it. Dark brown.

Just this wall between me and him. That's all. One wall. One door. Then I'll have him. Then I'll save her. I'll save them all.

As quick as it started, the adrenaline shuts off.

I stop moving.

I've succeeded in flaking off some tiny flecks of glass, no bigger than my smallest fingernail.

I am meat and bone under the will of gravity and I slump into the wall, collapsing at the base of it.

My heart thuds limply into my chest.

I'm crying.

I think I might like to die here, burned and bleeding. Leave this weak flesh behind and be somewhere where only my spirit can go. Far beyond mortal concerns. Failing that, just to lie here in silence and never move again, never ever feel again.

I think that would be nice.

There is a screeching noise followed by a barrage of painful crackling as the rarely used internal speaker system bursts into life.

"Is this thing on?"

It's Charles. He seems out of breath. In the background there is distorted grunting and groaning drowning out a barely audible sobbing.

"Is it.. can you hear... it's working yes? Right. This is an official team broadcast people!" he pauses. "There are holes for everyone up here! Come on, it's party time, WOOO!"

A bouncy seventies disco tune starts playing as the shouts get louder.

I hear Inna scream.

I screw my eyes tightly shut.

I pull my arms up over my head, wrapping them over my ears

I want to fall away through the world to a better place, but he doesn't let me.

I hear everything.

I'm crying.

I'm crying.

I'm crying.

CHAPTER 40
MONDAY 17TH SEPTEMBER 2012

Martin sat on a high stool facing out the window of a small coffee shop a few streets away from Pullman Tower. A thick drizzly rain smeared the glass, melting the world outside. As people went by, their shapes broke into loose collections of coloured smudges, wriggling, trying to slither apart to find shelter.

He let the shifting curls of movement hypnotise him as he slowly turned the large cardboard cup of lukewarm coffee round in tiny circles, trying to feel for the subtle bump of the join down the side.

It had taken half the cup and nearly twenty minutes for him to stop shaking.

There had been times over the last eighteen years when his thoughts had become too much for him. All it took was one memory, and it would race around his head trying to reproduce itself in the smallest detail, never quite fully formed, frustrated. He would fight it, try to resolve it, calm it down, but with each restored fragment it became more painful and terrifying. It would carry on like this for hours, the furious memory needing to be finished, him running from it, throwing it scraps of the past in the hope it would leave him alone.

Then there had been other times when his mind had been as barren as a salt flat. He would sit on the sofa, or on his bed, or in the kitchen, staring straight through whatever was opposite him. Nothing came into his mind at those times. When he tried to entice a thought, there was no feature for it to cling to and it would just slide away from him to the horizon. Days would pass like this, broken only by the toilet, sleep or a glass of water, when his subconscious would take temporary control of him.

He couldn't bear to be near people any more. He would get this odd feeling that the closer he got to others the more his thoughts, his secrets would be exposed. He had nightmares where he was trapped in crowds. The more desperately he scrambled and pushed to get out, the more he broadcast his memories of what had happened, the more they knew. Eventually the crowd learned everything and they would stand back, avoiding him, staring at him in disgust, shaking their heads. He would run for the doors. It was always white outside, getting brighter the closer he came. He would scream "No!" and panic. He would dive for the doors and then he would wake up.

Then there were the nightmares set inside the HQ. Nightmares about Inna and the others in her room. Where his legs wouldn't work, or he couldn't quite get the door open enough to get in, no matter how hard he pushed. Dreams about him and Inna in the shower that morphed distressingly into nightmares about Inna and the others and him in the shower and her room. Vile, disgusting nightmares that would sicken him, make him shudder in disbelief the next day that his mind, his own mind, could conjure anything as depraved as that and present it to him without remorse.

That had been the first seven years after leaving The Pulse.

He never sought help. He couldn't. His brain convinced him nothing was wrong. He convinced himself nothing was wrong, and that if it was, he could fix it. And he couldn't tell anybody anyway. The only explanation for how he was, was the explanation he couldn't give. The only activities that helped were going to the park and reading the book his mother gave him as a child.

In Element Park he would sit in the same place each time, in the corner under a conifer. He had a view over everything from there. He could see where everyone was and he could be alone at the same time. He was safe and he could deal with his thoughts one by one.

The book from his mother was a gift to him when he was twelve, shortly after his father died. She told him to read it whenever he felt sad, whenever he felt alone and she couldn't be there for him. It was a story about a loving family where the father dies suddenly and those that are left behind have to work out how to carry on without him. It was a sad story, but full of hope. He had no idea whether the book was actually any good, he had never read that many books to compare it to, but it worked. And she left a surprise inside it for him that made him smile every time.

Gradually he started to go out more, but only at the quietest times of the day, getting used to the city outside his flat. Then he would make himself go out at a busy time, just to get some milk, then straight back. Testing himself.

He saw a news report or a documentary, he forgot which, about how exercise was one of the best ways to help control depression and other mental illnesses. He never admitted to himself that was what he had, but all the same he remembered how many hours he used to put in at the team gym so he went and bought some weights. He started walking more, walking further, too self conscious to jog.

He would still have the nightmares, still have times when thoughts would either pursue or abandon him, but they became less frequent, less distressing. There were times too when he would push himself too much, think he was OK when he wasn't, and end up running from a shop, or collapsing in a corner somewhere. He would wake up to medics giving him oxygen, saying it was OK, it was a panic attack, they're common, no need to be ashamed, it was OK. Each time that happened he felt like he had lost a year of progress and would get disheartened. The thoughts would return for a while and he had to try to pick himself up again.

That had been the next six years after leaving The Pulse.

Then he saw an article in the free newspaper about a local charity in his old neighbourhood struggling for funds. They ran services for children who either couldn't, or didn't, go to school, groups where they could learn skills, get basic reading and writing tuition, self-defence classes, anything to keep them out of the drugs and poverty which had taken hold there again.

He had bought his flat in a different area. He hadn't wanted any reminder of his Hero days, even the good ones, wanting them washed away. But he felt guilty about not helping. He wasn't a Hero any more and here he was sitting on a big pile of hush money that would last him three lifetimes. So he decided to give them a large donation. The next week there was a follow up article, staff pictured with beaming faces: "Anonymous donor keeps centre open for next ten years", and that wasn't even a quarter of the money he had.

Something about that act sorted something, fixed something that had come loose inside. It wasn't overnight and he wasn't all better, but he felt more grounded, more real. Over the coming years he would make more secret donations, would volunteer for charity work or area "clean ups" when he was feeling particularly settled in himself.

It was around this time that Vincent was finally released from care. Martin had received a letter from Maria to tell him that she was going to help Vincent get a house somewhere, a decent place. Martin sent a cheque, the majority of what remained of his cash, saying she should get him somewhere nice, quiet, not too near, yet not too far from people. There was no reply for a couple of months and he did wonder if he had been stupid, sending a cheque like that. Was that an acceptable thing to do? Then he got a reply thanking him. His donation, combined with hers, had allowed them to purchase a nice detached house in a quiet area and Vincent had moved in the previous week. She said she knew he would love to see him, Martin being the only one who had ever written or enquired as to how he was. It was only now he wondered whether she had wanted to see him too, whether that had been between the lines.

The first time he went round to see Vincent he pulled up at the house so nervous that he had already slipped into the wrong gear and nearly stalled several times. The house was in darkness apart from one light. He got out of his car, picked up the bottle of whisky he had brought and, when he turned back round, Vincent was at the door. There was silence for a while until Vincent called: "I said 'Come in', but I guess you didn't hear me," and smiled.

He had expected all the memories to resurface, the nightmares to come back into sharp focus again. That had been the only reason he could come up with for not going to see him. But thankfully, they didn't. He came to enjoy his weekend chats, the phone calls when he needed something. Even after all this time, what they had both been through, the camaraderie was still there.

But helping buy Vincent's house had drained him of cash and he needed a job. Luckily he had been thinking about that for some time. Night work would suit him best, security work ideal. Not a bouncer though, too many people to deal with, too much pressure. He felt guilty lying on the application forms, but that tallied up with him not being registered, so it all worked out OK.

That had been the last five years.

Now Vincent was dead, he was registered, he would have no job as of today, Jack had tried to kill him, his flat was gone, PCA were digging up secrets, and he had just learned exactly what the others had thought of him all this time. Yet, here he was, sitting in a coffee shop window while it pissed it down outside, with the strangest feeling of focus he had ever had. His mind wasn't sending thoughts after him and he wasn't alone on that endless flat plain of consciousness. Instead, all of his thoughts were there, hanging in the air in front of him. He could look at any one, analyse it, step back, look at another, put similar ones together, break apart ones that should never have co-existed, and all the while he was calm, all the while he felt fine. He knew how strange this was. He should be curled up in the corner crying, customers staring at him as he struggled to prevent his mind flashing back in time to the horrible memories again. He should be overwhelmed by emotion, overcome by the past, but he was fine. Actually he was more than fine. He was angry and his thoughts couldn't be clearer.

Meeting Jack, walking along that fake lab corridor.

"You are a coward Martin. A fucking coward!"

Inna's tear track gouged face, eyes red, staring at him. *"...please..."*

The coolness of the lab glass against his shoulder as he lay there for hours, huddled against it.

Charles trying to ingratiate himself so he could get him to hand over the memoirs.

Maria reminding him about their vow of silence, warning him away from investigating too far.

Both of them playing the "all for the team" card while communicating with each other behind his back. It occurred to him that the memoirs weren't the biggest threat to them, *he* was, and they were all keeping tabs on him, who he had talked too and what he had said, with Maria in the middle, coordinating it all. But coordinating how much?

Martin looked down at the coffee. A little froth halo of bubbles clung to the sides of the cup. Maria must have known it was Jack from the moment she saw Vincent's body. But what about before then? She must have told them all about the memoirs after Vincent mentioned it to her. Had they discussed what would be done? Had it been left open, with the assumption that one of them would take care of it? At the very least she can't have been so naive as to not think that one of them would want to bury this, realising the danger Vincent now presented. Martin didn't want to think she had a hand in the decision. Jack must have been the one to decide Vincent had to go, it wouldn't have been her, she wouldn't have agreed to it. Surely?

And now what? He had done what Vincent had asked and was no closer to finding any password to the memoirs. What was it Jack said… what did Vincent write about *after* the split? Why was that important at all? He already knew what would be in them, there would be no surprises. Jack had been right too, Martin was the last person to want them published anyway, so what had been the point of any of this?

They just wanted to bury this with Inna, like it never happened. And he decided there and then he was going to let them.

Why should he care any more? He couldn't do anything else, it was all sewn up. He was going to burn the bloody thing when he got back, destroy it and tell Maria, and that would be it. Done. He wouldn't have to speak to any of them again. Suited him fine. Screw them. Screw them all.

He looked through the window to the wet world outside. He tried to think forward, plan something. Hopefully the insurance would cover the apartment, but from what he'd heard from work colleagues they always tried their best not to pay, so he may have a fight on his hands with that one, considering how it happened. And the fact he'd lied on the application form about being powered. That was going to void it. "Shit." He said to himself, as he remembered he had lied on *every* application form.

Finding work was going to be near impossible being registered, and having lied to get his current job wouldn't help matters. He now had nothing and was stuck at Charles's for the foreseeable. His stomach clenched at the thought.

And Hayley... He felt bad about her. She was so keen to help, so genuine, but she couldn't get involved in this. Things were too... complicated now, and he just wanted it finished. He was going to end it and that was that.

In any case, he no longer cared what the police investigation found, or PCA for that matter. It was unlikely they could tie it to Jack even if they worked out it was him. As long as Morris and Barclay didn't hassle him too much, ("the weak link" he thought to himself), he would ride it out.

Yep.

He sat up suddenly, the small of his back reminding him it was still knitting itself back together, and took a gulp of coffee. Tasted like nothing. He looked at his watch. He would have to meet Hayley at ten at their Sunny Food Palace HQ. Hours to go yet. He would just have to wander around town until then.

CHAPTER 41
TUESDAY 20TH JULY 1993

Wandering.

Up and down.

Back and forth.

The ritual of a disturbed zoo animal.

That's all I do now.

I feel rage. Impotent rage that tugs at me from the inside until I emerge from a delirious sickness, hours later. The churning threatens to drag me away with it unless I keep moving. Got to keep moving.

Into my room, rearrange chairs, smooth my duvet down.

Out of my room, along the corridors, hugging the wall.

If I don't hear anybody about I go down to the kitchen to grab some food before running back up.

If I do hear voices or footsteps I hurry back into my room and close the door. Then I usually hear laughter.

I know it's odd. I can't stop it. Find it hard to form thoughts for long. Anything promising tears itself apart before it gets fully formed, shredded in the whirlwind of my mind.

I shower again. Fifth time today.

My ankle is puffy and painful. Two fingers are swollen and red. My eyelids are pink and stick together. My eyes are still watery from the flames in my face. Every movement gives me pain.

I can't sleep. My thoughts, my pain, the sex sounds, their latest TV interviews on repeat play all night keep me awake. When I *do* doze off I see terrible things. So I don't want to sleep.

I don't go into the lounge any more. Lost count of the number of sex acts I've stumbled across. No coincidence. All choreographed for my benefit. I know this.

They go out on missions still. I stay behind. They no longer ask me to come. Is he bored of me now? I don't know if that's a good thing. They come back bragging about the damage they have done, the criminals they've killed and how they'll get away with it. They've lost count how many are dead now.

Inna has been fine. Of course she hasn't really, but he makes her appear so. He makes her smile and joke with the others. I hear their laughter coming from the kitchen and their rooms at night. He makes her act like she's fine.

Bastard.

I want to talk to her, tell her I'm sorry, tell her I'm sorry I was so useless, make her understand that I will stop this, I just don't know how yet. But I know if I do, I'd be talking to him. I'd be telling him my thoughts, fears, helping him get inside my head, which is what he wants. So I don't talk to her. I don't talk to any of them. I stay in my room, only coming out when it's quiet, when they are away on a mission or finally asleep.

Then I wander.

Up and down.

Back and forth.

I go to the lab. I sometimes think I see movement inside, through the thick glass wall, but it's only fleeting. Is he in there watching me? I stare. I test. I push, pull, prise. I can't get in. I can't get out.

Today, now, the team is away receiving some award at the City Hall. Today, now, I am trying to force my fat shaking fingers into a hairs breadth of a gap between the two doors. I fail again. I slap my hand on it. There is no echo. I give up again.

I turn round and go down the corridor. I turn sideways now, when I'm halfway down, closing my eyes. I feel like the curving walls are trying to crush me, but they can't if I can't see them.

I know it's odd. I can't stop it.

I'm through. I jog away to the top of the staircase, breathing freely again.

I look over the railing on the small balcony here and the floor of the atrium rushes up to meet me, making me pull my head back. I think about it. Every time I come up here, I think about doing it. Can't see any other way. Not many options right now. But I push myself away from it, because I know I can't leave them like this. There must be something I can do, if only I can clear my head and think of it.

I go down the stairs to the apartments. As I reach the next floor I hear crying.

Vincent? He's been locked in his room for weeks now. I've been to his door and knocked a few times, but he's not replied. I hate to think what's happened to him, but I'm too afraid to find out. No, that's not Vincent, it's female.

I keep one hand on the inner handrail and slowly walk round to the top of the next flight of stairs down. There, between floors, is Inna. She is leaning against the wall, arms tightly crossed in front of her. She is looking down, sobbing, sniffing.

I move back out of sight. It's got to be a trap. Another one of his games. What this time? She'll need my "help" again and try to seduce me? He can piss off. I go walk away.

"Martin?"

My heart pains. It sounds like her. Normal her. But that's what he does, suckers you in, then guts you. That's his M.O.

"Is that you?"

I close my eyes. Tears escape. I rub them away. I have to talk to her. Just in case. Tell her I'm sorry.

I walk back round to the top of the stairs. She is still standing by the wall on the semicircular landing between flights. We both stand looking at each other, both of us panting, trying to hold our emotions in. She is dressed in her full costume, all done up. She should have gone with the others to the ceremony. Her eyes are bright pink. Tears have created tracks in the powder over her cheeks.

"Inna."

It could be her, but it could be him. Want her to make the first move so I can work it out. Her eyes look into mine. Her terrified face from the other night appears in my mind. The silence screams at me. She glances down, then steps forward, uncrossing her arms. She is wearing blue nail polish. For some reason that stands out to me. I don't think I've ever seen her wear any before…

"This… this was dream." She looks out past the stairs and across the atrium. "To be part of The Pulse. Thought my life, my career was over when I was found out. Then I got call up. Found something I could do. Something to make my family proud."

I shiver. Is this genuine?

"My father… he don't speak to me. Not since he found out I was a Hero. Too much history in my country, Heroes being used by state. Couldn't see past, no matter what I did. Tried to make them all proud. Then this…"

She steps forward again and grips onto the railing, her arms gently shaking, lower lip curled up tight.

"He made me kill. He made me…"

She seems to be searching for the word, but when she gets it she doesn't say it.

"…with the men. He let me be aware, but I could not move!"

She puts one hand to her chest, taps her sternum.

"I couldn't… he stopped my powers… I tried to be strong…"

I want to say it wasn't her fault, that nobody could be that strong, but my jaws grip tight. Her hand clenches into a fist as she keeps it clasped to her.

"He likes to give control sometimes. Just enough to do what you really want, but not say you are his puppet, yes? Then he twist it."

She dips her head then looks up only with her eyes, almost embarrassed.

"That time in shower."

I swallow hard. I feel unbelievably awkward.

"That was one."

She starts blinking, fighting back more tears.

"I needed you Martin."

"I'm so sorry, I couldn't... couldn't do anything."

I barely get the words out. I brace myself for a retort from the lips of The Controller, but it doesn't come.

"You were there. You tried. I know."

"I couldn't help."

"You were there."

She nods at me, a weak smile forces its way through the despair.

She puts her other hand up to her chest and crosses her wrists. Her arms start to glow brighter and brighter until I can no longer make out the outlines of her hands. Her whole body is glowing now, her hair being picked up by her light and curling around her face.

"Inna, what...?"

"I can't... it's too much now."

Fresh tears pour out and are turned to steam. I suddenly realise what's happening.

"No, what is this? Controller... don't!"

"Not him! This is me."

She looks back at me. Her eyes are empty. Oh God, this *is* her. He knows what she wants to do and he's letting her.

"I can't be strong any more. My family... don't tell them, please."

She grimaces.

"Inna, NO!"

Her whole body becomes light. I start to move down the stairs towards her. There is a ringing sound in my ears as the whole world falls silent. Her light soaks through my body. It forces me backwards and I stumble to sitting on the steps. There is a sound like a pebble landing in soft sand and for a moment I find myself staring into the heart of a sun. Then suddenly everything is too dark, the world too empty.

All that is left of her are her feet, slowly crumbling from the ankles down into a fine powder. From her heels stretches a giant charcoal grey scorch mark, across the carpet and onto the wall behind. In the centre, a void, bright and pure, the shape of everything she was.

CHAPTER 42
MONDAY 17TH SEPTEMBER 2012

"You want me gone. Why?"

Hayley still had the last of her burger in her mouth. She slapped both hands on the table and sat rigid, staring at Martin as she chewed it and swallowed. It had taken him the whole of her meal to bring up the topic of ending this. It hadn't helped that she had launched into a stream of information about the investigation from the moment he sat down. Martin felt a flood of guilt wash through his chest, but he knew he had to press on.

"It's just easier this way. Trust me. I'm sorry. I didn't mean to make you think…"

"What, that I'm capable of making up my own mind about what I want to do? Who I want to help? Because I will. I'm not going to stop."

"Hayley, please…"

"No, I'm not. I know you Martin. You think I don't but I do. Plus, I'm a police officer, which means I can tell from that look in your eyes you've found out something you didn't want to."

Martin stayed silent.

"You met with Jack today didn't you?"

Martin stayed silent for a bit longer, then sighed deeply.

"Yes. I did."

"Yeah, I know you did, 'cos I've been following him like I said I would. Watching his movements and all that?"

Martin looked up, stunned.

"How?"

"Me jumping to rooftops, and surveillance info from the investigative team and PCA, courtesy of Gary."

She leaned forward on her elbows, her eyes staring into his.

"He never leaves the place, Pullman Tower that is. He never leaves. Hasn't left the place since The Pulse broke up apparently. All meetings have to take place there, or by holo-link or he sends someone else instead."

"Bloody hell, and I thought *I* was a hermit…"

"I know. Anyway, PCA spotted you going in…"

Martin sat back, frustrated.

"Knew the bastards would be watching me."

"…so that's how I know you were there."

Silence. They looked at each other across the empty burger wrappers and cardboard cups.

This was supposed to have been the end of the relationship. Martin had gone in confident to finish it there and then, cut her loose so he could extricate himself from events cleanly. Hayley had turned out to be more persistent than he had feared. She would make a good detective one day he thought to himself. Right now though, she was starting to annoy him.

"So, what did he say?"

Martin found it an effort to continue.

"He didn't admit to anything. I tried, but I'm not a detective, I don't know how to question somebody. Anyway, Jack's far too smart for a detective let alone me. I got nothing. It's over."

"What do you mean? You're giving up?"

"It's not as simple as 'giving up' Hayley. You have no idea how complicated it all is, it's…"

Martin's forehead ached. He clutched it with his hand and squeezed.

"There's just…"

The ache subsided and he clasped both hands together on the table. Hayley looked concerned.

"…history, Hayley. A whole lot of history. Stuff you don't know. Stuff that nobody but the team knows. Stuff that nobody else ever will."

"Oh trust me, if something is there, PCA will find it."

"Not this."

Hayley twisted her mouth up one side of her face.

"Vow of silence?"

Martin shrugged.

"Something like that. What it means is that there is no longer anything to investigate. Let the police and PCA faff around not finding out anything until they decide to drop it. It's… for the best."

Hayley sat back and crossed her arms, puffing her cheeks out.

"OK. No worries then. So, you know Jack murdered your best friend and you're going to let it slide because of something between you guys. That about it?"

She was decidedly annoying him now.

"No, I…"

"Did he threaten to beat you up again? That it? I wouldn't have thought that would stop you. Not *you*. So it must be something else, some information he has. But what can he have on *you* that would bother you, you've already lost pretty much everything as it is?"

"Yeah, cheers for the reminder. Look he doesn't… 'have' anything on me, OK? There's just a lot I can't tell you."

"And whatever it is means he can murder whoever he likes with impunity."

"NO!"

The three men behind the counter froze and looked over at them sat by the window. Loud pop songs from Radio Elemental drowned out most noise in the place but they had heard that outburst. Hayley, her back to them, turned her head slightly. Her hoodie was up as always and concealed her face.

"It's OK, he's my stepdad. Caught him shagging my sister. We're sorting it out."

The boss looked worried but went back to preparing salad. The smaller assistant looked at Martin and shook his head in disgust. The tall one grinned and gave him a thumbs up.

Martin stared down at his hands. She was right. Jack was going to get away with it because exposing the truth would expose them all. The battle inside him was slowly being won by the convenience of keeping the status quo. That thought made him so sick and angry, he didn't want to think about it any more.

"Look, Martin, whatever is going on, you do realise you are the only one who can stop it?"

"Christ. Not that again." He felt anguish in his bones. "We're done, OK?"

Martin stood up to go.

"Give me your phone."

"What?"

"Phone!"

She held her arm out straight, flicking her fingers in a "come on" motion. Martin pulled out the inanimate black slab and dropped it in her palm. Hayley snatched it away. She tutted when she discovered it wasn't turned on. After a short pause, during which Martin sat down again, she started tapping on the screen. There was a string of chiming noises.

"Whoa, someone's being trying to get in touch with *you* Captain Popular. There."

She held the phone out to him.

"I've put my number in your contact list, OK? First off, it helps if you have it switched on granddad. Handy one to remember that. Secondly, whatever has happened, whatever he said or threatened you with, it can't be worth more than somebody else's life."

Martin thought about Inna. This secret had already taken her life. Now Vincent's too.

"Call me when you figure things out, when you want to talk. Whenever you need my help I'll be there for you. I always will. I always have been, you just didn't know it," she smiled.

Martin took back the phone and looked at the screen. It had what looked like a card file on it with a number and the name "Gas Emergency".

Hayley tapped the side of her nose and grinned. Martin just nodded as the screen went dark then turned itself off. He was never going to call. He got up again, slipping the phone into his inside pocket.

"Thanks for… my life. I still owe you for that I guess. You take care, OK?"

"Sure thing boss."

"No, I mean *really*, with everything you know? You're secret's safe with me."

"Likewise. You can trust me. Really."

She did tiny, urgent nods. Right there and then he felt an urge to tell her everything, but he fought it back. It must be buried.

As he left the takeaway the three men chorused "Bye." He gave them a half-hearted acknowledgement and stepped outside, closing the door behind him. He knew Hayley would be staring at him through the window, so he didn't look back. He stood for a moment in the chill night air, gathering his thoughts. What was left to do? Oh yes, destroy that damn book before anyone else died for it.

He started walking up the hill to find a taxi rank. It was then that his phone rang. Within moments he was running. Running faster than he had in years.

CHAPTER 43
MONDAY 17TH SEPTEMBER 2012

Martin arrived at her house before the ambulance. The front door was unlocked and she was lying against the sideboard in the hallway like a smashed marionette tossed into a corner.

He wasn't sure she was still alive at first as she was perfectly still, a black silk nightgown lying over her. He instantly saw the bone jutting from her right lower leg, bent as it was into an unnatural boomerang shape, covered in rivulets of drying blood. Then the cuts, bright red slashes across her pale skin. Then the bruises, already appearing all over her exposed limbs. He couldn't see her face yet, that was hidden out of his view. He realised he was still standing there staring. His mind flashed back to how he answered the phone call when he saw her name on the screen:

"Oh, Maria, Hi Thanks for telling everybody I was coming, that's really helped you know, it gave

everyone plenty of time to work out exactly how to tell me to bugger off."

He quietly called her name, afraid to speak too loud in case the force of his voice broke her even more. No response.

"Look, just tell everyone they needn't worry, they won't see my ugly face again. And neither will you. Problem solved."

He moved towards her gingerly. He knelt over her, his hands outstretched as if trying to keep balance on a windswept ledge. He called her name again. No response.

"Please Martin, help..."

He was trembling now, panicking, eyes darting around. There was the cordless phone a few inches from her left hand, there was the massive, swollen, oozing plum of a bruise over the right side of her face, there were the streaks of blood where she had dragged herself from the living room to the hallway, there was the dashed bookcase, contents scattered across the carpet, standard lamp broken in two, the leg of a coffee table, bits of glass and other random debris that he could see in the orange light of the living room through the door frame.

"He tried... to kill... I'm broken..."

Suddenly she gasped heavily, startling him. Bubbles of blood popped and spattered her lips as she breathed out in short judders. He put his hands on her arm and hip, gently, and talked to her. He didn't know what else to do.

He stayed there until the paramedics arrived. Thankfully they knew what to do. Within moments they had a tube down her throat and one in each arm. They kept trying to get a response from her, flashing a small light in her eyes, checking her pulse in her neck and ankle. Then she was strapped into a bright yellow stretcher, head taped to a black foam headrest, and lifted into the back of the ambulance where he joined her.

He stayed with her until the doctors in A&E told him to wait outside, after he inadvertently burst into their resuscitation room with her.

He tried to peer in through the distorted glass portholes of the swing doors and decipher the medical jargon he could hear being spat out inside, but he was thwarted with both. A young nurse wearing a face mask came rushing out. She stopped in her tracks, put a plastic gloved hand on his arm to reassure him and said he would be the first to know what was happening and that he really should take a seat after having such a shock.

Martin reluctantly walked back to the waiting area, and found a seat at the end of a row as near to the room as possible.

He didn't feel shocked, at least not now. He just felt odd, as if this was an alternate reality he was observing, a "what would happen if" scenario that he would be able to rid himself of with a splash of cold water to the face.

He looked down at his hands and they seemed even fatter than normal, swollen, sensitive to the touch. A few spots and smears of blood had dried into the lines of his fingers and palms. He rubbed at them with his thumbs but they stained him.

The speckled vinyl floor started to blur and he realised he was going to pass out. He rubbed his face hard with the inside of his wrists then sat back in the chair, taking slow deep breaths until prickles ran down from his forehead to his cheeks and his arms began to feel heavy again. He became aware of his clothes, coarse, digging into his flesh. Noises bothered him: scraping chair legs, a whirring printer behind reception, the slightly worrying creak of the curved plastic chair under him, a distant phone that no-one was picking up, the swish and bang of a double door opening suddenly and a gaggle of urgent voices.

He stood up too quickly and had to steady himself on the back of the chair in front before running after the trolley. Doctors and nurses were flapping around it like vultures around a corpse, as they jogged it towards a pair of lifts.

"Is she? How is she?" he called. No-one seemed to notice.

He caught brief snatches of her between arms and heads. She was naked apart from her bra and the white sheet covering up to her waist. He could see more bruising around her stomach and ribs. The side of her face was even more swollen now, almost unrecognisable. A white tube ran from her mouth to nothing. She now had a second tube poking out from the front of her throat, leading to a plastic sac being squeezed by a doctor. Another nurse was diligently checking a cluster of blood and fluid bags hanging from a metal rail attached to the side of the trolley. She punched her finger at a small plastic coated computer with colour coded buttons that hung below them. The left side of Maria's chest had a scarlet dent in it like a meteorite crater which had been filled with gauze and covered in a sticky plastic film. A tube was sucking frothy blood into a bag swinging below the trolley. Her broken leg had blue foam packed around and into the wound, taped down at the ends. The foam was slowly turning purple as blood seeped through it.

The small nurse who had almost knocked him over earlier spotted him and, after hitting a button on the lift panel, came over. She pulled down her face mask and Martin was briefly surprised at how young she looked.

"She's OK. Battered but OK. We're breathing for her for now until the swelling goes down around her face and neck. We think she has internal bleeding so we're going to do some scans to find out where and then get her into theatre to fix whatever that shows us. We're also going to do a brain scan to make sure she hasn't got any damage there. The leg we'll fix later, after we're sure she's stable."

The lift tinged and rushed open. She turned back to the trolley and helped guide it in as the other staff adjusted bits of equipment and themselves so they could all fit in. As she went in after it, she turned back to Martin.

"You can wait in the theatre waiting room on floor three."

Martin nodded and went to get into the lift before she put her hand out to stop him. Martin noticed it was covered in blood.

"Sorry, this isn't a public lift." The doors started closing. "Floor three!" she said as they clunk-clunked shut.

The tiny square window of yellow light sped away upwards, leaving a dark mirror in its place.

Martin stared at his twisted reflection for a moment, before nodding to no-one in particular and muttering "Floor three, yes" and heading up the stairs.

CHAPTER 44
TUESDAY 18TH SEPTEMBER 2012

Martin sat for hours, drifting in and out of a fitful doze, jerking awake with the pings of the lift, metal trolleys crashing over carpet cover strips, shrill phone rings.

No-one had been to speak to him since Maria went into surgery. The worst thing was knowing that, somewhere within this building, she was in so much danger and he couldn't do a thing to help her. That anxiety again. It burned the inside of his chest. Guilt too. However complicit she was in all of this, however pissed off he was with her, he didn't want his last words to her to be the ones he spoke on the phone. He didn't want her to die thinking he hated her. Time and space had helped fade many of his feelings for her, but they had never gone completely.

Minutes caught on his clothes as they tried to slowly squeeze past. Every now and again he had to get up and shake them off him, looking at the clock down the corridor to confirm that time had indeed passed. He couldn't concentrate to read the magazines on the small table next to the row of seats. There was no-one to talk to, to unburden him of his worries. There was nothing to do here other than slowly suffocate in antiseptic anxiety. Then the agents arrived. Agent Morris was smiling inappropriately.

"Ah Mr Molloy, I see you beat us to the victim this time, or is that a poor choice of words?"

"Screw you."

Agent Morris put his hands together as if praying and dug the ends of his fingers under his chin as he walked up to where Martin sat.

"Oh, Mr Molloy, you seem tense and agitated by our presence. I had hoped you would be more relaxed with us now that we know each other."

Martin didn't stand up for them as they stood only a couple of feet away from his seat.

"Look, with respect I am really not in the mood for any of your mind games, especially after the stunt you pulled on me at the station, so if you have any questions, ask them normally then piss off."

"Did you assault Ms Gionchetta?"

"No."

"Did you break into her apartment?"

"No, the door was already open…"

"What did you do to her after you arrived?"

"Nothing. I mean I just watched over her. I'm no medic. I just made sure she was breathing."

"When was the last time you saw her?"

"Sunday. We met after I came to the police station to give my statement."

"Did you assault Ms Gionchetta?"

"No."

"Good."

Agent Morris sat down next to him, fingers still buried under his chin. Agent Barclay sat down at the far end of the row. Martin itched to move away from him.

"That all tallies up with what we already know from both of your phone records, her movements over the last few days and what the paramedics told us."

"Then why bloody ask me?" Martin thought to himself as he sank into the chair.

"It's just procedure you know. A quick way of gathering and comparing basic information from different sources. I often think it gets in the way of a more useful conversation, don't you agree?"

He twisted his head on the points of his fingers to look at him.

"I wouldn't know."

"How is she?"

It was Barclay who spoke. Martin and Morris both turned in surprise.

"Uh... she's in surgery. Has been for a while now. I'm not a doctor, but when you hear phrases like 'collapsed lung', 'internal bleeding', 'complex open fracture' etcetera, etcetera you know it's not good. I don't know." He stared down the corridor towards the theatres, but there was only a surgeon in scrubs writing into a patient's file. "I don't know."

He relaxed a little and rubbed a hand through his hair, squeezing his scalp to relleve the tension.

"Well they are experts in surgery and medical things Mr Molloy, I'm sure she is being well looked after. What did she say to you?"

Martin was almost used to this switch now.

"She called me and said she needed my help. Said someone had attacked her."

"No, she said 'he' and this 'he' had tried to 'kill' her. Not attacked. We have that recorded."

Martin shook his head in defeat.

"Yes. Yes, fine she said 'he' and he had tried to kill her. If you have the call recorded then why even…"

"Horrible, horrible procedure I'm afraid. It really is shocking."

Agent Morris slowly uncoupled his hands, wrung them together then carefully placed them, one under each thigh and extended his legs out in a stretch, pulling his toes back.

"Now some more useful conversation."

Martin wished he had the power to make himself fall into a permanent slumber.

"Please, you know this isn't a good time. She almost died. She… might still, I don't… oh just ask and go."

"Who do you think did this to her?"

"I don't know who did this."

"No, my question was 'Who do you *think* did this?'. The answer comes in the form of a name."

The agent looked around, gazing up and down corridors, eyes following different members of staff in and out of doors.

"To be honest I'm trying not to think too hard about any of this."

"Mm."

It was true. It hadn't even crossed Martin's mind who had done this, all he had thought about since the phone call was Maria. How he couldn't bear to lose her. Not after Vincent. Not at all. As the question sunk in he supposed it had to be Jack. But why?

"In any case, asking me who I 'think' might have done this… that wouldn't be admissible in court would it?"

"No no no, this is *conversation* Mr Molloy, not questioning. Conversation can elicit many more useful leads that would normally be uncovered by questioning you see? It's a useful tool. Do you think it's the same person that killed Mr Hayden-Phillips? That attacked you?"

"What?"

"That did this? Gave Ms Gionchetta a collapsed lung, internal bleeding, a complex open fracture etcetera, etcetera? Nearly killed her?"

He was still jerking his head around following the busy staff.

"I guess so."

"The same person who has been looking for something all this time?"

"I suppose."

"So…"

He suddenly swung his legs back, right under the chair and held them there. He looked down at the ground.

"...the killer wants something that Mr Hayden-Phillips has in his possession. Doesn't find it. He then believes you have it in your possession and either doesn't find it or is interrupted by yourself before he has a chance to. Then he beats Ms Gionchetta to within an inch of her life and doesn't even search her place for it."

Martin followed his thinking carefully.

"Of course he might have fled, worried that the noise would have prompted the neighbours to call the police which, incidentally, it didn't. Sad state of society today when even that sort of disturbance doesn't elicit a response..." he shook his head, frowning "...or maybe he knew she didn't have it but instead had information that might lead to its whereabouts, and intended to get that information from her."

Maria was the hub of information in the team. Anything new would have been communicated instantly to all of them. But there wasn't any new information. There had been nothing from the investigation that he knew of and all he had done since he last met Maria was move into Charles's place, which she helped organise anyway, and meet Mitchell and Jack. He hadn't uncovered anything apart from how much they all hated him. Nothing had changed, nobody had found out anything new...

Something pricked Martin's brain. He sat forward, leaning on his thighs, hands clasped over his knees. Actually, there *was* something new, and he was the one responsible for it.

"Gaps. So. Many. Gaps. They are the bane of my existence and yet the reason for it, to get them filled in."

Morris extracted his hands from under his legs and inspected the chair material weave imprint on his palms.

"There are patterns to everything Mr Molloy, stretching backwards and forwards in time. Some are trivial, some are incredibly intricate, some are interconnected, some unravel on their own and some just take longer to pick apart than others."

He stood up suddenly, making Martin flinch. Barclay stood up with him and Martin got up, more as a reflex than out of courtesy

"Help me fill in the gaps." He said, staring Martin in the eyes.

"I'll do my best."

Agent Morris smiled and was off down the corridor in one quick moment. Agent Barclay was left standing there. He took two careful steps towards Martin, stopped and put a hand on his shoulder.

"She will do fine, you just need to watch over her."

"Agent!" Morris gestured with his fingers over his shoulder and Barclay hurriedly jogged after him.

Martin stood for a long time, slowly going over things over in his head. He wasn't quick-witted like the others, but that didn't mean he couldn't work out a puzzle given time and enough of the pieces.

He took out the phone and skimmed through the missed texts and calls he'd had when it was turned off.

That confirmed it.

When he was sure he had everything in the right place, with only a small degree of bother he managed to call the right person. To his surprise, she picked up straight away.

"Hayley, you know you said 'whenever I needed help'?"

CHAPTER 45
TUESDAY 18TH SEPTEMBER 2012

It was early morning by the time Hayley dropped him off at Charles's, outside the gates this time. The code Maria gave him open them, and the automated security system recognised his face as he approached the front door, greeting him by name. Inside, the place was quiet apart from the noises of the central heating and the ticks of mechanical clocks. Martin climbed the stairs, warily eyeing the giant portrait.

In his room he looked for what he would need. One was a cheap plastic storage crate, hidden at the bottom of the largest box. He lifted the lid and inspected the contents. Apart from the "old clothes" smell everything seemed to be there. He closed the lid and placed it on the bed. He found the boots in a plastic bag of shoes and placed them on top of the crate.

Then he went over to the bookcase and picked up the book his mother gave him. The story of a family with a surprise inside. The crisp, burned cover crumbled under his fingers as he opened it into two halves to reveal Vincent's memoirs lying in a square space inside. He picked them up.

"I'm sorry my friend, but to prevent anyone trying to psychically force this you'll need a password to read it. Our old friends will help you out."

Martin sat down on the edge of the bed turning the blank book around in his hands, studying it as if waiting for another secret compartment to pop open.

"Vincent, Vincent," he muttered to himself, "I've met them all OK? I've spoken to them all, well all of them I could find. None of them knew anything about a password for these memoirs of yours. There was nothing they could tell me. All I found out was that they only care about themselves."

He held the book by the spine in one hand and waved it so the open end flapped like a fan. Nothing fell out.

"You know buddy, I think I know who killed you. Just something I need to check first, but I reckon I got him. But this…"

He held the book in the air in front of him.

"You told Maria about it. You knew she'd tell everyone. You knew someone, if not all of them would try to stop you, but I don't get why. You wanted to prove what selfish bastards they were, how far they would go to keep it all a secret? Well done, you found out. So what, you had some bloody death wish, was that it?"

He slapped the book down on the bed next to him.

"I found out about the Maria Information Network, everyone keeping tabs on me and you to make sure we weren't going to crack and spill it all. Found out too just what everyone thinks of me. I mean, *really* thinks of me, you know, behind my back. So thanks for that."

Martin clasped his hands and closed his eyes, rocking back and forth slowly.

"Why did you do it? You've only stirred up shit that should have stayed where it was. My life's gone now! Not to be selfish or anything, but my whole life as I knew it is gone. And Maria is…"

He stopped himself as his voice choked.

"Called the hospital. She's out of surgery and in intensive care. Touch and go. She'll probably lose the eye, but they won't know whether she has any brain damage until she regains consciousness, and they are keeping her sedated until the swelling goes down, so… And here am I, dragging all my old gear out, heading off tonight with a young girl I've only just met to take on one of the most powerful men I know. Do you see what you've done? I'm… uh, probably going to die."

He picked up the notebook again

"I'm sorry my friend…"

"So what's this about? This damn book…"

He flipped through the blank pages again.

"What password? The old team will help me? Something they said? OK. Let's try: 'Fuck off'."

The pages started back at him. He frowned.

"Coward!"

Blank,

"No, only Jack gave me that one. Several times mind you. The others? They are either pissed that I 'got away' with not being controlled, angry that I didn't save them sooner, didn't save Inna or resentful that I saved them at all. Especially Mitchell, seems to think I want him to look up to me, like I'm his..."

"So we figured you might need a saviour"

"Oh Vincent buddy, no."

"Only you get to be our untouchable saviour"

"I'm not. I'm not. I never was."

"Who made you our saviour, eh?"

He closed the notebook and held it in both hands at the edges.

"I could have done more. I could have saved her. I could have. I should have."

Tears dripped onto the cover. He didn't feel them rolling down his face.

"I didn't have the fucking balls. You bastard, don't make me say this."

He wiped the tear spatters off the cover.

"There was nothing I could do, I'm not..."

He felt his vision bending as the word passed his lips.

"Saviour."

His sight warped like a large stone dropping into the centre of a dark lake, tearing a reflection of the world apart. Then it quickly snapped back into focus.

"Vincent Hayden-Phillips AKA The Seeker: A Memoir" was gold leaf embossed into the red leather cover of the book. Martin could smell it now. A musty comforting smell. He could feel the texture under his fingertips and the dent of the binding. He opened to the first page.

"To most people, trust is finding out as much about another person as you can. Their fears, their dreams, learning how they think about you, about themselves, about the world. I knew everything about almost everybody, and I didn't trust a single one of them. I dedicate this book to Martin, the only person I ever truly trusted."

He turned to the first chapter and started reading.

"When it comes to our actions in life sometimes it's not our biggest secret that guides our hand, but that which is most personal…"

.

CHAPTER 46
THURSDAY 29TH JULY 1993

Secrets. So many secrets flitting around in here, like razor winged butterflies, cutting at you if you dare to go too close. No more.

I stretch my arms wide and grab hold of the two thick cables that puncture the bottom of the two dull grey cabinets in the basement. Wedging my feet in the angle of the wall I lean back and pull. With less resistance than I thought, I wrench them free, sparks skittering across the uneven concrete floor. The lights go out a few seconds later. I wait. I don't know where the backup generator is until I hear it kick in somewhere nearby. I find it behind a flimsy metal fence in a small room. Neither withstands my fists and soon it's very quiet indeed.

I can only imagine his panic right now. He'll know it's me of course. He'll be surprised for a short while, think I've lost it completely, but then he'll get angry and send them after me. But they are blind in the dark. No cameras. No Sunlight to help them and I have the only night vision goggles. The others lie crushed on the floor in storage 3.

I was worried he might spot me grabbing the stuff from there, but I think he was distracted making them do sex games in the kitchen. I make sure the goggles are on tight and turn them on. I know who will be first on the scene.

Andrea speeds in holding a torch. Crap, where were *they* hidden? She stands in front of one of the grey boxes, waving the light over the torn cabling, cursing aloud. In one move I slide out of the dark, grab the back of her head and slam her face into the box. It dents and I catch her as she drops to the ground unconscious. I make sure she's OK and leave her there, wedging the basement door shut behind me.

These stairs eventually lead up towards the back of the storage area. In fact they go all the way to the roof, but I won't need to go that far. As I quietly run up two at a time I wonder if anyone else will come down here after me? Probably not. Too risky. They will more than likely take positions on the main floors, around the atrium, by the lab.

He'll be worried now. That's where I need him, on the back foot with one man down and no eyes. Maybe he'll lose his grip on them if he panics enough. I hear a fire door scrape open above me.

"Right, take this you fucker!" A pillar of fire descends through the gap in the stairwell, bursting out sideways as it reaches each flight. Yep, he's panicking.

I climb faster, flames twisting around me. They lick over Charles's used fire retardant costume that he dumped in storage. Luckily he's a good foot taller than me, so I pull it up over my head. I can't see now, so I feel for the wall on my right, guessing where the steps are. It gets hotter the higher I get. I feel like I'm going to combust before I get there. Finally the furnace stops.

"That should have got…"

I cut him short as I leap up two, four, six steps and dive at him, landing both fists into the middle of his chest as he starts to come down. He collapses against the wall, coughing as I pick myself up off the floor where I fell. His face tightens and he puts both fists together, a hot flame starts to burn from them. I backhand him across the face and the flame goes out, his arms falling limp by his sides.

I tear at the smouldering costume, ripping it off in pieces. Some of it has melted, sticking to my own costume underneath.

I creep out through the opened door into the darkness. I am in the gym, I can tell by the echo in here. I hear a voice, Maria's, muttering "Shit, shit," to herself. In the goggles she is a paler green than the background, her eyes shining brightly. She is holding a large kitchen knife.

"I know you're here Martin. You've hurt the others, but that's fine. Come to me Martin. Relax and come towards me."

As I had hoped she, or rather The Controller, is so anxious she can't use her ability properly. Just like at the riots. Except this time I'm not here to calm her down. At least, not in that way. I easily sneak behind her before getting her into a sleeper hold. She tries to stab backwards at me but any contact she makes glances off my arms. I eventually feel her go limp as she passes out. Jesus, that made me feel like crap. I put her on a crash mat by the wall and throw the knife to the other side of the room.

Right. Business. I leave the gym, across the walkway above storage and towards the living quarters. The atrium is quiet with the TV off and no screams in the air. Through my fuzzy green view I can see Mitchell standing on the other side at the base of the stairs. I look up and spot Jack on the top gallery looking down. I'm most concerned about these two. At least they are separated, that should give me a chance. Then again as soon as I take out one, the other will know exactly where I am, so I'll have seconds at best.

Keeping low I creep out from the lounge doorway to the balcony and move round on the left. I see the two peering into the darkness but they still haven't spotted me. Suddenly, I hear a voice I don't recognise over the speaker system:

"And God said, let there be light, and there was light."

There is the sizzling sound of dozens of light bulbs turning on at the same time, followed by sparking explosions as a couple blow out. I tear the goggles off my face, but not before I'm overwhelmed with a buzz of bright green that gouges a furrow into my brain.

"Whoops! A bit too much power there I think…"

Hand over my eyes I try to back up to where I think an alcove is. I hear movement. They've spotted me. I peer through my fingers and through a haze of molten light I see two figures moving. I get into a fighting stance as best I can.

A burning punch catches me in the stomach and I stumble backwards. I push forward, swinging at a hazy figure. Shards of electricity hit me. I feel my feet lift off the floor. I land on a table, crushing it. All I can taste is metal in my mouth.

He shocks me again while I'm down. I'm screwed. My muscles are twitching so hard I can't right myself. Then it feels like the ceiling has fallen in again as Jack lands a pulse blast on me. The broken table works its way into my back as I cough blood out onto my face. Can't catch my breath.

Definitely screwed.

Bright world going dark…

***

My vision slowly returns, glowing bands of colour form hard edges as I blink. I see Jack and Mitchell standing a few feet away from me, just grinning. I try to curl up to sitting, but end up shaking like a wriggling baby on its back. Muscles all still buggered.

I give up and lie back down, trembling and waiting to die. It doesn't come.

I hear footsteps coming down the stairs and across the balcony towards us. I try to crane my head up, but instead it just nods and twists oddly.

Then I see him. The Controller stands between my two teammates and looks at me. He's young, like us. He's not how I imagined him, whatever damn difference that makes.

"Well, this has been beautiful. Exquisite even."

He runs a hand through his straw blonde hair, brushing one half of his fringe behind an ear. Across his centre parting, the other half curls down, hanging in front of his eye.

"I mean, controlling hundreds, creating chaos on the streets was an amazing rush, energising, but nothing like this. This… reminds me of my family, knowing all their secrets, little foibles, perversions. Just being able to drop in the smallest of comments, or make them do one tiny thing… it was like rolling a grenade across the floor, then watching the ensuing explosion…"

He trails off, a wistful look in his eyes.

"Hah! And then I'd make them fuck each other. And make them remember it, but not know why."

He grins. Dark glassy eyes.

"Martin, can I call you Martin? I feel like we've known each other for a long time even though we've never met. Either in mind, or face to face. It's always so interesting to meet a passive blocker. I've always had the most fun with people like you. Until I kill them. I've enjoyed playing with you, but now you just irritate me. You see, in the long run your type poses too much of a danger, obviously, and have to be dealt with. You were supposed to break like that piss wreaked streak of flesh Vincent but instead…"

He motions towards me on the ground, then sighs.

"I admire your adaptability and knack for improvisation. I'll give you that. Although I don't know that you had anything planned for these two."

He thumbs left and right. Jack and Mitchell look at him and smile.

"I think you were just hoping to sneak past them in the dark. Wing it. Unfortunately for you I had a separate backup generator installed in the lab. Some might say I'm paranoid, personally I just like to cover every eventuality."

My chest muscles twitch as I try to keep my torso off the ground, keep eye contact with him.

"Won't... get... away... bastard..."

"Oh, but I will Martin. I will. I'll get away with everything, because it doesn't matter who finds out. I can make them forget instantly and if I can't make them forget, I can have them killed. And any witnesses will forget instantly or be killed, and so on, and so forth."

"Someone will... stop you..."

The Controller leans forward towards me, sweeping an arm out to the side.

"Are you fucking blind you imbecile? Did you *see* the riots? I had hundreds, HUNDREDS under my control! Uneducated plebs, yes, but when you've got the numbers and the know-how and you get people like that into that situation they just feed off each other naturally." He rolls his hands over each other. "And then it's just up to me to nudge them the way I need them to go."

He stands up, tucking his pale blue tie into his trousers, buttoning up his dark grey suit jacket.

"But I've, 'been there done that', as they say. Not much new I can do with them. I reckon I could control about three hundred people max. But where do you take it? Ho, the riots were a blast."

He grins, eyes misting over.

"Amazing moment. The city will never forget that. Scars like that run deep, I should know. Then the shopping centre was fun, but lacked something…" he clasps his thumb to his fingers, brings them to his mouth, then releases them, smacking his lips like a chef delighting in a flavour, "… I don't know. Ah! I don't want to feel I've peaked. That's why I was so happy to meet you guys."

He puts his arms around Jack's and Mitchell's shoulders, pulling them closer to him. He grimaces, making a "Grr!" noise and clenching his fists. His puppets laugh and share the joke.

"I can't believe I never thought of it before. Take over my own Hero team. Hah, it seems so obvious now! It didn't before because I could never conceive myself being part of a team, but like this I'm not part of a team, I *am* the team. I am them. They are me. We are a team. In fact we are more of a team than we have ever been. I am the glue that binds them, and they will do whatever I want. The fun I've had, sharing their abilities, pushing them further than you ever would. The fun I've had sharing your women…"

He grins again while I try to get up to smash his teeth through the back of his skull, but my abs and thigh muscles lock.

"…and the fun I've had with you. Making you run around in circles in your head, because I know minds even if I can't get into them. I know what makes you tick. And you know, you are a good man Martin. A good Hero. Element City should be proud of you."

He makes a fist and clutches it to his chest. Jack and Mitchell copy him, looking up to the sky proudly.

"But you bore me now."

All three men drop their arms and look at me, scowling.

"You're in the way of what I want to do next."

"Which is?"

He shrugs.

"Fucked if I know. But I *do* know it will be INCREDIBLE!"

His scream echoes around the atrium.

"Heh, I just love the acoustics in this place. It really gives my voice a resonant quality, don't you think? Of course, you don't care, you're about to die now."

He turns to walk away as Jack builds up a pulse blast and Mitchell flicks sparks between his hands.

This can't be it. I've come so far. The bastard's right in front of me! I've got to be able to do *something*. In another universe I stand up calmly, dramatically getting to my feet as the three of them look on in horror; "how on earth is he doing this", "he's going to ruin our plans", but in the real world, nothing happens.

"Oh, actually, one thing I *know* I will be doing… joining in our team bonding sessions, if you know what I mean? Could never do that with you mooching around the place."

Red mist descends and I feel my heart straining to burst out through my ribcage. He stares me right in the eyes.

"Non. Stop. Fucking."

My neck feels like it's swelling to twice its size as my body gets ready to die. I realise I'm curled up and not trembling any more.

"Kill him slow guys... no, just get it over with actually."

Do my legs work now? Do they work? Come ON, WORK!

"I'm sick of the sight of the... AAAH!"

All three men suddenly clutch at their heads. Jack and Mitchell are wide-eyed, babbling loudly as if trying to speak their first words. The Controller tears at his hair as he spins round to find his mental attacker. Vincent stands on the opposite balcony, hands white to his wrists as he clings onto the railing, every vein in his face writhing under his skin as he shouts at me.

"NOWNOWNOWNOW..."

Muscles still twitching like pecked worms I lift my arms above my head, then swing them down palms flat onto the floor, tensing my neck and pushing in hard to the ground. I feel my back tear as I hurl myself up onto my feet.

Vincent is screaming, blood pouring from his nostrils as he clasps the railing like he's hanging onto a moving train.

My legs spasm. Carry me, that's all I ask, just a few steps, then you can give up, but not now! To my relief my thighs go solid as my bodyweight falls on them and I push forward, down through the balls of my feet, and charge straight forwards. I catch The Controller in the middle of his back, his head snapping over my shoulder and we crash through the railings.

I feel wind across my face. We plunge together, both head first towards the solid floor below. He is screaming incoherently. I am oddly calm about this. The world makes perfect sense right now. I can't describe it, but I feel it. It just feels right. I could burst out laughing.

There is a hard tugging at my legs and I come to a dead stop in mid-air. The Controller is wrenched from my arms by gravity, turned round to look upwards. He carries on falling, staring up at me. There is horror in his eyes. Anger. Disbelief. Getting smaller. Then he twists and bounces with a crunch and doesn't move any more. A human body shouldn't have angles like that.

A small, dark pool of blood starts to expand around his head and I close my eyes as Jack slowly lifts me back up to the balcony by the pulse field around my feet.

CHAPTER 47
TUESDAY 18TH SEPTEMBER 2012

"Oh my God, I can't believe this is happening!"

Martin looked at the items laid out on Hayley's bed. Little pieces of history. To be exact, little pieces of history he hoped he could still fit into.

"You and me both."

She had been slipping back and forth into the room in various states of dress since she jumped him from outside Charles's, out of sight of all his cameras.

"Do you think this is OK?"

He turned to look at her. This time she had on a green military style body warmer with dozens of zips and pockets and was wearing tight PVC leggings capped off with red and white trainers.

"Dark."

"You what?"

"Dark clothes only. It's going to be night outside and no lights turned on inside. Cold too."

"Right you are," she grinned and disappeared again.

"Oh, and as little metal as possible, don't want to set anything off we don't need to."

"Got it boss!"

His old dark brown and tan Roadblock costume looked twisted. He turned the waist so it was straight, but now the shoulders were off.

Sure, he was nervous. He had no problem admitting that to himself. He was always nervous before missions, he just never showed it, kept himself composed for the team. Now it was for Hayley. If she knew how nervous he really was there was no way she would... he laughed to himself. Who was he kidding, she'd teleport them into the middle of the sun if he asked her to. This girl had no fear. Then again he hadn't told her all the details, just enough.

So, this was it then. This was either the night he lived or the night he died. He loosened his belt and dropped his jeans to the floor. As he lifted his feet out he felt a twinge around the bottom of his ribcage, just to let him know it was still there.

"Wish I was in better shape for it."

"You what?"

"Oh... nothing, just talking to myself."

"Yeah, age will do that."

His chest ached as he unbuttoned his shirt, but he let it slip off his arms. Standing there in his boxers, socks and vest he looked at his body in the full length mirror beside the bed. He flexed his muscles and tried to loosen himself up. It had been a good while since he had gone to the gym. He wished he had kept up his membership, but he got put off by the number of people trying to strike up conversations. He chastised himself at that thought as he picked up the costume bottoms. He stopped going because of people talking to him? Christ, what kind of a person had he been turning into?

The bottoms went on easily enough. A little tight at the waist, but looser around the thighs than he remembered. He must have lost some muscle mass. Back to the gym it was then.

"Better?"

Hayley was still wearing the leggings, but had changed into a pair of black ballerina shoes and a short, black designer jacket tied at the waist by a belt. She had some kind of mask over her face.

"What is that?"

"Wore it at the masquerade ball we had last year." She shrugged "It's the only thing I got to cover my face."

"What about your hoodie?"

"This is better!" she grinned.

"It *is* cold out there you know…"

"I'll be fine granddad! Now come on, get yourself dressed before I call the nurse to help you."

She left. He picked up the top and unzipped the front. This wasn't as difficult as he had imagined it would be. He thought that digging out his old costume would bring back too many painful memories, but then he realised that there were no more to dig up. Maybe he was just resigned to his fate, like a death row inmate putting on his final set of clothes, trying to keep some last piece of dignity before he went to the chair. No, this was something else. He couldn't quite pin it down.

He slid his arms in and tugged the jacket across his chest, zipping it up. He had to pull in his belly to do that and felt bones cricking around as the zip closed. It felt reassuringly snug, the Kevlar panels helping keep his ribs in the right place. He buttoned the flap over the zip and tugged it down at the waist and sleeves. He put on the boots next. Big workmen's boots with thick soles and metal toe caps. Unnecessary protection, just part of the show, part of the costume. As he bent over, clicking down the heavy duty straps, he flashed back to the van. Sometimes he just had time to grab his boots from the locker before leaping in the back as it sped off. The thrill of it, was that what he had missed? The excitement of another mission, did that encompass the nervousness he felt now?

He clicked the last strap and stood up. Just the mask to go.

"Hang on, gotta go pee!"

He heard a door close and Martin stared at the flat, empty eyes of the mask looking back at him from the bed. No, this wasn't about thrill seeking. He was never *excited* to go on a mission. The fear wasn't of some potential scrap with another power, flinging each other through walls. That was a hazard, not the point. The fear was what had happened to innocent people, what tragedy, what danger they were in. That was his fear, always, that no matter how strong or how fast he was, there would be somebody he couldn't save. Heroes were meant to save everyone, and he was a Hero.

He picked up the mask. It felt lighter in his hands than he remembered. The stitching was worn around one of the eye sockets and there was a hole under the chin where the material had thinned. He would have to fix those later. Then again, why? Why fix it at all. This was just a one-off, wasn't it? Settle things for Vincent, finally put the past to rest and burn the costume. But then that would render this whole episode pointless. After all he had gone through, all the baggage he had waded through and everything he had found again, he was just going to destroy it?

No. That feeling, the reason he went on those missions back then, the reason he was doing this now, it was the feeling of doing something worthwhile. Using the gifts you had to help others less able than you. The feeling of having a purpose in life. That's what this feeling was. He remembered now. He remembered how that felt. He was a Hero.

Martin turned the mask round, put his hands inside the neck opening and lifted it over his head.

***

I pull the mask over my face, tugging the elasticated neck down over my chin. I make sure it's settled where it needs to be and make sure no hair is sticking out the top at an odd angle. I needn't have worried, seems I haven't got enough hair left for that to happen as both sides of my balding forehead peep out over the top of it. Yeah, I'll fix that.

I hear a toilet flush and Hayley slips into the room.

"You done ye…"

I wait for her to laugh but she just eyes me up and down, perhaps for a little too long, smiling.

"Yeah, you're good."

I hold my hand out towards her.

"Are you ready?" I say, feeling a smile creep across my face.

"Am I ever!"

She takes my hand and we jump.

***

We jump back and, apologising, I reach over and pick up the gloves from the bed.

"I forgot these."

"Hmm, it's been a good while hasn't it?"

I nod, feeling sheepish as I start to pull them on.

"You know, I swear these have shrunk…"

"Oh come *on*!"

Hayley grabs my arm and we're gone.

CHAPTER 48
TUESDAY 18TH SEPTEMBER 2012

"Shit, you can see my nipples through this jacket it's so cold up here!"

I ignore her as I scan the front façade of Pullman Tower window by window through a pair of hastily acquired binoculars. Every window is covered by blinds. Horizontal, vertical, roller, all kinds and no gap anywhere to see inside.

The wind flutters around us half-heartedly, but on the roof of the MMP Insurance building each buffet is a wave of icy water sliding down through our clothes.

"Nothing this side."

"Damn it! We're running out of sides."

She's nervous now. She should be, after all, I'm shitting it myself.

I point over to the Avery Tower, a tall block of office spaces for rent.

"Let's try there, I should get a good view of the south side of the building. Hopefully there will be a gap you can see through to get us in, otherwise it's the hard way."

The hard way would be teleport to the roof and, without counter surveillance or counter detection equipment, try to break into a high security research building before...

"...having to get down twenty two floors past all the cameras, automated defence systems and security staff. I prefer the easy way."

She remembered. Don't know why I'm surprised. I guess I'm still treating her as if she's tagging along for the ride, which is unfair on her. For a start she's a trained police officer, not a random civilian. I need to bear that in mind. Saying that, I'm still not sure how much experience of Hero work she has. She mentioned muggers and stopping fights, but this is a league above that and I feel responsible for her, can't let her get hurt. I say that... I haven't done anything like this for best part of two decades myself, and I'm not sure it's going to work. Or is a good idea to start with.

No Martin! Indecision bad! There is a plan. There are two of us. Stop treating her like a bystander, start treating her like a teammate.

"Exactly."

She grabs my arm. Next thing my soles are scrunching on small stone chippings and we're surrounded by a tranquillity garden.

"Camera!"

Way ahead of me. Must be a natural response for her to scan for cameras after a jump. No excuses, I should have thought of checking. I wonder who's looking after who here. What am I talking about, we're both looking after each other, that's what a team does.

She jumps us out of its field of view before I even begin to turn to spot it.

"Sorry, kind of an instinct that."

"A handy one."

I walk over to the safety railing at the edge of the roof, making sure I'm not going to get my legs in camera shot.

"This is fine, I can see what I need to from here."

The daylight is tearing away past the horizon already and the purple grey shroud of night starts to blend everything into one shape. It's a difficult angle but I lean over the barrier and lift up the binoculars from around my neck. None of the five central floors that used to make up our HQ are lit and there isn't much natural light left to illuminate them through any clear windows.

It's then I see it. One end of a set of blinds has come loose and is pulled down under its own weight, the vertical blinds curling up against each other like soft pasta. I fumble for the tiny buttons on the side of the binoculars that zoom in and I manage to get a shot of a table and, more importantly, a piece of the floor.

"Hayley?"

I hand them over to her.

"That good enough for you?"

***

We arrive near the middle of the room, only a few centimetres above the carpet. The tiny drop sends my guts running screaming to my lungs for help.

I'm next to the classic chair. We stand still for a second, but it stays quiet. No alarms go off. I had expected it to be different somehow, remodelled into offices or storage, but everything is where it was the last time I sat in here. Dust covers the coffee table and a musty smell of deteriorating cloth fills the air.

"Christ, it's like a tomb in here" she mutters.

"It is."

I walk to where the swing doors should lead towards the lobby stairwell. They're gone, replaced by a thick metal blast door. It's cold to the touch. I go up the couple of steps and towards the kitchen. It's dark. I flick the switch and the light comes on in two beats, just like it used to. The circle of ceiling still lies on the broken table at the far end of the room. I feel the muscles in my back twitch at the sight of it. Hayley appears at my shoulder.

"What happened in..."

"This way."

I turn off the light and lead her back through the lounge to the atrium. Faint light seeps in around the edges of the closed blinds as dust sparkles in the dead air. The silence hits me and I choke on the memories. Not now you bloody fool, you've got work to do.

The railing is still smashed from where I charged through it. I peer over the edge of the balcony opposite the door, down through the gloom, and I'm relieved that he isn't there. I never looked at his body again at the time so I suppose part of my brain expected it to still be there, an ever widening pool of blood still expanding outwards. Past and present seem to collapse into one point right now. In here, everything might as well have happened yesterday. Hayley was right, it was a tomb. A tomb where we had buried all our memories.

We quietly run along the opposite balcony. Hayley keeps glancing at the items hung on the pillars. Pictures and medals and souvenirs of past conquests. This must be like visiting a museum after hours for her. I envy her detachment.

We reach the stairs at the far end. There is no other way up to the lab. I'm going to have to walk right past it. I assume it is untouched like everything else in here. I pause at the bottom of the stairs.

"You out of breath already? Fucking hell, come on granddad."

She runs up ahead. I take a deep breath and follow. Each step up feels like a hundred metre descent into the ocean. Before I know it I'm miles down in darkness and can feel the weight of the world squashing me. I meet Hayley three flights up. She is staring at the ghostly black outline on the wall and floor. It is faded with time, but it's still there. She points at it as I get near.

"What...?"

"Nothing."

My legs feel like they're stuck in setting concrete. I heave them off the ground with each step. I run past Hayley and Inna's shadow and keep going. We reach the top together and I can see all the way down the corridor to the lab door. I put an arm out to hold her back and we creep down slowly. No security systems activate. Either he's confident the door will hold or they are silent and he already knows we're here. The corridor ends and opens out. Hayley makes a quiet "whoa" as the curving glass wall comes into view. There is a dim green light coming from within that is casting a glow over the whole passage.

There is the chipped patch of glass, although my blood has been cleaned off. The smashed iris and voice scanner has been fixed and there is just a single plate of brushed steel secured over it. In the centre is etched the outline of a hand.

"Can you get us in there?"

Hayley screws up her eyes and peers in through the glass the other side of the door. Then she is gone. Seconds later she returns next to me.

"Yup."

She grabs my arm and we pass through the glass.

***

We are a few metres the other side of the door. It's unexpectedly warm in here. I hear a background thrum of dozens of fans as I squint into the green dimness. The layout looks to be pretty much the same: glass cabinets filled with old costumes either side of the metal stairs leading down to the work floor, four rectangular workbenches at the bottom, equipment stored either side, machines on pulleys hanging from the ceiling, the large central "danger" lab raised off the floor.

The only difference is the covering of thick power cables and piping sprawling across the ground like ancient jungle vines. They snake under the benches and scrunch together as they collect under the lab supports. The central room itself has been blacked out but a green glow escapes through the ventilation system on top.

"Wow, I remember seeing this on TV when I was a kid," Hayley whispers. "This is cool, but I'm also shitting myself."

I gently shush her and motion right. She nods and moves to the far side of the stairs. We walk down together. I pass Mitchell's old costume, hanging on a blank plastic dummy like some odd scarecrow. I see Hayley stare at one of Maria's early dresses on her side. Don't get distracted girl. Focus. I say that and then find myself looking at a display of Inna's costume. This mannequin is more detailed than the faceless, sexless ones around it. It's a female model, almost exactly the same shape and build as she was. It's a copy of the costume she wore when she died that day, the grey outline on the stairs.

"I think about her every day you know."

I hear Hayley gasp and I press myself against the wall. Pointless reflex. He already knows we're here and where we are. I hold my palm out to Hayley and she nods as I move away from the wall and step slowly down the stairs, scanning the grey and green scene for any sign of him. That wasn't over the speakers, that was from in here.

"So do I Jack."

Step. Step.

"She needs to be remembered as she was."

He doesn't reply. Step. Step. Floor.

I look towards the partitions along the walls. They are filled with humming computers and pumps and cooling units. The cabling stretches up from the ground and digs into their exposed backs like dark probing fingers, tiny LEDs flashing around the wounds.

The workbench in front of me has old, chunky equipment on it. All four of them do, they have hardly been touched in years.

"I've found myself thinking about the past a lot, recently."

That came from near the lab, perhaps down the side of it, shrouded in darkness.

"I know what you mean. Always seems to find its way back to you however you try and escape it."

"Oh, you can't escape it. You can't do that, it would be like trying to run from your own shadow."

I hear movement, not sure from where. The voice is too far away and echoing too much to pinpoint it. I move forward, brushing my hand over the worktop as I pass it. I glance at Hayley crouching along the far wall and into the shadows.

"You can never escape your past Martin, it's what defines you as a man, what you did, what you didn't do. The decisions you make don't 'haunt' you as the popular phrase goes, they *make* you."

He is by the supports of the lab, next to a fat bundle of pipes. I think.

"And you have made two very bad decisions in coming here tonight."

"Is it really a bad decision Jack, when it is the only thing I can do?"

He steps forward out of the darkness and stands framed by the green light, a dark silhouette about twelve metres in front of me. I can just make out the edges of his jaw and cheek as the light curls around them, and I know he's staring right at me.

"Oh but it isn't Martin. You could have decided to die. You could have died back at your apartment. That would have solved several problems in one fell swoop. You could have decided to do nothing, go back to your lonely night shifts except..." he gasped "...oh, you can't any more can you?"

He shook his head.

"I had hoped that you would give up, that it would all be too much for you and that you would do the honourable thing, do what you have surely contemplated several times over the years, and take your own life. Save me the trouble."

I clench my fists and stare into the blank shadow face.

"Well I guess you never knew me that well."

Jack suddenly laughs. It sounds strange and I realise I have never heard him laugh before. He stops just as suddenly.

"Where are the memoirs Martin?"

"Somewhere safe."

"Nowhere is safe from me, Martin."

"It is when the only person that knows is me."

Jack gives a single chuckle and shrugs.

"Look at you standing there all costumed up and confident. It's cute in a way. Like eighteen years never went by."

He steps forward into the light and I can see he is wearing his old Pulse one-piece, minus the head and boots. He is smirking.

"We know this can only end in one of two ways" he says.

"Yeah, I know."

With a deep breath in, I brace my abdomen, grab the edge of the workbench, and I pull it quickly towards me. The bolts fixing the legs to the floor snap. He is readying a pulse blast, split seconds left. Ribs scream to be left alone to heal as I tip the bench over to face him while pulling it across me, layers of dust left behind in the air.

The pulse is almost fully formed over his hands and forearms, he is about to throw his arms forward. I grab part of the frame underneath the bench and manage to haul it up in front of my face as the blast shoots out from his body. I barely keep my footing as it hits the surface, denting it and is reflected back at him. There is a scream as he is hit by his own blast. I drop the bench and see the pulse scatter, tearing apart cables and pipes, ripping open big square machines that spill their metal guts across the floor.

I quickly look back to the other side of the room but Hayley isn't there. Fine, as long as she's safe I don't care if she's bailed.

Stupid, distracted. Jack launches himself at me, fists glowing bright blue. A punch lands in my stomach and my intestines shrivel. It feels like a long steel pole has been fired at me end on as the force sends me flying backwards. I hear the wind in my ears and then a dull thud in my spine as I hit the outer glass wall next to the door. I land on all fours, spitting saliva and trying to keep my bowels from escaping out of my mouth. I need my lungs. Where are they? No air. I look up and see the empty damaged lab through blurry eyes. I hear him running around somewhere.

"No! Nooo, I need that! I needed that! Dammit!"

I spot him by one of the machines tearing out damaged circuit boards and trying to fit in replacements grabbed from a nearby shelf. Now *he's* distracted. Still on the ground, I slide myself down the other side of the stairs, where Hayley was, before getting to my feet. I stay low and make my way to the storage cabinets. No time to be subtle. I punch the locks and rip off the doors. It takes me a moment to pick out what I need and I grab it before shrinking into the dark behind the lab. It's gone silent. I awkwardly step over a bunch of cables as thick as a fallen trunk.

"The damage you've done..." he starts muttering from the other side of the lab. "I should have killed you as soon as I knew. You are too dangerous. I should have known. One stupid mistake and it could all be over. Stupid. Stupid! Stupid!"

I see him round the corner of the glass lab. He is hitting the sides of his head repeatedly. Then he stops and cranes his neck round into the back of the lab where I am hiding.

"It's got to be now. Got to kill you now."

I press myself next to a shelving unit, keeping him in view. He moves around the back wall of the glass box and scans the darkness. He turns to look at the opposite corner and hovers for a moment.

"What have you got there?"

He covers himself in a pulse shield and steps back.

"Do you think that's any use to you now? Enough of this... LIGHTS!"

Rows of halogen ceiling lights frizz into life in quick succession from the front of the room towards the back. As they bleach the air around me I'm already standing in front of him. My legs are wide, knees bent and I'm leaning forwards, a cylinder of compressed air jammed into my abdomen, nozzle end facing him. He looks at me quizzically, almost amused.

"Remember the market?"

I grab the nozzle and swiftly wrench it off. The explosive burst of compressed air escapes in a jet in front of me. It passes right through his shield, tearing at his costume as his body is lifted off the floor and up through the rear wall of the lab. The wall dissolves into tiny chunks of glass that skitter out across every surface. The blue glow of his pulse shield fades and is replaced by the green glow from inside the lab.

I drop the canister to the floor and try not to be sick as my guts settle again. No time to dawdle, I've got him on the back foot. I jump up through the gap after him. He is on his back at the other end of the lab, clutching his face, coughing. I see blood trickling from between his fingers.

I look down and see all the cables below me. The floor isn't solid as it used to be, it has been replaced by metal grating with access hatches to small control panels bulging out of the plastic spaghetti. I follow their line of travel under my feet as they converge in the centre of the room, sprouting out of the ground like roots of some ancient tree, forcing themselves into dozens of orifices of a black circular disc of a machine. I look up and see a long glass cylinder filled with fluid, a soaring green monument on its plinth. Inside is the offering, a shrivelled comma of flesh, tubes and wires bursting out from it, as The Controller slowly rolls his eyes to meet my gaze.

"Holy. Fuck."

"Eighteen years locked in here."

Jack is speaking. He's on his feet, eyes streaming tears and thin slips of blood.

"It took all my mental effort to take him over when he came to dispose of my 'body'. Almost killed me, again. For years I couldn't let him get too far away, only had the strength to maintain control of him alone."

Jack coughs and clutches at his chest, pulling at shreds of spandex.

"Do you know how many times I wish I'd died in that fall? Ended up in the incinerator, so much dust in the air?"

The horror of the reality sinks in. When I read the memoirs I had hoped Vincent had been wrong, that this was all some mistake, some misreading brought on by his illness or his medication. But then I hadn't picked up that Jack never said "saviour" when we met, which meant Vincent hadn't been able to imprint him with the password to say to me, which meant he must have been under the control of another psychic.

"Vincent knew."

"Yes, but thankfully I'd fucked him up enough to keep him on medication for years. He barely remembered his own name let alone what happened here. In the meantime I managed to keep myself alive thanks to my handyman here."

Jack waves as The Controller speaks through him.

"There was nothing that could be done for me though. This contraption keeps me alive but can't fix me or make me stronger. So there was nothing for it."

Jack shrugs.

"I had to be him, this… for the rest of my days. There are worse bodies to be stuck in to be sure, but keeping up his boringly, painfully stoic persona all these years has been an incredible strain. But oh yes, I've partied outside the limelight, I've had fun that you couldn't imagine. Well actually… you could, you've been there."

The Controller's contorted face twists into a weak grin around the plastic mask and tubing shoved in his mouth and nostrils. I tighten my fists, stepping sideways to keep the The Controller between myself and Jack. He won't send a blast at me with himself in the way.

"I should thank you though, Martin. I say that honestly. This whole incident has helped me mature as a person. After all I was only, what, twenty four back then? All I could think of was fucking over a city, in many ways literally."

Jack rubs the tears from his swollen, red eyes and puts his hands on his hips as he steps around the cylinder too. We keep eye contact.

"But when you put me in here you gave me the opportunity to think deeply about what I wanted to achieve in life outside of the moment to moment fun. You do realise it's not easy for psychopaths to make long term plans? Spent years just fucking around in anger before I realised I had to think long term. And the answer came to me: I wanted everything to die. Total chaos, end of the world, Armageddon."

My feet crunch on broken cubes of glass.

Jack shrugs.

"I mean, why not? Hah! So through him I helped create one of the largest technology companies in Britain. In fact we've just won a huge contract to supply psychic-suppressing machines for all major government buildings. That's what years of research gets you when you have nothing else to do!"

His ranting starts to grate.

"You are nothing, you're just a psychopath in a tube of jelly who should have died years ago. Armageddon my arse."

"You really don't see the big picture do you? You have no idea the plans I've made. These machines…"

"Frankly, I couldn't give a shit."

I reckon a well aimed punch should smash this tube in. I quickly sidestep out of Jack's view and raise my fist to strike.

"Martin!"

I see Jack through the cylinder, body contorted by the fluid inside. He is holding out his arm, but there is no pulse energy around him.

"Haven't you forgotten something?"

I rack my brains for a moment. Nothing, he's just distracting me.

"Actually yeah... Jack, you may have been a massive dick, but you never deserved this."

"Ha ha! No, I mean what I said earlier about you making 'two' very bad decisions in coming here."

I glance around nervously. I feel very exposed and unsure. Jack leans around the bend of the glass and whispers.

"Bad decision one: not giving up or dying. Bad decision two: bringing somebody else with you. I'm strong enough to take over *two* people now."

Jack grins. I feel a separating of air behind me then Hayley wraps her arms around my body, one round my waist that grabs onto my belt and another up and across my face, grabbing at my eyes and nose. There is a thin moment when I try and call to her but the next is purple and white shapes and then I suddenly feel very light and cold.

She lets go of me and I look round to see her grinning, waving at me before jumping. The hole she leaves behind sucks in the surrounding clouds as I start falling. The air buffets me. My nostrils and throat fill with ice when I try to breathe in.

I break the clouds and recognise the shape of the city painted in lights below me. Spreading my arms and legs out into a skydiver pose makes me feel like I'm doing something useful but I know I'm pretty much screwed. Probably less than a minute before I hit one of those skyscrapers wobbling around below me. If I'm lucky they are shoddily constructed and the multiple floors will slow me down enough to survive. Or just enough so that they can identify the body.

Oh shit.

Maria, if I could be by your bedside now, just to say how sorry I am for everything, to tell you that I tried. Because that's all we can do isn't it? Just try. Otherwise nothing will change. If I hadn't tried I would still be hiding away in my flat, in my job, in plain sight. If I die right now, it's because I finally decided to change something, not because I gave up. I guess that's enough.

That looks like the telecoms mast on top of the BBC tower. That would make one hell of a front page picture tomorrow if I hit that dead on.

Vincent, if I could see you again buddy I would thank you. Even as I plunge through the night air, I would thank you for getting me here, for saving my life from purposelessness.

I'm crying.

Oh god, is this it?

Inna, I'm just sorry. I thought I got him for you, thought I'd ended his sick games, but he's still alive, and now I'm *really* not going to be able to stop him.

The tiny point lights have changed into large globs of colour, smears across the earth.

Christ, that thing looks like it's going to be hard.

"Ma..."

"..in."

"..uck!"

I stop looking at the ground and twist myself around to face the sky. Hayley pops into view above me, reaching out, but too far away.

"..aa.."

Gone. I see sky.

Back. Closer.

"Nuh.."

Grim face. Gone.

I reach up into the sky as windows whizz past me.

"Shi.."

***

We slam into the stack of mattresses so hard they all burst. Springs and shredded filling fly out and bounce off the walls. Hayley cracks her jaw off my forehead and bounces away from me, tumbling out of sight with an "Ow".

I feel like the sky has collapsed into my face, as I find myself staring up into a dirty concrete ceiling only a few feet from my nose. My guts rebound into my abdomen and I'm overcome with a queasiness of stillness. I'm still falling inside my mind.

Hayley scrambles into view and stares at me, face racked with terror.

"Oh my fucking Jesus Christ! He got me! He took over me and made me drop you. I didn't mean to do that, that was him, oh God, but then I jumped back here by instinct which I always do if I jump when I'm falling 'cos I carry momentum with me you see and that sudden distance change broke his mind-fuck-link thing whatever he does but then I had to try and remember where you were and I've never tried to catch someone falling at terminal velocity trying to work out where you'd be next in the time I jumped not helped that I was panicking and kept coming back here when I didn't want to and I thought..."

I grab hold of her arms and she stops.

"I think that just about covers everything."

Her eyes look to her right as she thinks.

"Yeah."

"Thanks for saving my life."

She laughs nervously.

"I guess I did didn't I? That's two you owe me."

She sits back and almost tumbles off the edge of the mattresses again but I keep hold of her arm. I sit up, balancing myself on the broken bedding. I'm about eight feet up on a huge pile of old mattresses, pillows, duvets and boxes. It tastes of concrete dust and stale air in here.

I stumble down to the ground as the last few minutes catch up with me. Damn, feels good to have solid crunchy ground under my feet again. I lean on my thighs and take some deep breaths, coughing as the dust laminates my throat.

"I'm sorry Martin, I couldn't help it, he made me..."

"I know, that's what he does."

"Oh God, we can't do anything, we'll get taken over as soon as we try and go back!"

The Controller. Jack. I feel a sudden urgency and my heart starts pounding. This has to end now. If I delay he'll move himself somewhere else, somewhere I'll never find him. I look over at Hayley leaning against the wall next to a collection of battery powered lamps. Momentum. Momentum and surprise, that's all I have in my arsenal. I run down the tunnel into the darkness.

"You can't get out that way, it's all underground and locked up, I'll jump us out!"

"No, stay there!"

I come to a halt about forty metres away, all dust and darkness around me. I turn round and she is silhouetted by the lights, a dozen shadow Hayleys stretched across the walls of this bunker.

"I've got one idea and we're going to do it right now. Listen up…"

With that, I start running at her.

***

Jack is kneeling down, working at a terminal on the far side of the lab when we reappear at the same spot we left from. Hayley instantly jumps away as instructed. I am running full pelt, full momentum, pounding on the metal floor. They both look at me. I think he manages to work out what I'm doing in the split second before I charge into the glass cylinder, shoulder first.

A moment. It doesn't move. I have a vision of myself bouncing back onto the floor like an idiot. Then the next moment it gives like a stubborn shell, splitting into large blade like shards. I keep running through the thick green fluid. It sticks to my clothes, to my face, smelling faintly of urine. I reach out and grab The Controller, slippery skin and plastic tubes. I pull him to my chest as I charge on. My feet slip on the floor of the container and I fall forwards. I feel tugging at me as his tubes and wires reach the end of their slack and either snap in half or come sliding out of him.

The fluid is in my eyes, sticking to my teeth as I hit the far glass wall. This one smashes instantly, the whole tube weakened, and we both tumble and slide out onto the lab floor. I must have been running fast as we roll several times, smashing through piles of boxes, until I lose my grip on him. He almost slips out of his own skin, a thick layer of cells left plastered over my arms and chest, and bounces away towards Jack. A reddening, shrivelled bean that curls up into itself, gasping a sigh of pain.

I slam into the wall next to the door, denting it, cracking the glass. I spit out bits of jelly and slip around as I try to get up. I use the wall as support to get to my feet and decide to stay where I am. Everything is oddly quiet now.

Jack walks towards the shivering body on the floor. His eyes are wide and fierce. Pulse energy forms around his fists. I see The Controller try to look up at him, gently lifting an arm before twisting away in agony.

The first punch caves the side of his skull in.

The second bursts it open at the back, forcing his brains out.

The following punches reduce his head to a smear as Jack, crying, hits him again and again and again. The metal floor bends and gives under him, flecks of flesh flying up with each drawing back of the arm. Something shatters and sparks buzz around him as Jack stares intently at the tattered rag of a skull flattening under his fists, each punch tugging on the spine, the body jerking as it is slowly dragged down into the deepening hole.

Jack is screaming now. All I can make out is "Eighteen years!" repeated over and over. Spittle runs down his chin, his eyes are red and streaming tears. After a minute I slowly turn round and leave by the lab door. I sit on the steps outside, listening to the roars behind me and wait for him to finish.

CHAPTER 49
FRIDAY 30TH JULY 1993

"We tell no-one. Ever. Anyone who breaks that rule will find themselves in the incinerator along with The Controller."

Nobody said anything.

"The team no longer exists as of the end of this meeting. You will each receive a considerable deposit into your bank accounts in three days time. Call it a golden handshake, call it hush money, I don't fucking care. You will take it."

The team sat in the lounge, Martin on the steps by the doorway to the kitchen corridor, Maria and Andrea on the sofa near each other. Maria had her arms folded tightly across her chest, legs pressed together, sitting back. She was the only one in costume, wearing her black Gothic dress and make-up. Andrea had her legs folded up under her. She had a bulky knitted jumper on and was picking balls of fluff off it, dropping them on the carpet.

"Vincent has been committed to a secure mental hospital. I have informed his family of this and that myself and Maria will make sure he's taken care of and monitored. The official line, which will be confirmed by the doctors, is acute psychic psychosis brought on by fighting The Controller."

Charles sat opposite the girls in the large classic chair. He was leaning forward, elbows on his thighs, hands clasped together. His face was tight and unreadable. Mitchell was leaning on the wall by the doorway to the atrium, hands in jeans pockets, staring at the ground. He looked like he was sobbing gently.

"I will send Inna's personal possessions back to her family in the Ukraine. The official line is that she was atomised by a villain during a secret mission. She was guarding some civilians when she was attacked and killed. Suicide for any reason just wouldn't have been in character and would be a smear on her whole life, especially back home. She died protecting others, as she would have wanted."

Jack stood at the far end of the room in front of the windows. His arms were down by his sides, rigid, fisted, as he spoke.

"There will be an official press release tomorrow. It will say that, in saving the city from The Controller, events took their toll on us and we each need to take time out to reflect on our next move. We thank the city and its people for their support. It will also say this doesn't mean the end of The Pulse, that there is always a chance we will reform if the time is right."

Maria looked up at Jack.

"It's bullshit of course."

Andrea squeaked the sofa as she changed the position of her legs. Something electrical clicked and a fan came on in the kitchen.

"You have as long as you need to clear your personal items from your rooms. But as quickly as you can. I don't imagine you'll want to hang around for long anyway."

Charles brought his clasped hands up to his face and leant his nose on top of them. Mitchell sniffed back tears.

"Our public actions while we were under his control are all covered by our previous press releases and interviews. Any members of the press contacting you for comment on the split or recent missions, bounce them straight to me and I will deal."

Maria cleared her throat and swallowed.

"And that's it."

Jack seemed uncertain for a moment, then nodded to nobody in particular and left the lounge to the atrium. Mitchell put his hand to his face and slipped out, head bowed. Andrea watched him go, then slid her legs out and followed him, clutching the ends of her long sleeves. Charles stood up purposefully. He tugged down the bottom ends of his black jacket, said "Sort my things," to nobody, and left.

Only Martin and Maria were left in the room. There was an awkward moment where they both wanted to say something but didn't know if they should. Martin wanted to ask her if she was OK, ask about her and Jack, their marriage, the future. But there just didn't seem to be any words that made sense in any kind of sentence right now. Maria couldn't find any either and, after a moment, she stood up and walked out of the door towards the stairwell to the front lobby.

"It's over," thought Martin, even though a sizeable part of him knew it never would be. The Controller may be dead, but he would always be with them.

His things were already in boxes and bags sitting on his bed. The plan was to stay in a hotel not far from here until the pay-off arrived, then start looking for a small flat. Begin again.

He wanted to think of a future where none of what had happened mattered. A future where they were still The Pulse, Heroes of the city and were out there making a difference, doing good and saving lives. But he couldn't seem to see it, it kept getting smothered and killed by the darkness in his mind.

The sun slowly shifted towards the horizon, long bars of light sliding through the long vertical blinds, across the room and up the wall. Martin sat alone in the quiet room as the walls pressed in on him.

CHAPTER 50
TUESDAY 18TH SEPTEMBER 2012

It takes a good five minutes before the screaming and pounding of metal stops. Then another ten filled with crying and quiet sobs before I hear Jack slowly get to his feet. Another five before he comes to the doorway. I stay sitting on the stairs as he stands next to me holding on to the handrail. I don't look up. He wouldn't want me to see his face right now.

We stay like this for some time, nothing being said. We don't need to. In my head we have a conversation about everything he has gone through, everything I have done and we come to an agreement that certain things should stay unsaid. I guess he has thought the same conversation too when he suddenly grunts, nods his head and says:

"The incinerator still works. I can disable the cameras from here until it's done, so you won't be recorded."

I nod slowly in understanding.

"Anything else you need me to do? All this... equipment?" I look around at the bundles of cables and racks of hardware.

"No. No. All... re-purposed. Labs can use it."

"Sure."

I nod again and sit up straight as I feel my loosened ribs grinding together sharply.

"That... that girl..."

"Won't say a thing. Won't tell her any more than she's already seen. Doesn't need to know."

"Doesn't need to know."

He stands there, breathing in and out deeply, wiping his hand over his face, trying to settle his consciousness. I stand up and turn to face him. He looks shrunken and exhausted. He doesn't look at me.

"Thank you," he says quietly.

Then he walks past me down the steps to a computer console with a bank of monitors displaying CCTV footage. He taps at the keyboard.

I feel like crying, but I manage to hold it in before it bursts over me. So much needs to be said yet we already know most of it and so we don't bother. In any case I don't want to think about the past any more. I'm done with it. Well, almost.

The Controller's carcass is half buried in a pit of mangled metal near the broken cylinder. I go and look for something to wrap it in.

***

About an hour later, having cleaned myself up, I emerge on to the roof of the building. When the security door clicks shut behind me I feel a fleeting desperation to force it open, to get back inside. But then I take a breath and realise I have no need.

I walk to the edge of the roof and look out over the city. The patterns of colour are different from when I was up here last, but I can still make out the bridge, the strings of light along the banks of the river, the constellations of the suburbs. All those lights, all those people. I imagine myself as one of them, sleeping soundly, waking up in the morning ready for another day at work, oblivious. I laugh at the craziness of it. There was so much torment and pain involved, how could they *not* know what has happened here? Surely it would seep through the air, affecting the whole city until everyone knew? But of course not, that only happens in my nightmares. Nobody else will ever know what has happened here, either eighteen years ago or today.

What was it The Controller said through Jack at our first meeting? "The past is a shared delusion until it is given form." Fine. A delusion it is, existing only in our minds, mine and Jack's, far away from the reality in front of me. It makes more sense this way.

I put my hand up and wave to the city. Hayley jumps next to me.

"Camera..."

"They're turned off until we go."

"Shit! I was worried, I almost went back in there, like, thirty times but stopped myself..."

"Good. You did good."

"Everything OK? I mean is he...? That was... that wasn't *him* was it?"

Her face is scrunched up with confusion. Not wanting to spread the delusion any further I put a hand on her arm.

"It's almost done now."

"Almost? Done? But I thought you'd got your revenge! Didn't you? What... I don't get it."

I smile at her.

"Sometimes you don't get it. Sometimes you just have to go with your gut and know you did something right. Tonight you just proved yourself. You did really good."

She smiles back, still confused but happier at least.

"As for revenge, no. This was a favour for an old teammate, to help free somebody trapped in the past just like I was. The revenge part is yet to come. Just one more thing to do. You ready for a trip to London?"

CHAPTER 51
WEDNESDAY 19TH SEPTEMBER
2012

I'm sitting in one of the armchairs by the fire when Charles draws up outside in his Jaguar. It's just gone four in the morning and faint moonlight peers around the edges of the heavy curtains. I hear footsteps crunching up to the door. I hear the "beep-clunk" of the security system as it scans his retina and disengages the magnetic locks. I take a deep breath in and steel myself.

"Martin? I got your message – you deciphered the memoirs, yes? Martin...?"

"In here."

The heavy footsteps move across the polished wood floor of the entrance hall then across the carpet of the hallway. Thud. Thud. Thud. Charles swings the door open vigorously. He stands there for a moment, pausing expectantly, holding onto the doorknob, but I ignore him.

"Well old chap?"

He half runs over to me, then slows down as he approaches the second, empty chair angled opposite me. He places his hands on the back of it and stares at me.

"What does it say? Do you still have it here? Where is it? Jesus, what's that smell... what the fuck happened to you?"

I take my time.

"It said everything Charles."

"Everything?" his face droops. He's shaking.

"Absolutely everything. Everything about The Controller. How he infiltrated us, took over us, what he made us do, what really happened to Inna..."

"Yes, tragic I know." Charles seems distracted. He grips the chair back so tightly his knuckles whiten. I start to smell singeing fabric. "A horrible, horrible thing..."

"I know."

I stand and walk over to a group photo of us on the mantelpiece. Taken before things went bad, we were all smiling. Even Inna had cracked a one sided grin for the camera.

"Problem is... I've been thinking about who would want to keep that secret. Who would want to keep that secret so much that they would kill for it."

"We know who it is Martin!" Charles seems irritated. "It's Jack! His company is worth billions, it would ruin him if this got out."

Charles starts to crack a smile. "You went for him didn't you? You got him didn't you?"

"It would ruin all of us Charles." I turn to face him. He grips on to the chair. It starts to smoke around his hands. "And that's the problem. None of us would want that getting out, most of all Vincent."

Charles eyes dance all over my face, desperately trying to decipher me. His smile recedes into confusion.

"But that's not why he wrote his memoirs. He never had any intention of publishing them."

"What?" Charles looks lost.

"They were only ever meant for me to read. Only I can."

"You? I don't understand. Why write them for you?" Charles lets go of the chair leaving two shiny molasses brown, smouldering hand prints.

"Because he had suspicions. Suspicions of things he couldn't tell me on the phone or to my face in case we were overheard. Suspicions about someone that he could only confirm when the book was finished and he told Maria about it. He didn't have to die for me to find out, but he was expecting to."

"Expecting to?" Charles seems to gather his thoughts. He's looking at the floor.

"Thing is, he hadn't realised that another one of us would kill for something else. Something personal, not life ruining, no dangerous revelation, not even a huge secret. Something never spoken out loud but understood or assumed by everyone. Nothing worth killing over. Nothing worth beating the shit out of Maria over."

Charles is shaking.

"How.. how is she? I've been busy I haven't..."

"Don't give me that shit you fucking bastard."

Charles stares me in the eyes.

"What are you suggesting?"

"I don't suggest a thing. I know."

Charles clenches his fists.

"It was Jack, Martin. He's the one you need to be going after. He killed Vincent. He attacked you. He attacked Maria. Isn't it obvious? We talked about this, I thought you understood?"

I nod and look thoughtful.

"Well one out of three isn't bad I guess. He definitely attacked me at my flat, no argument with you there. But that was a delayed reaction you see. It took a few days for Maria's message about me having the memoirs to get through to him. That PA of his is ruthless with the admin."

Charles' face is turning red.

"The others? No, that was someone else entirely."

"Give me the memoirs."

"No. You see I've not long spoken to a very nice, if extremely anxious porter at The Dorchester in London, who tells me that for certain celebrities who ask, and slip him some cash, he'll let them in and out of an emergency exit where, incidentally, there is no security camera. You don't have to go past reception at all. In just over an hour you could be back up here and as far as anyone knows you're still in your hotel room."

His face is contorted and fixed, his fists glowing.

"And can you remember which nights he happened to let you slip out undetected? Do you need me to jog your memory?"

"Give. Me..."

"No." I shake my head. "Because they're not yours to have. You know, they are actually very well written. Well of course they would be, Vincent was an English literature graduate you know. Now I come to think of it, the brother of one of the girls I work with at the shopping centre has contacts in the publishing industry."

"What?"

"Sure, it would take me some time to transcribe it all from psychic text to actual text, but…"

"You wouldn't do that."

"Or I could just release it on the World Wide Web. You can do that now, so I'm told. These little book reading devices you get. I'd sell it for ninety nine cents, the whole sordid history of our team."

"You can't do that." Charles' clothes billow away from him as the heated air around his skin escapes. "Don't you fucking do that."

"No? Oh. OK then. How about this then 'buddy': how about tomorrow, you go to the police station and confess to what you've done. And when they ask why, you can tell them it's only because you didn't have the balls to come out."

"How dare you! You have NO RIGHT to say that to me!"

Charles is burning now, smoke and flames lick around his body. I can barely stand the heat at this distance. The log fire barely registers. For a moment I wonder if I'm doing the right thing, but then I remember Maria's crushed body in her apartment and tighten my fingers into a fist, preparing myself.

"Everyone knows Charles. Everybody already knows. Every fan of yours, every interviewer, every panellist, every publicist, every make-up girl, every fucking tea boy knows. Everyone knows your marriage is a sham and wonders why the fuck you did it since it's so bloody obvious you're gay."

"NOBODY KNOWS!"

"We all knew. Everyone who followed the team even back then knew. There are whole websites dedicated to gay Heroes. You're on there, filed under 'in the closet'. Just come out! No-one will be surprised or shocked. It's not going to ruin your showbiz career. Unless you think it's worth killing all of us over?"

"No-one can know!" he spits through gritted teeth.

"To be honest, I hardly care any more, especially after what I've seen today. Seriously Charles, I always respected the fact you didn't want to openly admit it. That's your choice after all. I do get how important that is to people like yourself; when, how and if they come out and all that. But you know, after what you've done... you can burn in hell because I'm telling the whole bloody world!"

"NO!"

Charles swings his arms together in front of him, slams the sides of his fists together and unleashes a massive jet of flame towards where I stood a split second ago. It slams into the wall next to the fireplace, charring a hole through into the kitchen, melting a water pipe which starts to gurgle its contents down the wall.

I knew him well enough to know how he was going to attack and how long it took him to ready it. I roll out from behind the other chair and I'm running along the far wall towards the door to the hallway. Charles roars as he turns to track me. I grab an antique sideboard as I run past it and fling it towards him. Charles disintegrates it with a flash burst. By the time the embers clear the air I'm out of the door.

"NO!"

As I run, I hear him pounding across the room behind me. I nip through the doorway, recoiling from the heat as a billowing cloak of fire bursts through it, setting it on fire immediately.

"You selfish bastard!" I cry.

I really don't think I need to goad him into following me, but I can't help it.

"Shut up!"

I'd seen him angry before, heard rumours of his artistic temper tantrums, witnessed him let rip with his powers, but now I'm worried. Inside his mind he has everything to lose by letting me live.

I run up the stairs.

"MARTIN!"

I stop underneath the massive painting and turn to see him at the bottom of the stairs in full flame. His whole body crackles as fire erupts from his skin and is drawn back around him like the tail of a comet. I've never seen him like this. I guess I was right to be worried.

"Vincent didn't deserve to die Charles! Not after everything he'd been through, those lost years. He helped save our lives. The most decent, harmless man I've met in my entire life. Was he worth it?"

501

"He didn't need to say anything, write anything or do anything. He just needed to keep his mouth fucking shut and the snivelling wretch couldn't even do that!"

"Or what about Maria. She might have permanent brain damage! She's lost an eye! All for what?"

Charles stares.

"You? Your peace of mind? Your privacy? Were they worth it? Do you feel safer now Charles, is the world better for you?"

"You don't know."

"Don't know what Charles? Educate me." I fling my arms wide.

"You didn't have him in your head. You didn't have him rummaging around your personal..."

"Oh Jesus Christ, don't tell me this is about The Controller?"

"Only you can say that you smug bastard. Look at you running around confused at how we're all so fucked up in the head. It's because he was in here…" Charles points to the side of his head, then at me, "…but you got away with it. You were immune. You have NO IDEA what it was like!"

That image of Inna in her room with the three men crowded around her flashes unbidden into my head. My neck stiffens with rage.

"Don't you dare say I have no idea what it was like. With all the horrors you committed you at least have the excuse that you were under his control. Everything I did and didn't do, couldn't do, was all me. All my fault. And you know what? I'm done hiding from it. I'm ready to accept that now. I'm ready to be judged for what I did. For what I am."

I point at Charles.

"Those memoirs are going public, and we'll all be judged for what we are."

Charles screams and slams his fists down on the ground. A wave of fire rushes up the stairs, engulfing me. It breaks on the landing wall, shatters an antique chest of drawers, explodes vases and decorative plates and ignites the massive portrait. Paint bubbles and fizzes from the frame inwards. I hold my breath and screw my eyes shut as I dive up the left hand flight of stairs. Too slow, stupid. I knew that this flame retardant gel Hayley nabbed from the fire station would only buy me one mistake and that was it.

I run up to the balcony and down the picture corridor, wiping hot burning chunks of congealing jelly from my legs and chest. They drop onto the carpet, sticking like lava bombs.

Got to keep moving, keep my distance. Shit, nearly overran. Stop here, wait for him.

The corridor is dark and quiet apart from the orange rectangle of moving light at the end. It gets brighter as he walks up the stairs, edges of picture frames shining in C-shapes like tiny doors to a furnace raging behind the walls. He fills the end of the corridor, his flame rumbling loudly like masses of tumbling, shattering concrete. Apart from his face it envelopes his whole body, licking the walls and ceiling. He steps on a blob of gel that hisses angrily underfoot.

"You can't escape me Martin. Not in my own mansion."

He calmly strides down the corridor as black curls of paper and paint drop to the floor around him. Picture glass crackles and explodes. Wooden frames burst into flames, metal ones soften and sag down the walls ahead of him. Carpet, wallpaper, ceiling all scorch black as he approaches, peeling to reveal bony white plaster inside which browns and cracks open like a parched river. Wooden floorboards darken and split. Photographs of the team, newspaper cuttings are gone in a breath of fire. Memories die, years disappear in seconds.

He reaches out wide with his arms, pressing his palms into opposite walls and sends two streaks of fire towards me. They tear through the walls, getting wider, covering the whole width of the corridor as they approach me. I duck into the guest room, flames exploding through the doorway above my head. I scramble to my feet. This had better work.

I stare at the doorway. I see the corridor getting blacker, then turning orange. The door frame browns, tiny cracks in the paint spider out towards the walls. The wall to the left of the door starts smoking, dark oval shapes stain the wallpaper. Something snaps loudly as the frame buckles with the heat. Smoke and floating embers rush into the room.

I adjust the foam stuffed inside my costume. Not as good as the gel, but should stop me from immediately turning to ash at least. Don't think that! Don't let your mind wander either. Stay in the moment. I grab the book from the sideboard behind me.

Flames curl round the door frame like fiery hands of a giant monster, pushing the wood away so it can squeeze through. Charles turns the corner. His silhouette is black inside his cloak of fire.

"This ends now Martin. I really wish it didn't have to be this way you know? If you'd given me the book when I first asked no-one else would have needed to die. Because of your inaction, people have died. Sound familiar?"

I don't react. I hold the memoirs out towards him. For a moment, in his rage, he doesn't see anything else but me, but then his eyes drop to the black notebook and he stops dead. His flames disappear instantly, ash and burnt paper is sucked towards him then floats to the floor. He stares, wide-eyed, breathing heavily.

"That... is, is that it? The journal?"

He holds out a pointed finger, trembling as though being offered a gift by the Gods.

"Yep. Everything is in here. He was very thorough."

"Please?"

His whole body shakes, lip trembling, suddenly on the verge of tears.

"Please give it me."

He only has eyes for the journal. He shuffles forwards one tiny step as if the floor is about to give under him.

"Please Martin, buddy, please give that to Charles. Charles needs it."

"No. MAIL!"

Hayley jumps in next to me from the room opposite, hood over her face. Charles doesn't notice at first, then looks confused when he does.

"Who, what..."

I hand the journal to her.

"Delivery for PCA agents Morris and Barclay at Element City Police Headquarters please."

"On it boss!"

She gives a little wave to Charles and is gone.

Charles sinks to his knees in slow motion. He tears up, arm still outstretched, trying to grasp the piece of the past he almost touched.

"No, no, no... where's it gone?"

He looks at me, puppy dog eyes pouring water, creating pink tracks through the black dust on his face.

"It was there! Where is it Martin?"

He shakes with the tears as he drops his arm.

"Where's it gone! Where's she taken it? Who... does she know, tell me she doesn't know! No. Get it back, get it back Martin!"

He sobs like he's lost a loved one. I almost feel sorry for him, then I remember he's not crying because of what he's done, he's crying because he's about to be found out.

I walk over and crouch down next to him. He puts a hand up on my shoulder, eyes puffy red and streaming tears.

"You have a choice Charles, you can either go to the police tomorrow and admit to killing Vincent and attacking Maria for whatever reasons you want to make up, I don't care what, or the PCA will get Vincent's memoirs in their inbox at two p.m. and then you'll be outed and we'll all be screwed, forever."

Charles grabs onto what's left of my costume and pulls me closer. The tears have formed a tangle of white channels through the smoke on his face.

"Don't make me. You can't make me. Bring it back, BRING HER BACK!"

"She's gone Charles. And you know me and mobile phones, couldn't contact her even if I wanted to."

I shrug, picking Charles' hands off me, holding them tightly.

"It's time to take one for the team... buddy." I manage to not spit the word out as Charles stares at me. "Only you can do it. You're our saviour now."

I stand up and back away from him. I don't want to be here any longer, near him any more. Charles hugs himself and slowly lies down on the floor, curling up into a ball, crying to himself. I walk out of the room.

The corridor is like the inside of a charred, hollow tree trunk. I cover my mouth and jog through the smoke, before slowly picking my way around the burnt patches of floor down the stairs and into the lounge. Hayley stands there with the journal, gazing around.

"This place is amazing."

I nod and take the black book as she holds it out to me. As I touch it it becomes a red leather book with gold embossed lettering. I open it to the first page.

"To most people, trust is finding out as much about another person as you can. Their fears, their dreams, learning how they think about you, about themselves, about the world. I knew everything about almost everybody, and I didn't trust a single one of them. I dedicate this book to Martin, the only person I ever truly trusted."

"So... that was pretty intense. Earlier too."

I don't respond.

"Must be some pretty deep stuff that went on between all of you back then. Still think you're cool though, despite the raping of my childhood memories. Thanks for that."

I flinch at her choice of words, but she doesn't know, I couldn't tell her that. Not everything. Just enough.

"So, you're not going to give that to the police or tell me what the hell just happened are you?"

"Nope."

Hayley sighs.

"Didn't think so. But you *do* realise you guys are well fucked up yeah?"

"Yeah."

I close the journal and throw it into the log fire. It bursts into flames in seconds, shrivelling, blackening, fading until it is nothing more than a grey, crumbling ghost. Hayley stares into the fire, eyes wide.

"Er... didn't you need that for something? You know, like, evidence to help keep you alive?"

"Trust isn't about knowing everything..."

"Well count me in there."

"...it's about understanding."

This damn foam has been itching me for a while now. I pull out a handful of long pieces of it from around my waist and throw them on the fire too. They shrivel and snap, melting into shape around the wood.

"He'll go to the police tomorrow and confess everything. He won't mention any memoirs. And that will be it. Done."

"You certain?"

I nod. Hayley puts her hand on my bare arm and meets my gaze. She seems to search me for a while, trying to read my thoughts, then breaks into a smile.

"Done then. Where to next, boss?"

I smile back at her.

"Home."

"And that is *where* exactly?"

We stand still for a moment, both racking our brains, then start laughing.

I spot Charles' burnt hand prints across the back of the chair and shake my head.

"Buggered if I know, just... not here."

"Don't worry, I'll get you home," she winks.

Then we jump.

EPILOGUE

It's still bloody cold. Not October yet and even *I* can feel the chill. Especially up here. All the years I've been in Element Park I've never gone out the north-east entrance and into Heroes Graveyard, and now I know why. It's depressing. Beautifully depressing.

There are hundreds of headstones here from fully carved life-size statues, to symbols, to small granite plaques. Some are arranged on plots by team, some have a mausoleum dedicated to them, the rest are by date. Some have their real names carved on them, most just have their Hero name in large letters. The one I'm standing in front of is a full statue in white marble. Exquisitely carved. It's a perfect likeness. I can almost imagine it coming to life. I wish it would, there is so much to say to her, so much she's missed.

"SUNLIGHT" is carved in large letters on the circular plinth beneath her feet.

"1971-1994

SHE GAVE HER LIFE DEFENDING THOSE WHO COULD NOT DEFEND THEMSELVES"

That's the way she should have gone. What's the point in having these abilities if we don't use them to help others?

I place the small bunch of yellow daisies in the chrome flower holder at the base of the statue. I remember she had a little vase of these in her room. Wouldn't have thought she would be bothered by flowers but there you go. I wonder what significance they had for her. Her mother liked them? They grew in the countryside near where she lived? Gift from her first boyfriend? Never know now. So much lost, a whole history of a person.

I'm only just getting my head round the paperwork and responsibilities of being an executor but I want Vincent to be interred here when his body is released. There are some empty plots nearby, but I don't want people crowding him, even now. Somewhere quiet, just for him.

"Ah, Mr Molloy."

Agent Morris stands about twenty feet away, outside the marble dais the statue stands on. I glance at him through the corner of one eye, before looking back to the statue.

"I do apologise for disturbing you here of all places, that.. is an incredible likeness. It's almost as if she could start moving..."

"What do you want?"

Morris stands tall, hands in pockets and draws his face down into his chest, creating furrows of deep wrinkles curving from ear to ear under his chin.

"I thought you might like to know that Mr Heathcote came into the station a few days ago and offered us a full confession of the murder of Mr Hayden-Phillips. Furthermore he admitted to the assault on Ms Gionchetta. He was afraid she had worked out he was the culprit after identifying the body, apparently."

Knew he would. I just nod slowly.

"As to why he killed him, something about an ill-advised romantic pass on the deceased in a moment of emotional weakness, followed by anger at the rebuttal and fear of being exposed. He said he couldn't live with the self-hating guilt any more and had to tell his side of the story."

Typical of Charles. Even in his moment of contrition he manages to make himself the centre of the drama.

"We haven't made a public statement yet, but I thought you should know before we did. We have our man now, we are not looking for anyone else in connection with this case. "

"Good."

The cold makes my fingers tingle and my chest ache as we stand in this silent place.

"The attack on you and the destruction of your flat by persons unknown is still ongoing of course. Strange, we would have thought it was all the same person but of course Mr Heathcote cannot fly as per your description of the attacker. But then there's the fact that Mr Heathcote confessed to that also…"

He what? OK, I hadn't expected that. Then again I guess he is only doing what he's programmed to do, protect the team.

"I guess I must have been mistaken about that part then."

Agent Morris shrugs up his shoulders, deepening the furrows.

"It is to be expected as a result of such a vicious attack, at night, in the dark. Details are lost or confused, only to clarify themselves after a period of time."

"I apologise. If you need me to change my statement..."

"Three o'clock will be fine."

I look at Agent Morris, not quite sure what is happening here. Surprised that it might be, but wary, that it's some kind of trap.

"It's always nice to wrap things up. I don't like gaps, you see."

"No. I understand."

Morris looks around at all the statues and headstones.

"You know Mr Molloy, I have always wondered what it would be like to have abilities such as yours, or Miss Nesvyaschenko's here, or my colleague's. The power, the difficulties that come with it, having a weapon on you at all times, having to constantly keep it in check lest you harm those around you that you care about. Would I be able to bear the responsibility that comes with it? Take on the role expected of me by society?"

He looks at me.

"I don't think that I could. I don't think I'd want it truth be told."

He takes a few steps forward, stopping just outside the dais.

"It is never easy doing the right thing, when the 'right thing' is so fluid and dependant on the context and the law is so rigid and defined by centuries old moralities. It's not an easy choice Mr Molloy, but I would like to think you are the kind of person who understands that."

"I would like to think that too."

His shoulders drop, elbows bending as his hands stay in his pockets, his head lifts and he seems alert.

"Actually I believe I just lied to you earlier!"

"I'm sorry?"

"About having a power. If I could have one, if you could indulge me to be selfish for a brief moment... teleportation!"

A huge smile crosses his face. I feel the chill down to my bones. Does he know?

"I love teleporters, jumping around like little people-grasshoppers, although not so much the bank robberies they tend to go in for. Major headaches. But to be able to leap around at my will, go wherever I pleased, ha! I am a frustrated traveller, if I can allow myself to admit such a thing. There are so many places I would love to visit, places never seen by the human eye. I would spend my lifetime, just, seeing..."

He drifts off into a reverie for a moment, eyes bright and relaxed. Then his eyelids drop back to their default position halfway down his eyeballs, his smile shrinks to a horizontal line and his chin drops.

"But of course, the one place you can never travel is the past, even if you might want to change it for the better. What is done is done and you cannot let it define you Mr Molloy, you must find yourself in the present and act on that alone."

He is looking at me intensely, hoping I understand. And I do.

"I know, Agent Morris."

"You know Mr Molloy, we have an unofficial motto in the PCA: 'You are only as strong as the people around you'. It's all very well being a lone wolf but nothing gives a sense of purpose more than having someone to fight for, knowing that they will fight for you too."

He steps back from the dais.

"I hear Ms Gionchetta is recovering well, if slowly. I do hope there isn't too much long-term damage, that would be tragic for someone of her talents. I have found that it aids recovery if there is somebody there for them that cares for their well-being. Other than the clinical staff I mean."

"No need to worry, I'll look after her."

"Good. Good."

He seems distracted now and makes steps to move away.

"Well, that's another case closed, and the people of the city live safely for another day. All good work Mr Molloy."

"Thank you Agent Morris."

"Goodbye Mr Molloy."

Maybe it's where we are, the sense of peace and purpose affecting me. Maybe it's the statue of Inna right in front of me, and the fact I can look her in the eyes and not feel guilty any more. Maybe something has changed over the last week or so. Whatever it is, it makes me call after him as he walks away.

"Agent Morris?"

He spins on the spot.

"The name is Roadblock."

One corner of his mouth curves upwards.

"Yes. Yes it is isn't it?"

***

ABOUT THE AUTHOR

Thank you for reading POWERLESS. I hope you enjoyed it as much as I did writing and editing it! Whatever your thoughts I would love it if you left a review on the site you got this book from, or left your comments on my blog.

In total it took me about a year, starting very slowly in January 2012. I worked on it in dribs and drabs until June/July when I realised that I actually had enough of a story to make a full novel and I was interested enough in the characters and premise to want to finish it.

If you ever want to ask me any questions about the book, writing or self-publishing ebooks then feel free to drop me an email, tweet, forum post or Facebook comment (see overleaf).

And if you are already wanting more of these damaged Heroes and the world they inhabit, then there is no need to wait any longer. The sequel, KILLING GODS, is out now (the first chapter of which you can read in a few pages time) and the third book is underway.

Thanks again for reading,
Tony.

My blog

www.hungryblackbird.com

Facebook

www.facebook.com/TonyCooperAuthor

Twitter

@_tonycooper

Email

tonycooperauthor@gmail.com

Amazon

amazon.com/author/tonycooper

Smashwords

www.smashwords.com/profile/view/TonyCooper

Goodreads

www.goodreads.com/user/show/7234993

OTHER TITLES

POWERLESS
The first book in the 'Powerless' series

When the best friend of a retired superhero is killed by another power, Martin must drag himself out of his self-imposed isolation to find out who is responsible. In doing so he finds himself digging up a past he would rather forget, risking exposing the secret of why the team split up and destroying all their lives in the process.

KILLING GODS
The second book in the 'Powerless' series

When the baby son of a physically mutated eighties villain goes missing from protective care, he goes on a rampage to try and find him.

In his way stand a Child Protection Officer following her heart above her duty, a violent anti-hero group desperate for media attention, a seemingly benevolent hero-worshipping cult and Martin and Hayley struggling to work out who they can trust.

THE RESURRECTION TREE AND OTHER STORIES

A collection of nine short stories about life, death and consequences.

A mix of creepy, disturbing contemporary fantasy and science fiction stories in one book.

KILLING GODS

PROLOGUE

They had picked out the old woman easily and had been following her for a few days now. They had watched where she went and who she met up with, and from that had found another couple of names that weren't on the list. She always shopped for her groceries at a small corner supermarket with only four aisles, one chest freezer, a small counter by the door and a lottery machine. Even though she was now much older than in the photo they had of her, her features were still strong and she did her hair the same way. Right now she was trying to decide between custard creams or a pack of chocolate-covered biscuits on offer, just past their sell-by date. Either would be fine with a cup of tea, she thought to herself, but it would depend if she was in a chocolatey mood or not. She fiddled with a ring on her finger, set with a black stone, while she tried to decide, tugging her sleeve down to hide the faint pink scarring on the back of her arm.

They had watched her go in and waited a minute before two of them followed her. All three knew their places and their roles. The tall one in the black hooded top found the aisle she was in and stood at the end of it. He turned away from her towards the newspapers, which lay on three white, angled metal shelves in front of the long windows. The one in the dark blue top knew from where his mate was standing which aisle she was in, and moved around to the other end. The one in the grey and white top was to come in after and keep the shopkeeper busy, while the other two, "got it done".

The guy in black scanned the headlines in front of him, something about a Hero being sentenced for murder, some red-headed old guy. He snorted and opened The Sun to page three where, "Melanie from Bristol", was worried that Hero Registration alone wasn't enough to stop these dangerous people from committing serious crimes.

"Not fucking Heroes," he muttered to himself and looked down the shop to the counter. Carl, the one in grey, had just come in the door. They glanced at each other, as Carl went up to the counter. The shopkeeper, a middle-aged Indian man wearing a pale blue turban, was busy sorting boxes and ticking things off a sheet behind the counter. A small girl with big auburn hair bustled back and forth through an open doorway to the back of the shop. Carl picked his time just as she disappeared.

"Twenty Bensons mate."

The man looked flustered as he dropped his list and turned to the curtains behind him.

"Hood down please."

"You what?"

"I said hood down. No hoods up in here, there's a poster up in the bloody door that tells you this. That goes for you too son…" he called out to the tall guy in black by the papers. The shopkeeper pulled back one curtain and grabbed the packet, while shaking his head. "Damn kids can't read nowadays."

The tall guy in black squeezed the round end of the baseball bat hidden up his baggy sleeve, while the one in dark blue, now waiting at the other end of the aisle, gripped the flick-knife inside his front pouch pocket. Carl turned and nodded at his friend, who left the paper open on the shelf and walked down the aisle and out of sight. Carl looked up from under his hood at the small TV on a shelf behind the counter showing four black and white scenes of the inside of the shop from different angles. He could see the two figures moving in on the old lady.

"I said drop the hood OK?" The shopkeeper slapped the packet down on the counter. "I'm not going to serve you if you don't. I don't have to you know, I've got the law on my side, OK?"

"Yeah, yeah, all right mate. Another pack of Bensons please."

The man scowled at him, leaning on the counter with both arms.

"Are you taking the piss yeah? I get your sort in here all the time and I know how to deal with you. Hood down or you're out!"

"Sure. Twenty Bensons please mate."

The man jerked up straight, cheeks flushed and lips twisted in anger.

"I said get that fucking hood down!" He reached over to flick Carl's hood back, but Carl was quicker. He grabbed the arm and pulled and twisted it towards him, making the guy bend forwards, then he slammed him down on the counter. The man cried out in pain as the side of his chest hit the counter hard. As he looked up from his pinned position he saw a knife pointed at his face.

"You do nothing mate."

The other two moved towards the old lady. She had finally decided to go with the chocolate biscuits, a nice treat with her tea. The money she saved would go towards a coffee and cake at Mandy's at the weekend. It was then she noticed a tall lad in a black hoodie close to her.

"Is everything…?"

"Catherine Forbes, yeah?"

"Well… yes, how do you know…"

The guy in black let the baseball bat slip out of his sleeve, catching it by the grip.

"We know everything you've done." He nodded to somewhere behind her left shoulder. Catherine turned round to see another, shorter lad in a blue top standing behind her. He pulled out the knife and flicked it open in front of her face as the guy in black took a swing.

"What are you guys up to?" asked the shopkeeper, as he lay stretched out over his counter. He was confused and worried, shoplifters didn't usually announce themselves and this guy wasn't interested in the till.

"You'll know," said Carl.

There was a shout. He assumed it was the old lady he'd seen coming in a few minutes ago. He heard her say, "What are you...", before she screamed again. He heard voices calling her terrible names, he heard the sickening crack of bone.

"Stop it ... ah!" cried the man, as Carl twisted his arm tight, making him bring his other arm over to clutch at his shoulder. The small girl appeared through the doorway with a cardboard box full of chocolate bars and a concerned look on her face. Carl pointed the knife at her.

"You! Get back in there now and stay there!"

She hovered for a second before running away. Carl started to get nervous. This was taking too long. How long could it take to beat up an old woman?

"Come on guys, we've got to..."

There was a roar, like an angry animal, but unmistakably human. Then there was a piercing screech of rending metal as the shelves around the central aisle were torn apart, flung away from each other. Packets and jars and bags were hurled in all directions, punching holes in the polystyrene ceiling tiles which shattered above them. Jars of curry sauce and bolognese barrelled through the outer two shelves, peppering Carl in the back of his body and head. He lost his grasp on the shopkeeper's arm as cans of lager thudded into the back of his knees, making him drop. He managed to stop himself falling to the ground by grasping onto the wooden surface like it was the edge of a cliff. Bottles of wine exploded on the counter around him as he closed his eyes and waited for everything to go quiet. He looked back and saw the air full of shredded food bouncing off the windows and walls.

"Jed!"

He scrambled to his feet and ran, almost slipping on spilt beetroot and pickled onions, to where the tall guy in black had landed on the racks of papers. He was clutching his back as he bent down to pick up the baseball bat.

The middle of the shop was now clear, the two sets of shelves that had been there were compressed against the outer ones. The shelf furthest from the counter had tipped over and crashed into the vegetables in the chilled cabinet. The guy in blue was lying on the ground at the back of the store groaning, half buried in cereals. The old lady was on her back on the floor in the middle of it all, propped up on one elbow. Blood seeped through the fingers of her hand holding her stomach. Her grey hair was wild in all directions, her eyes bright and bloodshot.

"You fucking bitch! You freak!" roared Jed, as he leapt forward past Carl and swung the bat down at her head. There was a crack and a squelch and all tension left her body. Her dented head dropped away from the bat and thudded against the floor as her arms flopped outwards. "Fucking freak!" He swung again and hit her face just under her left eye, with an even louder crack.

"Jed, let's go."

Jed was about to take another swing when Carl grabbed his arm.

"We got her! Let's go already!" He stepped over her and lifted the guy in blue off the floor from where he was looking for his knife. "Leave it, come on!" Carl pulled him past Jed and out the front door. Jed looked down at his handiwork. His shoulders relaxed as he stretched up taller. Blood dripped off the end of the bat as he turned to see the shopkeeper peering horrified over the top of the counter. Jed smiled and lifted the end of the bat so it pointed at him.

"Hero freaks must die!"

CHAPTER 1
BITTERFIELD INDUSTRIAL PARK

"Got any crisps?"

"Nope."

The street below them glowed a pastel orange as the street lamps illuminated the fine mist kicked up from the pouring rain. It was quiet apart from the white noise hiss, the cacophony of thousands of raindrops spatting off every surface. Martin blinked as a fat drop fell onto his eyelashes, making him attempt to squeeze his bulky frame even further under the shallow overhang. They were huddled together, him and Hayley pressed against the boarded-up loft windows of an old empty warehouse, five floors up on the roof. Martin had cramp in his thighs and a pain in one buttock as he sat, one foot out, bracing himself on a guttering of dubious solidity. His other arm grasped a metal bar, a part of the overhang above him.

Hayley seemed to be quite comfortable sitting squat, arms wrapped round her shins. She even swayed back and forth gently now and again, seemingly oblivious to the few centimetres between her feet and the drop to the pavement below. Martin had read about so-called, "free climbers", people with no powers who have such belief in their skills that they scale cliffs and skyscrapers with their bare hands and no safety line. The very idea terrified him. It was sheer recklessness. However good you thought you were, you always had to have a backup plan. Even when he was solo, before he joined The Pulse in the 'nineties, he would plan before a mission to make sure he never boxed himself in or took on more than he could deal with. There was always an escape route. He reckoned that Hayley must be so used to being able to teleport at will that she had lost that healthy fear of danger through knowing she could be anywhere else in a split-second. It was good to have that confidence, but he would have to keep an eye on her, to make sure she didn't put herself in danger unnecessarily. Not that he had seen anything like that yet. She was very keen to get into Heroics properly, willing to do anything he asked, and she had a cool head about her most of the time.

Probably being a police Constable helped. She had told him about the training they had to go through, all the different duties they performed, (most of which Martin would never have guessed), and all the strange and sobering things she had witnessed in the three years she had been doing it. There was no room for recklessness in that job, it was all about rules and procedures, and putting the safety of others first.

But she hadn't yet been in the heat of action. Aside from giving muggers and drug dealers surprise meetings with walls, she hadn't actively gone up against a serious opponent, particularly a Hero. Martin didn't know how she would behave in such a situation, and that meant he had to train her, contrary to his own best advice to himself. Then again, he'd been out of a job since he was outed as a Hero at the end of last year and, despite his best efforts to try to return to a normal life, Hayley had been persistently insistent about what he needed to do. She had saved his life twice after all, so he owed her that much, but none of this had been in his plans for his middle years. Well, they hadn't been particularly detailed or exciting plans anyway, but then that was the point. A quiet life, a bit of security work here, a few cans of beer in his flat there, and nothing much of interest in between.

Hayley suddenly leaned forwards over the edge of the roof. Martin winced. There was a dark car coming towards them, tyres tearing through the water on the road. It was impossible to see any details at this time of night, especially through the spray. The car didn't slow down and drove on past. Hayley pulled herself back, the edge of her hood now wet and drooping onto her forehead. Her costume wasn't anything fancy or custom-made. Fancy meant too easily traceable from CCTV analysis, while custom-made took a lot of time and mistakes, and time wasn't something they had a lot of tonight. She had grabbed an old hoodie, a pair of PVC trousers and some heavy black boots that reminded him of the old Doc Martens from the 'eighties. His original costume had been so utterly ruined, that night back in September, that in the end he ripped it into pieces and burned it. The charred remains went in a black bag and were dumped in a cauldron bin round the back of a supermarket. No great ceremony for the past. No great memories from it. It was too recognisable as a signature costume anyway, useless now that his identity was public knowledge. His replacement was a black leather bikers' jacket, (bought from a charity shop years ago), a knitted balaclava, a pair of dark brown waxed workman's trousers and his old boots, the only useful item from his past. One boot was now utterly sodden.

"Any biscuits?"

"Nope."

The noise of the car blended into the hiss of the rain as Martin felt his back go stiff.

Hayley had discovered information during one of her "unofficial" night-shifts about a group of thieves targeting office supplies. Martin initially laughed it off, cracking a joke about "very well organised crime" that didn't seem to go down too well. He regretted his levity when Hayley said they had already stolen goods worth over forty thousand pounds in the last few months alone.

"Never underestimate the market for stuff you don't think about or you take for granted. Big companies spend thousands every year on stationery and other consumables. Trust me, it's huge."

Martin knew that Hayley was in a bit of a situation. Nobody with powers is allowed to join the police force, or any emergency service for that matter, and being a Hero and patrolling the streets means you inevitably come across information that the police would find very useful. Too worried about her voice being recognised if she called in a tip-off, or someone tracing an email or text back to her, she always had to try and deal with the situation herself. It was the larger stuff she knew she couldn't take on alone, the gangs, the drugs, the powered crime. That frustrated her. She knew stuff that her colleagues didn't, but couldn't tell them, and she was powerless to sort it out alone. She felt she was betraying her force and herself, but now that she had found Martin, "that was all going to change", apparently. Martin had smiled weakly at the time, wishing himself somewhere else, wondering how far she thought this partnership would go. Then he felt guilty for feeling exasperated with her, after all, she had saved his life. Twice.

She had told him that she knew where the group held the stolen goods before they were moved across the country in a small fleet of vans. There were six guys, no firearms she knew of, very careful people. She had laid out surveillance photos of the warehouse on her kitchen table and pointed to all the entrances, adding a rough marker pen drawing of the internal layout. As they sat drinking tea she had told him of her plan of attack. Instantly he had disagreed with her, pointing out the weaknesses, the blind-spots she hadn't thought about.

At first he was worried she would take offence at him suddenly butting in, but instead she was rapt, eyeing him intently, nodding, both hands curled round her mug. She was taking everything in like a good student. Did that make him her teacher? Her mentor? He supposed it did, and he wasn't yet sure how that made him feel. What he was worried about was how easy this came back to him. It had been nearly two decades since he had been part of a team but here he was, plotting entry and exit points, lines of sight, kill-zones, cover locations. He identified where the targets would most likely be, where they would be themselves and their path and timing through the inside, and alternate scenarios if the men were armed, ran, or stayed to fight. Within half an hour they had a detailed plan and that's when Martin realised he had just talked himself into it. He had sighed and finished his tea as Hayley stared at the photos with a huge grin on her face.

He wished he had a cup of tea now. Anything warm. They had been cooped up here for nearly fifty minutes. The vans were supposed to have arrived twenty minutes ago. The goods were being shipped up to Leeds and Manchester overnight, two big orders. It looked like the stationery business was moving! Martin kept that joke to himself. His mind had begun to wander when one of the men appeared from a small door at the front of the building, mobile phone pressed up against his ear. He pulled the hood of his jacket over his head and stood, sheltering under a corrugated iron awning.

"Here we go."

Two white unmarked Ford Transits sped up the road from where the earlier car had disappeared. Martin could see the face of the driver at the front, illuminated by the pale blue glow of a phone as he drove with one hand. The man waiting put his phone away and jogged up to the gates as the vans pulled up. After a minor struggle with the lock, he opened the gates and the vans drove through, driving down the side of the building to two large shutters. Closing the front gates, the man ran down to meet them as the drivers hopped out, clutching jackets around their chests. There was a short moment of waving hands and a loud conversation that they only caught bits of, before the gate-opener banged on the shutter near him. As they waited, one of the drivers lit up a cigarette. The gate man slapped it out of his hands, pointing at the shutters, then the van. The hand waving began again.

"At least it's not just us that's pissed off they're late." Martin observed.

"We wait until they're all inside yeah?"

"Yeah. You got the knife?" Hayley tapped her hoodie pocket. "OK. I think we're ready." There was a harsh rasping sound as the shutter opened on a chain. The three men ducked under it when it reached waist height.

"Now!"

Hayley squeezed his shoulder and in a soft huff of air they were gone from the roof.

50724643R00295

Made in the USA
Charleston, SC
06 January 2016